"All I want is unconditional, complete love that will last forever."

"And how do you know when you've got it?" Alana asked.

"My heart will tell me," Pax answered. "Grandpa told me that he knew right here"—he tapped his chest—"when he'd found the right woman. I'm depending on the same feeling to hit me."

"I'd like something a lot more concrete, like the name of my forever soul mate to be written in the stars, or maybe for a halo to appear over his head when we're sitting beside each other in church," she said.

"That's not asking for much," he chuckled, but his tone suggested the opposite.

"I don't think so." She laid her head on his shoulder. "As my friend, I believe you could arrange that for me, right?"

"Happy, happy birthday, my dear friend!" Pax kissed her on the top of her head. "Anything for you, darlin'."

COWBOY REBEL

"Brown's capable fourth Longhorn Canyon contemporary western romance...suggests that love can make even the baddest of bad boy cowboys want to settle down. Sweet, sexy romance and a strong heroine elevate the story. Fans of romance series filled with small-town charm and a cast of supportive family and friends will appreciate this installment and seek out earlier ones."

—Publishers Weekly

COWBOY BRAVE

"Sizzling romance between believable characters is the mainstay of this whimsical novel, which is enhanced by plenty of romantic yearning."

—Publishers Weekly

"Over 300 pages of warmth, humor and sweet romance... Carolyn Brown always manages to write feel-good stories, and this is definitely a...special read."

—Harlequin Junkie, Top Pick

COWBOY HONOR

"The slow-simmering romance between Claire and Levi is enhanced by the kind supporting characters and the simple pleasures of ranch life in a story that's sure to please fans of cowboy romances."

—Publishers Weekly

"Friendship, family, love, and trust abound in *Cowboy Honor*."

—Fresh Fiction

COWBOY BOLD

"Lighthearted banter, heart-tugging emotion, and a good-natured Sooner/Longhorn football rivalry make this a delightful romance and terrific launch for the new series."

—*Library Journal*

"*Cowboy Bold* is the start of a new and amazing series by an author that really knows how to hook her readers with sexy cowboys, strong women, and a bunch of humor... Everything about this book is a roaring good time."

—Harlequin Junkie, Top Pick

"Everything you could ever ask for in a cowboy romance."

—The Genre Minx

"Western romance lovers are in for a treat. This wickedly saucy series is unputdownable. There's no one who creates a rancher with a heart of gold like Carolyn Brown."

—*RT Book Reviews*

Cowboy Strong

Also by Carolyn Brown

The Longhorn Canyon Series

Cowboy Bold
Cowboy Honor
Cowboy Brave
Cowboy Rebel
Christmas with a Cowboy
Cowboy Courage

The Happy, Texas Series

Luckiest Cowboy of All
Long, Tall Cowboy Christmas
Toughest Cowboy in Texas

The Lucky Penny Ranch Series

Wild Cowboy Ways
Hot Cowboy Nights
Merry Cowboy Christmas
Wicked Cowboy Charm

Digital Novellas

Wildflower Ranch
Sunrise Ranch

Cowboy Strong

Carolyn Brown

FOREVER

New York   Boston

Copyright © 2020 by Carolyn Brown
Sunrise Ranch copyright © 2020 by Carolyn Brown

Cover design by Elizabeth Turner Stokes. Cover images by Rob Lang.
Cover copyright © 2020 by Hachette Book Group, Inc.

Forever
Hachette Book Group
1290 Avenue of the Americas, New York, NY 10104
read-forever.com
twitter.com/readforeverpub

First Mass Market Edition: June 2020

Forever is an imprint of Grand Central Publishing. The Forever name and logo are trademarks of Hachette Book Group, Inc.

The publisher is not responsible for websites (or their content) that are not owned by the publisher.

The Hachette Speakers Bureau provides a wide range of authors for speaking events. To find out more, go to www.hachettespeakersbureau.com or call (866) 376-6591.

ISBNs: 978-1-5387-4878-7 (mass market); 978-1-5387-4880-0 (ebook)

Printed in the United States of America

OPM

10 9 8 7 6 5 4 3 2

ATTENTION CORPORATIONS AND ORGANIZATIONS:

Most Hachette Book Group books are available at quantity discounts with bulk purchase for educational, business, or sales promotional use. For information, please call or write:

Special Markets Department, Hachette Book Group
1290 Avenue of the Americas, New York, NY 10104
Telephone: 1-800-222-6747 Fax: 1-800-477-5925

*This book is for
Lynette and Ryan Giovinco
With much love!*

Chapter One

The only thing Alana Carey's father ever wanted was to live long enough to see his daughter, Alana, get married and settled down. Alana was only twenty-nine years old, so she had plenty of time to make her daddy a happy man—right up until she came in at noon on a bright, sunny day in the middle of the week and found him sitting in the kitchen in his Sunday jeans and shirt.

"Where have you been, all dressed up?" She rolled the sleeves of her chambray work shirt up to her elbows and washed her hands at the kitchen sink.

"Been to Amarillo." His voice sounded like it was about to crack.

Matt Carey was an old-school rancher and a cowboy. His kind were as tough as nails, and they held their emotions inside their hearts. They didn't cry or whine about anything. He was Alana's rock and had been her only parent since her mother's death when she was a girl. He was all the family she had left—no siblings, no grandparents, and only a handful of cousins that were scattered from coast to coast. He was also her mentor—he'd taught her everything about how to operate a ranch from the ground up.

She'd heard sadness in his voice before, had seen him worry, but she'd never seen such a bewildered expression on his face.

"You didn't tell me about a cattlemen's meeting." She opened the refrigerator and got out some cold cuts to make sandwiches.

"Leave that and come sit down." He used his boot to slide a chair out from the table. "I didn't go to Amarillo for a cattlemen's meeting. I went to talk to a doctor."

Alana felt as if someone had dropped a chunk of ice down the back of her shirt. "Why did you go all the way up there? Doctor Wilson has taken care of us forever."

"I haven't been feelin' too good lately, so Doc Wilson sent me to a specialist for some tests. I didn't want to worry you until the results came back," Matt said. "I never was any good at beating around the bush, so I'm just going to spit it out. I've got stage four cancer, an inoperable tumor in my brain. They told me it's very aggressive, and even if they managed to take it out I might live six months, but there's a high probability I'd be in a coma all that time."

Alana's chest tightened, her breath came in short gasps, and words wouldn't form in her mouth. Matt Carey was a big strong man. He couldn't have cancer, and what did "stage four" mean anyway?

Matt reached out and took both of her hands in his. "If it continues to grow the way it has been, I've got about six weeks."

"Oh, Daddy, what…" A sob caught in her chest. Her mind couldn't begin to process the words he'd said. Her heart seemed to understand better and had tightened into a ball of pain in her chest. Her hands shook, and for a few seconds she thought she might faint.

"Promise me that you'll let me do as much as I'm able and not mollycoddle me in the time I've got left." Matt squeezed her hands. "I want to go out with my boots on, not in a hospital gown with no dignity. Promise me that much. Let me do what I can on my own terms as long as I can."

"I'll do whatever you want, Daddy," she said, tears streaming down her face. "But…" Her voice caught, and the heaviness in her chest felt as if rocks had been piled up on her heart.

He stood up, rounded the end of the table, and gathered her into his arms. His warm tears mingled with hers. "I hate this for you, sugar. On one hand I want to go be with your mother. On the other, I can't bear to leave you."

"Daddy, isn't there anything…" She dried her eyes and straightened her back to try to get her composure. Her father needed her to be strong, but she couldn't do it. She sobbed until the front of his shirt was wet, and she had the hiccups.

"Honey, think of it this way," Matt said as he took a step back from her. "If I'd had a heart attack or a stroke and dropped out in the barn, you would have had no forewarning. The way it is, we've got six weeks. The doctor says that last couple of weeks, I'll sleep a lot more, and then one time when I take a nap, I'll take that final step from earth to eternity." He went to the bar and started making sandwiches. "We're going to live each day to its fullest. Now, let's have some dinner and then get back out there in the hay field. I'll drive the truck, and the kids who've got hired for summer help can throw the bales."

He didn't have to say the words. She had heard them

often enough that they echoed through her heart and her mind. "If I can live long enough to know that Alana is settled down with a good man, I'll be happy to go on to heaven with my sweet Joy." The fact that he'd said those words so often the past year made her wonder if somehow in his subconscious he'd known that his time was limited, and he'd soon be in eternity with his beloved wife. "I've had a good life, and my only regret is that I can't walk you down the aisle at your wedding. I'd like to leave this world knowing that you've got a partner in your life, like I had with your mama. You're a strong woman, Alana, but I'd rest easier knowing that someone was beside you to share in your joys and halve your sorrows."

What he said wasn't anything new. The same thing had come up often in the past, more so this last year. She'd figured it was because she was getting closer to thirty years old. Alana couldn't snap her fingers and give him more than six weeks to live. She couldn't wish the tumor away or even make it less serious so the doctors could remove it. She sure couldn't pull a boyfriend out of her cowboy hat and plan a wedding so he could walk her down the aisle. Or could she?

The only trouble with the plan that popped into her head was that it would involve a huge lie. Still, it would make her father rest easy, and he'd never have to know she hadn't told him the truth.

No, she told herself. *I need to spend every waking minute with my daddy, and Daddy would be so disappointed in me if he found out.* The little devil in her head kept showing her smiling, happy pictures of her father's face as he walked her down the aisle and left her in the care of a loving man.

I don't need a man to care for me, she argued.

No, but think how happy it will make your dad, the pesky voice whispered.

There was only one man who might be willing to say yes to such a wild plan—Paxton Callahan. Her father liked him as a man and a cowboy, but Pax had a wild reputation. Scenarios played through her head—one after another until she couldn't think about anything else.

She dried her tears, took a deep breath, and pushed back her chair. She got out a jar of pickles from the refrigerator and set out a banana cream pie she'd made the day before.

She draped her arm around her father's shoulders. They did seem a little bonier than they had been. Why hadn't she noticed that he was losing weight?

Because you see him as the big, strong cowboy he's always been. The voice in her head was definitely her mother's that time. *Make him happy, Alana. Don't let him leave with a single worry.*

She hugged him a little tighter and then sat down in her chair. "Have you gotten a second opinion?"

"Don't need one," her father said. "I trust our doctor and the team that took care of me in Amarillo. Besides, I can feel it."

Alana took a deep breath. "I have something to say, and you might not like it." Her father was going to have his wish, and by damn, Paxton had better agree or else.

"It's not bad news, is it?" All the color had left his face.

Alana stood up, crossed the kitchen, and picked up the coffeepot and two mugs. That gave her another minute to put into the hardest words that would ever come out of her mouth. "It all depends on how you look at it, I guess, but it doesn't have anything to do with my health." She set the mugs on the table, filled them, and then returned the pot.

"All right then." His blue eyes stared right into her brown ones.

She sat back down, took a deep breath, and said, "Daddy, don't get mad, but I've been dating Paxton Callahan since he came home a few months ago. We both got tired of the way we were running from the attraction we've kind of had for each other for all these years, and well..." She let the sentence trail off.

"Why would I be mad?" Matt asked. "Paxton and I get along fine."

"Well, he and his brother were pretty wild before Granny Iris turned the ranch over to them." She was amazed that she could talk rationally about anything after the emotional bomb her dad had dropped on her. But she knew she had to stay strong to pull this off. She had to be strong for her father.

"I wasn't a saint either until I married your mother." Matt smiled for the first time. "So how serious is this relationship?"

"Very serious." She stood up and and got the chips from the cabinet to keep from meeting her father's gaze. "We've kept it secret because you know how people in Daisy are with their gossiping and spreading rumors. They'd have me pregnant and married by the end of summer."

"I wouldn't mind that one bit. I could walk you down the aisle, and to know I have a grandchild on the way would be the icing on the cake." Matt's tone got lighter with every word.

"Daddy!" Alana rolled her eyes.

How could they be talking about anything but what was going to happen and what needed to be done the next six weeks? There was all kinds of legal stuff to take care of, she thought, and they'd never discussed things like funerals.

That last word put a lump the size of a grapefruit in her throat.

"Don't take that tone with me," Matt chuckled. "I'm telling the truth. If y'all are very serious like you say, then you could move things along a little faster, couldn't you?"

"How can you laugh when…" Tears flooded her cheeks again.

He handed her a napkin. "We'll talk about serious things like my will, the ranch, and my burial another day. Right now, I want to feel alive and not think about the end. I don't mind checking out of this life, but I sure hate to leave you alone."

"You won't." She took a deep breath and forged ahead. "Pax proposed to me a week ago and we planned to elope to Las Vegas this summer, but if walking me down the aisle will make you happy, then we'll have a wedding right here in Daisy. How about we have a small, family-only type ceremony at the church?" She glanced at the calendar on the wall to the right of the sink. "Does June sixth sound good? That gives us a month."

"That's the day that me and your mama got married." Matt's eyes welled up, and he took the napkin from her. "I can't think of a better going-away present. I don't see a ring on your hand. Didn't he give you one?"

"Don't talk about going away." She wiped her new tears on her shirtsleeve. "We were going to pick out a ring this weekend."

"All right then," Matt said. "I'd love it if you used your mama's engagement ring. It's in the safe. I'll get it out for you right now. And, honey, for the next month, we're going to focus on your wedding. Your mama made me promise that you'd have a wedding to remember, and I'll see to it that you do. This shouldn't be a little family affair at the ranch. We're goin' to have a big event that folks will talk about for years and years."

Oh boy. How was Alana going to convince Paxton Callahan that they were getting married in a month when they hadn't even been dating?

* * *

Paxton Callahan was soaked in sweat when he brought the last load of small hay bales to the barn. The calendar might say it was the first week in May, but the temperature disagreed and insisted it was the middle of July. At least the heat wave had dried the hay that was down in the field so they could get it baled. He and his brother, Maverick, had noticed dark clouds over in the southwest, so they hadn't even taken a noon break. Maverick's wife, Bridget, had brought sandwiches and a gallon of chilled sweet tea to them right out to the field so they could eat and keep on working. The first big drops of rain hit as he drove the truck into the barn.

Pax removed his cowboy hat from his head and wiped his forehead with a red bandanna. "That was close, but at least we've got it all inside."

"Luck is with us today, brother." Maverick jumped out of the passenger seat of the old farm truck.

"Luck," Pax whispered under his breath as he pulled his work gloves from the hip pocket of his Wranglers and grabbed hay hooks from a nail on the barn wall. "I'll finish this if you want to go on to the house," he said. "It's only forty bales, and Bridget has an appointment up in Amarillo, doesn't she? If you hurry, you'll have time to get cleaned up and go with her."

"Thank you. I'll sure take you up on that. Getting U.S.

citizenship takes a lot of paperwork. I'm glad we've got a good lawyer working with us." Maverick hung his pair of hooks back on a nail and took off his gloves. He removed his hat and wiped his brow, then resettled it. "We might have supper up there, and maybe even take Laela to the park before we come home."

"I can fend for myself." Pax sunk the hooks into a bale and tossed it off the side of the truck.

"All right then, see you later." Maverick jogged from the open barn doors out to his pickup.

Pax tossed off a few more bales, then hopped over the side of the truck bed and started stacking them. That word *luck* kept playing through his mind. Little Laela was lucky to have parents like Mav and Bridget in her life. His own father had died when he and Mav were young, and then their mother remarried and handed them off to their grandparents to raise. Fortunately, their grandparents were amazing people who did their best to bring them up right.

"Laela won't have a mother who ever leaves her behind for another man," he muttered as he stacked the last bale.

He was jumping out of the back of the truck when he caught a movement in his peripheral vision.

"Hey, Pax."

He'd know that husky, sultry voice anywhere. He glanced up to find Alana Carey not two feet from him.

Like he'd been doing since high school, he paused to take in her beauty: blond hair and big brown eyes and legs that seemed to go on forever. She was so tall that she looked him right in the eye, and he was over six feet. But even more awe-inspiring than her looks was her attitude. She could outride, out-ranch, and out-dance every cowboy in the Texas panhandle—and she could most likely out-drink all of them, too. Truth be told, she intimidated the hell out of him—and yet her presence was like a magnet at the same time.

But the pain and misery in her normally sparkling eyes brought him up short. "Alana, what's wrong?"

"It's Daddy." She could barely get the words out before she started sobbing as if her heart was broken. Nothing ever rattled Alana, and he'd never heard her voice crack like that.

"What happened?" Paxton stepped forward and wrapped his arms around her, coaxing her head to his shoulder. "Let it all out and tell me what I can do to help."

"The doctor said he's got cancer. And only six weeks to live."

"Oh, sweetie." The soothing words came naturally to Pax. He knew Alana wasn't the type who needed to be coddled, but he hated seeing her so upset.

"He doesn't want anyone to know, but..." Another round of weeping began. "I have to talk to you before the whole town finds out."

"I won't tell a soul," he promised. "And I'm glad you came to me. You can't carry around something this big and this sad all on your own."

Alana pulled back and wiped at her eyes with her sleeve. "I'm sorry for getting all emotional on you." She took a step back and sat down on the nearest bale of hay.

"Hey, that's what friends are for. When is he starting treatments? Do you need me to take him to the doctor or help you on the ranch? Tell me what to do."

"No treatments." She hiccupped. "It's an inoperable brain tumor, and Daddy says he wants to die with dignity."

"Alana, I'm so, so sorry." Pax blinked back tears of his own. It was hard to imagine the strapping man he'd known his whole life wouldn't be with them for much longer.

"Please know that I'm here for you and for Matt. I'd do anything at all for y'all."

She took a deep breath, and he could tell she was fighting to get words past the lump in her throat. "Daddy has said"— her lip quivered and she took a second to compose herself— "so many times that he wants to live to see me settled down and married, and that his biggest wish is that he gets to walk me down the aisle someday."

Pax gave Alana a bittersweet smile. "I've heard Matt say those very words several times, myself."

"I want his wish to come true, Pax." She took another deep breath and then began to talk very fast, as if she had to get the words out in a hurry. "I told him that we'd been dating ever since you came back to Daisy, and that we'd been planning to elope sometime this summer. So you can either fake break up with me right now, and I can go home and tell him the sad news, or you can go along with my story. I said we'd planned to get married on June sixth in a small family ceremony at the church here in Daisy. It'll be a small thing, and after he's"—she sniffled—"after he's...I can't say the word. When he's with Mama in heaven, we'll have it annulled."

"Whoa!" Pax threw up both palms defensively. "You did what?" He couldn't wrap his mind around what she'd asked of him. They'd been neighbors and friends their whole lives. They'd attended the same small rural school and the same church. And there was no doubt that there'd been sparks between them, but to marry her? Sweet Jesus in heaven! "You want me to pretend that we're engaged? To lie to a dying man?"

"But it will make my daddy so happy in his last days," she said. "And you can't tell anyone that it's all fake, not even Maverick, because we have to make Daddy truly believe it. He'd be devastated if he knew I made it all up. Please, Pax. It's not for very long." Her big brown eyes shimmered with tears.

He couldn't say yes to such a crazy idea! But then he couldn't very well say no, either, now, could he? God, he hated to see a woman cry. If he agreed to what she was asking, he'd be a married man in a month.

"I know it's a lot to ask," Alana said. "I shouldn't have told him that we were dating until I asked you if you were willing to go along with it."

Pax took her hand in his and tapped her ring finger. "I wouldn't be the kind of cowboy who didn't even buy you a ring."

"I've got Mama's engagement ring," she said. "That way you're not even out money on this deal."

"All right," Pax said before he lost his courage. "I'll do it."

She threw her arms around him and said, "One more thing, and it's a big one. Would you please, please ask Daddy for my hand in marriage?" He's old-fashioned and..."

Pax liked the feeling of her body pressed against his chest. "Of course," he whispered. "I hope he don't see right through the lie."

"He'll be so happy that he'll never know." Alana hugged him even tighter and then moved back. "Thank you, Pax. From the bottom of my heart and soul, I thank you. It'll mean a lot of pretending, but..."

He leaned over and kissed her on the cheek. "I'll get cleaned up and go talk to your dad this afternoon, and please put that ring on your finger," Pax said. "If we're going to do this, let's make it believable for Matt's sake."

She pulled a beautiful diamond ring from her pocket and handed it to him.

It's only pretend, he told himself as he took the ring

from her, *and I'd do anything for Matt.* "If we're going to do this, then let's make it as real as possible," he said as he got down on one knee and said, "Alana Joy Carey, will you marry me?"

This might be the right way to propose to a woman, down on one knee with the ring in his hand, but Pax had always figured when he popped the question to a woman it would be in a more romantic place than the barn. In his mind, he'd be dressed up in his Sunday finery and everything surrounding them would be ultraromantic.

"Yes." She smiled.

He slipped the ring on her finger and kissed her on the cheek.

"Thank you," she said with a rather sisterly peck on his forehead. "Now we won't be lying about the proposal."

Chapter Two

Not much made Paxton Callahan nervous. Usually, he was as solid and steady as a rock. He could walk right up to a woman in a bar and have her in his arms and dancing in five seconds. He could sweet-talk his way around a deal when it came to buying cattle for the ranch without blinking an eye. But that afternoon, he was sweating bullets when he climbed the three stairs up onto the porch at the Carey house. On the way over to talk to Matt that afternoon he'd practiced several different versions of what he would say, but now none of them sounded right or even plausible in his head.

He raised his hand to knock on the door, and Matt swung it open.

"Come on in, Pax." Matt stood to one side.

Paxton wiped his feet and stepped out of the blistering heat into the cool foyer. He removed his cowboy hat and ran his fingers through his dark brown hair.

"This humidity is a killer, ain't it?" Matt said as he led the way into the living room. "Never seen it this damn hot in May. I hate to think about what it'll be like in July, but then…" He stopped talking and sat down in a recliner. "Have a seat. Want a beer or sweet tea or something?"

"Alana told me, sir." Pax sat down on the end of the sofa and laid his hat on the end table. "I'm so sorry. If you need anything at all, call me, and I'll come runnin'. And I'll pass on the beer for now."

"Thank you, son," Matt sighed. "I'm glad y'all have moved the wedding up. Getting prepared for the big day will keep Alana so busy she won't have time to worry."

Pax cleared his throat. No matter what he said or how he said it, the next words out of his mouth weren't going to be easy. "I really came to ask for your blessing on our marriage." He spit the words out so nervously that he was sure Matt would figure out something was up.

"Most fathers would ask a future son-in-law to take care of their daughter. Alana doesn't need that from you." Matt's tone and expression were serious, "She can take care of herself and this ranch. What she needs is for you to love her, respect her, and stand beside her until death parts you, like the wedding vows say. You think you can do that?"

Pax nodded slowly as he tried to figure out a way to agree to the terms without it being a big ugly lie. To love her, respect her, and stand beside her he could do, but that until-death-parts-you thing was throwing butcher knives at his heart. Then he realized that it would be death that parted them—maybe not with his death or Alana's death, but Matt passing on. "I can do that," he finally said. "I've always respected Alana and loved her. Standing beside her won't be a problem, sir."

"Stop calling me that." Matt shook his finger at Pax. "You've both got my blessing, and I'd sure like it if you'd call me Dad after y'all are married." He slid his phone from his shirt pocket and touched the screen.

He waited a minute and then said, "Alana, honey, can you come to the house?" Whatever she said put a grin on his face. He ended the call and turned back to Pax. "She'll be here in a few minutes. I want to thank you so much for agreeing to move the date up so I can walk her down the aisle. We're both struggling with this whole thing, Pax. I'm trying to be strong for her, but this sucks."

"I can't even imagine," Pax said. "But like I said before, I'm here for both of you. All either of you have to do is pick up the phone and call me."

"Thank God for that," Matt said. "Knowing she won't be alone will make it easier to go when I have to leave."

Not knowing what to say, Pax nodded.

"I don't want you kids to worry about a thing. I'll take care of the whole wedding so you can enjoy your short engagement. I've already called the preacher and got the date on the church calendar. That's one thing y'all don't have to worry about."

"That's great," Pax said with a smile. But thoughts circled in his head like buzzards flying over a dead bull out in the pasture.

How fast would word get around? The preacher would have told Trudy Mason, the church secretary, to put the date on the calendar. Then she was sure to tell her son, Billy Ray, who had worked on Callahan Ranch for several šummers while he was in high school. Pax hoped he had a chance to tell Maverick and their grandmother the news before they heard it through the grapevine.

Alana arrived before either Matt or Pax could continue

their conversation. She removed a pair of work gloves, nodded toward her father, and crossed the room to kiss Pax on the cheek.

"I've given you two my blessing." Matt inhaled deeply. "I want you to respect Pax in this relationship and not be as bullheaded as you usually are."

Alana sat down on the arm of the sofa and slung her arm around Pax's shoulder. "I'll do my best, Daddy."

Pax had danced with Alana at the Wild Cowboy Saloon more than once. Hell, they'd been dancing around each other for years, and his heart had never skipped a beat one time—except in elementary school, when he literally ran from her and got winded. Maybe it was the fact that she was wearing an engagement ring, but something was definitely different now. Her touch had caused a stir down deep inside of his heart like nothing he'd ever felt before.

He sensed that he should do something so he laid a hand on her knee. "We both will, darlin'." He smiled up at her, hoping that it was enough to convince Matt he was serious.

"Let's all have a good cold beer," Alana said. "Then I'll get changed and ready for our date to celebrate us telling the world. The way this town likes to gossip, I'm surprised that we weren't found out months ago."

Date?

They hadn't talked about a date or a celebration.

"I'll skip the beer and be back in half an hour to pick you up." Pax stood up and gave her a quick peck on the lips. That almost breathless feeling in his heart got even stronger.

"Better make it an hour. Where did we decide to go?" She raised an eyebrow.

"It's a surprise," he said, "Wear something nice. I guarantee it's better than going to a hamburger joint."

"Ahh, shucks." She played along. "I had my heart set on a double meat and cheese from The Burger Palace."

"I remember when Joy and I got engaged," Matt said. "We went to The Silver Dove in Amarillo to celebrate. I actually got down on one knee at that restaurant and gave her the ring. I took her back there to celebrate every one of our anniversaries, and I've gone back every year since she passed away on our anniversary for the memories."

A single tear left a silver streak down Alana's cheek. "Daddy, we don't have to go out tonight. We can stay right here, and the three of us can have supper together. It's the first day that…" She couldn't finish the sentence.

"No way!" Matt declared. "This is an important night for the two of you. Go make memories that will last as long as mine have. Besides, you gave me your word that you'd let me live life as normal as possible, and now I'm asking that neither of you smother me."

"That's a tall request," Pax said.

"I'd rather live for the moment than worry about the end," he said.

"Then that's what we'll do. Besides, don't you have a poker game tonight with your buddies?" Alana reminded him. "It is Wednesday, after all."

"Yep. We're playing over at Carlton's tonight."

"They're your closest friends, Daddy. Are you going to tell them?"

"Nope, and neither of you are either. We're going to spend our time planning a wedding, not a damn funeral," Matt answered. "Now, Alana, you get on upstairs and make yourself presentable. Pax, you go do whatever it is you need to do to take my baby girl to a nice place, and I'm going to Clayton's. We've got things to do, so let's get after them."

"Nothing has curbed your bossiness," Alana smarted off.

"That's my girl," Matt chuckled. "That's what I want to hear and see. We've had our time of cryin', now let's do what that song says, let's live like we were dying."

"That was my buddy Tag Baker's favorite song for a long time," Pax said.

"Yep, and it's a good one." Matt stood up and held out a hand toward Pax. "Welcome to the family."

"Thank you, sir." Pax had panicked when Alana first told him her plans, but things had gone more smoothly than he could have imagined. One month out of his entire life wasn't so long, and God only knew what a wonderful neighbor Matt had been. Matt had been there to help Pax and Mav out of plenty of scrapes. He owed the man. And Matt deserved to rest in peace.

Pax settled his hat back on his head. "I'll be back in an hour."

Alana slipped her hand into his and walked with him out onto the porch. Her hand fit into his as if it had been formed specially for him. "Thank you so much, again."

"Hey, that's enough thanks." He gave her a hug because she looked like she needed one. She'd known about her father's diagnosis for less than a day. The real sorrow hadn't even had time to settle into her heart and soul. "You'd do the same for me if Mam was in Matt's boots. Besides, if this was real, you wouldn't thank me all the time."

"All right then." She hugged him back. "Are we really going somewhere fancy or can I wear jeans?"

"Put on your prettiest dress, darlin'," he said. "I'm takin' you out for a celebration."

He waved from the window of his truck when he got inside, then quickly rolled up the window and turned on the air-conditioning. He got the call from Maverick about the time he pulled into the driveway at his ranch. He figured his brother had already heard the news, and Pax dreaded answering the phone, but he finally hit the accept icon. "How mad are you?" he asked.

"About what?" Maverick said. "Bridget and I are here with Mam. We got done at the lawyer's a little early so we stopped by, and then we're going to have supper before we come on home."

"Hello, Pax," his grandmother said.

"You're on speaker." Bridget's Irish accent had faded a little in the five months she'd been in the States, but not a lot. "You've got me, Maverick, Mam, and Laela."

"Well, y'all only have me, and I've got some big news," Pax said.

"You got the old tractor fixed that we've been workin' on?" Maverick asked.

"Why did you think Mav was mad at you?" Mam asked.

"I asked Alana to marry me, and she said yes." He spit it out all at once before they could ask another question. "We've been kind of secretly dating since I've been home, and—"

"Bullshit!" Maverick cut him off. "That's the biggest crock of crap I've ever heard out of you. Last week you couldn't wait to get to the Wild Cowboy to blow off steam."

"Alana was there, too." Pax wasn't lying. Alana *had* been there, and he'd avoided her all evening.

"I'm not a bit surprised," Mam said. "Y'all have both fought the attraction between you since you were teenagers. I don't know why it took you this long to admit it."

"I'm not surprised, either," Bridget said. "When you're in the room together, I can see the heat between y'all."

"I still don't believe it," Maverick said. "You're either yankin' my chain or you've lost your mind."

"I gave her an engagement ring today. I went over to ask Matt for his blessing this afternoon. Alana and I are about to go out to celebrate this evening." Pax heard another phone ringing in the background.

"Hello, Trudy," Mam said.

Pax rolled his eyes toward the ceiling. *Thank you, God,* he mouthed.

"Yes, we've already heard. Pax told us all about it, and yes, ma'am, I'm all for having a wedding shower at the church sometime this month. Let me know what you need me to do. Bye now," Mam said. "Okay, I'm back. I guess you heard me talking to Trudy?"

"Yes, I did. Matt told me that he'd called the church and put the date on the calendar," Pax said.

"I'll believe it when I hear the preacher pronounce you man and wife," Maverick said. "I don't know what you and Alana have going, but you'd have told me if you were dating her."

"Like you told him all about me, right?" Bridget asked.

"That was different," Maverick said.

"And on that note, I'm going to go get ready for my celebration date with Alana tonight. See y'all at breakfast, and I'll be up to visit you soon, Mam. Bye." He ended the call.

When Pax and Maverick had inherited Callahan Ranch, their Mam's dog and cat came right along with the house. Mam had named the dog Ducky because he had short legs, and she said that he waddled when he walked. To Pax, he looked like a cross between a Catahoula and a dachshund with a lot of pure old mutt thrown in. Dolly was named after Dolly Parton, and when she meowed, it kind of did sound like she was singing.

Ducky was waiting on the porch and made a beeline inside

the house as soon as Pax opened the door. He touched noses with Dolly, who was sleeping in front of the cold fireplace, and then headed over to the rug under the coffee table.

"Guess what?" Pax said. "I'm getting married in about four and a half weeks. Can you believe that? I damn sure can't."

The dog barked. The cat meowed pitifully. And Pax's phone rang again.

"Hello, Billy Ray," he said.

"Mom just told me the news, and I wanted to congratulate you," Billy Ray said. Pax had known Billy Ray for ages. If Mav weren't already Pax's best friend, Billy Ray would've been close.

"Thanks. I'm still a bit shocked myself."

"Well, I'm a little jealous," Billy Ray continued. "I've always had a crush on Alana, and when I was a little kid, I even planned our wedding. I got to admit, y'all sure did a fine job of keeping the secret."

Pax moved down the hall to his bedroom. "We didn't want to go public with the news because we live so close together. What if we'd broken up? Then it would be awkward for our families."

"Well, now it all makes perfect sense why she rejected me," Billy Ray chuckled. "Call me if you need anything. Mama's already planning a wedding shower."

"Thanks," Pax said again.

"Be seein' you around," Billy Ray said and ended the call with a goodbye.

Pax tossed his phone over on the bed and stripped out of his clothing. He'd shoved his legs down into his jeans when the phone rang again. When he saw Hud's face pop up on the screen, he groaned. "Surely to God, the news hasn't gotten halfway across the state already!"

"Hey, what's going on in Sunset?" he asked.

"Congratulations!" Hud chuckled. "I knew if Alana chased you long enough that you'd catch her."

"How did you find out so fast? We only told her dad today," Pax asked.

"Billy Ray called me," Hud replied. "Why didn't *you* tell me?"

"I was going to tell y'all first, but Matt got all excited and reserved the date at the church before Alana and I could tell our families and personal friends. Damn Billy Ray anyway. He's a bigger gossip than his mama." It was amazing how fast Pax was falling into the part of Alana's fiancé.

"Always has been. They're good people, but they do like to spread the news," Hud chuckled again. "How come the wedding is so quick? I figured Alana would be one that wanted the big church thing with everyone in Daisy invited."

"Alana? You must not really know her. She wanted us to elope to Las Vegas." He made a mental note to tell her that bit of information. "Her father made her promise to at least have a small ceremony and reception right here in Daisy."

"June six, right?" Hud asked. "I've got the pen in my hand, and you know the rule. Remember the rule—if it's on the calendar here in the ranch house, it's written in stone."

"Start writing," Pax replied, surprised that he wasn't stammering even a little bit. "I'll see you in a month."

"Wouldn't miss it for the world. Got to go tell Tag and all the folks over on Longhorn Canyon. They're going to be as shocked as I was. Bye now."

The screen went dark, and Dolly came wandering into the room. She jumped up on his bed and started purring. Pax stopped what he was doing long enough to pet her. "When I woke up this morning, I had no idea I'd be getting married in a month, but I couldn't turn Alana down. Who knows, maybe by being around her so much, I'll get over this infatuation I've had for her since I was a kid."

The cat looked up at him and meowed.

"I know it's crazy as hell, and it sure doesn't go along with my plans."

The cat meowed again.

"My dream was to have my own house built and ready for a bride before that time came. Maybe I'd even have enough money in the bank for a decent little honeymoon. Until then, I'd work hard, party hard, and enjoy my life as a freewheeling cowboy."

Dolly curled up in a ball and shut her eyes.

"Some friend you are," Pax griped. "It's written in stone now. I just hope we don't get trapped in our own web of lies now."

Chapter Three

Alana slumped down into the rocking chair in her bedroom and took a deep breath. The ball was rolling now, and there was no way to stop it. She thought back to the time when she and Pax were kids. She'd chased him on the playground. He'd stolen a ribbon from her hair one day and refused to give it back, so she'd taken his pencil that afternoon in English. It was still in her memory box where she kept her prize things, like the rock they'd both found on a science trip in the sixth grade. He'd let her have it, and she'd thought he liked her.

She checked the time and realized she needed to get a shower and figure out what she would wear, so with a long sigh, she pushed up out of the chair. She opened the memory box, took out the pencil and rock, and smiled at the vision of Pax as a young kid when his voice hadn't even changed yet.

Maybe things would have been different if both of them

hadn't been so damned stubborn after that incident behind the barn when they were thirteen. She'd snuck back there to get away from all the people who were still hanging around after the fall ranch sale and dinner. Paxton had appeared out of nowhere and sat down beside her—and out of nowhere he'd kissed her. She drew back her fist, opened it before it made contact, and slapped the fire out of his cheek.

She could still see him jumping to his feet and grabbing his face. His voice had cracked when he said, "Why'd you do that? I thought you liked me."

"Not like that," she'd said. "And don't you never try something like that again or next time I'll hit you harder."

He'd crossed his arms over his chest and glared at her. "Don't worry. I wouldn't kiss you again if you was the only girl on earth." Then he'd stormed off into the dark, and they had both run from the emotions of that first kiss all these years.

"He didn't have to go and kiss another girl the very next day at school," she muttered. "I don't know if he really liked me or if he wanted to start kissing, and I was available."

A shiver ran down Alana's back when she thought of how Pax's touch still affected her like that first kiss had—leaving her a little bit breathless and speeding up her pulse.

She stared at her reflection in the mirror. "Maybe this month will get him out of my system. God knows I need to if I'm ever going to move forward with a real relationship."

She hated lying to her father, but in the last few hours, the sadness had left his eyes, and he'd talked about nothing but the wedding. If he passed away before the wedding, she and Paxton would simply break up. If not, then they'd get an annulment or a divorce. Either scenario would bring on the gossip mongers like ants to an open sugar bowl. She could handle all that if her daddy could die a happy man.

Just thinking those last few words caused a lump in her throat that was difficult to swallow. She shook her finger at her reflection in the mirror and whispered, "You are making Daddy's wishes come true. It doesn't matter how much flack you get over it all or how *you* might feel. This is for Daddy, and you will pull it off, no matter what it takes. No one will ever, ever know that it wasn't all real until the breakup, and then I'll even take the blame for it, so that Pax's reputation won't be ruined."

With new resolve, she turned away from the mirror and went into her bathroom to take a shower and wash her hair. She came out of the bathroom with a towel around her hair and another wrapped around her body. She had thirty-five minutes to get ready. She quickly dried her long, blonde, naturally wavy hair and drew up the sides with a pretty silver and turquoise clamp. Then she slapped on a bit of makeup—a tiny bit of eye shadow and a little lipstick. She opened the closet doors and picked out a lovely off-white dress with spaghetti straps, a tight bodice, and a flowing skirt that stopped at her knees.

It took her awhile to decide between a pair of light brown sandals or the cowboy boots that she'd gotten got for her birthday last spring—brown with a turquoise inlay of a phoenix with outstretched wings. She caught her reflection in the mirror again and frowned. "Why am I worrying about this anyway? This isn't real. I'm not really engaged."

But you're playing an important part. Her mother's voice was so clear in her head that she whipped around to see if she'd come back to life and was in the room with her. *You and Pax are doing a sweet thing. It'll keep your father from counting the days and worrying about you when he's gone.*

"Yes, ma'am," she said aloud and smiled.

Joy Carey didn't pop into her head very often, and when she did have a memory or a moment, it meant a lot to Alana.

She slipped her feet down into the boots, picked up her purse and an ivory lace shawl. When she reached the bottom of the stairs, she heard the sound of a truck pulling up in the front yard. Her phone rang before she could open the front door, so she fished it out of the purse and answered it.

"Hi, Emily," she said.

"Congratulations!" Emily yelled into the phone. "I could wring your neck for not telling me that you and Pax were dating. We've talked every couple of weeks since Christmas, and you didn't say a word. Hud came in to tell us that y'all are engaged. We've already got the date on the calendar. I wouldn't miss it for the world."

Emily had always been her best friend, even though they attended different high schools. Daisy and Tulia weren't that far apart, and the two girls were always thrown together at rodeos and ranch parties. Then when they got their driver's license, they were back and forth between the two ranches every weekend or chance they got. Emily was the one that she'd gone to when Pax kissed that other girl. She smiled at what Emily had told her. "He's pretty, but he's a dumb boy to do that. You should hit him again."

"It's going to be a small affair with family and close friends, but you know that includes everyone on Callahan Ranch as well as Longhorn Canyon Ranch and Canyon Creek Ranch. That'll be a pretty big crowd right there." Alana heard boots on the wooden porch and then a rap on the door. "Got to go now. Pax is here to take me out to celebrate our engagement."

"I'll come a week early if you need help," Emily offered.

"Thank you. I'll keep that in mind. Bye now," Alana said.

She slipped the phone back into her purse, opened the door, and stood face-to-face with Pax. He filled out his Wranglers just right, and his western shirt stretched across his broad chest like it had been tailor-made for his body. She inhaled deeply and let it out slowly as she stepped out onto the porch and closed the door behind her. "You clean up very well, Paxton."

"So do you, Alana Joy." He offered her his arm. "Matter of fact, you are downright gorgeous tonight, but then you always are."

"Why are you double-naming me?" she asked as they headed toward his truck.

"Kind of nice not having to shorten my stride." He opened the truck door for her. "And I double-named you because you called me Paxton. You only do that when you're mad at me."

"It's real nice not to have to watch the length of *my* steps, too," she replied as she fastened her seat belt. "Most men shy away from a six-foot giant like me, but lots of the guys I've dated were shorter than me."

He rounded the front of the vehicle and got behind the wheel. "Hud already called me."

"Emily called me."

"I guess we both dove right into the deep water with this, didn't we? Was it hard to lie to Emily?" He started the engine and turned on the air-conditioning.

"Strangely enough, not so much. It was a lot tougher to tell Daddy that we were dating and seriously thinking about getting married. And believe me..." She stared him right in the eyes. "It was sure enough harder to ask you to go along with the idea."

"We're over the first hurdle at least," he said.

"Momma knows, too." She told him about her mother being in her head. "Do you ever feel like someone is talking to you, only it's not even possible because they've passed away?"

"Oh, yeah." He put the truck in gear and drove away from the house. "Mostly it's my grandpa, but sometimes Mam fusses at me, and she's even still alive. Your mama is right. This is for Matt, but we've got to keep our heads in the game like it's real. One missed step and we'll break his heart. I'm glad that he gave us his blessing."

"And the ring." She held it up to catch what little light was left in the day. "You could have bought a fake one, but this is so much better."

"It's ruined for the time when you really get engaged, though, isn't it?" Pax turned at the end of the lane and started toward Daisy.

"Oh, any real engagement in my life is a long ways away, so I might be fine with using this ring again. It's nice to have something of my mother's. And at least Daddy won't know anything about it when the times comes," she answered. "You know we could go there," she said when they passed The Burger Palace.

"Oh, honey, that wouldn't be right," Pax said. "This is our engagement celebration—real or not—and everyone in Daisy will know where we went by the time we get home."

"You're right," she conceded. "So where are we going?"

"The Silver Dove. Reservations at eight," he told her. "Your dad deserves all the happiness we can give him."

Alana laid her hand on Pax's shoulder. "You are a good man."

"Thank you for that. Now, from this moment on, we're engaged," he said.

She drew in a long breath and let it out slowly. "I'm not going to thank you, but I am going to say it again—you are an amazing friend and a good man."

"Did you ever look back and try to figure out when we became friends instead of enemies and competitors?" he asked.

"I think it was that night you brought me home after the prom. God, Pax, I wanted to go with you so bad, but you went stag rather than ask me," she said.

"I figured if I couldn't take you—and believe me, that time I kissed you and you tried to knock my teeth out taught me that you didn't want anything to do with me," he said. "Anyway, if I couldn't be with you, then I wouldn't ask anyone. But, honey, I couldn't let you go to that after-party. Darrin Wilson had bragged in the boys' bathroom that he was going to..." He hesitated.

"Darrin said that?"

"Yep, he'd been refilling your punch cup and adding vodka to it all evening so you'd be drunk enough to"—another pause—"not tell him no. So when the prom was over, I talked you into letting me take you home."

"I guess that's when we started being friends all right," she agreed. "But it's taken us both a long time to build up to now, hasn't it?"

"You got that right."

* * *

Pax had seen a blooper reel of *Friends* a few years back, and one of the cast members had said "Get in character" as she ran her hand down her face. When she did that, she'd changed into the woman she was playing. As he escorted Alana into The Silver Dove, he told himself the same thing.

He liked Alana—that was a fact. He respected Matt—that was absolute truth.

"We're going to be together a lot in the next few weeks," Alana said.

He slipped his arm around her shoulders, and leaned in to whisper, "It won't be difficult. Did you get all your hay in before the rain hit?"

She looked into his eyes, let a sweet smile play at the corners of her mouth, and answered, "Yes, I did, and I bet we get another cutting in a month."

"It's not what people hear, it's what they see that gets their imagination in gear." He kissed her on the tip of her nose and remembered that first kiss he'd stolen out behind the barn a lifetime ago. Who would have ever thought that they'd be where they were today after that fiasco?

"This way, please." A hostess motioned for them to follow her and showed them to a table in the middle of the room. "Vicky will be your waitress, and she'll be with you soon."

Pax seated Alana and adjusted her shawl before he sat down. "Looks like we got center court, and I see two tables of folks from Tulia and from Daisy."

She glanced around and waved to those she knew. "I thought this was a place for a special occasion."

Pax leaned across the table and took both her hands in his. "Me, too. See that older couple to our left. I bet they're here to celebrate his retirement."

"You'd lose that bet. See that big diamond ring on her hand and the way they keep smiling. I think they got engaged too," she said.

"They're too old for..." he started.

"Honey, haven't you read that there's more Viagra pills sold than antibiotics these days?" A mischievous grin tilted her lips. "I bet they think we're talking about how much in love we are."

"Let's hope so." He gently squeezed her hands.

"Good evening. Well, hello, Pax Callahan." The waitress batted her eyelashes at him. "I heard you'd moved back, but I haven't been out to the Wild Cowboy in ages."

"Vicky, meet my fiancée, Alana. Alana, this is Vicky," Pax said.

"Nice to meet you." Vicky nodded toward Alana, then turned back to Pax. "Never thought I'd see the day that a woman would lasso you."

Pax kept his eyes on Alana and a smile on his face. "It took someone who understands me and loves me for what I am: a plain old cowboy."

"Well, I'm here to take your drink order, and then I'm going to leave you with another waitress," Vicky said. "I'm already dipping into overtime, and The Silver Dove doesn't like us to do that. So what can I get you?"

"A bottle of your best champagne," Pax answered. "And bring us an assortment of appetizers to nibble on while we study the menu."

"Coming right up, and congratulations to you both." She winked at Pax.

"What was that all about?" Alana asked.

"We danced a few times at the Wild Cowboy and flirted a lot," he admitted.

"Are you going to miss those times this next little while?" she asked.

"Maybe, but then I'm engaged to the prettiest girl in this part of Texas, so I kind of doubt it. We'll be so busy with all the wedding stuff that the time will go fast." The smile disappeared, and he tilted his head to the side. "I'm sorry. You don't want the time to go by lightning fast. You'll want to enjoy every moment you can spend with Matt."

"This whole thing has me so wound up in knots that I'm not sure what I want," she said. "The full impact of what is about to happen hasn't even sunk in. I've cried, and Daddy and I've talked a little, but not enough. He doesn't seem to want to say much about it, other than that he wants life to be as normal as it can possibly be. Looking back now, I realize that something's been wrong for a while. He hasn't had much of an appetite, and he's been taking a nap after we come in at noon for a break. Maybe if I'd been less involved with the ranch, I would've made him go to the doctor sooner."

"You can't blame yourself," Pax said. "And Matt wouldn't want you to anyway."

"But I do," she argued. "I'm an only child. He's raised me all by himself after Mama died. I never thought of him as aging. I guess I figured that he'd live to be a hundred or at least ninety, like his father did."

"That's what I thought about my grandpa too, so I understand what you're saying. He was taken from me in the blink of an eye, but he died the way he wanted. He used to tell me that he wanted to drop at the end of a long day, right there on the ranch, and that's exactly what happened." Pax locked gazes with her. "Your dad has been given some time and what he wants is to see you settled and happy. We can give him that."

"Hello, I'm Deanna." Their new waitress set a silver ice bucket with a bottle of champagne in it on the table. "Shall I pour for you?"

"Yes, please." Pax's eyes never left Alana's.

Deanna poured champagne into two flutes. "I'll be right back with your appetizers."

Pax picked up his glass and held it up. "To an amazing engagement and wedding."

She touched hers to his. "To making wishes come true."

They each took a sip.

Alana leaned forward and said, "I'd really rather have beer, but it's nice to try something a little different every now and then."

"Me too," Pax said. "These bubbles make my nose tickle."

Deanna brought out the appetizers and asked if they were ready to order. Alana reached for a grilled shrimp, looked at the menu once more, and said, "I'll have the nine-ounce rib eye, a loaded baked potato, fried okra, and sliced tomatoes."

Pax handed Deanna his menu. "Make that two of the same, only I want the twelve-ounce rib eye."

"Well, if you're going for the big steak, then change my order to that one too." Alana gave her menu to Deanna.

"How do you want the steaks cooked?" Deanna asked.

"Medium rare," Pax and Alana said at the same time and then laughed.

"Got it." Deanna hurried in the direction of the kitchen.

"We've got a lot in common, ranchin' being the biggest thing, but I was thinking about what it would be like for us if we were really getting married." Pax refilled their glasses and then picked up a fried cheese stick. "We both like tomatoes with our okra and our steaks cooked the same way. Think there's more to us than that?"

"We'd make a fine couple. We can talk cows and ranchin' for hours. We understand each other, and we make a damn good-lookin' couple." She reached for another shrimp.

"Yep." He picked up a slice of fried green tomato. "Do we have kids in this dream?"

Their hands brushed, and Pax wondered if she felt the same tingling sensation that he had.

She doesn't feel anything but sadness right now, the voice in his head scolded him.

He refilled her glass one more time, but not his.

"It gets better with each glass," she said. "Of course we have children. The ranch house was built for a lot of kids, and as you can see"—she made a motion that took in her body—"I'm built for having kids. You aren't drinkin' anymore? Does the husband in the dream give up alcohol?"

"I'm the designated driver tonight, and Matt would shoot me dead on the spot if I drove after drinking," he told her. "You have all you want. I'll throw you over my shoulder like a bag of chicken feed and carry you into the house if you pass out."

"Honey, it'd take more than this to knock me on my butt. I'll admit to being a little tipsy a few times, but only one time did I even have a hangover, and that was prom night, and I've never passed out in my life." She popped a tiny stuffed mushroom into her mouth and took a sip of champagne. "It's pretty damn good when you blend the two flavors. Here. Try one." She leaned across the table and fed him one, then handed him her glass.

He nodded in agreement. "You are so right. We'll have to have this at our wedding reception."

"I agree. I'm thinking a small wedding and then a reception at the church fellowship hall. What's your opinion of that?" she asked.

"Honey, it's your day, so you plan it any way you please. I'll show up and smile for the pictures," he answered.

"The smaller the better as far as I'm concerned. I don't know why I didn't tell Daddy that we'd already eloped to Las Vegas." She sighed.

"Then we'd have to be married, not engaged, and he wouldn't get to walk you down the aisle." Pax had a sudden image of them really living in the same house together. Sleeping in the same bed. He felt his cheeks flush and his blood stir at the thought.

"Holy smoke!" She clamped a hand over her mouth and whispered, "What happens if Daddy insists we go on a honeymoon?"

"We'll cross that bridge when we get to it." He laid his hand back on hers and squeezed her fingers ever so gently, willing his mind to think of anything but her on a beach in a bikini.

Chapter Four

"Hey, sweet baby." Pax stopped at the high chair to kiss Laela on the cheek when he reached the kitchen the next morning. He could still hardly believe his brother was now married with a newly walking toddler. As godmother to Laela, Bridget had taken charge of her when the baby's mother and father had both been killed in an automobile accident back in Ireland. Luckily, Pax loved Bridget like a sister, and he adored Laela.

"Don't you act like nothing has happened." Bridget turned away from the stove and punctuated every word with a fork. She might be petite, but dynamite came in small packages, and Bridget was a force to be reckoned with when she walked into a room.

Maverick poured two mugs of coffee and handed one off to Pax, and then they both sat down at the kitchen table. "You and Alana? When did y'all stop runnin' from each other?"

In that moment, Pax understood how hard it had been for Alana to lie to her father. He and Maverick had shared everything since they were little kids. They'd cried together when their dad died and again when their grandpa passed away. They'd moved away to the Rockin' B Ranch right out of high school to work with a couple of their friends, Tag and Hud Baker. Then when Tag and Hud bought a ranch of their own halfway across the state, they'd gone with them to help out. After Mam moved into an assisted-living facility and left Pax and Mav her ranch, he'd come back home, and they'd worked side by side to restore the place.

"We had to stop sometime and see if any of the vibes we've felt for the past ten years are real or if they were a flash in the pan," Pax said, trying to skirt around the issue.

"So why didn't you tell me that y'all were dating?" Maverick asked. "I thought you were still enemies."

Pax raised one shoulder in half a shrug. "We were what they call frenemies, I guess. That's somewhere between friends and enemies, and then somehow the enemy part kind of went by the wayside, a little at a time, and we became friends. We started talking, and then it led to more." That much wasn't a lie. After he had come home from Sunset in the winter, they had begun to talk about ranching stuff when they'd meet at the feed store or the burger joint. Then they'd started calling each other a couple of times a week to talk about other things.

"Why didn't you tell me that?" Mav asked.

"Things were going so well between us that we didn't want to jinx it," Pax answered. "We talked about eloping to Las Vegas, but Matt has always had this dream of walking her down the aisle." That part was true, so he looked his brother in the eye and smiled. "Be happy for me."

"Happy for you?" Maverick raised his voice. "You don't

even say the word *marriage* out loud, and you've been running from Alana since y'all were kids. Now you tell me you've proposed to her?"

"Marriage," Pax said with a grin on his face. "There I said it."

"All right." Maverick narrowed his eyes. "Now you said it, but when you even mentioned settling down, it was always after you were thirty."

"I'm almost twenty-nine," Pax shot back at his brother. "That's pretty damn close."

"I think you're rushing things because you think you want what we've all got," Maverick said.

Pax shrugged. "Maybe so, but it is what it is. I'm going to marry Alana, so get used to it. Will you be my best man?" Pax asked. "It's going to be a real small wedding with family and very close friends with a little reception in the fellowship hall."

"Of course." Maverick finally smiled. "But why the rush? Is she pregnant or something?"

"No, she's not pregnant and the rush is that we want to get married. God!" He raked his hands through his hair. "Geez, with this kind of interrogation, maybe we should've eloped to Las Vegas like we talked about doing."

"I don't know her so well," Bridget said, "but she seems like the type who'd want a big wedding. She's lived in this place all her life, and knows everyone. I'd think she'd want the big dress and all the frills."

"You got her pegged wrong. She's pretty down-to-earth once you get to know her. She didn't even want me to buy a ring. She's so sentimental that she wants to use her mother's wedding rings." Pax pushed back his chair, stood up, and re-filled their coffee mugs, then helped Bridget bring breakfast to the table.

Maverick said a short grace, and Bridget passed the platter of biscuits to him first.

"So from what I've heard, you and Alana have had some chemistry between you and you've been running from each other for a while?" Bridget asked.

"Since they were big enough to walk," Maverick answered.

"Why would you do that if you felt something for one another?" She handed the bowl of scrambled eggs to Pax.

"She'll be the sole owner of the Bar C when Matt passes away," Pax explained. "Until Mam deeded this place over to us, I had nothing to offer her, and besides once you've been runnin' as long as we were, it was kind of hard to stop and admit defeat. And"—he paused and decided to tell the truth—"it all started when we were thirteen." He went on to tell the story of their first kiss. "I decided right then I wasn't going to give her the time of day. I liked her and thought she liked me. I was wrong, and the rejection right along with that slap in the face sure enough smarted. I wasn't going to be rejected again."

"What was the exact day you decided to let her catch you?" Bridget asked.

"We both showed up at the assisted-living center to visit Mam and wound up going out for a burger. We figured out later that Mam had asked us both to come at the same time, and no doubt about it, she was playing matchmaker. Then the very next Saturday night we were both at the Wild Cowboy. We were dancing with other people and her partner tapped me on the shoulder, so I stepped back, and there she was, lookin' kind of hurt. So I opened up my arms and she walked into them. From then on, we kind of..." He kept the story as close to the truth as possible.

"Kind of fell in love," Bridget sighed.

"That's right." He made a mental note to call Alana later to tell her that he'd told that much of their story.

"And when did you actually propose?" Maverick finished biscuits and eggs and put a stack of three pancakes on his plate.

"Yesterday afternoon out in the barn," Pax answered. "She came over to see me right after you left. It wasn't nearly as romantic as I'd planned, but I did take her out to The Silver Dove for supper last night to make up for it."

"It doesn't have to be romantic." Bridget gave Laela small bites of egg while she ate. "You know in your heart when you love a person enough to ask them to marry you."

"That's the way I figured it." At least he didn't have to tell Alana how that happened.

"What did you say?" Bridget asked.

"I said, 'Alana Joy Carey will you marry me?'" He was damn sure glad he'd actually gotten down on one knee and done it up right.

"With no ring?" Maverick asked.

"We'd talked about eloping and having matching bands. Besides, I knew she loved her mother's ring. This was a fine breakfast, Bridget."

"Where are you going to live after the wedding?" Bridget asked.

"Over at her place." He hoped Alana wasn't having to answer this many questions. "But don't worry, I'll be over here every morning. This is our ranch, and I'll be here to help take care of it like always. I just won't sleep here."

"I guess your wild days are over." Maverick snapped his fingers. "That quick."

"So were yours," Bridget reminded him.

"Yes, but..." Maverick started.

"There are no buts when it comes to love," Bridget told him.

Pax chuckled as he got up, took his plate to the sink, and rinsed it. "I can only hope that Alana and I have as good a relationship as y'all have got."

He hurried out the back door before either of them could ask another question, went to his truck, and drove out to the barn where he and Maverick would be working on a tractor that morning. As soon as he was inside, he fished his phone from his hip pocket and called Alana.

* * *

"Hi, Pax." Alana was already in her truck and headed out to the barn on her place to tell the hired hands where she wanted them to work that morning. "I hope you survived the interrogation at your ranch this morning," she said.

"I kept everything as close to the truth as possible." He told her what he'd told his brother and Bridget.

She smiled at the sound of his voice—and at the memory of that night, when she danced in his arms. She'd felt as if she belonged there and wished that the song would never end.

"Got it," she said. "Daddy wasn't so interested in particulars about when we decided that we were in love. He's more wound up about this wedding. He's called a wedding planner, and we're supposed to meet with her tomorrow evening. And he says that he doesn't think the church will hold all our close friends, so he wants to have the wedding here at the ranch. You okay with that?" She'd come close to fainting that morning when he told her that her plan for a small wedding idea wasn't going to work, and that they were going to invite everyone they'd ever known.

"I don't even know what a wedding planner is, and whatever makes Matt happy is fine with me," Pax said. "So what are you doing today?"

"I'm helping Daddy measure our sale barn, and then we're going to make out a wedding list so the planner can get the invitations sent. That means you need to get your guest list done by tomorrow evening. Some of our people will be the same, but Daddy says the planner will sort it all out."

"I'm sure she will. How are you holding up?" Pax asked.

"Trying to keep busy. Otherwise I worry too much— about Daddy's..." She couldn't even say the word. "And whether we're doing the right thing."

"Hang in there, Alana. He seems to be getting a lot of joy with all this wedding planning. Focus on that."

His deep voice soothed her, like a hug right over the phone.

"Thanks, Pax. Can you come over for supper to help with some of the planning stuff?"

"I'll be there, darlin'."

When Alana got back to the house, her dad was sitting at the dining room table with folders and papers all around him. He looked up over the wire-rimmed reading glasses perched on his nose and smiled. "Sit down. I want to go over some of the books with you, and then we can start talking about the guest list. I don't want to leave anyone out and hurt their feelings."

"Daddy, I hate paperwork," Alana groaned, "and Pax and I really want to keep the wedding a small affair."

He patted the chair beside him. "Honey, we both hate to do the office work, but it has to be done if we want the ranch to be successful. Pick one day a week to take care of it all so it doesn't pile up. Your mama loved all the organization and books, so she did it before she left us."

Her father almost never said *when your mama died* or even *when your mama passed away*. It was always *when she left us.*

Alana sat down and kicked off her boots under the table. "All right then, let's get with it. What do I need to learn today?"

He pushed a whole stack of folders to one side. "Let's go over my will first and get that out of the way. I've left everything I own to you, of course, but since you're getting married and Pax will be living here, I'm wondering if I should put it in both your names. Until you have a child to inherit the place, it could be a nightmare if, God forbid, something happened to you. Pax wouldn't even be able to pay for a sack of cattle feed."

"Let's not talk wills today, Daddy," she sniffled. "It makes me too sad. That can always be changed after the wedding is over and done with."

"All right, but you need to keep that on the back burner," Matt said. "As soon as you get back from your honeymoon, we'll revisit this folder." He laid it to the side. "Now, let's get into finances. You already know what the operating cash is for the ranch and how much we've put into savings in case we have a bad year down the road, but I've had some personal accounts for years. I'm meeting with my lawyer tomorrow to sign all those over to you as well. One is for your wedding, so I don't want you to give a thought to how much anything costs."

All Alana heard was *honeymoon.* "Pax and I thought we'd wait until later to take a trip. I want to spend as much time with you as I possibly can, Daddy. I couldn't bear it if..." She couldn't say the words.

Matt wiped a tear from her cheek. "Don't cry. We need to talk about it like it's a second honeymoon for me and your mama. We'll be together again, and I'm so looking forward to looking at her all I want. After the wedding, I want you kids to at least have a long weekend honeymoon."

"But that would be time I could spend with you," Alana argued.

"It's important for you and Pax to have some time away from the ranches and from family. It'll make your marriage stronger." Matt patted her back. "So, where do you and Pax want to go? What's always been your dream vacation? We never went on anything that didn't have to do with Cattlemen's Conventions or rodeos. I'm sorry for that. I should have taken you to the beach or the mountains or even to New York City," he said.

"I loved going to the places we went to," she said.

"Close your eyes," he said.

She did what he asked.

"Now open them and say the first place that comes into your mind," he said.

"Right here on the ranch," she said.

"Oh, no, you're at least going somewhere for two or three days," he argued.

"Maybe Galveston to the beach then," she agreed, but she had no intentions of leaving the ranch after the wedding. Like Pax said, she'd cross the bridge when it came time, but today, she wasn't wasting precious time on a fake honeymoon.

* * *

"Well, don't you look all fine?" Bridget looked up from the counter where she was putting together a salad.

"Thank you." Pax smiled and then chuckled when a movement in his peripheral vision caught his eye. Ducky,

Dolly, and Laela marched into the room, looking like a little parade coming to see him off to the Bar C.

"She follows them everywhere, now that she can walk," Bridget said. "I don't know if they're trying to get away from her or helping her exercise, but whatever it is, she loves them."

Pax picked the toddler up and kissed her on the cheek. "A kiss for good luck and"—he kissed the other cheek—"another one because I love you so much."

Maverick came through the back door and Laela held out her arms to him. "Da-Dee," she said loud and clear. His brother removed his work gloves, stuffed them into his hip pockets, and took the baby.

Pax's felt like someone pricked his heart as he saw the love that flowed from the baby to her father. He opened the refrigerator to get out a couple of six-packs of beer and noticed the glance that passed between Maverick and Bridget. That's what he wanted when he *really* got engaged—a love so strong that everyone in the room could feel it.

"See y'all later," he said as he headed out the back door, reluctant to intrude on their private moment.

Laela waved at him and said, "Bye-bye."

"She's going to miss you when you move across to the Bar C," Bridget said.

Pax waved back at her. "I'll still see her every day."

He couldn't tell them that he wouldn't really be jumping the barbed-wire fence that separated the Callahan Ranch from the Bar C and actually moving into the big two-story house over there. "This is a helluva lot tougher than I thought it would be when I agreed to it," he muttered as he crossed the yard and got into his pickup truck.

As the crow flies, it would have taken only two minutes to get over to the neighboring ranch, but as the truck drove, it took longer. Pax had to drive down the lane a quarter of a mile, make a left-hand turn and drive a few hundred yards, and turn left into the lane leading up to the Carey house. When he arrived, Alana waved from the porch swing, then came to the truck and opened the door for him.

"We'll put that in the fridge," she said, pointing to the beer. "Daddy says he's in charge of dinner and that we're to spend a little time together." She motioned for him to follow her inside, took two beers from one of the six packs, and put the rest in the refrigerator. She twisted the tops off and handed one to Pax. "Let's sit out on the porch. I've always thought these walls have ears and that they report back to Daddy every night at bedtime. Somehow, I've never been able to keep anything from him." She tucked her free hand into Pax's and led him through the den, the foyer, and back outside.

"I used to think that about our house too," Pax said, "but I found out later it was Mam's hotline with the gossipers in Daisy." He waited for her to sit down beside her and then eased down on the porch swing.

She scooted over closer to him. "Just in case the drama gossips have spies out," she whispered. "This is our first night after the official engagement. If there's three feet of space between us, they'll think we're already fighting."

"You sure do look pretty tonight," he said, "and that's real, not pretend. Orange is a good color on you."

"Glad you like it." She smiled up at him.

Was this the same girl that had slapped him and told him in a loud voice to never touch her again?

That's when you were a kid, and you felt awkward about the kiss too, since it was your first one, Mam scolded him.

Pax remembered that night vividly. He'd watched Alana from the sidelines all evening, and when she'd gone out the back door, he'd followed her. The kids at school said that she liked him and wanted him to be her boyfriend. He'd never kissed a girl before so his heart was doing double-time and his hands were clammy. It didn't take long until his face was burning, not only from a hard slap but also from rejection.

"I'm planning on using yellow and orange for the wedding. It looks so summery." She took a long drink from her beer. "I didn't realize there was going to be so many details. I figured we'd go to the church, get married with a few friends and family watching, and then we'd get it annulled when"—she took another drink from the bottle—"when, well you know."

Pax slipped an arm around her shoulders. "Let's concentrate on getting through this a day at a time. It doesn't matter to me how big or how small the wedding is, and I'll even take the blame for the breakup when it comes, so long as you don't tell folks I was unfaithful." The thought of folks thinking that about him would be worse than being rejected by the one girl he'd admired up until that fatal night when they were thirteen.

"I'd never do that," Alana said. "I think the best scenario is that we rushed into marriage too quick because I knew my dad was dying, and I wanted to make him happy. It's the truth, so it's believable."

"And my excuse will be that Matt wanted to walk you down the aisle so I proposed. It's the truth, even if it isn't the whole truth and nothing but the truth," he said.

"One more thing out of the way," Alana agreed.

Matt opened the door and said, "Food's on the table, so if you two lovebirds can quit making eyes at each other, we'll eat now."

Pax stood first and extended a hand toward Alana. She

put hers in his, and together, they walked across the porch. To Matt and to anyone looking on, they looked like a couple in love.

"Alana sure looks pretty tonight, doesn't she?" Matt held the door open for them. "Seeing her wear a dress twice in twenty-four hours might break all records around here."

"Daddy!" Alana scolded. "I wear a dress to church almost every Sunday."

"And you always look gorgeous." Pax leaned over and kissed her on the cheek. He liked that he didn't have to bend down to her and the smell of her hair, but what he liked most was the way she fit against him when he hugged her up tight.

"Well, thank you both. Now, can we eat while the steaks are still hot?" Alana went straight to the kitchen table. "Look at this." She waved her hand to take in the whole setting. "You even got the table set all pretty. Mama would be proud of you."

Matt wiggled his dark eyebrows. "It ain't my first rodeo. I used to grill every week for your mama. Friday nights, she'd dress up, and I'd put a steak dinner on the table. That was our date night when we were first married, and we were trying to keep the ranch out of the red."

"We should do that." Pax held Alana's chair for her. "I can grill a mean steak."

Matt sat down and put a huge T-bone on his plate and then passed the platter to Alana. "We always found it was something we both looked forward to all week, and it beats the devil out of going out to eat. After all"—he lowered his voice and raised his eyebrows—"the bedroom is a lot closer when the meal is done."

"Daddy!" Alana's face flushed with a crimson blush as she slid a steak onto her plate and handed the platter to Pax.

Pax couldn't remember the last time he had blushed, but he had no trouble recognizing the heat traveling from his neck to his face.

"Oh, come on," Matt teased, "don't tell me that—"

Alana held up a palm and butted in before he could go any further. "I'm already blushing, and you've always said that cowboys don't kiss and tell. Well, neither do cowgirls."

"Fair enough," Matt chuckled. "But while both of y'all have red faces—and I didn't know Pax was even capable of blushing—if you ever have a daughter, please keep the name Joy in the family. Your great-grandmother was Joy. Your grandmother was Alice Joy and then your mama's name is Joy Rose."

Alana nodded. "If we have a daughter, you've got my promise that we'll keep the family name."

A daughter of his own—Pax wasn't sure how he felt about that idea, but this marriage wasn't real, so he didn't have to worry about it. Yet, the idea kept nagging at him, and he figured if he had one like Laela, that would be great.

Matt used present tense when he talked about Joy, and he'd teased them about already having sex. That wasn't the quiet, solemn Matt Carey that Pax had always known. Whatever was in his brain had to be already affecting him, but by golly he could still grill a mighty fine steak.

"This is really good," Pax said between bites.

"Good Carey beef," Matt said. "Before I forget, and I'll do a lot of that in the days ahead according to the doctor, the wedding planner is coming over tomorrow night at seven. She'll need your guest list, Pax, since we're short on time."

"Yes, sir. I'll bring it with me." Pax made a mental note to call his grandmother the next morning and ask her to help him with that.

"Good, and Alana, you need to choose your bridesmaids because Saturday, you've got an appointment at that fancy bridal shop in Amarillo to pick out dresses for you and them," Matt said. "When I called Trudy to tell her to put us on the charge calendar, she told me about the shop and offered to make an appointment for you. She said that she'd be getting in touch with you to set up a wedding shower. Several ladies have already offered to be hostesses with her."

"Thank you so much for taking all this on," Pax said.

"But, Daddy, we really don't need all this fuss," she said.

Matt shook his head. "No, ma'am. This is going to be the biggest, prettiest wedding the Panhandle has ever seen. I insist on it. And same with your honeymoon."

Alana reached under the table and squeezed Pax's knee. The gesture and the fact that Matt had mentioned a honeymoon startled him so badly that he dropped a bite of steak off his fork back onto his plate.

"I forgot to tell you that Daddy wants to give us a honeymoon." Alana locked gazes with him. "I've picked a beach in Florida, maybe Destin. What do you think?"

"That sounds wonderful, and I'd love to spend a few days with Alana on the beach, with our toes in the sand, but Matt, I believe the groom takes care of the honeymoon. I'll make all the arrangements for that. You take care of this big ranch wedding," Pax told him.

Thank you, Alana mouthed when her father wasn't looking.

Pax gave her a brief nod and went back to eating.

Chapter Five

While other little girls were playing with dolls and having play dates that involved tea parties, Alana had been tagging along after her father on the ranch. She was helping round up cattle on a four-wheeler at the age of six and roping calves before she went to school. She had been the tallest kid in her kindergarten class and had held that position until ninth grade, when Pax finally matched her in height. She'd always preferred to sit with the guys at lunch or play football with them on the playground. Alana liked getting dressed up for church on Sunday, but when she got home, she was more than ready to get back into her jeans and work shirts.

"So who do I ask to be my bridesmaids, since I didn't form those kind of friendships when I was growing up?" she asked herself as she climbed the stairs to her room that night. "Maybe Rose, Emily, and Bridget?"

She thought about those three as she undressed, hung her

clothing back in the closet, and adjusted the water in the shower. She and Emily had known each other through their family's ranching businesses. Bridget was Pax's sister-in-law. Rose had gone to school with her here in Daisy back when they were in junior high school, and she'd been nice to Alana.

"But then there's Retta, Claire, and Nikki over at Longhorn Ranch. They're all kind of like extended family." Alana peeled off her bikini underpants and tossed them into the hamper. "I guess if Daddy wants a big wedding, then by damn, he can have one. I'll ask all six of them."

She showered and dried off, shrugged into nightclothes and climbed into bed. Thoughts swirled through her mind so much that she couldn't sleep. Finally, she slipped out of bed, picked up her phone, and tiptoed downstairs. She took a cold beer from the refrigerator and carried it out to the porch. A full lover's moon sat in the night sky like a queen on her throne with a gazillion stars twinkling around her like her adoring subjects. She sent Pax a text to ask if he was awake.

His reply came back immediately: *Yes, got too much on my mind to sleep.*

Her thumbs were a blur as she typed: *Want to call it off?*

Her phone rang in seconds.

"Hello, Pax," she said. "What's keeping you awake?"

"I'm worried that I might mess up and say or do something wrong. Matt would be devastated if he found out, and now we need to plan a honeymoon, right?"

"Only a long weekend one, and we're planning it to please Daddy"—she paused—"but by then we won't even have to go on one."

"There's a mountain resort not far from Pueblo, Colorado, that might be nice," he suggested.

"Yes!" she said without hesitation.

"Then I'll get the arrangements made," Pax said. "There's a four-day package and a seven-day."

"Four," she answered. "And we can drive rather than fly. I've been up there with Daddy on a Cattlemen's Convention. It's beautiful this time of year, and we can be home in half a day if he gets sick. I've read all I could find about his illness. From what the papers he brought home from the doctor's say, his memory and motor skills should be fine, but he'll get to where he sleeps more and more. With the medication they gave him, the tumor might stop growing, but even if it does, then six months is all they've given him." She paused.

"We'll hope that he stays well until this wedding is over."

His calm tone comforted her. Who'd have thought that a big strapping cowboy like Paxton Callahan would have such a soft heart? She was so lucky that he was her friend and that he'd jumped right in when she asked him to marry her.

"Did you decide on how many women you're going to have in the wedding party?"

"Yep," she said. "If Daddy wants a big wedding, then by damn, he'll get one. I'm having six." She named them off. "I don't know any of them as well as I know their husbands. I've only met Levi and Claire at a couple of weddings, and Rose adores her."

"That's great," Pax replied. "Now I can ask Levi, Tag, Hud, Justin, Cade, and Maverick and not have to choose between them. They can each come down the aisle with their wives, right?"

"Sure thing." She didn't care how the wedding planner set it all up, so long as her father had a good time.

"Dealing with grief and all this at the same time must be tough," Pax said.

"It's sure not easy," she sighed.

"I can be over there in five minutes if I jump the fence," he said.

"I'm on the swing in my nightshirt and shorts," she told him.

"I'll be there in four," he laughed.

"I'll have a beer waiting for you." She ended the call.

She took a minute to actually put on a pair of shorts before she went to the kitchen and got a beer out of the fridge. She was surprised to see him already sitting on the swing when she returned to the porch.

"That was fast." She handed him a beer and sat down on the other end of the swing.

"I was motivated." He smiled and took a couple of long gulps. "It don't take long to get here when I come across the pasture. There's a nice breeze this evening, and the moon is throwing good light, so it was a pleasant walk. Are you okay? You sounded a little frazzled on the phone."

"I am," she answered. "A couple of days ago the only thing on my mind was whether I'd go to the Wild Cowboy tomorrow night. I was listening to music while I took a bath and Vince Gill started singing 'Go Rest High on That Mountain.' Ever since it came out, Dad has said that he wants the song sung at his funeral, and I don't know if I can bear it."

"I'll be right there with you, I promise," he said. "I'm gonna be right beside you through all of this, Alana."

She moved over closer to him and laid her head on his shoulder. God, but it felt good to have someone to lean on and share her burden with. "This is one screwed-up mess we've gotten ourselves into. Planning a wedding one minute, and an annulment the next, and a funeral somewhere in between," she whispered.

He set his beer on the porch and put an arm around her. "One step at a time. Wedding is first. When are you calling the ladies? I thought I'd get in touch with the guys tomorrow morning and get that set down before we meet with that wedding planner."

"I'll do it in the morning." She yawned.

* * *

Pax felt her go slack in his arms and knew she was asleep. He couldn't bring himself to wake her. It was actually kind of nice to be needed, so he kept the swing moving. His eyes grew heavier and heavier until finally they closed and he fell asleep with his cheek braced on the top of her head.

He dreamed that she was walking down the aisle toward him. She wore a beautiful white dress and a veil that trailed out all the way to the back of the church. His friends were standing beside him, and the ladies were lined up on the other side. A lovely breeze whipped the veil away from her face, and then he realized that instead of a preacher, there was a lawyer behind the podium, and a gray casket was where the altar should have been.

He awoke with a start and a severe kink in his neck. The sun was a glimmer of orange trying to make its way over the few mesquite and scrub oak trees between the Bar C and his ranch. He thought of the pretty dress that Alana had worn the night before and how gorgeous her blond hair had been, hanging down her back. Now it was splayed out over his shoulder. He tucked a few strands back behind her ear.

"Sweet Lord!" She jumped up off the swing. "I had the most horrible dream. Daddy wasn't here for the wedding, and they told me he'd passed before it was time to walk down the aisle. What would we do if that happened?"

Pax put his hand on her cheek and looked deep into her worried brown eyes. "Don't borrow trouble from tomorrow. Simply walk down the path life gives you today. That's what Mam used to tell us."

"That's a pretty tall order," she said.

"Well, good mornin'." Matt joined them on the porch. "Coffee is made. I hope you're not comin' in dressed like that, Alana."

"We were talkin' about the bridesmaids and groomsmen and fell asleep on the swing," Alana explained.

"I remember when me and Joy slept on that very swing a few times, but it was after we were married. My mama would have had a hissy fit if she'd caught us out here before we got hitched," he teased. "Y'all come on in here and we'll make some breakfast. How does ham and eggs sound?"

"Sounds real good, but I should be getting on across the fence to my house." Pax stood up and rolled the kinks from his neck. "Thanks for the offer, though."

Alana gave Pax a quick peck on the cheek. "See you this evening. Don't forget your list."

"I'm putting Mam on it right after breakfast. Call me if you need anything else," he said. "Love you."

"Love you," she said, and it didn't feel awkward at all to say the words.

Matt was beaming when Pax left the porch and started jogging across the pasture. Running through knee-deep grass still wet with morning dew dampened his jeans. The sun looked like an orange ball sitting on the edge of the earth when he put a hand on a wooden fence post and sailed over it like he was a professional hurdle jumper. He hoped that he'd be able to sneak into the house without being heard, but no such luck. Maverick was busy making the first pot of coffee for the day when Pax opened the back door.

He really wasn't in the mood for a lot of questions, but he braced himself for them anyway.

"Dum, dum, de dum," Maverick sang the wedding march. "So the groom has either been out sowing wild oats or else he's putting the cart before the pony and spent the night with his bride before the wedding. Which is it?"

"I walked over to Alana's last night so we could talk about wedding plans?" Pax asked. "We fell asleep on the porch swing, end of story."

"So who's her maid of honor going to be?" Maverick asked.

"She's inviting all the girls to be in the wedding party. So I'll have you, Tag, Justin, Levi, Hud, and Cade as my groomsmen. I need to get in touch with them today." As soon as the coffee quit dripping, Pax poured a mugful and sat down at the table.

"That's getting to be a pretty big wedding." Maverick got his own coffee and joined him.

"What's going on?" Bridget covered a yawn with her hand as she entered the room. "Did I hear 'big wedding'? I thought this was going to be a small affair."

"It was until Matt decided that since Alana is his only child, he wants a big to-do."

"I still think this is too fast," Maverick said.

"We've done beat on that dead horse long enough. Let's have some waffles and then get out to the hay field. That back pasture is ready to cut, and the forecast says there's sunshine for the next three days." Pax changed the subject.

He wanted to talk about hay, cattle, or even building a fence. He didn't want to talk about weddings or Alana. But that was impossible, since every single detail of the night before kept running through his mind.

Not even his favorite country music playing in the tractor

that morning helped. Every song reminded him of her and how it felt to sit on that swing with Alana right next to him. She was adorable in those boxer shorts with Minnie Mouse printed on them, and the faded pink nightshirt. A tingle shot through his body when he thought about her long, long legs, and those kissable lips.

She'd been adorable in that shirt and those shorts, but his holding her and comforting her was the best part of the night. He hadn't felt like a fake fiancé at all the night before. In fact, he'd felt pretty damn good.

Chapter Six

W hen Alana opened the door promptly at seven o'clock that evening she found a woman about her own age wearing cute black slacks, a white button-up shirt, and high-heeled shoes. Her blue eyes looked out of place with her jet-black hair, and she barely reached Alana's shoulder.

All of those qualities made Alana feel like a giant sunflower growing wild in a bed of pretty little pansies. "Hello, I'm Alana." She stuck out her hand.

"Crystal Taylor." The lady shook with her and then picked up the case she'd set on the porch.

"Come right in. We're going to set things up on the dining room table." Alana led the way to the dining room like a good hostess, even if she did feel a bit intimidated.

"Please to meet you, Alana," Crystal said. "Your father has already given me lots of information over the phone." She followed Alana across the foyer and into the dining room. When she saw Pax, her blue eyes lit up like sparklers on the Fourth of July. "Are you the groom?"

"Yes, ma'am." He stood up and shook hands with her. "Paxton Callahan. Pleasure to meet you. Please have a seat."

"Well, you two make a good-looking couple. Your wedding pictures should be stunning." She opened her briefcase, took out a legal-size yellow pad, and sat down across the table from Pax and Alana. "Let's start with how many will be in the wedding party."

"Six bridesmaids and six groomsmen." Alana took a seat beside Pax. "We called them all this morning and they've agreed."

He took her hand in his and gave it a gentle squeeze.

"How many guests are you inviting?" Crystal asked. "We usually find that about seventy-five percent send back the RSVP card, and maybe eighty percent of those actually attend, but we'll need a rough number for the catering service."

Pax slid his list across the table.

"And here's mine." Alana handed hers over. "There's sure to be duplicate names."

"We can take care of overlaps when names get entered into the computer tomorrow for invitation labels. Can you give me an estimated guess?" Crystal glanced across the table at Pax.

Slow down lady, Alana thought. *I'm not trading places with you no matter how much you look at him like that.*

"Five to six hundred," Matt suggested, walking in from the kitchen. "I overheard you say coffee." He glanced at Crystal and set a tray with cookies to the table. "I'm the father of the bride, Matt Carey. What can I get y'all to drink? Coffee or maybe a glass of sweet tea?"

"Pleased to meet you, Mr. Carey," Crystal said, "and a cup of black coffee would be nice."

A triple shot of Knob Creek Smoked Maple, Alana thought, but she said, "Sweet tea will be fine, Daddy, but I can get it."

"Honey, y'all keep plannin'. I can take care of that," Matt told her.

"That's a big wedding. Is your venue large enough to accommodate that many?" Crystal asked.

"We're using our sale barn, and yes, ma'am, it will hold that many people. The wedding and the reception will both be in the same barn. We'll make an aisle through the tables," Alana answered. "I want the reception to be buffet style."

"Okay." Crystal wrote as fast as she could. "That's about fifty tables for ten. What color tablecloths?"

"Yellow," Alana told her. "With shades of orange in the centerpieces."

"Well, you certainly know what you want." Crystal talked to her but smiled at Pax.

If you could see him in his tank top and black cowboy hat like he was wearing last night, you'd be panting by now, Alana thought. *Why am I mentally fighting with a woman for eyeballing Pax?*

Because you've always had a crush on him so admit it, the voice in her head smarted off.

"I'll have my flower people make up several different centerpieces, then send you pictures so you can have a choice," Crystal continued. "What do you have in mind for your corsages and boutonnières? I can also have them make some samples of those, too? Also, artificial flowers or real?"

"Real," Matt answered as he brought in coffee and tea

for everyone. "We want real flowers everywhere. On the tables, on the archway where they will get married, and for the corsages and boots—yellow roses. That's Joy's favorite, and Alana has always loved them too."

"My mother passed almost twenty years ago," Alana explained.

"I'm so sorry. My mother is my best friend," Crystal said.

"Mine was too, and yes, yellow roses maybe mixed with those pretty peach-colored ones would be nice," Alana said.

"We should plan on sending out your invitations no later than Tuesday." Crystal pulled a book of samples from her case and turned it around so that Pax and Alana could thumb through it. "While you're picking out a design, let's discuss what you want me to do for you."

"All of it," Matt said. "You and I can talk food while they're deciding on the invitations. We want three meats. Steak is number one. Chicken is next, and smoked ribs for number three. Then all the sides to go with it."

"Yes, sir." Crystal kept writing. "When they have decided on a design, I may have enough to get started. After the invitations are sent, I'll be in touch about the next items on my list. Do you want me to provide the photographer and the band, also? I can work up prices with each of those and without them."

"Just do it all." Matt shoved an envelope across the table. "A country band for sure. That's what we all like. Here's a check already made out to help you get started. When you get everything together, I'll give you the rest. I don't want Alana to worry about anything at all, and she will have everything she wants."

Guilt lay on Alana's shoulders like a heavy blanket at the thought of all the money being spent on a fake wedding. *What I want is for you to be well and our lives to be back like they used to be.* Alana's hand shook when she turned the next page of the sample invitations.

Pax quickly laced her fingers in his and turned the pages for her. "What do you think of this one?" He pointed to a simple invitation with a long-stemmed yellow rose printed on the side. "That one would tie in well with the yellow roses, but you should make the decision."

"That's the one," she said. "You can use it for the napkins, the thank-you cards, and everything else."

"Want to change the wording?" Crystal asked.

"No, what's on there is perfect." Alana's voice caught in her throat. Her father was giving her the wedding that most women would die for, and yet when she really got married, she'd probably go to the courthouse in her jeans. "Except you'll need to change the names to Alana Joy Carey and Paxton Callahan."

"Middle name for Paxton?" Crystal asked.

"No, ma'am," he answered as he slid the book back to her. "You can really get those printed, ordered, and sent all by Tuesday?"

"Yes, I can," Crystal said.

"I told you that she came highly recommended," Matt said.

Alana stood up and gave her dad a hug. "Thank you for everything, Daddy."

"I believe that's all we need for tonight." Crystal shoved all the paperwork across the table. "Who wants to sign this contract?"

"I will," Alana said as she put her signature at the bottom of several pages.

When she finished, Crystal gave her a copy of each page, stuffed everything into her case, and stood up. "Thank you for the coffee. I'll be in touch with you"—she glanced over at Alana—"the first of the week. This will be the fastest wedding I've ever planned. I'm not putting anything else on my calendar until it's over."

"Thank you for that," Matt said.

"I'll walk you to the door." Alana pushed her chair back and got to her feet.

"I've never done a barn wedding, but it's really exciting thinking about it. I was thinking of using fairy lights to romanticize the barn a little. What do you think of that?" Crystal said as they crossed the foyer.

Alana opened the door for her, and the two of them stepped out on the porch. "That's a wonderful idea, and maybe use some tulle to soften things up a bit?" She inhaled deeply, taking in the fresh night air.

"Think you could get me the dimensions of the barn by the first of the week so I'll know what size we're working with?" Crystal asked.

"I'll put Daddy on that job." Alana nodded. "Thank you for driving out here and getting all this together in such a short time. I should explain something, though. My dad has some short-term memory loss, and it seems to be getting worse, so maybe you should run things by me instead of him."

"I'm sorry to hear about your dad. That's a tough thing to see looming in the future. I'll sure enough keep you in the loop," Crystal agreed. "Would you consider letting me use your pictures on my website? I'll give you a ten percent discount on the entire wedding if you'll agree. Of course, I'd have to get permission from the photographer, but since she's a cousin, I don't think that she'll mind."

"I'd have to ask Pax before I said yes." She couldn't very well tell Miss Pretty-Blue-Eyes Crystal that this was really a fake wedding to please her father and there was already an annulment or divorce in the planning.

"Fair enough, let me know by the wedding day. If you agree, I'll take the ten percent off the final payment, and thanks again." Crystal headed out across the yard toward her van.

Pax chose that very moment to slip his arms around her from behind and rest his chin on her shoulder. "Might as well make a good impression on the lady," he whispered.

"You already did," Alana told him. "If you weren't marrying me, she would have dragged you off to a hayloft and tossed her clothes in the corner."

"Oh, honey," Pax said, "she's not a hayloft girl. She's more of a fancy dinner, five-star-hotel woman. Did she make you a little jealous?"

"Not a bit." Alana whipped around and put her arms around his neck. "You're a hayloft cowboy, not a satin sheets guy." She heard the sound of the van's engine starting, and asked, "Is she looking this way?"

"Oh, yeah," he answered, "and the window is rolled down."

Alana leaned in, and her lips met Pax's in a fiery kiss. Her knees went weak and she felt as if she were floating. Every nerve in her body tingled, and her pulse raced so fast that she had trouble catching her breath. When she finally took half a step back, she had forgotten all about Crystal.

"I'd hate to see what a jealous kiss would be like," Pax teased. "That knocked my boots clean over into New Mexico."

"You'll probably find mine pretty close to yours." She took another step back.

He chuckled. "Want to go get some ice cream to cool us both down?"

"Love to," she answered. "Let me tell Daddy. You go on

and get the truck started and turn the A/C on high. We both need to cool down."

"Yes, ma'am, but you do know that after we're married you can't boss me so much, don't you?" He flashed her another grin.

"But until then?" She cocked her head to one side.

"We'll talk about that over ice cream." He took a step forward and kissed her on the cheek.

* * *

Pax got behind the wheel and took a couple of long, deep breaths in an effort to settle his racing pulse and ease the pressure behind the zipper of his jeans. Usually, thinking about stacking hay in a barn would work, but not that evening. Neither did picturing himself wearing a fleece-lined leather jacket to keep warm while fishing in a calm river on a cold December night.

It startled him so bad when the passenger door flew open that he forgot all about the desire shooting through his body. "It's not cooled down much, but it was damn hot when I got inside," he said.

"As hot as that kiss was?" she asked.

"Oh, no, honey." He shook his head as he drove away from the yard. "Hell ain't even that hot."

"Do you think things would've ever been different between us if we hadn't gotten involved with this wedding stuff?" she asked.

"Never know now, but I doubt it," he answered.

"Why?" she asked.

"I've always had a crush on you, Alana, but you're about to inherit the second biggest ranch in the Panhandle. I don't have a thing to bring to a table like that, and I felt that folks would think I'd married you for your money. I'm too proud for that, I guess," he replied. "And besides you hurt my little heart when you slapped the hell out of my cheek when I kissed you behind the barn. Remember?"

"Evidently I didn't do too good of a job, because you've been raisin' hell ever since then," she smarted off.

"I've been tryin' to prove that some girls like my kisses," he told her.

"Got that job done yet?" she asked.

"Maybe." He shrugged. "I wanted to ask you to the prom when we were seniors but when I finally got the courage to even walk up to you in the hallway at school, you gave me a dirty look."

"I did not," she protested.

"Yep, you did. You glared at me like if I took another step toward you, you'd knock me square on my ass," he said.

She clamped a hand over her mouth and giggled.

"What's so funny?" he asked.

"I remember that day now. Wyatt Downing was right behind you and he"—she suddenly got serious—"and he made a rude hand gesture. I was giving him the dirty look, not you."

"Would you have gone with me if I'd asked?" Pax asked.

"Probably," she answered. "That was a long time ago, and by the way, so was that kiss. I shouldn't have slapped you, but you went right out and kissed another girl the next day, so..." She raised an eyebrow.

"I had to do something to restore my thirteen-year-old manhood."

Even if it was years later, he felt like a king that she'd liked him enough even in those days to be jealous. "Did you go kiss another boy?"

"Hell, no!" she said. "I didn't kiss another boy until I was sixteen."

"Did you like it then?" he asked.

"No, he didn't do much better than you did," she teased.

"Ouch!" he groaned. "I'd been practicing for weeks on the back of my hand. I thought I had it down, and, honey, let me tell you something." He brought her hand to his lips and kissed each knuckle. "When my lips touched yours, my heart skipped at least two beats."

"So did mine," she admitted. "But we need to talk about the business of the ranch now."

"Party pooper," he joked.

"One of us has to be," she told him. "Now then, you're half owner of the Callahan Ranch, right?"

"That's right, and, honey, it's not a big ranch, so you're sure not marryin' me for my money," he continued to tease her.

"How do you know? I might be wanting to add the Callahan Ranch to the Bar C," she said.

"No way." He shook his head. "That's Callahan land. How many acres does the Bar C cover? How many permanent hired hands does the ranch employ? How many temporary kids do you hire in the summer?" he asked.

"You thinkin' about suing me for half of my ranch when we get the divorce?" she asked.

"No, I'm making you see what I'm talking about." He turned out of the lane and onto the county road.

"Well, the Bar C isn't as big as the King Ranch," she said, "or even the Rockin' B. It's not listed on the top ten biggest ranches in Texas by a longshot, but we've got ninety thousand acres, twenty hired hands who stay in the bunkhouse with Lucas, and we usually hire about fifty local kids in the summer. Does that answer your questions?"

"Yep, and it's pretty close to what I figured. The Callahan Ranch has a little over a thousand acres. Maverick and I are trying to take care of it with only ourselves and a handful of summertime help. You get the picture?" He turned off the county road onto the highway leading into town.

She folded her arms over her chest. "No, I don't and never will."

It was his turn to ask, "Why?"

"Because no one should marry for money, but then again, no one should ever let money keep them from a happy relationship," she told him.

"Not if you live by the Cowboy Code," Pax said.

"I know that code as well as you do," she asked.

"Then you know you should never let anyone take your courage, your strength, or your dignity."

"I guess it would take a strong cowboy to follow his heart and not let what other people say influence his decision to fall in love with a woman because she owns more dirt than he does," Alana said.

He pulled the truck into the parking spot at Mama's Little Ice Cream Parlor and turned off the engine. "Yep, it would, but I'm not so sure we're really made for each other—not for the long haul. You can outdo me in everything, including ranchin'. I'd kind of feel like a kept man.

"Hey, don't say that," she scolded. "If we were really engaged and getting married, you'd be bringing a lot to the partnership. You're the kindest man I know, and there's not a rancher out there who takes his job as serious as you do. No way in the world would you ever be a kept man, and believe me, you are my equal in everything, Paxton Callahan."

"Oh, really," he countered, "who won the most trophies in bareback bronc riding?"

"Who got thrown the most in practice and has back

trouble now?" she asked right back. "And if we're throwin' around stuff, who's been known to haul hay by the light of a truck so he can get it in before the rain hits the next morning, or who's come over here more than once to help Daddy when the hired help couldn't make it to the ranch because there was a foot of snow on the ground."

"This is all a crazy conversation anyway," he said. "If we weren't getting married already, neither of us would even begin to think about the *M* word on the basis of one hot kiss."

"I sure wouldn't." She opened the truck door. "And, Pax, thanks for being honest with me."

"Hey, that's my job," he told her as he got out and went around the front of the vehicle to extend his hand to help her out. "Want to try another of those kisses again right here to see if maybe that was beginner's luck?"

She shook her head and tucked her hand into his. "Nope. I still need ice cream to cool down that last one."

"Rain check?" he suggested as the automatic doors into the store swung open.

"Maybe." She went straight to the counter and looked up at the menu. "I want a double dip of chocolate almond and a glass of sweet tea."

"And you, sir?"

He pointed at the menu. "I want a double fudge brownie sundae like that picture right up there, and a big glass of ice water," he answered, as if he was oblivious to her charms.

"I want to change my order." Alana laid her left hand on the counter. "I'll have the same thing as my fiancé."

"Congratulations," the gray-haired woman said. "You might not remember me, but I took care of the nursery when you kids were babies. This one is on the house from me to celebrate your engagement."

"Well, thank you," Pax said.

"You're Wilma," Alana said. "I didn't recognize you without your red hair."

"I got tired of dyeing it and let it go natural," Wilma told them. "I'll have that ice cream out to you in a few minutes."

"Thank you so much. That's sweet of you." Alana smiled.

"Small world," Pax said as he ushered Alana to a booth.

"Yep, and speaking of that, did you notice that Trudy is sitting right over there with Billy Ray?" Alana asked.

Pax glanced over his shoulder and waved at the mother and son. "Anyone else?"

"The place is packed." She slid into a booth. "And some of them already have their cell phones out."

Pax took his place across from her and reached across the table to hold both her hands. "Ignore them and look right into my eyes. We've come out of hiding, and we're so much in love that we can't get enough of each other."

"Do you really think this is the way that engaged couples act?" she giggled. "We're almost thirty for God's sake, not sixteen."

"Yep, we are." He laughed with her. "But think how much gossip fodder we're giving Trudy right now. She doesn't know that you basically told me that I'm full of crap. She thinks we're really making eyes at each other."

"And here they come," Alana whispered as she slipped her hands away from his and looked up at Trudy. "Well, hello there. Did y'all have a cravin' for ice cream tonight too?"

"Ice cream is always good on a hot night," Billy Ray said.

"I wanted to come over and congratulate you in person," Trudy said. "I'm so excited about your engagement, and so is your dad. I could hear it in his voice when he called to be sure the church was available for that day. I've already got half a dozen ladies who are going to help with the wedding shower. Have you registered for gifts yet?"

"Thank you, and no, ma'am. We met with the wedding planner tonight. Since things are moving so fast, you could wait a few weeks to give us a shower, maybe after the honeymoon, even."

"Oh, no!" Trudy talked with her hands. "We've already got the ball rolling, and we're so excited about giving y'all a shower. I've talked to your granny, Iris, several times and the other ladies in the church group." She leaned forward and lowered her voice. "Don't forget to register with Amanda's Gifts, since she's local or it'll hurt her feelings, and besides she's one of the shower hostesses."

Billy Ray stepped up from behind his mother. "Got your best man all picked out?"

"Maverick, of course," Pax answered, "and the guys out at the ranches where we worked are going to be groomsmen."

"Well, if y'all need me for anything, holler," Billy Ray said.

"We'll sure keep that in mind." Alana smiled up at him. "And thanks so much, Billy Ray."

Trudy patted her on the shoulder. "Here comes Wilma with your ice cream. Y'all better get after it before it melts. We'll be in touch the first of the week to get your colors for the shower." Mother and son turned and made their way back through the crowd.

"Cravin'?" Pax's green eyes twinkled. "Don't pregnant women get cravin's? Are you tryin' to tell me something here tonight?"

"Dammit!" Alana gasped.

"And here y'all are." Wilma set the two sundaes and the ice water on the table. "If y'all need anything else let me know."

Pax picked up a spoon and dug into the ice cream. "Want

me to call her back for a side order of dill pickles? And what was that about not wanting a shower?"

Paxton had thought that she'd blush, but instead she ran the back of her hand down his cheek and whispered in a seductive voice, "Not yet. I think I have to be in the second trimester before the pickle craving starts. And I feel guilty about getting gifts for a sham wedding. We'll have to give them all back when we get the annulment."

The sensation of her touch and the sound of her voice sent another wave of heat through Pax's body. He might need to spill the ice water in his lap if she did that again.

Chapter Seven

Pax was hot, sweaty, and out of sorts when he made it to the house on Saturday evening. Three of their weekend hired hands were off to a baseball tournament, so he and Maverick had worked double-time with the two who remained. The sun had already set, and he wished that he and Alana hadn't made plans to go to the Wild Cowboy that night. Every bone in his body ached from stretching barbed wire fence from early that morning until now, and it was dusky dark.

"I'll sure be glad to see those boys get back to work next week," Pax groaned.

"Are you tellin' me that you're too old at twenty-nine to be ranchin'?" Maverick teased. "You do realize that you'll have a helluva lot more to do after y'all are married."

"I kept up with you all day, didn't I?" Pax said. "And now, the most strenuous thing you'll do this evening is stack up blocks for Laela to knock down. I happen to be going to the Wild Cowboy to dance until they close the place down."

"Does Alana know?" Maverick asked.

"She's going with me," Pax shot over his shoulder as he headed down the hallway to the shower.

He let the cool water beat down on his tired shoulders for a long time and wondered how the evening would go at the bar. He and Alana were both regulars there, right along with lots of cowboys, cowgirls, and bar bunnies in the area. But tonight would be different—being engaged changed everything. No flirting with other women, very little dancing with other gals, and for sure no going to a motel with one of them or bringing one of them home.

He'd stood under the water longer than he'd thought, so he had to hustle to get ready. He got out his lucky Saturday night boots, the black ones that hardly ever let him down.

Alana was supposed to be ready at eight o'clock, and he knocked on her door with five minutes to spare. No one answered, so he rapped harder.

"Hey," Matt came from around the end of the house. "Alana told me to tell you to meet her in the barn. I've got a cattlemen's meeting I can't miss tonight over in Tulia. I'm already going to be a few minutes late, so I'll let her explain." Matt hurried over to his truck, settled in behind the wheel, and sped off.

Pax crawled back into his vehicle, picked up his phone from the passenger seat, and called Alana. She was breathless when she answered. "I'm so sorry, Pax, but I can't go to the Wild Cowboy. I've got two heifers having trouble delivering. I'm in the first barn, and I could use some help."

"Be there in five minutes," he said and ended the call.

He drove down the rutted path to the barn closest to the house. He got out and jerked off his good boots, grabbed his old black rubber boots from the bed of the truck, and shoved his feet down in them. His jeans and shirt could be washed, but he sure didn't want to ruin his lucky boots.

The barn door squeaked when he slid it open, and Alana yelled, "I'm back here." She came out from a hallway between rows of stalls and met him in the middle of the floor. She wore jeans with holes in the knees, a chambray shirt over a dirty white tank top. Strands of blond hair had escaped her ponytail, which had a piece of straw dangling from the end. "I'm a mess, but I can't leave the heifers, and all the hired hands are gone, and Daddy has a meeting…"

He took her in his arms and said, "We're ranchers. This is what we signed up for. There'll be other Saturday nights when we can dance at the Wild Cowboy. Let's check on those two heifers."

"You're a good man, Paxton." She led the way back to the stalls. "I did so enjoy the thought of dancing with you all night, but I'm sure glad that as ranchers we understand each other."

"I was feelin' the same way about you," he said as he opened the stall and checked the first heifer. "First calf, right?"

Alana nodded. "She and the other one are both out of my personal herd. They belong to me, not the ranch. I've raised them from babies. I probably shouldn't have bred them to our prime bull, since he always throws big calves."

"This ain't my first time pullin' calves." Pax went over to the other stall and dropped to his knees. "This one will come first. If we're lucky, she won't need much help. She's a little bigger than that one over there. Now, all we can do is wait, and I had a mind to do some dancin'. I got to warn you, I'm not nearly as smooth in rubber boots, though."

"Here in the barn?" She frowned.

"Come on now, Alana." He stood up, took her by the hand, and led her out into the middle of the barn.

"You got a country music band hiding in the bed of your truck?" she asked.

"Nope, don't even have a jukebox." He laid his phone on a bale of hay and hit the playlist that he listened to when he was plowing. "But I don't need either one to make enough music so I can dance with a pretty lady."

"So you think I'm pretty?" She wrapped both her arms around his neck.

"No, Alana, I think you're beautiful." He pulled her close to him and dropped his hands to her waist. Having her in his arms set off the same jolts of desire that he'd felt every time he touched her—crazy thing was that even though he'd been with lots of women, he'd never gotten such a feeling with any one of them.

They swayed to Kenny Chesney and David Lee Murphy singing "Everything's Gonna Be Alright."

"You really believe what they're saying?" she asked.

"You don't?" he shot right back.

"No, I do not. My daddy won't be with me at Christmas. By then I'll be divorced, and everyone in town will be saying that I wasted his money on a lavish wedding instead of using it to find a cure for him," she muttered.

"This wise woman, a tall blonde to be exact, told me that we shouldn't care what other people say. Besides, honey, I'll stick by your side until the baby is born anyway," he teased.

"Oh, you are so funny," Alana said. "I bet Trudy is already making notes about a baby shower sometime this fall."

"Well, you did say you were cravin' ice cream." He did some fancy footwork when Travis Tritt started singing

"T-R-O-U-B-L-E." Pax swung Alana to one side, brought her back to his chest, and together they did some fancy swing dancing all the way through the song.

Alana was giggling when that song ended, but before another one began, one of the heifers let out a bellow loud enough to rattle the sheet metal siding on the barn. Alana whipped around and ran back to the second stall with Pax right behind her.

She peeked over the top of the gate in time to see the hooves of the calf come out. The cow's sides bunched up with another contraction, and a big black head popped out. After that the rest was easy, and in minutes, the mother was on her feet, taking care of her newborn.

"Is it going to live?" Alana whispered.

"Give it a minute. She's only been cleaning it up for a few seconds." Pax slipped an arm around her waist. "Look. She took her first breath. That's one good-lookin' girl you got there."

"Yes, she is." Alana nodded. "She'll grow up to be a breeder."

"You do know that you are going to own everything on this ranch, so why do you have a personal herd?" Pax asked.

The baby struggled up onto its wobbly legs and bawled. The mama nudged it toward her udder, and the calf began to have its first meal.

"I started my own herd when we were showing cattle at the county fair. Remember, you and I competed a lot of times in FFA?" She didn't take her eyes off the mother and baby.

"Of course I remember," he said. "One of my proudest moments was when my steer beat out yours when we were seniors."

"Daddy *told* me not to show that animal, but I wouldn't

listen to him. God, I feel sorry for parents of kids who are seniors now," she said.

"Amen!" Pax remembered all the things he'd put his grandmother through when he was a senior in high school. "We knew everything about everything that year, didn't we? If we were half as smart now as we thought we were then, we'd be runnin' the whole world."

"We were going to set the world on fire, for sure." Alana nodded. "Anyway, I've built up my own little herd, but I've never spent a dime of the money I made from it. It's all going into a savings account for my first child's college fund."

"Oh, so the second and third ones don't get to go to college?" he teased.

"No, that's on you to provide for the rest of them," she giggled.

"Now who's being funny?" he asked.

* * *

The heifer in the other stall bawled, and Alana whipped around to go see about her. By the time she opened the gate, Pax was right beside her. This time, there were no hooves in sight and the heifer was heaving with the contractions that were coming every few seconds.

"She's in distress." Alana wasn't worried, though. With Pax's help she was confident that the two of them would take care of her prize heifer. She dropped to her knees, threw off her chambray shirt, and rubbed the animal's sides. "Come on, sweetheart. You can do this. I know you can."

Minutes seemed like hours before the calf finally entered the world, hooves first like it was supposed to. Pax held a hand out to her. She let him help her to her feet, and then the two of them watched the young mother take care of her baby like nature had taught her to do.

"I never get tired of the feeling I get when there's a new calf born on the ranch." She sighed. "It's like the next generation coming on."

"It really is, and I feel the same way," Pax agreed.

"You ever wonder if we could read a mama cow's expression, would it be like new parents staring at their baby through a hospital nursery window?" Alana asked.

"I expect that mothers feel the same no matter what the species. Think about a mama cat. She would take on an elephant if it tried to mess with her kittens," Pax answered.

Alana caught a whiff of his shaving lotion—something woodsy and sexy. Meantime, her hair was a fright from working outside all day. She had perspired so much her skin felt to her like she'd been rolled in salt. Her tank top was dirty and her work shirt likely ruined.

Pax let go of her hand and reached out to brush her hair away from her face. "Congratulations on a job well done, ma'am." He bent to brush a sweet kiss across her lips.

* * *

"One of each." Pax smiled at Alana. She might look like a mess right then, but to him she was beautiful. He recognized the pride at having two new calves to add to her herd and knew exactly what she was feeling. He'd had the same bursting feeling in his heart when any new calf was born over on the Callahan Ranch.

"You got a girl over there." He nodded in the direction of the other stall. "And a boy right here. Both seem healthy, and that bull calf looks to me like he could be a good enough breeder to pay for a semester of college."

"Yep," she said. "Thanks for being here with me."

"Aw, shucks!" He kicked at the straw on the barn floor. "You would've done fine without me."

She looked him right in the eyes without blinking. "Maybe, but it felt good to have you here, Pax."

"Then you are so welcome. Bringing those calves into the world meant more than going out dancing," he admitted.

"Spoken like a true rancher." She took a deep breath, as if she was about to say something else, but changed the subject. "I need a shower. I can feel dirt growing on me."

"I guess I should go," he said.

"Why?" She grabbed him by the hand and pulled him along with her. "I'm too nasty to even get in either of our trucks. There's a bathroom off the tack room. I'll take a shower there and then we can watch a little television or talk."

She opened the door to the neatest tack room he'd ever been in. Most barns that had a storage room for things like saddles and tools smelled like old sweaty leather and had no air-conditioning. This place was spic-and-span, clean and cool. Alana went to a small refrigerator and took out a beer for him. "Remote is on the end table. Is something wrong?"

"No, but our tack room sure doesn't look or feel like this," he said.

"Daddy turned it into his little poker cave a few years ago, back when we sold the last of our horses and went to four-wheelers to round up cattle. Then he built a room on the back side of the barn to store what was left in here when he got rid of the saddles. The only ones left on the place are my saddles. The one that I used to ride my Shetland when I started training to barrel race, and a couple of others are at the house on display in Daddy's den."

"I thought you were a bronc rider." Pax turned the bottle up and drank from it.

"I was until a couple of years ago. I got tired of the aches and pains," she admitted as she disappeared behind a door.

Pax sunk down in a buttery-soft leather futon and looked around. A poker table, complete with chips in the middle of it, was to his left and a desk with a computer on the top sat to his right. When he and his friends played poker, it was usually around the kitchen table. He picked up the remote, but before he could push the power button, he caught the reflection of pictures on the wall behind him on the television screen. He stood up and turned around to see a collection of photos of Alana. The center one was of her on a Shetland pony, holding a blue ribbon. A couple of the pictures had Alana's mother, Joy, in them with her and her pony.

"She sure looks like Joy did," he muttered.

His eyes went back to the first photo, and he remembered Alana wearing her hair in two braids like that when they were in elementary school. She'd always been tall, but to him, she'd been beautiful even then.

"And she intimidated the hell out of me," he whispered as he studied several more shots of her in her bronc riding days. Those would have been right after high school, when he had begun to really compete with her to prove to himself— and to her—that she shouldn't have slapped him over that first kiss, or given him dirty looks all through high school. Mam used to tell him that things happened when they were supposed to, not necessarily when folks wanted them to. Maybe he and Alana weren't supposed to be friends or even more until now.

"If that's the case," he muttered, "then what has a fake engagement got to do with anything, and where is it leading us?" Finally, he sat back down, turned on the television, and started channel surfing.

He was watching a bull-riding event when she finally came out of the bathroom. She'd twisted a white towel around her head, and a pair of bright red shorts with turquoise trim peeked out from under an oversize T-shirt. She smelled like vanilla and roses mixed together, and there was a whiff of coconut when she removed the towel and shook her blond hair out.

"Oh, I love bull riding," she said as she sat down beside him, reached across him, and picked up his beer. She took a long drink and then handed the bottle to him. "Thank you. I needed that."

"I don't mind sharing with a beautiful woman." He winked at her.

"I sure don't feel pretty with wet hair and dressed like this," she said.

"Well, darlin', Mam always said that beauty from the inside outshines anything on the outside," he told her.

"My mama said the same thing," she said and then got quiet.

"What's wrong?" he asked.

"Tomorrow will be the first Sunday since Daddy told me...about...his...time," she stammered.

Pax scooted over and put his arm around her. "I'll be right there beside you. After all, we *are* engaged."

"I'm scared, Pax," she whispered. "I've always plowed ahead like a bull going through a flimsy fence, but I look at this huge ranch, at everything I'll need to do. Daddy has taught me well, but to think about making all those decisions I'll have to make without him is terrifying."

"You could run this place with one hand tied behind your back, woman, but remember you've got good neighbors, as in a cowboy sitting right here, who's willing to help. All you have to do is holler, and I'll come runnin'. Not only through however long we're married, but as long as you need me. And you can talk with me about any decisions you need to make." He assured her with a sideways hug.

"I couldn't get through this without you." She rested her head on his shoulder. "Having someone to talk to is a comfort."

"I can't begin to imagine what you're going through, darlin'." He tipped her chin up and gave her a soft kiss.

She cupped his face in her hands and brought his lips to hers in a long, lingering kiss. That led to even hotter kisses and then she tugged his shirt out of his jeans, unfastened all the pearl snaps with one tug, and ran her fingers over the hair on his chest.

"My God, Alana, I can't take much more of this," Pax groaned.

"Me, either." She panted as she undid his buckle.

"Whoa!" Pax leaned back and put his hands on her shoulders. "Is this going to complicate things?"

She covered his mouth with another kiss. "I can't worry about tomorrow. Let's live for the moment right now."

Pax ran the back of his hand down her cheek. "You are so damned gorgeous that it takes my breath away."

"Why didn't you tell me that ten years ago?" She traced his lips with her forefinger.

"Because I was young and stupid," he said.

He was already throbbing with desire. He ran his hand up under her nightshirt, expecting to find a bra, but there was none. Her breast filled his hand like it had been formed purposely for him. Then she whipped the shirt off over her head and tossed it on the floor. She unzipped his pants, asked him to stand up, and tugged them down. She pushed him back down and pulled pants, boots, and socks off with one fell swoop and peeled off her shorts.

His breath caught in his chest at the sight of her, standing there like a goddess. Then she was beside him on the futon, her warm naked body next to his, and the kisses began again. Making love to Alana was more intense than he'd ever thought it could be, and the cuddling afterward was even better. She fell asleep snuggled up to his side with the quilt thrown over both of them.

He awoke sometime after midnight to find her still sleeping in his arms. He'd been with a lot of women, spent the night with more than a few, but he'd never felt like this afterward. He couldn't put it into words, but being with her was like completing something in his life. Light from the television lit up the room enough that he could see every eyelash resting on her high cheekbones.

Her eyes opened slowly, and she smiled at him. "No regrets?"

"Nope, not a single one. That was amazing." He gave her a sweet kiss on the lips. "But I reckon maybe I should go home. It's only a few hours until I pick you up for church. We really should go together, don't you think?"

"I'd rather stay here the rest of the night and all day tomorrow." She yawned.

"Me too, but Trudy would think that you had morning sickness for sure, if we did that," he chuckled as he pushed back the quilt.

She sat up and reached for her shirt. "You're right. I suppose we shouldn't make a habit of this, either, should we?"

"Why not?" he asked.

"Friends with benefits, huh?" She slipped her shirt on over her head.

"Doesn't have to have a title." He started getting dressed.

She laced her hands around his neck and hugged him. "I'll see you in a few hours."

"I wish we could stay right here all day." He buried his face in her hair and inhaled deeply.

"We'd have to face a thousand questions from my dad and your family if we did," she teased as she pressed even closer to him.

"You're so right." He gave her a steamy hot kiss.

"The devil is telling me to see where this goes, but I think I'd better tell him to get behind me and leave me alone," she giggled as she wiggled her naked butt into her shorts. "I'll be ready by ten forty-five. I'm going to wear bright red so no one can miss seeing that I'm with the sexiest cowboy in the state."

"I'll get my best swagger on when I walk you into the church on my arm." He kissed her once more on his way out the door.

Chapter Eight

The preacher started off his sermon that Sunday morning with an old saying—"O, what a tangled web we weave when first we practice to deceive," he said. "That comes from Sir Walter Scott, and in a shorter form, straight from the Ten Commandments. Thou shalt not lie."

Alana squeezed Pax's hand hard.

"That doesn't simply mean lying as we think of it," the preacher went on, and Alana could swear that he was staring straight at her. "It also includes lying to ourselves. If we aren't truly honest with ourselves, then we're living a lie."

"Do you think he knows?" Alana whispered.

"No way," he answered. "It's our secret. We didn't even tell God."

"God knows everything." She sat up straight and tried to listen, but she kept visualizing a gray casket up there in front of the altar. Finally, she bowed her head, closed her eyes, and sent up a silent prayer for God to help her. When she opened her eyes, the weight had left her heart. Her thoughts went back to the night before. Had she opened a big can of worms by having sex with Pax?

"Oh, shit," she murmured and then clamped a hand over her mouth.

"What did you say?" Pax asked.

"Protection," she muttered.

"What?" Pax frowned.

"Later," she said.

The preacher finally closed his Bible and tucked his notes down onto the shelf under the lectern and smiled at the congregation. "Before I ask Matt Carey to deliver the benediction, I'd like to congratulate Paxton Callahan and Alana Carey on their engagement. Matt has given me permission this morning to invite everyone in our church to the wedding, which will be held on the Bar C ranch on June sixth, and to the reception afterward. Time is seven o'clock, so save the date. Alana and Paxton, we want y'all to be happy and have a long and happy marriage. And one more thing, I'd like to take a moment to say happy Mother's Day to all our mothers, grandmothers, and expectant mothers in church this morning. Now, God bless all y'all."

He stepped away from the lectern, and Matt stood up. He thanked God for everything that had happened or been done since the day that dirt was first formed on the earth. Alana thought that her head might explode if he didn't get through his prayer so she could talk to Pax. It seemed to her like everyone in the church sighed when he got around to saying, "Amen."

Then, as luck would have it, everyone in the church wanted to stop them, shake hands, hug them, and wish them well. Her father beamed. Pax was the perfect gentleman. And Alana couldn't wait to get outside so she could tell him that she'd been off the pill for a month. She'd been so busy with spring planting, calving season, and getting the first cutting of hay in the barns between the rains that she'd forgotten to fill her prescription.

"You kids are on your own for Sunday dinner," Matt said as they left the church. "I'm meeting my poker buddies for Mexican in Tulia."

"But Daddy, we always have Sunday dinner together," Alana said. "It's Mother's Day."

"That was before you got engaged." Matt patted her on the shoulder. "You go on with Pax and have a good time. Don't worry. Joy understands." He disappeared into the crowd heading for the door.

"I thought we might go up to Amarillo. We always take Mam to a little pizza parlor on Mother's Day," Pax said. "Is that all right with you?"

She looped her arm into his and pulled him along. "I'd love to see Iris. Haven't talked to her in months."

As she and Pax made their way across the parking lot to his truck the folks that had missed them in the church kept stopping them to have a few words. When they finally reached his truck and climbed inside, she let out a heavy sigh and blurted out, "I've been off the pill for a month."

"Don't worry, honey, I used protection." He smiled across the console.

"Praying for a crop failure during church doesn't work so well," she said.

"I used a condom," he told her.

"I didn't see you..." She blushed.

"I guess I was distracting you well, then," he chuckled.

She slapped him on the arm. "Did you come prepared for that? Dammit! Did you plan on having sex?"

"Plan on it? No, but I always stay prepared." He wiggled his eyebrows.

"And you planned on seducing me?" she asked.

"I did not," Pax protested, "and if I remember right, you started it."

Alana let out a whoosh of pent-up air. "Thank God for that. All I need is for Trudy to be right about me being pregnant."

"Well, honey, if you were, I'd marry you," Pax said.

"You already are," she reminded him.

"My kids are going to grow up with a father and, hopefully, a mother who sticks around to see them ride broncs, graduate from high school, and attend all the other important events in their lives." He drove out of the parking lot and headed out of town.

"You're pretty definite about that." Alana was so relieved that Pax had used protection that she had to concentrate on the countryside out her window to keep her tears at bay. Someday she wanted children, but not now. She had too much on her plate to even think about bringing a baby into her chaotic world.

"Yes, I am," Pax said. "Grandpa and Mam were good to us and raised us well, but I was always envious of you kids who had both your parents."

Alana knew the story about Pax and Maverick's life, how Iris and Tommy Callahan, their grandparents, had stepped up and done what parents should do. Iris had brought cupcakes to school. She and Tommy had both made sure that the boys got to their rodeo events, helped them with animals to show at the fairs, and even attended FFA dinners with them. There couldn't have had better grandparents than the Callahans, but she could see his point.

"I always envied you having Iris," she whispered. "When Mama died, I wished that she was my grandma."

"Well, I damn sure was jealous that you had Matt," Pax told her. "Especially after Grandpa died."

She turned her head so she could look at him. "Guess life don't promise us beds of roses."

"Yeah, it does," he argued. "Only life don't take the thorns off."

"You got that right," she told him. "But I'm sure looking forward to having Sunday dinner with her."

"Even though it's only pizza?" he asked.

"Yep," she answered. "Sounds wonderful."

"Cravin' it, are you?" he teased.

"Yep, and you get to get up with the baby at the three o'clock feeding every night," she popped off.

"Oh, man!" he groaned. "You really know how to hurt a cowboy."

"You're strong. You can do it. After all you're marrying me, and you know what the gossip hounds say, don't you?" she asked.

"That I'm a lucky man?" he ventured.

"Nope, they say it'll take a strong cowboy to marry Alana Joy Carey, because she's taller than most men and she's more stubborn than all of them." She sighed.

* * *

Pax had heard that said before, and he agreed with it whole-heartedly. Alana could out-ride, out-shoot and out-ranch nearly every cowboy in the state, but not one of those other men had held her when she sobbed because her daddy was dying. That didn't make him so strong—it made him a good friend that she trusted enough to let him see her at her most vulnerable.

"It used to hurt my feelings and make me feel ugly," she

went on, "but then I figured that if I was gonna have the name, then by damn, I'd have the game. I'd beat out all the cowboys at whatever game they were playing. Did you know that I even tried to go out for football, but the school and my daddy said no?"

"Didn't know that, but can't say as I'm surprised," Pax answered as he drove past the WELCOME TO AMARILLO sign. "Do you like football that much, or were you on a mission?"

"Love to watch it on TV with Daddy, but at that time I was pretty much trying to live up to what folks said about me," she admitted.

"Darlin', you might not realize it, but when you walk into a room or a bar, every man in the place can't take his eyes off you. I've considered selling bibs at the door of the Wild Cowboy so the drool don't ruin their shirts," he said.

"I don't believe a word of that bullshit, but thank you." She smiled at him as they pulled into Iris's parking lot. Iris waved from the bench by the front door and stood up. The second the vehicle came to a stop, Alana hopped out and met Iris halfway. She bent and gave Iris a hug, and then held out her hand so Iris could see the engagement ring. When they'd finished talking about the ring, Alana helped Iris into the backseat.

"Happy Mother's Day, Mam," Pax said. "You've got a present back there somewhere."

She fastened her seat belt and then dug into the gift bag. "Oh. My. Goodness. There's enough little chocolate bars in here to keep me happy for a month, and this card is lovely. You always pick out the prettiest Mother's Day cards." She reached between the seats and laid a hand on his shoulder. "Thank you. I love you kids so much."

"You deserve a truckload of candy for raising Maverick and Pax," Alana said.

"I can't think of a better Mother's Day than spending the afternoon with y'all. I'm so glad y'all came to your senses and realized you were made for each other. I've known for years that you would wind up together. It was written in the stars when you were little kids."

"I looked at the stars every night, and I didn't see anything like that," Alana said.

"Me, neither," Pax agreed.

"Well, y'all didn't have my binoculars," Iris smarted off.

Pax drove out of the parking lot and back toward town while the two ladies chattered about the wedding details. His mind was on pizza, not the wedding.

"I'm going to come home for a week or two before the wedding so I don't miss out on anything." Iris's voice took Pax's mind off food. "Besides, I want to spend some time with Bridget and Laela. Living at the center is great, and I love it there. I've settled in, and I've made lots of friends, but nothing beats spending time with family."

"Call me whenever you're ready, and I'll be here to pick you up." Pax looked in the rearview and smiled at his grandmother.

Iris opened up a miniature candy bar and popped it into her mouth. "A couple of these will be my little appetizers before my pizza. I love that you're getting married in the barn. You're both ranchers, so that's perfect. I guess you'll be living at the Bar C?"

"Yep, but I'll still help run our ranch." Pax drove right up to the front door of the pizza place. "You ladies can get out here. I'll park and be right in."

"That's wonderful. Thank you," Iris said as she slid out of the backseat.

Pax had been worrying that Mam would see right through their ruse, but so far things had gone much better than he had expected. She was excited about the wedding and that he'd be keeping his hands in the Callahan Ranch. She'd always loved Alana, so that was a plus. Still, he hated the guilty feeling that wrapped around his heart and soul. Mam and Matt wanted the same thing—to see their kids settled and happy. Matt would be gone so he'd never know what happened, but Mam's heart would be broken.

Chapter Nine

Alana went over her mental list as she made her way downstairs that morning. She and Lucas had to rake a field of hay up into windrows. Some of the hired hands would move cattle. Others would repair fence lines. She stopped so fast when she got to the kitchen that she almost fell over her own feet. Her father was not at the table with a newspaper in front of his face, and the coffee wasn't made.

She whipped around and headed back up to his bedroom but before she'd taken a step, the back door opened and Matt came into the house. "I had breakfast in the bunkhouse with the guys this morning, so don't make anything for me. I'll get a pot of coffee going and have a cup with my morning paper"—he held it up—"and we can visit while you eat."

"Daddy, you scared me," Alana fussed at him. "I thought . . ."

"Lucas is right behind me," he whispered.

"Hey, kiddo. Did you decide to be lazy and sleep in this morning?" Lucas teased as he pushed open the back door.

"It's only five o'clock," Alana argued.

"We've already had breakfast and have given the hired hands their chores for the day."

A short, round man who lived in bibbed overalls and a wide-brimmed straw hat, Lucas had been foreman on the Bar C for all of Alana's life. She could even remember him when he had a head full of dark hair. Now, all he had was rim of gray that circled his bald head above his ears. His brown eyes were set in a bed of wrinkles, but they were always happy.

"Must be that love bug that bit you that's makin' you lazy," he continued to tease her. "I'm glad I didn't ever settle down with a woman if that's what happens."

"No woman would have had you for more than a weekend," Alana shot back at him.

"Thank God. I'd hate to think that one woman would get all this." He made a gesture to take in his whole body. "That would deprive so many others of a chance to spend a night with such a fine cowboy."

"On that note, I'm going to get my newspaper off the porch," Matt said.

"You, Lucas Nighthawk, are full of bullshit." Alana put on a pot of coffee and got her favorite cereal from the cabinet.

"And that's why all the women love me." He lowered his voice. "Is Matt all right? He's seemed a little off the past several weeks. He needs to see a doctor."

"What do you mean?" Alana asked.

"Sometimes he talks about Joy like she's still alive, especially since y'all announced that you were getting married so quick," Lucas said. "Folks say that this is a shotgun wedding."

"That's only a rumor. Don't pay any attention to it." Alana concentrated on pouring cereal into a bowl and avoided looking Lucas in the eye. When she was growing up, she could fool her father some of the time, her mother very rarely, but never Lucas. He'd been the uncle that she'd never had, since both her parents were only children, and he always knew when she was lying.

"Well, dammit!" Lucas slapped his thigh. "I was hopin' it was true. I'd like to see the next generation before I die."

"Don't talk to me about dying." She shivered at the thought. "You old cowboys are supposed to live forever, don't you know that?"

"Old cowboys never die. They just kick the dust." Matt brought his newspaper to the table and sat down to read it.

"I've heard that they never die, but they smell like they have after a long day on the ranch." Alana poured three cups of coffee and set one in front of her father.

Lucas picked up the other two and carried them to the table. "I hate to see you eat nothing but that dried-up crap with sugar on it. A workin' woman needs something that will stick to her ribs, something like ham and eggs."

"I'll take a couple of energy bars with me." She sat down and set about eating her Lucky Charms.

"Huh," Lucas snorted. "You should pack some beef jerky, not those newfangled bar things you kids think are so great."

Matt laid his paper to the side and took a sip of his coffee. "The wedding planner called me last night. The invitations are going in the mail today."

"I damn sure want one," Lucas said. "I'm going to take it up to that place in Amarillo that does custom framing, and it's going on the wall out in the bunkhouse. I'll want a wedding picture too, so we can hang it above the mantel."

Alana shoved a bite of cereal in her mouth to give herself time to collect her thoughts. When she'd swallowed, she asked, "How big do you want that picture?"

"Huge." Lucas made measurements with his hands. "Wide as the fireplace and tall as it needs to be. I'll take them steer horns down and put it right up there where they're hangin'."

"I was thinkin' we'd hang one over our fireplace too," Matt said. "I want the whole wedding party in mine. Maybe the photographer can take y'all outside and take it with the setting sun back behind you."

"That would be beautiful. We'll have to talk to whoever Crystal sends to do the pictures about it." Alana managed to get out the words around the grapefruit-size lump in her throat. "But we don't need to sit around the table jawin' all day about me and Pax. We've got hay to rake, don't we?"

"That's my girl," Matt said. "I'm going to run up to Amarillo today. Y'all need anything?"

"Bridget and I are going tomorrow to look at wedding dresses. You want to wait and go with us?" She took her bowl and mug to the sink.

"Nope." Matt shook his head. "I'd be bored to tears. I've scheduled a cattlemen's meeting this morning. I'll be back by noon. Want me to pick up some fried chicken on my way home?"

"Yes," Lucas said on his way outside. "I'm inviting myself to eat with y'all. I do love fried chicken. And get extra potato salad."

"Got it." Matt winked at Alana.

As soon as the back door shut behind Lucas, Alana went back to the table and hugged Matt. "Now, tell me why you're really going to Amarillo. You don't have cattlemen's meetings in the middle of the week."

"Doctor's visit," he said.

She folded her arms over her chest. "I'm going with you."

"No, you are not," he protested. "I'll be seeing him every week on Tuesday morning, and until I absolutely can't go on my own, you are not going with me. Lucas is already fussing at me about going to the doctor. He says that something is wrong with me, and I need to see about it. If you start going with me, he'll smell a rat. I plan on telling him after the wedding, but not a day before."

"All right, Daddy." Alana remembered from the research she had done that she shouldn't argue with him. "But if you ever want me to go, or if you don't feel like driving, I'll make an excuse that I need to check on wedding dress alterations or something."

"Sounds good." His voice was back to normal. "Now get on out there. Lucas is waiting for you."

She stuffed a couple of energy bars into her shirt pocket and waved over her shoulder as she went out the back door. "See you at noon." Dealing with the stress of a wedding planner who had called her three times in the past two days, the grief over her father that ate at her soul, and the way she felt the past couple of days after sleeping with Pax, was not an easy task.

* * *

Pax awoke that morning to the sound of a giggling baby and the aroma of bacon. He flipped on a bedside lamp and crawled out of bed. He and Maverick had put in a grueling day on Monday getting the rest of their hay cut. Today, they'd rake it into windrows. The weatherman was calling for rain later in the week, so if they could get their round bales done before it started, that would be wonderful.

Two days had passed now since he'd seen Alana. On the one hand, he'd missed spending time with her. On the other, he'd enjoyed the hard work, something he was used to and could do without much thought—and not having to worry about being the perfect fiancé. He got dressed for work in faded jeans and a tank top, slipped into a soft chambray work shirt, and headed for the kitchen.

Maverick was putting a platter of biscuits on the table. "Did you stay out all night again?"

"Nope, I was too tired to do anything more than send a text to Alana and tell her good night, and then I fell right to sleep." Pax poured himself a cup of coffee and turned to Bridget. "She says the wedding invitations are going out today, and that y'all have an appointment at the bridal shop tomorrow afternoon."

"That means you two better get the hay baled," Bridget said, "because Maverick is going to Amarillo with me. He's going to take Laela to the park while Alana and I both try on dresses, so it's either get the job done today or you'll be doing it on your own tomorrow afternoon, Pax."

"I'll hold down the fort," Pax offered.

"Thanks." Bridget put the rest of the breakfast on the table.

"Wedding invitations?" Maverick asked. "You really are serious about this, aren't you?"

Pax put two biscuits on his plate and passed them on to Maverick. "Maybe when you go get fitted for the tux, you'll believe me."

"You mean it's going to be that formal? So us guys will have to wear one of those hot monkey suits?" Maverick frowned.

"Yes, but Alana says you can wear your cowboy boots if they're black. And she's going to let the girls wear boots too. She says that's only right since it's a barn wedding," Pax said.

"Guess I'll be shopping for cowboy boots today too, then." Bridget smiled. "I've wanted a pair for a while, and this gives me the perfect excuse to buy them."

"Wonderful," Pax said. "You're turning into a real Texan." Anything to change the subject, because Pax would be glad when the wedding was over and done with so everyone would stop talking about it.

An hour later, he was in the cab of an air-conditioned tractor mowing hay, and all he could think about was the wedding. It seemed like every song that came on his favorite country station that morning had to do with weddings. First Thomas Rhett sang "Marry Me." The lyrics reminded Pax that he would likely have to sit by someday and watch Alana marry someone else.

A shot of jealousy ran through him. He didn't want to be the one sitting at the back of the church when she was saying her I dos. He didn't even want her walking by with a wedding ring on her finger that had been put there by another man.

Then Scotty McCreery came in with "This Is It." The words talked about a bride walking down the aisle and how the two of them would be on top of the world together forever. Pax knew that Scotty had written the song for his own wife, and Pax would see Alana walking down the aisle, but there would be none of that forever stuff for them.

When Blake Shelton started singing "God Gave Me You," Pax turned the radio off and called Alana.

She answered on the first ring, and he could hear the beat of music in the background. "I hear a tractor. Are you rakin' or cuttin'?" she sniffled.

"Are you crying?" he asked. "Is it Matt? Is he all right?"

"He's fine, but he told me this morning, he's got a doctor's appointment every Tuesday. He won't let me go with him." She broke down and sobbed.

"Do I need to come over there?" he asked.

"No, I was thinking about a song for the daughter-daddy dance at the wedding," Alana answered, "and found one by Heartland called 'I Loved Her First.' It's perfect, but it reminds me that he'll never see his grandchildren, and he won't be there when I get married for real," Alana said. "The real reason behind this wedding makes it as heart-breaking as a funeral."

"I should stop this tractor and come over there. You need me," he said.

"I'm in a tractor too. Lucas and I are raking hay. First and foremost right now, we're ranchers, and you can't come runnin' every single time I'm sad, so keep working. Talk to me," she said.

"Turn off the music," he suggested. "I had to turn off my radio."

"Okay," she said, "but then my thoughts make me cry. I'm going to put on a good audiobook I've been listening to. Maybe that will take my mind off things," she said. "I'll call you when I'm not such a mess."

"I can be there in five minutes if you change your mind," he said.

He'd barely ended the call when his phone rang again. This time it was Matt.

"Hello," he said.

"Pax, I want to tell you something, and I want you to promise that you won't say a thing to Alana," Matt said.

"That might be tough," Pax said.

"I know y'all are engaged and all, but this has nothing to do with anything between the two of you. The thing is, she's takin' this business of my upcoming death pretty hard. I don't want to talk about the funeral with her, but she needs to know the arrangements have already been made. I've even taken care of the clothes I'll be buried in and ordered the flowers for the top of the casket. Everything is taken care of, so when the time comes, I want you to hold her and comfort her, and tell her that all she has to do is show up at the graveside services." Matt took a deep breath. "It will be easier for her if the service is short and sweet. A song, a few words from the preacher, and then you take her home and love her for the rest of your lives. Promise me that, son."

"I promise." By his reasoning, it wasn't a lie. He wasn't giving his word to stay married to her, but only to love her. He could do that as a friend. A lump stuck in Pax's throat when he thought about having to go to Matt's funeral. The man had been there for him countless times through the years.

"Thank you. I hear the engine of a tractor, so I won't keep you," Matt said and the call ended.

Impulsively, Pax reached out and turned the radio on. Vince Gill was singing "Whenever You Come Around." The words of the song said that whenever his lady came around and smiled that his world turned upside down.

"That's the truth," Pax muttered.

Chapter Ten

Alana parked her truck in front of Clara's Bridal Shop at the same time Bridget pulled into the spot right beside her. They got out of their vehicles and had five minutes to spare when they entered the store. A petite lady who had to be at least sixty years old asked Bridget if she was Alana Carey.

"No, ma'am," Bridget said. "This is Alana. I'm the maid of honor and soon-to-be her sister-in-law."

"I so, so sorry," the woman apologized to Alana. "Are you a professional model?"

"Nope, a ranchin' woman," Alana answered.

"Well, you missed your callin'. By the way, I'm Sadie, and I'll be the one seeing to your needs today," she said. "Honey, I would have given anything for some of your height when I was younger."

"Thank you for that. I would have been glad to have shared some of my height," Alana said. "Where do we start with this business?"

"What is your budget?" Sadie asked.

"She doesn't have one." Bridget held up a credit card. "Her father gave me this and said that she's to have whatever she wants."

"Well, the first thing we'll have you do is pick out about six or eight dresses that you like from the racks. Don't pay any attention to size. I'll look at the dresses, and we'll get as close to your size as possible for the trying-on stage. While you do that, I'll get the dressing room ready." Sadie beamed.

"I have no idea what I want," Alana whispered when Sadie disappeared around a rack of dresses. "Something that goes with my new boots, maybe?"

"I heard that we get to wear boots under our fancy dresses." Bridget started flipping through the dresses. "That's so exciting. We should have a picture made of all of us girls with our dresses raised up so everyone can see our boots."

"Great idea," Alana said, "but we have to remember, Emily is six feet tall like me, and she's eight months pregnant. She might not be comfortable in something too formfitting. We need to choose dresses that are all the same color but maybe not the same style."

"First, the wedding dress, then the bridesmaids'," Bridget told her. "How about this one?"

"Too much skirt and bling." Alana shook her head. "Something way simpler with no sequins."

"Like these." Sadie held up two dresses.

Alana looked at the sleeveless satin sheath dress with its deep V-neck. She imagined wearing her mother's pearl necklace and maybe some simple pearl earrings, and nodded. "Yes, much better. Do you think Daddy will like it, Bridget?"

"You are the bride," Bridget reminded her. "You're the one who has to feel special and pretty in the dress."

Alana hadn't given a wedding dress a second thought—hell, for that matter, she hadn't given the dress a first thought—when she had set out on this path. What was it the preacher had said about tangled webs? Well, this was a step up from anything that a spider's web had ever produced. It was more like a highway of self-destruction.

"Whoa!" she said as Bridget flipped past a dress. "I kind of like that one." She thought about the picture of her mother and father on their wedding day that sat on the mantel above the fireplace. Her mother had been a tall woman too, and she'd worn a Cinderella-type gown with a big skirt and a train that went on forever. There was even a picture in their wedding album of the little flower girl and the ring bearer sitting on the train and looking up at the bride.

Why don't you wear that dress? the voice in her head asked.

Because Mama was a lot thinner than I am. It would never fit. She went back to the first dresses on the rack and soon found four that she thought would work.

"Now I'm ready to try on," she said.

"Then follow me." Sadie led the way through the maze of dress racks to the fitting room.

The dressing room had Alana's name printed on the chalkboard hanging on the door. Sadie hung seven dresses on the rack outside and waved Bridget over to a comfortable chair. "So am I to understand that y'all will be picking out bridesmaids dresses today also?" she asked.

"Yes, ma'am," Alana said. "We'd like to get it all done today if possible, but we'll only be taking Bridget's dress with us. We need for you to coordinate with your sister store in Wichita Falls for the other five."

"The way we usually work is that we order you a brand-new dress that's never been tried on before. If you need alterations we will set aside a day for that," Sadie said.

"I'm getting married June sixth," Alana told her. "We won't have time for alterations."

"Then let's hope that whatever you choose fits perfectly," Sadie said. "Which one do you want to start with?"

"This one." Alana chose a sleeveless satin one with a square neckline.

Sadie went into the dressing room with Alana and helped her step into the dress. She'd barely gotten it zipped when Alana began to shake her head. "This thing weighs as much as a baby elephant."

"Satin is a heavy fabric, and there's a lot of yardage in the skirt." Sadie opened the door for her to step out and look at herself in the three-way mirror.

Bridget snapped a picture of her. "Before you say yes or no, I'm sending this to Matt."

Alana stared at her reflection. The dress would be good with her mother's pearls, all right, and she'd bet dollars to doughnuts that her dad would love it. She was blown away when Bridget shook her head. "Matt says if she wants it, that's fine, but he doesn't think it's the dress."

Back to the dressing room.

The second dress had a lovely belt that accentuated Alana's small waist and matched the beaded lace around the hem. Matt vetoed that one too. Thank God her father had said no because she would have argued with him if he'd liked it.

"Third's the charm." Sadie helped Alana into the sheath dress that she'd picked out for her.

It fit every curve of her six-foot body, and the flare

at the bottom extended to form a short train. The dress felt better than either of the other two that she had tried on, and it fit perfectly. It wouldn't have to be altered at all. She stepped out of the dressing room and stood in front of the mirror. Bridget snapped a picture and sent it to Matt.

That's the one, Matt sent back. *Buy it.*

"You were right, Sadie. Third time's the charm," Alana said.

"Now let's talk about shoes and a veil," Sadie recommended.

"We're all wearing western boots," Alana told her.

"It's a barn wedding," Bridget explained as she snapped several more pictures to send to Matt. "What about a cowboy hat instead of a veil?"

"I'm not sure about…" She stopped midsentence when Sadie held up a pearl-encrusted comb with a short veil attached to it.

Sadie pulled out a chair. "If you'll sit down here, I'll show you how this would look."

Alana was surprised to find that even when she was seated, the dress felt wonderful. Sadie twisted her hair up into a messy neckline bun and secured it in place with a couple of bobby pins. Then she positioned the comb at the top, letting the veil float about halfway down Alana's back.

"Now stand up and take a look," Sadie said.

"Perfect." Bridget took more pictures.

"It does match Mama's pearl necklace and her earrings." Alana sighed.

"Do we have our dress, then?" Sadie asked.

"I believe we have," Alana said. "I love all of it."

"Then we'll get it ordered. You can take the veil home

today, and I'll put a rush on your dress. It should be here within a week," Sadie said.

"Thank you." Alana looked at her reflection once more. An icy cold chill chased down her back, and the smile left her face. She felt beautiful in the dress, and evidently her father loved it, but...she closed her eyes and tried to keep the tears at bay.

"Matt sent a text," Bridget said. "Listen to this, *Knew the dress was the right one by Alana's expression. She's beaming, and that's the way I want to see her on her wedding day.*"

Alana thought about walking down the aisle on her father's arm and him putting her hand into Pax's. She found herself hoping that on this wedding day, she could make her father's wishes come true even if hers couldn't—that this was really the wedding of his dreams. Someday she would marry a man who had really proposed to her, not a friend who was doing her a big favor.

"You look like you're about to cry," Bridget said. "I can't let anyone cry alone, and I don't want to mess up my makeup before I try on dresses."

"It's all so overwhelming." Alana pulled a tissue from her purse and dabbed at her eyes with it.

"That's why I didn't want a big to-do when Maverick and I got married, but you've got a whole different situation," Bridget said.

"Truth is, I didn't want a big wedding," Alana admitted as she headed back into the dressing room. "I wanted me and Pax, you and Maverick in the church with family around us, and then a small reception. Daddy's the one who wants this huge affair."

"It's because he loves you," Bridget said. "Don't lose sight of that."

"Thanks, and I'll try, but every time I turn around he wants to do more." Alana managed a weak smile. "If Mama were here, she'd put the reins on him."

She closed the dressing room door. Sadie started undoing all the small buttons down her back and asked, "What are your colors, and do you want long dresses or short ones for your bridesmaids?"

"Long dresses," Alana told her, "and my colors are yellow and orange. We're having lots of yellow roses because they were my mama's favorite, and shades of orange worked into the centerpieces and bouquets. I was thinking something in a soft peach for the bridesmaids. One of them is eight months pregnant, as tall as me, and red-haired. One is as tall as I am and dark haired, but she's not pregnant. The other three are shorter—one is a redhead, one is a strawberry blond, and one is a brunette, and Bridget is the one who came with me today. I don't really want their dresses to be alike but all of them in the same color would be nice." She realized she was talking too much to cover up her own anxiety. The whole idea of getting married to please her father hadn't hit her so hard until she saw her reflection in the mirror in that perfect dress.

"I think I've got what you need," Sadie said. "While you get dressed, I'll take your dress and veil up to the front and help Bridget pick out an assortment of peach-colored ones."

Alana waited until the women were gone, and then she sat down in a wingback chair, put her hands over her eyes, and wept as silently as she possibly could. The past week had gone by so fast that it was nothing but a blur. She wished she could slow time down to savor every single moment. She knew whatever time she had left with her dad would go all too quickly.

"Stop it!" she scolded herself as she took her hands away from her face. "Some folks don't get even one extra hour with their loved ones. Think about Pax and Maverick's grandpa. He dropped with a heart attack right where he stood. They didn't have any time to get goodbyes said and things arranged."

She wasn't sure which was worse—the shock of a death when it happened suddenly or having time but knowing that it was fast coming to an end.

"I've got to stop this and enjoy what time I have left with him. This should be a wonderful time, not one of sorrow," she whispered to her reflection in the mirror.

She left the dressing room and went out to sit in the chair that Bridget had vacated. She'd just sat down when her phone rang. Expecting it to be her father, she answered it without even looking at the screen.

"So you like the dress, do you?" she asked.

"Wouldn't know," Pax said. "If you'll send over a picture of you in it, I'll be glad to pass judgment."

"Oh, no, the groom can't see the bride in the dress until the wedding day. That's bad luck." Her spirits lifted at hearing his voice. "And we sure wouldn't want any of that, now would we?"

"No, ma'am, we're going to have a beautiful wedding, and, honey, you'd look good in a dress made from a feed sack and tied up in the middle with a calf rope," he teased. "Want to take a drive to the creek this evening? We could throw down a quilt, have a few beers, and watch the stars. We might even see a shooting star and share the good luck."

"I would love it," she said. "Pick me up at eight. You bring the beer, and I'll bring the quilt."

"Sounds like a plan."

"Before I forget," she continued, "our high school reunion is Friday evening. Want to go?"

"I thought that was in June," he said.

"They changed it to May this year. The excuse was that so many people take vacations in June that we were having a small turnout. And you'll never believe it, but we're having it in the school cafeteria. The committee thought that it would be nostalgic, but there'll only be nonalcoholic drinks." She stood up with the phone still to her ear and walked through the store to see where Bridget might be. Surely it didn't take that long to find some peach dresses.

"Sure," Pax answered. "Let's go show 'em that we're engaged."

"Billy Ray is in charge of everything this year. I'll call him and tell him that we'll be attending." She finally located Bridget.

"Tell him there will be four of us. I'm sure Maverick will want to be there with Bridget," he said.

"Will do. See you this evening," she said and ended the call.

A real girlfriend or fiancée would have ended with I love you. Alana wondered if she and Pax should say it too so what they were doing would be more convincing.

Bridget waved her over and pointed to a large bunch of dresses on a rolling rack. "We found so many in the same color that we couldn't carry them."

* * *

At dusk that evening, Pax hit the house in a dead run, went straight to the bathroom for a quick shower, got dressed in clean jeans and a T-shirt, and was ready to go pick Alana up. He was in his truck and halfway down the lane when he remembered the beer he'd left behind in the refrigerator. Gravel and dust billowed up behind him when he stomped the brakes. The gray fog hadn't cleared when he whipped his vehicle around in a three-point turn and headed back to the house.

He waved at Maverick and Laela, who were sitting on the porch swing, as he raced inside the house and came out with a six-pack of beer in his hand. "See y'all later."

Laela whimpered and reached for him. He set the beer on the porch railing and crossed the porch in a couple of long strides. "It's all right, darlin'. You'll always be my favorite girl, and I'll be back in time for breakfast."

"Don't believe him, Laela," Maverick said. "If he's telling the truth, then that means something fishy is going on with this wedding business, because Alana should be his favorite girl."

"Alana is my favorite woman. Laela is my favorite girl." He gave the toddler a kiss on the forehead. "And don't you ever doubt that. But right now I've got to go. Being late for a date does not start off the night well."

"Got dinner reservations somewhere?" Maverick asked.

"Nope, we're going to find a place to relax and lay back to watch the stars," Pax answered and then set Laela on the swing beside Maverick.

"Watch the stars?" Maverick chuckled. "Yeah, right."

Pax poked him on the arm. "Well, we'll start by watching the stars."

Maverick's laughter rang out across the ranch. "You should marry her already."

"I intend to, and you'll be standing right beside me." Pax got into his truck again and then remembered he'd left the beer sitting on the porch. He slapped himself on the forehead, slung open the door, and jogged across the yard—again.

"I'm starting to believe this might be real after all," Maverick hollered from the swing. "Only a cowboy in love would be so forgetful."

Pax grabbed the beer and headed back to his truck. "Don't wait up for me."

"Wouldn't think of it," Maverick called out.

Pax arrived at the Bar C two minutes late, knocked on the door, and was surprised when Matt threw it open. "Come on in. Alana's runnin' a little late. After she and Bridget got home from that dress business today, she went out to the hay field and worked until about thirty minutes ago."

"How are you feeling?" He followed Matt into the living room and took a seat on the sofa.

"I get tired more each day, but usually after a little nap, I'm ready to go again. I'm glad that I'm able to do what I can," Matt answered.

"Does Lucas know?" Pax asked.

Matt shook his head. "No, and I'm not telling him until after the wedding. The only people who know are God, my doctor, you, and Alana, and that's the way I want to keep it. I can't stand the idea of discussing the issue with everyone in the county or having folks bringing food to the house like I'm already dead. Alana needs this to be a happy time."

"Did I hear my name?" Alana entered the room, crossed over to the sofa, and planted a kiss on the top of Pax's head. "I'm ready to go."

"Yes, you are, and you look beautiful, as usual." Pax stood up and laced his fingers in hers.

"Well, thank you." Alana beamed. "Sorry I was a little late."

"Takes a rancher to understand a rancher," he said. "We both have jobs to take care of."

"God, I'm glad you aren't marrying a city slicker." Matt picked up the remote, popped the footrest up on his recliner, and started surfing through the channels.

"See you later, Daddy," Alana called out as she and Pax left the room. She picked up a quilt from the bottom stair step on her way out. "See, still in the package. I saved it for a special occasion."

"I'm honored." He raised her hand and kissed the knuckles.

He turned on the radio when they got into the truck and kept time to the music with his thumbs on the steering wheel as they drove toward an old abandoned homestead a couple of miles west of Daisy.

"We're going back to Baxter's pond, aren't we?" Alana asked when he turned right out of town.

"I thought that might be a nice quiet place," he said, "but, Alana, after tonight we really need to spend more time with your dad, even if it's watching television with him."

"Thank God you said that," she said. "I've been thinking the same thing. But tonight I'm glad for some time with you. I haven't been to Baxter's pond since we were in high school. I wonder if it's still as beautiful as it used to be." She turned off the radio. "I've always loved the way the moon and stars are reflected in the water."

"Me too." Pax drove another half a mile and slowed down to make the turn. The moon lit up an old weathered house with red roses still growing in front of the porch. He moved along at less than five miles an hour, keeping the tires in a path that was really only two ruts with weeds growing up in the middle.

When they got closer, the light from the moon also let

them see a dozen trucks parked around the pond. "Guess we're not the only ones who discovered Baxter's pond."

He braked and country music floated across the flat country right into the pickup with them. Alan Jackson was singing, "Good Time." A dozen or more teenagers were doing a line dance at the edge of the pond.

"Unless you want to party, I guess we had better go find us another place for our date tonight," he said.

"We're a little old to be out there with a bunch of high school kids like that. Oh, my!" She pointed.

When the song ended at least half of the kids peeled off their clothing, and jumped into the pond.

"Have you ever been skinny-dipping?" Pax turned the truck around and headed back to town.

"I was far too self-conscious about my size to do that in high school. Besides, that water is damn cold, coming up from the springs the way it does," she said.

"Then I guess there won't be any sex until they get out." He laughed.

"How about you?" she asked.

"Not in Baxter's pond, and not with a girl unless taking a shower together counts," he said.

"I know just the place," she said. "There's a shallow stream at the back of the Bar C that's pretty nice."

"Are we going to skinny-dip?" He wiggled his eyebrows at her.

"If we do, that'll be all we do, because our stream is every bit as cold as Baxter's pond," she giggled. "Not even a big old strong cowboy like you could keep things ready in that kind of icy water."

"Oh, honey, I bet we could get so hot we'd boil that water," he said.

"You know we really shouldn't," she said.

"Probably not, but it would be fun to try to see if we could warm the water wouldn't it?" he teased.

"Oh, yeah." She directed him to a dirt road leading off to the back side of the ranch. "I'll open and shut the gate. I hope that beer was good and cold."

"I had it in the freezer for more than an hour." He turned when she pointed and then braked when he came face-to-face with a gate.

She was out of the passenger's seat before the truck came to a full stop and opened the wide gate. When he pulled through it, she shut it and got back into the vehicle. "Straight ahead about a quarter of a mile. Stay in the ruts. You ever been back here?"

"Nope," he answered. "Is this where you take your fellers?"

She slapped his arm. "No, this is where I go when my fellers or my parents or anyone else upsets me. You've heard folks talk about someone being *their person*?" She put air quotes around the last two words. "Well, this is even better than having a person to tell all your darkest secrets to. This is *my place* where I sort out all my problems. I've never shared it with anyone. Park right there under that tree."

The clear water looked to be about knee deep and served as a mirror for the moon and stars. There were no kids playing loud music or skinny-dipping. Pax felt like he was walking on air when he got out of the truck, knowing that he was the first person she'd brought to her secret place. He grabbed the beer from the backseat and headed down the grassy embankment to the bubbling creek.

She followed right behind him with the quilt in her hands. She flipped it out on the grass close to the edge of the creek, sat down, and removed her boots and socks, then stuck her feet into the cool, clear water.

"Come right on in, the water is fine," she teased.

"I wish this creek passed through the back side of our land." He set the beer down and removed his boots. He whistled through his teeth when the cold water bubbled over his feet. "Damn that's cold!"

"My cowboy isn't as strong as I thought." She popped the top of a can of beer and handed it to him, then opened a second one and took a long drink. "So you still thinking about skinny-dippin' in my little creek?"

"No, ma'am, but I might be talked into skinny-dippin' in a big old Jacuzzi tub in a hotel room somewhere. Want to take this quilt and party up to Amarillo?" he asked.

"I'd rather stay right here," she said. "Like you've told me so many times, I'm a ranchin' woman, not a city girl. If you really want to go skinny-dippin' with me, then you have to do it right here."

He took that as a dare, downed the rest of his beer for some liquid courage, and got to his feet. He found Luke Bryan's "Knockin' Boots" on his phone and turned up the volume as loud as it would go. Moving his shoulders and hips to the music, he turned his back to her and teased her by taking off his shirt a little at a time. When he turned back, she was on her feet and was twirling her shirt around the top of her head.

"Guess I'm not getting a thing over on you, am I?" He pulled off his shirt and tossed it toward the tree.

"Never." Alana took down her hair and shook it loose.

He took off his belt and pulled it free of the loops.

She did the same. Lord, that woman could make a mint at a strip club the way she tormented him with the simple act of unzipping her jeans.

Slow piano music started the next song on his play list. Lorrie Morgan sang, "A Picture of Me Without You."

He opened his arms and they swayed together. He'd never danced completely naked with a woman. His heartbeat and pulse both jacked up several notches. Not even the cold water could take care of the erection pressing against her lower belly—at least he didn't think it could.

She touched his phone with her toe and then did the same to hers, and Whitney Duncan started singing "Skinny Dippin'." The lyrics told about chills from the water and chills from the way he kissed her. He pressed his lips to hers and felt both of those. She led him out into the creek, wrapped her arms around him, and then fell backward into the shallow water and brought him down on top of herself.

His lips found hers, and not even the chilly water could take away his need for her. She reached down between them and guided him in her. They forgot about the temperature of the water and all the crazy things going on in their lives. The world disappeared, and they were the only two people left on earth.

Sometime near dawn they awoke, wrapped up in the quilt like they were encased in a cocoon. Her head was on his shoulder. Their clothing was scattered around them in the grass that was now wet with dew. Both of their cell phones had been turned off and tossed to the side, and the only sounds they heard were the gentle bubbling of the creek as it went on about its business and the gentle cooing of a mourning dove.

"Good morning," Pax said.

"Mornin' to you," she responded. "Think maybe we better get our clothes on and go home?"

"Ten more minutes." He pulled her closer to him. "Now I see why you love it here. Thank you for letting me be the first one you shared it with."

"You deserve it. You're going to marry me." Her warm breath tickled his ear.

"Maybe fifteen minutes," he said.

"Make it twenty at least," she said as she rolled over on top of him.

Chapter Eleven

Not even sucking on lemons could have wiped the smile off Alana's face the next day when she thought about the night before. Her eyes widened as realization dawned, and she threw her hand over her mouth and moaned.

"What's the matter, honey?" Lucas wiped the grease from his hands and then tossed her the red rag.

She cleaned the dirt and grime from her hands. "Nothing, I just hope this damned old tractor starts up when I turn the key," she lied. "I hate to give it up, since it's the first one that Daddy let me drive when I was twelve years old, but poor old thing's wearin' out."

"Don't I know it," Lucas laughed. "She's runnin' on constant cussin', bubble gum, and bailing wire these days."

The tractor's engine turned over on the first try, and Alana drove it out of the barn. She was almost afraid to turn it off when she reached the pasture she was supposed to plow, but she simply had to talk to Pax.

For two people who ran from each other for so long, y'all are sure makin' up for lost time, the voice in her head pestered her.

"Oh shut up!" Alana sent up a prayer that had more to do with the red-hot sex in a cold creek than it did with being able to start a tractor again.

She slipped her phone from her shirt pocket, but before she could touch the screen, the damned thing rang. She had to scramble to keep from dropping it and was out of breath when she finally answered. "Hello, Pax. I was about to call you..."

"About last night? I'm so sorry, Alana. I got so caught up in the moment, and I wasn't thinking about us having sex, so I didn't come prepared," Pax said. "When can you take one of those tests?"

"I'll know in a week either way," she told him. "And I was caught up in the moment too, so part of the blame is on me. We can't do that again."

"Not even—" he started.

"Not even," she butted in. "It'll make the annulment that much tougher. Besides, we're going to be too busy between now and then for much time alone anyway."

"It was pretty amazing," he said.

"Yep," she agreed.

"So what's on our agenda for tonight?" he asked.

"If you want to come over, we could play dominoes with Daddy," she suggested.

"Sounds great. I'll be there at seven-thirty," he told her.

She sighed and put the phone back in her pocket. From the time she was old enough to know that boys were different from girls, she'd felt something for Paxton Baker. Then there was that incident when he kissed her. The next day she'd made up her mind to apologize for slapping him, but when she found him, he and Amanda Sue Williams were behind the school buses with their lips locked.

"Boys!" she muttered. "They think they're the only ones who feel rejection?"

She started up the tractor engine, put her earbuds in, and started the playlist in her phone.

* * *

Pax threw his tools in the back of the old ranch work truck and was about to get into the cab when his phone rang. He saw that it was Alana and answered it before he even started the engine.

"I need help," she said.

"Right now?" he asked.

"This very minute. I got a call from Daddy. Can you go with me to Plainview to get him? He's confused. I can drive him home, but I'll need someone to bring my vehicle back," she said. "He's sittin' on the side of the road."

"Broke down?" Pax started up the engine, then changed his mind.

"No, he's lost and doesn't know what to do."

"I can be there by the time you get your truck fired up if you don't mind me coming as I am," he said.

"I don't care how you look. I'm a mess too. I'd just walked into the house after plowing all day in an open cab tractor," she told him. "So I'm sure not a beauty queen right now, and I don't smell like roses."

"I'm on my way!"

"Thank you. I really appreciate you being able to help," she told him and ended the call.

Pax was completely out of breath when he jumped into Alana's passenger seat and strapped the seat belt across his chest. The truck's air-conditioning felt good on his sweaty body, but he sure would have preferred a dip in that cold creek where they'd spent the night before.

"What happened?" he asked.

"Daddy said that he was coming home from Tulia and got turned around." Her voice cracked. "He was going to the vet's for some calf medicine. I was out on the tractor when he called. I figured he'd driven over there and right back home, but he never made it." She gripped the steering wheel so hard that her knuckles were white. She sounded as if she would break into tears any minute.

"Pull over and let me drive," Pax said.

She shook her head. "It'll take too long."

"Hold one of your hands out."

"I can't." Those two words were tough for her to get out. "They're shaking too bad. I need them both to drive."

"You need to let me drive, darlin'." He kept his voice as steady as he could. "If you wreck and kill us, who'll take care of Matt?"

She braked so hard that she left skid marks on the pavement, hopped out of the truck, ran around the back side, and Pax met her coming the other way.

"Need a hug?" he asked.

"Maybe later." She passed him without even slowing down.

He got behind the wheel and sped down the dirt road. He didn't slow down until he had to turn south on Highway 27. With her hands still trembling, Alana pulled out her phone and punched in a phone number.

"This is Alana Carey. I'm Matthew Carey's daughter." She hit the speaker icon and laid the phone on the console between her and Pax.

"This is Doctor Winslow. What can I do for you?"

She explained the situation. "I read everything you sent home with him, plus I looked up everything I could find on the Internet. Nothing said anything about confusion or memory loss."

"That's a side effect of the medicine I gave him, hopefully to slow down the growth of the tumor. Now you have a decision to make. Do you want him to live a little longer or have a clear mind for what time he has left? If you decide on the latter, then simply throw away the pills. I'm so sorry to have to tell you this. The meds work for most of my patients, but about ten percent do have the side effects you described."

"If we decide to get rid of the pills, how long will it take him to get back to normal?" she asked.

"About forty-eight hours," the doctor answered.

"Do we need to taper him off them?" she asked.

"No, tell him not to take the one for tonight," he answered. "Any more questions?"

"That should do it. Thank you." Alana ended the call and heaved a long sigh of relief. "I'll talk to him, but I'd rather have all of him for less time than worry about him every time he walks out the door."

They found Matt on the north side of Plainview at the junction of Farm Road. He was sitting on the tailgate of his truck and waving at the cars that passed by. When Alana hopped out of the truck, he got down and slammed the tailgate shut. "What took you so long? I've been sitting here for hours."

"You all right? It's pretty warm out today," Pax asked.

"Sweatin' a little, but I'm used to that. I'm a rancher," Matt told him.

"Get in the truck, Daddy, and I'll take you home." Alana started around to the driver's side of the truck.

Matt folded his arms over his chest and propped a foot against a tire. "Don't you start thinkin' you can boss me around because I made a wrong turn and couldn't find my way back home. I'm still the head honcho, and don't you forget it."

"I'm glad to let you be the boss man, but you've been out here in the heat for a while, and I think you need a big cold glass of water or maybe a sweet tea. Why don't we go on to the house and see what we can find?" she asked.

"Fine." Matt got behind the wheel of his vehicle. "Now, y'all go on back in your truck, Alana. I'll follow you so I don't get lost again."

"I was going to drive you, Daddy, so we can talk on the way. I called your doctor, and he said that you and I need to discuss some things," Alana told him.

He tossed the keys to her. "Well, why in the hell didn't you say so to begin with?" He slid over into the passenger's seat. "See you at the house, Pax."

Paxton waved over his shoulder. "You get the sweet tea ready. I'll pick up a pizza on the way through town."

Alana was good with her dad, Pax thought—much, much better than he'd ever been with his grandmother. She had to be worried out of her mind, and yet, she knew exactly how to handle Matt. She'd be a wonderful mother someday if she managed her kids the way she was taking care of her father—with patience and kindness. Matt would never know how much he'd scared her that day, the same way her kids would never know how much she fretted every time they left her sight.

* * *

Alana waited until she could trust her voice not to shake and they were well underway before she told her dad what the doctor had said about the medicine. "So what do you think, Daddy? I can't make this decision for you."

"I wanted to live a few more months so I could go out knowing that you and Pax were going to have a baby to take over the ranch when y'all get old," he admitted. "But I don't want to burden you with having to come find me every time I leave the house, either. This is as much your decision, sweetheart, as it is mine. Is quality or quantity more important to you?"

Alana wiped a tear away with the back of her hand. "I don't want to lose you, but I sure don't want to lose you before you breathe your last either. Seems to me that if your memory is gone, then I have already lost you anyway."

"Then I'll quit taking the pills. My main focus right now is on your wedding, and I need to be lucid for that," he said. "Now how're things between you and Pax? Did I sense a little tension back there?"

She shook her head. "We're fine. We were both really worried about you."

He patted her on the shoulder. "It won't happen again. I'll stick close to home for a couple of days. Pax is a good man to come running out of the field when you call him."

"He really is," Alana agreed.

That part was the gospel truth for sure, and she could add an amazing friend and still not be lying in the least.

Pax must've called in an order for the pizza as he drove because he pulled into the yard right behind them. He took two boxes out of the backseat, carried them onto the porch, and said, "I really should've gone home and cleaned up. A feller shouldn't come to his fiancée's house looking like a field hand, but I thought y'all might be hungry."

"Son, Alana's going to see you in worse condition than you are right now when y'all are married," Matt told him. "She knows she's gettin' a rancher, thank God for that"—he rolled his eyes toward the ceiling—"and you'll see her as dirty as she is today many times too. So let's sit down at the table and enjoy a conversation over supper."

"Yes, sir. I'll set these pizzas on the table and help Alana get out some plates," Pax offered.

"Ain't no need for that. We got paper napkins on the table, and we can sure enough eat pizza without dirtying up plates or silverware," Matt said. "Joy says not havin' to do dishes is one of the joys of eatin' finger food."

Alana caught Pax's eye and nodded.

His head barely bobbed. He understood that she had talked to her father, and all was well. Without either of them saying a word, they'd read each other's minds. It might not be a huge thing to most people, but it amazed Alana and gave her something to think about.

Had it been anyone other than Pax sitting at her table that evening she might have snarled at the dirt on his shirt. But she saw right past the grime and even his bulging biceps and looked right at the heart of the man. He'd dropped what he was doing to go with her, had taken over the wheel to calm her down, and then hustled up a meal. Now that was a man that any woman should be proud to call her husband.

Any woman? A streak of jealousy shot through Alana. She'd known a touch of that feeling a few times when she'd seen a woman coming on to Pax in a bar, but she'd never experienced such a fiery surge before. Maybe it was because they'd had sex, or maybe it was because her crazy heart was beginning to think this engagement was the real deal.

When they finished eating, Matt got out the dominoes and shuffled them in the middle of the kitchen table. "Don't think because I got a little confused today that y'all are going to beat me at Shoot the Moon. I'm the king of this game." He chose his seven tiles.

"I remember the first time I beat you. I should've gotten a trophy to set up on the mantel. That was more exciting than when I won my first bronc ride." Alana nudged him on the shoulder as she passed by on the way to refill all their tea glasses.

"Well, darlin' daughter, don't expect to get a trophy tonight, because I'm feelin' real lucky." He set up his dominoes.

Alana looked across the room for a few seconds, and liked the feeling of having a family around the table. She wished she could freeze that moment in time so she wouldn't get her heart broken twice—once when she lost her father and the next when Pax left after the annulment.

Chapter Twelve

The days went by much too quickly and yet the hours in every one of them seemed to stump along like a hundred-year-old man on crutches. Nine days had passed since Matt had dropped the news of his cancer on his daughter. That Friday morning the pain in her heart was as raw as it had been when he told her. Would it still feel like this when a year had passed? she wondered.

Dust fogged up the tractor's window as Alana watched the baler open up and a round bale roll out. This would be the last year that she and her father could talk about the hay crop and compare it to years before. Had they gotten enough to last through the winter? Had rain spoiled a few bales? She turned on the windshield wipers to take away some of the dust, and wished that cleaning the tears off her face could be as easy as touching a button.

Her phone rang and Bridget's name popped up. She slid

the button on the screen and put it on speaker. "Hey, girl, what's goin' on?" she asked.

"I'm in a"—Bridget paused—"in a...I'm worried about this thing we're going to tonight for the class reunion. I don't want to look like a *culchie*, but I don't want to be overdressed, either. I want Maverick to be proud when he introduces me as his wife."

"Holy crap!" Alana exclaimed. "I'd actually forgotten about the reunion. What's a *culchie*?"

"You'd call it a country bumpkin," Bridget said. "How could you forget? I've been fretting over it for a week. What are you wearing?"

"It's very informal." Bridget tried to remember what was in her closet, since she hadn't taken time to shop for anything new. "I'll probably wear a pair of capris and maybe a sleeveless top."

"Thank God." Bridget heaved a sigh that Alana could hear on the phone. "I was afraid I needed a formal dress, and I've been kicking my arse because I hadn't shopped for something nice when we were out looking at bridal and bridesmaids' dresses."

"What you wore when we went shopping would be fine," Alana told her. "I'm sure glad that you called, because I'd forgotten all about the affair, what with all these fast wedding plans and the shower tomorrow afternoon."

"Thank you so much for sorting that out for me," Bridget said. "Maverick has gone to get Mam. She'd planned to come to the ranch tomorrow, but we needed a sitter for Laela this evening."

"You're very welcome," Alana told her. "Why don't we four all ride together?"

"That would be great," Bridget answered. "I won't feel like such a stranger if you're with me when we walk into the room. Meeting all of Maverick's old school friends is goin' to be a bit intimidatin'."

"I've always been tall and felt out of place, so Mama used to tell me to walk into a room with my head held high and act like I owned the place." Alana finished the final round and parked the tractor.

"Sounds like advice my grandmother told me," Bridget said. "You've turned off the engine to whatever machinery you were running, so I guess you're calling it a day?"

"I guess I'd better," Alana said. "Right now I look a lot like one of your *culchies*."

"Not you." Bridget laughed with her. "Pax says you look like a model no matter what you're wearing, and I agree."

"So he says that, does he?" Alana opened the tractor door and hopped down out of the cab. The sun was setting in the west, taking part of the heat with it, but the slight breeze that ruffled her hair was still hot enough to bake a cake—or so it seemed.

"Yes, he does. He's very much in love with you, Alana. Now, I've got to go start getting dressed for the party. See you later," Bridget said.

Alana said goodbye, tucked her phone into her hip pocket, and jogged all the way to the house. Matt looked up from the sofa as she passed through the living room. She gave him a smile.

She stopped and kissed him on the top of his head. "How're you feelin' today, Daddy?"

"Better than yesterday. Not as good as I hope to be tomorrow when all this medicine gets out of my system. But darlin', you don't have time to stop and worry about me. Pax will be here to get you for the reunion in an hour. Quite frankly, you look like hell right now," Matt told her.

"I always have time to talk to you, and thanks for boosting my ego," she told him.

He chuckled and pointed toward the stairs. "Get on about makin' yourself beautiful."

"Yes, sir!" She saluted smartly and raced up the stairs, started a shower, and shuddered at her reflection in the mirror. Her father was right. She did look like hell. Dirt clung to her sweaty T-shirt and was smeared across her face like war paint. A few blades of straw were stuck in strands of her hair. She'd been in such a hurry to get to the house that she hadn't even realized she'd stepped in a fresh cow patty until the smell hit her in the nose.

"So Pax is in love with me, is he?" she muttered as she peeled out of her clothing and stepped into the shower. "I bet if he saw me now, he'd run the other way."

She had finished putting on her lipstick an hour later when the doorbell rang. She heard the sound of two deep voices floating up the stairs, but she couldn't make out what they were saying. After one final glance in the mirror, she slipped on a pair of sandals and headed down the stairs.

"Aren't you going, Daddy? You went to school here in Daisy too, and I've never known you to miss a reunion," she asked when she got to the foyer. "You can ride with me and Pax."

"We'd be glad to have you go with us," Pax said.

"Not this year," Matt said. "Don't have the energy to deal with all that bullshit. You kids go and be the talk of the party with your engagement and all."

Pax took her by the hand and twirled her around. "We should've gotten a red carpet laid out for you and a limousine for you to ride in. You look like a movie star."

"You need to get your eyes checked." She picked up her

purse from the credenza. "Don't wait up, Daddy. We'll be late, but if you need us, call."

"If you get bored, you can pretend I called," Matt chuckled.

"Thanks, Matt"—Pax nodded—"but I'm going to be the one with the prettiest girl there. I plan to stay until they lock the doors and stay on the dance floor so long with Alana that I have to buy new boots tomorrow."

"That's exactly what I want y'all to do," Matt said. "Good night, now, and get on out of here."

Alana kissed him on the cheek and thought about the last word in that last sentence the whole way out to the truck. Not even the heat caused by Pax's hand on her lower back could shake the words from her mind. Waiting—that summed up what she was doing. Waiting for the end of both her father's life and the marriage that she was about to enter into with Pax. She'd read that there were several stages to the grieving process—denial, anger, bargaining, depression, and acceptance—and that often they didn't affect a person in that order, but they could jump around. According to the article, she might even experience more than one stage in a single day or hour.

As she got into the truck, anger washed over her, and she knew exactly who she was mad at—not her father but God, the Big Man Himself. How could He do this to them? There were serial killers out there on the loose that God could justify giving an inoperable brain tumor to. Those were the ones who should be dying instead of hurting other people. Her father was a good man, a Christian. He'd put her interests before his own after her mother died. He damn sure didn't deserve to be afflicted with something like this, she thought as she fastened her seat belt.

"You all right?" Pax laid a hand on her shoulder. "You look like you're mad at someone."

"Nope, not mad at anyone," she said.

Pax drove over to the Callahan Ranch and honked the horn. Bridget and Maverick came right out and got into the backseat.

Alana turned around in the seat enough to see her soon-to-be sister-in-law. "Bridget, we'll have to stick together tonight."

"Why's that?" Bridget asked.

"Because all those poor women who thought they would someday end up with these two Callahan boys might pick a fight with us," Alana answered.

"My grandmother said anything worth havin' was worth fightin' for," Bridget said. "If I have to go to battle for this sexy cowboy here then so be it."

Maverick picked up her hand and kissed the knuckles. "Thank you, darlin', but I reckon I should've brought droolin' bibs for my old classmates. When they see that I've married a gorgeous woman like you, they'll be slack-jawed."

"You sure know how to sweet-talk a woman," Bridget teased. "And what about those two? They're the ones that everyone's talkin' about right now." She nodded toward the front seat.

"That's because they managed to keep their dating a secret so long. I bet all the gossips are wondering how they did it," Maverick answered.

"Even you, huh?" Pax asked as he started the engine and backed out of the driveway.

"Especially me," Maverick said.

Pax changed the subject and the two guys went from one topic to another and still another while they drove from the ranch into the town of Daisy, and Alana was glad to be ignored and have some time to think. She needed to do some bargaining with God.

Lord, she thought, *if you'll let that tumor shrink and give me a few more years with my dad, I'll come clean with him about this fake engagement. I promise I'll never lie to him again.*

God didn't answer her, not even with a simple sign like a beautiful sunset. Maybe He wanted something bigger, like a promise that she'd never go to the Wild Cowboy again or that she'd change religions and become a nun. Right then, she would have been willing for almost anything, but no answers came and no agreement was reached. Pax nosed the truck into a parking space not far from the school cafeteria, and she put away all her bargaining tools with a sigh.

"You sure you're all right?" Pax asked.

"I'm fine," she said. "Just a lot on my mind."

"Well, let's go forget all about those wedding plans and have a good time," Bridget said. "I haven't been to a party in months. Thank goodness Iris decided to come to the ranch a little early and watch Laela. Now I can have a good time without worrying about the baby all evening. Iris told me that if I call more than once to check on them that I'm in trouble."

"That sounds like her," Alana said. "I sure wouldn't worry about my child if she was babysitting for me."

"So have y'all talked about kids?" Maverick asked.

"We've got to get through all this wedding stuff before we think about that," Pax said as he got out of the truck and opened the door for Alana.

"Well, I hope y'all don't wait too long. I want Laela to grow up with lots of cousins," Bridget said as she and Maverick got out of the truck and headed toward the door where music was floating out of the cafeteria.

Pax took Alana's hand in his. "Would you have done all

this again if you'd known about wedding showers, wedding planners, and now talk of kids?"

"Yep," she said. "I'd do anything to make Daddy happy."

They followed Maverick and Bridget through the doors and down the hallway.

"That was my locker right there." Maverick pointed.

"And mine was on the end," Alana told Bridget. "Pax's was beside his. Wouldn't it be something if these old things could talk?"

"I would imagine that they've been used by dozens and dozens of classes coming through the Daisy school, so each one could probably tell enough stories to fill a book," Bridget said.

"Yep." Pax nodded. "And Alana's would be a romance novel."

"Oh, hush!" She bumped him with her hip. "Mine would be a little Christian novel compared to yours and Maverick's. Y'all's would border on erotica."

"Tell me more," Bridget giggled.

"Later," Alana whispered. "Right now, we have to go inside and fight off the crowds of women who are probably already gossiping about us."

"Poor darlin's. At least we're giving them something to brighten their days," Bridget said as Maverick pushed open the door for her.

As soon as they were inside, several of the girls Alana had graduated with came over to make noises about her engagement ring. The lyrics from that old country song about always being sixteen in your hometown played through her mind as she held out her hand. No one among this group where she was the center of attention was a teenager anymore, but put them all together, and by damned if they really did act like they had in high school—all drama, flipping hair around and flirting. Most of them were married and had kids. A few were even on their second marriages, and at least two of them were past that and working on their third set of wedding plans. As far as Alana was concerned that last bunch was bat crap crazy. Thank God for the wedding planner her father had hired or she'd already be certifiably insane with all the preparations. Thinking about going through all the process three times was enough to give her a case of the hives.

"I can't believe that you're really going to marry Paxton," Melissa said. A short blonde who was thirty pounds heavier than when she'd been a high school cheerleader, she'd dressed in a skintight dress that barely reached her now chubby knees. She'd gotten a divorce from her second husband and kept scanning the room, as if she was looking for number three.

She went on her tiptoes and cupped a hand around Alana's ear. "But then I suppose you finally caught him with the oldest trick in the books."

"So when's the baby due?" Danielle asked. She'd been one of the other cheerleaders in high school and was still so thin that even skinny jeans looked like they were hanging on a hoe handle. She'd had quite the reputation for sleeping only with guys on the basketball team, and had actually married the star player. They had two kids, and Frankie was now the owner of the local gas station/convenience store.

"I'm not pregnant," Alana said.

"Sure, you're not." Danielle gave her a big wink. "If you weren't, you'd have taken a year to plan the biggest wedding in the whole state of Texas. You can't fool us, but we'll play along."

"But only after you tell us when the baby is due," Melissa giggled.

"In about two years," Alana whispered. "I'm really not pregnant."

"Bullshit!" Rachel Freeman, who'd been Alana's nemesis in high school, pushed her way through the crowd. "I've had my eye on Paxton for three years and was about ready to close the deal. I even learned how to drive a tractor so I could impress him. The only way he would have chosen a big old horse of a woman like you over this"—she swept her hands down over her body—"is if you tricked him with pregnancy."

Rachel had been a thorn in Alana's side since they'd been in junior high school. Alana's dad had told her that the girl had a severe jealousy issue, and he was so right. His advice was for Alana to ignore the girl and eventually karma would catch up to her. But Rachel's bullying had gone beyond jealousy. She'd told ugly tales about Alana, and then denied saying a word when confronted. She'd tried bronc riding and failed at that, then she'd raised a steer for the county fair and come in behind both Pax and Alana. The days of being able to ignore Rachel came to an end that very evening.

"Like I said, I'm not pregnant." Alana fought the urge to cross her fingers behind her back. "I don't have to catch a man—or even three—that way."

The woman had recently divorced her third husband and had claimed that she was pregnant all three times, but then after the wedding, she suddenly "had a miscarriage."

Rachel's hands knotted into fists. "What did you say to me?"

"You heard me," Alana said with a sweet smile on her face.

Bridget, bless her heart, must've overheard or maybe read the expressions of the women around Alana, because she chose that moment to make her way through the maze to hand Alana a glass of what looked like wine. "Hello, all. I'm Bridget, Maverick Callahan's wife. Alana is going to be my new sister-in-law in a few weeks. Pax tells me that he's been in love with her since they were barely knee-high to a grasshopper, but it's only been recently that she'd agree to go out with him. Have you seen her gorgeous ring?"

"So you're the Irish woman who had Maverick's baby," Rachel said. "I got to admit, y'all both"—her eyes shifted from Alana over to Bridget—"were smarter than we were."

"Come on, Rachel." Melissa took her by the arm. "I see two empty barstools, and I do believe that Billy Ray is making eyes at you. Let's go let him buy us a drink."

Rachel wobbled slightly on the three-inch spike-heeled shoes that she wore with her skintight designer jeans. "Poor old Billy Ray has been in love with me his whole life. Maybe I need a younger man in my life. I believe I'll make him a happy man tonight."

"Sorry about that," Danielle said. "Rachel never has been able to hold her liquor, and we all know that she's been jealous of you for years."

"I wish I knew why," Alana said.

Danielle smiled. "Because she had her eyes set on Paxton all these years. She even flirted with him every chance she got when she was married."

"But Pax and I didn't even start dating until this year," Alana said.

"You sure hid it well when you did."

"Poor Rachel," Bridget said. "She was married three times, and all the time wanted to be with someone else. That must've been miserable."

"She's definitely got some problems that would probably make a therapist pull out his hair." Danielle lowered her voice. "I don't think Rachel likes who she is, but we won't let her ruin our night. I'm going to go get another glass of wine. Can I bring you something?"

"We're good," Alana said.

Danielle nodded. "Great seeing you, Alana, and meeting you, Bridget. I'll see you both at the shower."

Bridget and Alana disappeared into the crowd. Bridget wiped her brow in mock fear and smiled up at Alana. "Thought for sure there we were goin' to have to go all superhero on that woman."

"She gets worse when she's drinkin'. Billy Ray may have to spend a lot of time on his knees." Alana took a sip of her wine. "God Almighty, this is terrible."

"Maverick says all we get is nonalcoholic everything since the reunion is held in the cafeteria. No drinking on school property," Bridget told her. "So Rachel is psychologically drunk or else she had her fair share before she got here. And why would Billy Ray have to do some praying, or were you referring to kinky sex?"

"Nope, I was talkin' about praying for sure." Alana set the rest of her fake wine on a table. "His mama, Trudy, is super religious and would have an acute cardiac arrest if she found out he'd slept with Rachel Freeman. That girl has always had a horrible reputation, and lies flow out of her mouth like hot lava from a volcano."

Alana caught Pax staring at her and pointed at her glass of wine. He returned the greeting by holding up a can of root beer. *Why?* she mouthed.

He shrugged and started her way. When he was close enough he set the can on a nearby table and opened up his arms for a dance. "School rules, even though most of us in this room are adults. I asked Billy Ray about why we couldn't have real alcohol, and he said that the alumni committee is mainly made up of older people now. Except for him, none of the younger folks want to step up and be a part of it. But he also said there's a keg in the back of his truck and plenty of red plastic cups right beside it. And that Bubba Joe has a private little bar set up in the old bullpen for anyone who wants to buy a real drink."

"Leave it to Billy Ray and Bubba Joe." She walked into his arms and the two of them began a smooth two step to "Lost in this Moment" by Big & Rich.

"Whoever was on the music committee got the songs right at least. Remember when this one came out?" Pax buried his face in her hair. "I'd pretend I was dancing with you around the kitchen floor with a mop."

"That's sweet," Alana said. "Did you really want to dance with me?"

"Oh, honey," he groaned.

"No one can hear us," she told him. "You don't have to pretend so well. And FYI, darlin', Rachel still has hopes of hookin' up with you when"—she did half a shrug—"when we get our divorce."

"No thanks," Pax said. "What makes you say that, anyway?"

"She was about to ask me outside for a catfight when Bridget came up with that awful wine. I'm going to get elected to the committee, and believe me, we're going to have the next reunion somewhere other than the school, even if we have to put it on ourselves out in the sale barn," she said. "This is ridiculous. We might as well have it in the church fellowship hall."

The song ended and "Don't Blink" by Kenny Chesney began. Alana listened to the words and tears dammed up in her eyes. The song talked about a man over a hundred years old being interviewed. His advice was that you shouldn't blink because time goes so fast. She couldn't hold the tears back when the lyrics talked about the love of his life lying in the bed dying, and said to take every breath God gives for what it's worth. She was sobbing when she heard the words saying that when the hourglass ran out of sand that she couldn't flip it over and start it again. She was so glad that Pax was holding her and she could bury her face in his shoulder so everyone around them couldn't see her crying.

* * *

"Don't cry, darlin'." Pax lifted her face and wiped away a tear with the pad of his thumb. "I know exactly what you're thinkin'. The time is going by so fast, but I'll be with you until…"

In that moment he wanted to say that he'd be with her until they were married fifty years like the song said, but he couldn't promise that.

"Until Daddy is gone and we get an annulment or a divorce?" she said.

"Until you are ready to be on your own," he said. "I'll stay with you longer than the day after." He stopped at that, but the week after, the month after, the year after, went through his mind.

"Thank you." She leaned back and locked gazes with him. "I might hold you to that. I'm going to need a friend to lean on when it happens."

He leaned in and kissed her on the lips. "You've got my word."

"Are you bored with this thing, yet?" she asked.

"Never," he replied. "Not when I'm dancing with the prettiest girl in the room. Besides, we're Maverick and Bridget's ride home, so we have to stay until the last dog is hung. They're having a great time."

"Let's slip outside, get a drink from Bubba Joe, and sit

on the tailgate of your truck," she said. "I can't deal with all this drama right now, Pax."

"We'll two-step over to the door, then sneak on out of here," he said. "I'll tell Maverick when we pass by him."

"At least we made an appearance," she said but then started falling.

He tried to grab her, but it was impossible to get a hold anywhere. She landed hard on her side, and then Rachel was on the floor right beside her. Pax figured they'd both slipped on root beer that was dripping from a table where a can had been turned over. He extended his hand toward Alana and helped her stand.

"You okay?" he asked.

"I'm fine."

Her tone and the pained expression on her face suggested that she was anything but fine. He turned to help Rachel, but Billy Ray was already at her side.

"That bitch grabbed my high heel and dragged me down," Rachel hissed.

"Aww, come on, sweetheart. It was all an accident." Billy Ray draped an arm around Rachel's shoulders and led her out the door. "Let's go find you a real beer. That'll make it all better."

Bridget and Maverick made their way across the floor and stopped in front of Alana. "Are you all right?" Bridget asked. "That was a nasty fall."

"I'll be fine," Alana said, again. "I need to get out of here and get a breath of fresh air. Y'all go on and enjoy the evening. Pax and I are going to visit Bubba Joe's bar out in the parking lot and buy a drink. Want me to send him back inside with something real for y'all?"

"Maybe later," Bridget said. "I can be the designated driver if y'all get more than one drink."

"Thanks." Alana tucked her arm into Pax's and leaned on him on the way out of the cafeteria.

"Do we need to run over to the emergency room and get an X-ray of your side?" Pax asked when they were out in the hallway. "That sounded like a pretty solid crack. You might have fractured a rib."

"I had cracked ribs back when I was bronc riding. This is only going to be a bruise. I know the difference," she told him. "It hurts like hell, but by damn Rachel is going to hurt too. I'll teach her to trip me."

"What?" Pax stopped in his tracks.

She pulled on his arm. "Let's get out to the truck, and let me stretch out in the bed, then we'll talk."

Pax scooped Alana up in his arms and carried her out to the truck. He set her on the ground, lowered the tailgate, and said, "Stand right here, darlin', while I get a blanket out of my truck."

"Right now I don't even care." She held her arm and groaned. "I hope the bruise is gone by the day of the wedding, but at least I won't be walking down the aisle with an arm in a cast."

Pax rushed to the backseat, grabbed an old patchwork quilt, and carried it to the pickup bed. He quickly spread it out, put his hands around her slim waist, and picked her up again. This time, he set her on the tailgate and motioned for her to slide on back. "Tell me what to do to help you, and I'll do it."

"I can do it without help." She managed a weak smile. "Thank you, though."

She scooted until her back was braced against the back of the cab. He did the same until he was right beside her. His heart threw in an extra beat when he gently pulled her to his side. "Now what's this about Rachel tripping you?"

"She was dancing with Billy Ray, and she snarled her nose at me, stuck out her foot, and kicked me in the shin about the same time I stepped in that spilled root beer. Then as I was falling, she gave me a shove with her elbow and called me a bitch. Man, she's really got the hots for you," Alana said.

"For me?" Pax frowned. "What have I got to do with anything? Like I told you, I never did like that girl."

"Well, honey, she sure had a mind to marry you. She told us that she even learned to run a tractor to impress you," Alana told him.

"She'd have to do more than that to make me take notice," Pax said. "You ready for a drink? Name your poison, and I'll have Bubba Joe mix it up for you."

"Jack Daniel's on the rocks, triple, please," she answered. "And if you've got a couple of aspirin in the glove compartment, I'll take those too."

"Yes, ma'am, to both," Pax said. "Guess she got her comeuppance when she went down with you."

"I suppose she did." Alana smiled. "Truth is that I grabbed her high heel and gave it a good solid twist. I was glad she didn't fall right on top of me. Drunk as she is, she might have upchucked all over me, and I'd hate to have that in my hair."

Pax chuckled, then laughed out loud. "And all this because she's mad at us?"

"Yep, she thinks I tricked you into getting married by getting pregnant," Alana confessed.

"People sure like to meddle in other folks' business, don't they?" He swung himself out over the side of the truck bed. "Two triple shots of Jack coming right up," he said.

Of all the dumb luck, Billy Ray and Rachel were in line

right in front of him. Rachel turned around and put both her hands on his chest.

"I can't believe you asked Alana to marry you." Rachel slurred her words. "We could've been good together, and we'd have made such pretty babies."

"Billy Ray would make gorgeous babies with you. Just look at his big old blue eyes." Pax grasped her hands in his and laid them on Billy Ray's arms.

Mama would kill me graveyard dead, Billy Ray mouthed over the top of Rachel's head.

"I don't have any doubts about that," Pax agreed. "But go for it anyway."

"Oh, Billy Ray, darlin', why didn't you speak up sooner? We've lost so much time. I don't care that you're younger than me. Age is numbers on paper," Rachel finally caught up.

Billy Ray narrowed his eyes at Pax. "Let's talk about it when we're both sober."

"You got it." Rachel pointed a finger at Pax. "Too bad. So sad, I'm over you now. You can go on and marry Alana Carey. I don't give a damn. I've got Billy Ray now, and he's goin' to be so good to me."

Billy Ray led her back to a line of folding chairs, helped get her seated, and then he returned to the line. "What in the hell is going on? I thought this would be a nice reunion, but it's worse than all the other ones I've been to put together. We should've rented the Wild Cowboy for the evening like you said last year."

"Yep," Pax said. "Good luck with Rachel."

"I hope to hell she doesn't remember anything when she sobers up," Billy Ray said. "Is Alana all right? Rachel told me that she tripped her on purpose."

"She'll be sore for a few days, but it'll wear off, and

take my advice, old friend." Pax laid a hand on Billy Ray's shoulder. "Get Rachel back inside, hand her off to her friends, and make yourself scarce, or you might find yourself walking down the aisle. She's lookin' for a husband, not a one-night stand."

"I hear you," Billy Ray said.

What are you lookin' for? His grandmother's voice popped into his head, and he remembered that Mam was coming to the ranch. She'd arrive sometime tomorrow for the wedding shower, and she planned to stay until after the wedding.

I'm lookin' for what Bridget and Maverick have, he answered honestly.

He waited for a few minutes, but Mam didn't offer any advice, one way or the other. No doubt, though, when she was at the ranch, and they were face-to-face, she'd give him plenty of sass about everything.

He finally reached the front of the line, got his drinks, and was carefully carrying them back to the truck when he realized that he hadn't missed flirting. He'd always spent most of his time at the alumni reunions flirting with all the ladies—but he'd had eyes for only Alana that evening.

Chapter Thirteen

Thank god it isn't raining, Alana thought as she waited for Pax to return with her whiskey. "Oh, no!" she muttered when she remembered that she'd been bargaining with God an hour before. Falling was her punishment for thinking that she as a mere human had anything that she could trade for more time with her father.

God doesn't punish people for talking to Him. He knows you love your daddy and that you are scared about life without him. Tonight is on Rachel, not God. Her mother's voice was so clear in her head that she looked to both sides to see if she was actually right there.

"Okay, I get it," she whispered.

"You get what?" Pax handed a red plastic cup over the side of the truck bed.

"That I can't bargain with God," she answered.

"I think we've all done that at some time in our lives," he said.

She took a sip of her whiskey. The smooth warmth of it flowed all the way down to her stomach. "What do you really want out of life, Paxton? I've been giving that question a lot of thought lately. When Daddy's gone, I'm going to have a lot of responsibility, so I need a plan. I need to think about where I'm going. I need to have my children now so I can teach them what they need to know so they can carry on the legacy that Daddy has worked so hard to leave to me."

Pax crawled up from the tailgate to sit beside her. He stretched his long legs out and took a sip of his whiskey. "That's some heavy thinkin' there. Maybe you should concentrate on getting through the wedding first. One-day-at-a-time stuff, you know."

"I need a plan to survive one day at a time," she said. "Surely you've got a chart of some kind for the rest of your life, even if it's a loose one." She thought of all the time she and Pax had wasted already. If she'd gotten married five years ago, she could already have at least two kids, maybe three, and her father would have gotten to spend some time with his grandchildren. Better yet, they would have gotten to know him.

"To tell you the truth, I don't," he said. "But now you've got me spooked. I need to think about more than just the day ahead. Grandpa and Mam built the Callahan Ranch with sweat, tears, and a lot of calluses. It wouldn't be right to let it go to ruin or sell it to strangers when my generation passes away. We have a responsibility to teach our children to love the land like we do, don't we?"

"So my plan is that I will have my first child by the time I'm thirty. *That* means that we should get our divorce or annulment as soon as possible so I can find a husband, and I'll need to get pregnant on my wedding night." The plan sounded good in her head, and completely doable.

"You plan on doing all that in less than eighteen months?" Pax took another sip of his whiskey. "If we have to get a divorce, you can't remarry for six months, then you'll have to find a husband and have a baby in one year. You better adjust your calendar, girl. Maybe that first child shouldn't come along until say thirty-five."

Now her new plan was ruined as quickly as it was formed. She couldn't wait until she was thirty-five to have kids, not if she got a brain tumor at fifty-five. There wasn't a twenty-year-old in the whole state of Texas who could be taught to run a ranch by that age. She'd have to make a new plan. Dammit! She should've gotten married right out of high school like her mama had.

She set the whiskey to the side. "I hope I *did* get pregnant when we had sex without protection."

Pax spit good whiskey all over the side of the truck bed. "Good God, Alana! What if your child, whenever you have one, has no interest in ranchin'? Ever think of that? Maybe you'll have a son who wants to be an artist or a schoolteacher."

"Sorry, but you can't convince me of that. Not with both our ranchin' blood. It would simplify things so much. I don't really need a husband. I'm perfectly capable of raising a baby as a single mother. If I am pregnant, I won't even ask you for child support. You can fade away into the foggy past," she said.

"I might not have a big plan, Alana Joy Carey, but like I told you before, I will always be a part of the life of whatever child I father, so forget that bullshit. If you're pregnant, I won't give you a divorce." He downed the rest of his whiskey in one gulp. "Look at us, trying to figure out the future, when we can't even get a good firm grip on the present."

"We ain't got a choice," Alana sighed. "Life says we've played too long, and now it's time for us both to be adults. Kind of scary ain't it? And Pax, I love you too much as a friend to rope you into a lifetime of marriage that you didn't want. But you never answered my question. What do you want?"

"I want what Maverick and Bridget have. Matter of fact, I want what Hud and Rose have, what Tag and Nikki have, and all the other couples at the ranches in Sunset. I want what Grandpa and Mam had," he answered without hesitation.

"And that is...?" she asked.

"Unconditional, complete love that will last forever," he said.

"And how do you know when you've got it?" Alana asked.

"My heart will tell me," he answered. "Grandpa told me that he knew right here"—Pax tapped his chest—"when he'd found the right woman. I'm depending on the same feeling to hit me."

"I'd like something a lot more concrete, like the name of my forever soul mate to be written in the stars, or maybe for a halo to appear over his head when we're sitting beside each other in church," she said.

"That's not asking for much," he chuckled, but his tone suggested the opposite.

"I don't think so." She laid her head on his shoulder. "As my friend, I believe you could arrange that for me, right?"

"Sure I can." Pax kissed her on the top of her head. "Anything for you, darlin'."

* * *

Alana chose a cute little white sundress with a red short-sleeved knit cardigan to cover up her farmer's tan for the wedding shower. She started to wear a pair of flat sandals but chose red wedge-heeled sandals, a luxury she would have never had with anyone else she'd dated. According to Trudy, the shower would last from two to four, but the bride and groom should plan to stay a little longer, since it might take extra time to open all the gifts.

Alana shook her head at her reflection in the mirror. "They'll all have to be sent back after the annulment. That'll be quite an undertaking for sure."

"Hey, are you excited?" Matt poked his head in her bedroom door. "I heard you talking. Were you on the phone?"

"No, I was mumbling," she answered, glad that he hadn't heard her exact words.

"Well, are you excited about the shower?" he asked. "I remember when they gave me and your mother a wedding shower, and we finally got to move into what's the bunkhouse now. My mother was already gone, but Dad let us have that place as our own, and your mama had such a good time putting homey touches on it." He stared off into space, as if he was reliving those first days of marriage. "We were happy there, and then a year later, your grandfather got killed, so we moved into the big house—this place. It took both of us a while to be as happy here as we were out in the bunkhouse."

"Yes, Daddy, I'm very excited," she said. "But we have everything we could possibly need right here already, so I'm wondering what we'll do with extra toasters and blenders. Not that I don't appreciate everything that will be done for us. Don't get me wrong." She finished brushing out her hair and turned to face him. "How do I look?"

"Like you're in love," Matt told her. "I'm glad that guys

go to these things nowadays. I don't want to miss a single moment of all this, and I'm real happy that Pax didn't mind you going with me. He and Iris are going to meet us at the door, so y'all can walk in together."

Alana looped her arm into her father's. "Let's go unwrap presents. That part I do love."

A hot wind swept across her face when they stepped out of the air-conditioned house onto the porch. Maybe that was the devil telling her that he owned her soul for so much lying lately—reminding her of how hot hell was going to be. If that was the case, then so be it. She wouldn't change a thing because her dad was happy. And since he'd stopped that medication, he was even lucid most of the time again.

On the way to the church fellowship hall, she replayed the conversation she'd had with Pax. Basically, he wanted the same thing she did. A home, a family, and someone to leave his ranch to when he was finished with life on this earth. She wondered if they'd remain friends and good neighbors after everything was over and done with.

When they reached the church, the parking lot was full. Matt nosed his truck in right beside Pax's out at the far edge of the lot, shut off the engine, and turned to face Alana. "We got so busy, I forgot to ask about the reunion last night."

"It went fine, Daddy," she answered. "Pax and I spent a lot of the time out in the bed of his truck, talking about the future. Having the party at the school wasn't a good idea. I'll have to tell you more about it this evening. Looks like Pax is on his way to escort me inside."

Matt climbed out of the truck and waved at his future son-in-law. "I'm going on in. Y'all hang back a minute or two so you can make an entrance. Folks love that," he told Alana. "Be sure to look around the room and thank every-one personally as you open the gifts."

"Yes, sir." Alana nodded. A month ago his saying that would have upset her, but now that she had only a limited amount of time with him, it was endearing.

"You look stunning," Pax said as he opened the truck door for her and extended a hand. "But then you always do."

"Thank you," she said. "You clean up pretty good too, for an old ranchin' cowboy."

"Do my best." He tipped his hat at her.

His hand on her lower back as he escorted her into the fellowship hall sent tingles of desire up her spine and through her body. When they walked through the doors, she gasped, not because of the heat created by his hand, but by all the gifts piled up on two ten-foot tables. Good God, it would take hours to open them, and sending them all back would take weeks. She thought about owning up to her deviousness right then and there and calling the whole thing off.

Matt slipped up beside her and whispered, "You are loved."

"Yes, I am," she said with a wide smile on her face. "Thank all y'all. I'm wondering how in the world we will get through all the presents in only two hours. You've outdone yourselves."

"You've always been willin' for anything from helping with the Christmas program to dinners. This is our little way of giving back to you," Trudy said. "And, honey, we're planning on giving you and the wedding party a little brunch the morning of the wedding right here in the hall."

"That's so kind of you." Alana blinked back tears when she glanced over at her father and saw the pride in his expression. "Thank you again. Where should we sit?"

"Right here beside me," Matt said. "Pax sits beside you, and Iris beside him."

Alana's heart felt like it had chains wrapped around it as she passed homemade quilts, fancy needlepoint pillows, and other handmade gifts to Trudy to display on the gift table. She had no idea so many of the folks in Daisy would send such priceless gifts, and guilt wrapped itself around her like a blanket made of ice.

When the last item, a lovely crocheted throw in the colors of a beautiful Texas sunset, had passed through her hands, she stood up with tears flowing down her cheeks and faced all the people. "Thank you for this wonderful outpouring of love. These gifts are really amazing and I love every one of you for your friendship and care y'all have given me and my daddy all these years. It's great to live in a small town, even if everyone does know everything that goes on."

Everyone chuckled and then gave her a standing ovation. She didn't even realize that Pax was standing beside her until he handed her his handkerchief. She dabbed her eyes with it, and said, "I'm overwhelmed with emotion."

"I'd like to thank all y'all too," Pax said. "I'm glad that I was raised amongst folks who love and take care of each other. Y'all are the best, and I've got to admit, I'm more than a little overwhelmed myself. When we decided to get married in only a month, we had no idea that the whole town would come together like this to support us."

"Most young couples are overwhelmed. Just keep that fresh love in your hearts, and it'll help you get through the tough times." Trudy dabbed at her eyes with a tissue. "Now let's have some refreshments. Instead of ordering a store-bought cake, we asked each of the hostesses to bring one. I hear that you're partial to lemon, Alana, so I brought that kind. Miz Minnie brought chocolate, and I think Darlene brought her better-than-sex cake, but since we're in church, we call it Hawaiian Delight," Trudy giggled.

"Church or not, it lives up to its name," Iris said. "You've gotten a good shower, kids, and most of your gifts are things you'll use and cherish. Folks know that y'all already have a house full of necessary things so they tried to give you handmade things that would touch your hearts."

"It really is pretty awesome." Pax looked at his grandmother. "We're so glad that you could be here, Mam."

"Wouldn't miss it for all the dirt in Texas," she said. "Now I'm going for some of Darlene's cake before it all gets served. It might not be better than sex for you two, but at my age, it damn sure is." She rolled her eyes toward the ceiling and said, "Pardon me, Lord, for swearing in church."

"Now y'all go sit down at the head table," Trudy said. "We'll bring a sampling of all the cakes for you to try."

Pax slid Alana's chair in for her and then took a seat in the one beside her. "Who'd have thought this would have gotten so out of hand."

"Want to go back and change your mind?" she asked.

He shook his head. "Look at Matt and Mam. I don't want to tell them that we've been lying to them."

"Daddy won't ever know, but you will have to tell Iris," she whispered.

"I think, since I agreed to this as a favor to you, that you should tell her," Pax told her.

"Oh, no, that's your job. It's in the agreement." She kissed him on the cheek. "Remember when you proposed, you said that you'd do anything to make me happy."

"Nope, I do not remember that." He frowned.

She patted his hand. "You were tired, and you'd probably spent the night before with some bar bunny, so you don't remember. Oh, look, darlin', at all the cake." She clapped her hands and squealed for the benefit of those watching.

Three of the hostesses had formed a parade and were coming right at them. One had a platter full of different cakes. Another had a tray that held two glasses and a pitcher of lemonade, and the last one had a platter of finger foods.

"This all looks amazing," Alana said. "I'm sure the cake testing for the wedding cake won't be nearly this good."

Trudy beamed. "We loved putting it together for you and wanted you to have something special."

"Well, you've all gone above and beyond," Pax said. "I'm starting with a bite of that chocolate cake."

"We've got to get back and serve all the folks. Y'all enjoy. I'm sure Matt and Iris and Bridget and Maverick will join y'all soon. I wish your whole wedding party could have been here, but we'll get to see them at the brunch," Trudy said.

"Yes, you will." Alana put a bite of lemon cake into her mouth. "Trudy, could I get you to make a couple of these for the wedding?"

Trudy really beamed at that request. "Honey, you tell me how many you need, and I'll deliver them the morning of the wedding?"

"Thank you." Alana nodded. "I'm thinking maybe we'll have a small wedding cake, something to cut for tradition, and then serve your cake to the people. It's always been my favorite at get-togethers."

Trudy laid a hand over her heart. "I would be honored, and I'll save back a big square for you today." She winked and hustled off to help serve.

"That was sweet of you," Pax said.

"I really do like this cake that much, and besides"— she looked around to be sure no one was listening—"she's going to blame me for the annulment. That means she damn sure won't offer to make lemon cakes for my second wedding if I ever have one. And you can bet your sexy little cowboy butt there won't be another shower, either."

Pax picked up a chicken salad sandwich. "Well, darlin', I'm right glad to get to be a part of your first wedding, and for the record, I don't imagine Trudy's going to lay all the blame on you. I bet I get my fair share."

She leaned over and brushed a kiss across his lips. "I really do thank you for everything."

"Anything for you, my darlin'." He laid his sandwich down, picked up her hand, and kissed her knuckles.

Chapter Fourteen

Two things that Alana had always envied were class-mates who had mothers to bring cupcakes to school instead of a nanny and those kids who had siblings. After church on Sunday morning, Iris insisted that Matt and Alana join them at the Callahan Ranch for dinner. She'd made a huge pot roast, and Bridget had made scones and a lovely peach pie. There was plenty, she said, and she wouldn't take no for an answer.

When Alana walked through the door at the Callahan Ranch, memories flooded over her like a warm spring rain. She'd spent time in the small farmhouse when she was a kid, and she'd always loved the bantering that went on between Maverick and Paxton. But what she'd liked even more was riding the bus to their house and walking in to the aroma of cookies or bread fresh from the oven. Her nanny didn't make supper and left as soon as Matt came in the back door, so Alana cherished the moments she spent at Iris's house.

"Still smells as wonderful as it did when I was a kid." Alana sniffed the air. "I've missed coming over here to visit with you the past six months, Iris."

"You always said that as a child." Iris pulled her into the kitchen. "I need a few minutes alone with you. It's a strange situation you and Pax have gotten yourselves into, isn't it?"

Alana's heart jumped up into her throat. Iris always could see through all three of them, even when they were children. Had she somehow found out about the whole ruse?

"How's that?" Alana's voice was high-pitched even in her own ears.

"Pax will need to be over on the Bar C Ranch helping you. Matt has told me that he's ready to hand it over to you kids and retire to the bunkhouse to live out his days with Lucas and the boys out there. He talked about the first year of his and Joy's marriage. I remember that time, and they were so happy. I think he wants to relive some of those memories that you and Pax gettin' married have brought back to mind," Iris answered.

Alana heaved a sigh of relief. "He has been talking about her more since Pax and I got engaged."

"So, I've made up my mind to change things a bit around here," Iris said. "I'm going to buy out Pax and hire a foreman to help Maverick. There's a young man up on the Rockin' B that I've had my eye on for a while. His father has been the foreman up there for years, so he knows the ropes, and it'll be good experience for him," Iris said. "I think if we enlarge the tack room a little, we can turn it into a nice little bunkhouse for him."

"But Pax and Maverick work so well together, and they'll miss each other," Alana argued. Those words the preacher had said about tangled webs came to her mind. "I've got lots of help on the Bar C. Have you talked to Maverick and Pax about this?" Poor old Pax was going to be divorced and not even have a ranch to call home.

"No, but after the wedding, we're going to have a long talk, and I don't think I'll get a bit of trouble out of them. Pax loves you, and he's going to want to be a part of the Bar C. Everything is actually working out beautifully," Iris said. "But for the next two weeks we're going to concentrate on the wedding, and then we'll make what plans we'll need for the changes."

Thank God for the wedding, Alana thought. It would keep everyone occupied. By the time Iris could get plans in motion, everything would be over and done with.

"What can I do to help get dinner on the table?" Alana changed the subject.

"You could get down the plates." Bridget came in from the living room. "And maybe the utensils. The guys are watching Laela for me until we can get things ready. We'll be sitting at the dining room table. It'll be cozy with the six of us and the baby, of course."

A memory of her mother teaching her how to properly set a table flashed through Alana's mind as she carried plates to the dining room. She'd been begging to help on a Sunday after church, a hot day much like this one, and Joy had finally handed her one plate and told her where to put it. She wasn't in school yet, so she must've been about five years old, but she remembered feeling very proud of herself.

Today, she was more than a little ashamed. Last week was Mother's Day. This year, for the first time since her mama had died, she hadn't put fresh flowers on her grave. She'd always spent time on holidays sitting in front of the tombstone that had both her parents' names on it. She'd even had a nice concrete bench put out there so she wouldn't have to sit on the ground, and she had always told her mother everything—when she was angry with her father, when she was mad at the girls at school for making fun of her, even when she lost her virginity.

But she'd never lied to her.

Alana was staring off into space with knives, forks, and spoons still in her hands when Pax came up behind her and slipped his arms around her waist. "Need some help? Maverick and Matt don't need me to take care of Laela right now, but I see why you'd like for Matt to have known his grandchildren. He's really good with kids."

"We've pretty well got things under control in here, and Daddy has always loved kids." She sighed. "This may sound crazy to you, but I need to go to the cemetery this afternoon."

"Great minds and all that," he said.

"What does that mean?" She stepped away from him and continued placing the rest of the cutlery around the table.

"I was thinking the same thing in church this morning," Pax said. "The preacher was talking about how we influence those around us, and his words made me think of Grandpa and my dad. I haven't been out to their graves since I came back to Daisy. We'll sneak away and go together."

Alana had wanted to go alone. She couldn't very well talk to her mother with Pax right there beside her—at least not out loud.

"That would be great," she said. "Would you mind if we drive down to Plainview first to get some flowers at Walmart?"

"Not a bit," he answered.

"Drive to Walmart for what?" Iris brought a basket of fresh scones to the table.

"Flowers to go on Mama's grave," Alana answered.

"I'm planning on going out to visit with Tommy and Barton this next week. I've ordered a custom-made silk arrangement for your grandpa's tombstone and one for your dad's. They'll be ready on Wednesday, so tell them I'll be out to see them then," Iris said.

Paxton nodded and headed back to the living room. "I sure will."

Iris stopped to give Alana a hug. "I know that my husband and son are dead, but sometimes I like to sit and talk to them. It brings me comfort."

"I know exactly how you feel." Alana wrapped her arms around Iris. "I talk to Mama all the time, and I should've been out there last weekend."

"Yep, you should've," Iris agreed. "So go tell her why you weren't today, and, honey, she will forgive you. I knew Joy well, and she understands how busy you and Pax are with this wedding."

"I hope so," Alana said.

* * *

Of all the bad luck, Rachel Freeman was the first person that Pax and Alana saw when they walked into Walmart that afternoon. Pax tried to steer Alana in the opposite direction, but Rachel had already spotted them and was pushing her cart in a beeline toward them.

"Dammit!" Alana swore.

"Guess we kind of had a little dustup, didn't we?" Rachel smiled and pointed toward the walking boot on her foot. "I'd had way too much to drink, and I apologize for tripping you. I was mad at my ex-husband for too many things to list, and I took it out on you."

"Apology accepted." Alana nodded but didn't smile. Her arm hadn't really hurt all day, but now it started throbbing. Of course, she knew the pain was psychological, but knowing that didn't help a lot.

"You could say it like you mean it," Rachel said through clenched teeth. "I believe you owe me an apology too, for pulling me down on top of you."

Pax pulled his phone from his pocket and answered it. "Oh, dear! Darlin', we have to go right now. Seems that Mam needs a ride to the cemetery. See you later, Rachel." He took Alana by the hand and pulled her toward the door.

"Bitch," Rachel hissed.

Alana stopped and turned around. "Would you be referring to me or Iris?"

"You, of course," Rachel said. "You almost broke my ankle, and you can't even apologize to me."

Alana took a couple of steps away from Pax and knotted both her hands into fists. "Are you angry because of the ankle or because I'm marrying Pax?"

"Both," Rachel said. "If you didn't have money and land, he wouldn't give a giant like you a second look."

"Hey, now," Pax cut in, "I happen to love Alana, and that's pretty harsh of you to judge us like this," Pax said.

"Talking or trying to explain anything to someone like you is a waste of time and breath." Alana relaxed her hands, turned around, and laced her fingers with Pax's. "Let's go see Iris now."

She let her anger smolder silently until she was back in the truck, and then exploded. "I should go back in there and wipe up aisle five with her. Apologize, my ass. She tripped me first, and I'm supposed to tell her that I'm sorry for retaliating? Is she crazy or plain stupid? I need to put someone on Rachel patrol at the wedding. You can bet your sexy cowboy ass that she'll be there for no other reason than to cause trouble."

"How about Trudy? I bet she'd do a fine job of keeping Rachel in line. By the end of the day, she might even have Rachel saved, sanctified, and dehorned," Pax chuckled.

Alana giggled, then laughed, and then guffawed until she got the hiccups. "I don't doubt that Trudy could save and sanctify her, but she'll have a helluva time trying to dehorn her."

Pax laughed right along with her. "I'm not sure even Lucifer could dehorn Rachel Freeman. She's had an itch that no cowboy could satisfy since she was thirteen."

"Sweet Jesus!" Alana threw a hand over her mouth. "How'd you know that?"

"It wasn't me, and I don't tattle on my friends," Pax said as he drove out of the parking lot. "I guess we'll get flowers at the Dollar Store."

Paxton Callahan really was a fantastic friend, Alana began to realize. All anger was gone now, and he'd already taken care of future problems. Putting Trudy in charge of Rachel at the wedding was a brilliant suggestion.

"That sounds great, but if Rachel follows us there..." She hesitated.

Pax butted in before she could finish the sentence. "I keep two good sharp shovels out in our tack room." He wiggled his eyebrows. "They'll never find the body."

Alana laid a hand on his thigh. "You are so good for me, Pax."

"Not nearly as much as you are for me." He squeezed her hand.

* * *

A soft breeze ruffled the leaves on the big pecan tree that shaded Joy and Matt's gray granite tombstone. The spring flowers that Alana had put out at Easter were faded. Recent storms had caused dirt to settle into the petals of the pastel-colored lilies and gladioli. Pecan tree pollen had settled on the tombstone, turning it a dirty orange in spots.

"You go on to see your granddad and your father," she told Pax. "I'd like to be alone for this."

"I understand," he said. "I'll be back in a little while. I've got a lot to discuss with Grandpa anyway, and their plots are on the other end of the cemetery."

"Thanks..." she said and then added, "...for everything."

"You are so welcome." He gave her a quick kiss on the forehead.

She set her tote bag of cleaning supplies and the bag of silk roses on the bench. "He's such an amazing man," she whispered to her mother as she began to polish the tombstone.

When Pax had driven away, she raised her voice. "I'm sorry I wasn't here last week," she said. "And speaking of sorry, Rachel Freeman's mama should have drowned her at birth." She went on to tell what all had happened that weekend as she cleaned. "She's been a bully to me ever since we started to kindergarten. I remember when you told me that I should pray for her."

When her mother had suggested that, Alana had protested quite loudly. "Pray for her! I want to kick her in the shins until she cries and then pull all her hair out for crying."

"Thanks for that memory, Mama," Alana said. "I'll try to pray for her, but I won't promise that it'll be nice. It'll be more like, 'Please God, send her a man from Russia to fall in love with and to take her back to his country where I'll

never see her again.' That's praying, isn't it?" She finished
with the tombstone, removed the old faded flowers from the
vase, and laid them on the ground.

"I guess I'd better back up and tell you what all has
happened since the first of the month," she said as she
arranged the new yellow and peach-colored flowers in the
vase. "I got these because that's the colors I chose for my
wedding. I'm marrying Pax, and it started out to be something I was doing so Daddy could walk me down the aisle
and die in peace. Did I tell you that he'll be joining you in
a few weeks? Well, he will, and I'm not a bit happy about
it." She stopped and ran her forefinger over Matthew Daniel
Carey's engraved name. Tears mixed with her mascara, and
black streaks flowed down her cheeks. "He's goin' to be
with you before the end of summer. The date of his death
will be written here, and, Mama, I'm not handling it worth
a damn. I'm putting on a pretty good show for him, but I'm
mad as hell. God took you from me so many years ago, and
now he's takin' Daddy, and it's not fair."

My child, God did not take either of us. Her mother's
voice was clear in her head. *He's spiritual, not physical.
Our bodies produced the cancer, not God. You can't be
mad at Him.*

"But, Mama, I've been taught all my life that God can do
whatever you ask Him to do. I was a little girl, but I prayed
that you would get well, and you didn't. Now I'm praying
the same thing for Daddy, and I know it's not going to be
answered," Alana argued.

*He hears your prayers but sometimes the answer is
no. He doesn't always do what folks want Him to do,
because He sees the big picture.* Joy continued, *but what
He does give you is the strength to endure the trials that
this life brings you.*

"Don't tell God how big your storm is. Tell your storm how big your God is." She recited what her mother had written in a letter to her the last week that she was alive. Alana had read it often in the past eighteen years, but right then she understood what Joy had been telling her.

He's sent Pax to help you get through this storm, Joy said.

"I think I might be falling in real love with him, Mama," she admitted. "It's complicated. He agreed to marry me, but he's only committed to this lie until Daddy has passed on. All of these emotions I'm feeling—all the grief—when Daddy is really still alive and the thought that I could possibly love Pax for more than a friend are confusing the hell out of me."

Evidently her mama had given her all the advice she would get that day. When she heard a truck approaching, she hurriedly cleaned up the area around the grave site and waited for Pax.

He sat down on the bench beside her, put an arm around her shoulders, and drew her close to him. "It never gets any easier, does it? And knowing Matt's death date will be on there before long, well…" His voice cracked.

"I don't want my tombstone put up until after I'm gone," she said. "Mama and Daddy have extra plots over that way." She pointed toward the pecan tree. "I definitely don't want my kids to have to look at it until after…" She used the back of her hand to wipe away more tears.

"Your dad didn't have a choice in the matter. He wanted to put one up for your mama and he wanted them to be together," Pax said. "It's not easy lookin' at Mam's name on that chunk of granite, either."

"Or your mother's?" Alana asked.

"When Mama remarried, she had the original stone removed and one put up with Daddy's name on it. I have no idea where she'll be buried. For a few years we saw her at Christmas, but that ended long years ago. She didn't even come back to Daisy for mine or Maverick's high school graduation," Pax told her.

Alana took his hand in hers. "I'm so, so sorry. I barely remember your mother."

"Me either, and most days I don't even think about her." He shrugged. "Mam has always been like a mother to me and Maverick, so we didn't ever feel like orphans."

"I never thought of you as an orphan, but I got to admit after Mama died, I kind of felt like one. Daddy did his best, but there were days when he grieved so hard. I was so young I didn't know what to do for him. The sadness didn't leave his eyes for a long, long time. I was glad in those times that I could spend time at Callahan Ranch with Iris and y'all."

She stood to her feet and pulled him up with her.

He led her away from the graveside. "I liked having you there, but then I ruined it with that kiss."

"We were two awkward kids who didn't know how to react," she said.

"Amen to that." He opened the truck's door for her. "Let's go get some ice cream."

He took one last look at the grave site from his truck before starting the engine. "The flowers look pretty. How often do you change them out?"

"Every couple of months," she answered. "More often if the weather's been bad or the sun fades them. Mama's always had flowers on her grave. Daddy and I see to that."

Pax fastened his seatbelt and said, "Mam takes care of Daddy's and Grandpa's, but when she's gone, I'll step up and do it. You might have to help me remember when and show me how to make them look good."

"Be glad to," she said. "We can take care of the grave sites together."

"Good, but I hope it's a long time before I have to do that. I want Mam to be with us for many, many years," he said.

"We don't always get what we want," Alana whispered.

Chapter Fifteen

For the next few days, everything seemed to move in slow motion. The wedding planner had things under control. Alana's dress had come in and now hung on the closet door in her bedroom, a constant reminder of the beautiful wedding that was wrapped up so snuggly in a great, big, fat black lie. Alana had spent the last two days in the office with Matt, learning the finer points of what she'd need to do with the computer work when the time came for her to take over everything.

Then suddenly, it was Thursday, and she realized that she hadn't seen Pax since Sunday evening. They'd sent texts back and forth all week long, and she'd called him a couple of times. She missed him, yes, but it wasn't an all-consuming ache to be with him. When people were first in love, they couldn't stay away from each other.

That's high school infatuation, that pesky voice in her head said.

"Where is your mind?" Matt asked from across the desk. "You've been looking off into space like you expect angels to float down from heaven."

"Might be nice if that was possible." She smiled at her father. "How do you feel today, Daddy? You didn't eat much lunch, and we're supposed to be out at the barn right after supper to start cleaning it up for the wedding. You need to keep your strength up."

"I don't have much appetite," Matt told her. "Iris is coming over, and we plan to sit back and supervise this evening, so I don't need a lot of energy to do that. You don't worry about me, darlin'. I've accepted things and I'm ready. Everything I wanted, other than getting to know my grandkids, is happening. I told Pax already, but I haven't told you. The funeral arrangements are taken care of, so you don't have to worry about decisions like that when the time comes. And I've talked to the lawyers. The minute the preacher pronounces you man and wife, the Bar C becomes y'all's joint property. Iris and I had a long talk after dinner on Sunday. She's having papers done up to give Maverick full ownership of the Callahan Ranch. Everything is working out perfectly."

Alana's chest tightened and the room did a couple of spins. She felt everything going dark and her body slipping out of the chair, then the phone rang and the noise jerked her back from the abyss.

"Yes, that's right," Matt was saying. "Tell the boys that we'll meet them there in half an hour. I've ordered pizza and beer to be delivered at five-thirty, and they get double pay for working overtime on this for us."

Alana had never fainted before in her life, but if the pain in her arms and the throbbing ache in her head were symptoms, she didn't want to do it again. "What was that all about?" she asked.

"The hired hands are going to help us with the barn business," Matt explained. "You're a little pale, honey. Are you all right?"

"I'm fine, Daddy," she assured him. He damn sure didn't need to be worrying about her. "I almost dozed off and almost fell out of this chair."

"Well, dammit! I thought maybe you were pregnant," he teased. "Your mama fainted a few times when she was first expecting you."

"Sorry to disappoint you." She had mixed feelings about the idea of being pregnant. Would she be sad or happy if it had happened that one time they hadn't used protection? And what would that mean for their future? "I haven't been sleeping well, and all this books stuff bores me. I dozed off there for a minute."

What had started off as a simple ceremony so her father could walk her down the aisle had snowballed into a huge nightmare. Iris might be waiting to draw up her papers until everything settled, but not her father. He had to have things signed, sealed, and delivered before he went to his grave. She hated herself for thinking such a thing, but it would probably be best if he went on to heaven before the wedding. Then she could simply postpone it because of his passing, and it would never come about at all.

Her chest tightened again, this time with guilt for even letting such a horrible thought filter through her mind. Everything around her spun at warp speed for half a second before it settled down.

Forgive me, she sent up a silent prayer. *Don't take him from me before you have to.*

"I reckon we could go on down to the barn and kind of get an idea about the lay of things," Matt said. "We'll get us a cold beer on the way through the kitchen. Pizza sounds good to me so I'll eat good tonight. This brain booger messes with my taste buds. Not much of anything tastes like it should anymore."

"Well, then"—Alana stood up slowly—"you decide what you want from now on, and I'll either make it or send out for it."

"Sounds like a good idea to me. Reckon you could whip up some western breakfast burritos in the morning? Spicy stuff is what sounds best." He settled his cowboy hat on his head. "We'll take the farm truck and you can drive."

"Burritos it is." She grabbed the keys from one of the hooks by the back door as they passed by. "Do you really think five hundred people will be at this wedding, Daddy?"

"Have no idea, but my motto is: Be prepared." He crossed the backyard, opened the gate, and went right to the twenty-year-old work truck. "If they don't eat up all the food, then we'll send it home with whoever wants it, or the hired hands can take it out to the bunkhouse and freeze it for later use. It won't go to waste, that's for sure."

Given a choice, Alana wouldn't have wanted to talk about entering data into a computer for days, or discussing what to do with the leftovers from the wedding. There wasn't a single conversation that she wanted to have with her father right then. All she wanted to do was sit with him and drink in every single breath he took, and see him smile that smile, which made his eyes twinkle. She wanted memories to hang on to when he'd taken that first step into eternity.

She parked the truck in front of the sale barn and got out. Matt was halfway to the barn when he passed Pax coming to meet her. They exchanged a few words that she couldn't hear, and Matt kept going. Was he walking slower, or was it her imagination? She was still trying to figure that out when Pax picked her up and swung her around several times.

"I missed you this week," he said before he set her down, tipped up her chin, and kissed her—long, hard, and with lots of passion.

"Me too," she admitted. "It's getting real, Pax. Are we really getting married in two weeks and two days?"

"Looks like it." He took her by the hand and led her toward the barn. "How much longer can we keep Matt's condition under wraps? He seems to have lost more weight since Sunday. His jeans are hanging on him."

"He's got to be the one to decide when to tell people," she whispered as they entered the huge building. Right now there were three tractors parked inside, and the floor was covered with loose hay that had fallen out of the small bales that had been stored in there. Alana couldn't remember when she hadn't helped her dad take care of the annual fall sale in that very place. On sale days, the bleachers and balconies always looked like a sea of cowboy hats. The cattle were brought in from the back door and the bidding wars began. Even the culls from the Bar C stock were coveted by ranchers—local, national, and some even international.

She took a deep breath, sucking in the smell of the hay and imagining the fast-talking auctioneer standing with his gavel up behind the old wooden lectern on the stage.

"Oh. My. Goodness." Crystal, the wedding planner, came out from the shadows and clapped her hands. "Man, this is one big space. It's going to be gorgeous." She gushed. "We can have the guests sit in the bleachers and the balconies, reserving the best seats for the family of course. We can put filmy curtains of tulle up around the tables to set them off from the actual ceremony staging. I can't wait to see how it's all going to look."

"I didn't know you'd be here tonight," Alana said, "but welcome to the sale barn. I'm glad you see possibilities."

"Oh, honey." Crystal almost swooned. "I'll gladly take twenty percent off the total tab if you'll let me use the pictures on my website, and if you'll grant me exclusive rights to have other weddings here."

"Yes, we will do both." Matt walked up beside her. "I wanted to introduce you around, Crystal. This is Iris, Pax's grandmother. And this is his brother, Maverick; his wife, Bridget; and their daughter, Laela."

"Pleased to meet all of you." Crystal's eyes were darting from one place to the other like a little kid in a candy store who had no limits on what she could spend. "So this lovely baby will be your new niece, Alana?"

"That's right." Alana hadn't thought of what all marrying Pax would bring into her life. A brother-in-law, a niece, a sister-in-law, and a grandmother. She loved Laela, but the idea of having Iris as her grandmother? Well, that might be the very thing that prevented her from divorcing Pax.

"We have to remember to tell the photographer we want a picture of the bride and groom with the baby. That's always such a sweet shot," Crystal said. "What do you think of putting white stadium chairs on the bleachers for the guests?"

"Might keep them from getting splinters in their butts," Iris said. "Got any that are engraved with a *C* on the back? That would be really nice."

Crystal made a note. "I'll check and see about that. If not, maybe wedding bells—better yet, a lucky horseshoe."

Pax pulled at Alana's hand. "Let's go move a tractor."

"Yes," she whispered.

"Where are y'all goin'?" Iris asked.

"Thought maybe we'd drive a tractor out of the barn so Crystal could see how big this place is, and the guys could get busy cleaning the stalls out," Alana answered.

"The hired hands will do all that." Matt pointed toward a table with a few chairs scattered around it. "Y'all sit down with Crystal and go over what she's planned. She and I've been talkin' every day, but this is your wedding, Alana Joy, and I want it to be perfect."

"Well, dammit!" Alana sighed. "I haven't seen Pax all week. We were going to make out a little bit."

"You can do that after we get done here tonight," Matt chuckled. "I'm not playing poker until the wedding is over, so you can even have the tack room for some privacy." He winked at her.

"And no curfew?" she teased.

"How about daylight?" Matt answered. "Now go on over there and sit down. Time is getting short, and there's lots to do. Me and Iris here have some things that we need to discuss, and y'all need to hear Crystal's plans."

Alana would far rather have heard what her father and Iris were talking about, but she and Pax followed Crystal over to the table. The woman quickly opened her case and began to show them pictures.

"This is going to be the most unusual wedding I've done yet. Let's start with the corsages and boutonnières that the florist has made as samples." She laid out three separate eight-by-ten color photographs.

Alana studied the first one and handed it to Pax. "What do you think?"

"Honey, I'm the groom. My job is to say my vows without stuttering and make you happy," he answered. "All three of those are nice, but that last one is downright cheesy."

Alana patted him on the cheek. "Thank you. I thought the same thing. I like this one best." She handed Crystal the picture. "Remember, I said to keep it simple. Now what's next?"

Crystal made a big green check mark on the back of the chosen picture and laid the other two aside. Then she brought out three more—this time of centerpieces. Without even handing one off to Pax, Alana picked up the middle one and gave it back to her. "I like the Mason jar idea better than that fancy crystal vase. Add a yellow ribbon around the neck and that's perfect."

Pax took her free hand in his and laid it on his thigh. "Maverick and I used to pick wildflowers and bring them to Mam. She'd put them in Mason jars."

"Mama did the same thing when I brought her bouquets from the pasture," Alana said.

"Now tablecloths," Crystal said. "I brought fabric swatches. Here's the configuration that I've come up with for the round tables. So try to picture that many covered with whatever color you choose."

Alana spent all of two minutes looking at the various shades of yellow before she chose one. "I like the idea of setting the tables and reception area apart from the actual wedding. This soft yellow should be pretty behind the filmy tulle you mentioned earlier."

"I agree," Crystal sighed. "I believe that's all for now, but we'll need to meet again next week to fine-tune everything, especially with the rehearsal dinner."

"I'll be taking care of that." Iris walked up behind her. "You kids go on now. We've kept you long enough. We'll have the rehearsal dinner in the fellowship hall at the church so all your wedding party can see your gifts. Go on, now, get on with your making-out session. Matt and I've agreed that neither of us would be disappointed if the first child was one of those jet airplane babies."

"What kind of baby?" Alana blushed.

"Jet airplanes that bring them faster than nine months,"

Matt chuckled. "All the rest in the marriage will take the full time, but the first one can come along in seven or eight months with no problem because they're ridin' on a jet airplane."

Alana blushed again. "Daddy!"

"Mam!" Pax shook his finger at his grandmother.

"Hey, the pizza is here," Matt said. "Y'all pick up one and take it with you to the tack room. There's beer in the fridge. I put it in there yesterday."

"Thanks, Daddy," Alana kissed him on the forehead and turned to Pax. "Let's get out of here before they embarrass me again."

* * *

Pax drove them from the larger sale barn on one side of the ranch to the smaller one all the way to the other side. He hadn't eaten since noon, and the smell of the pizza in the backseat made his stomach grumble.

"I'm starving too." Alana laid a hand on her stomach. "I keep thinking that I'll wake up and all this will have been a bad dream. Daddy will be fine, and you and I will still be dancing around the attraction we have had . . . whatever...for each other."

"Speaking of that attraction business." Pax parked the truck and turned to face her. "It's definitely still there and stronger than it's ever been. I really, really like you, Alana, and I've loved spending time with you."

She hesitated so long that his hands started to sweat, and his heart was on the way to his toes. "I like you too, but what do we do about all this, Pax? It was supposed to be until . . . well, you know."

"Maybe we shouldn't get in a hurry about a divorce," he said.

"Maybe we could put it off for a little while," she agreed. "Until I can get my bearings."

He picked up her hand and kissed the knuckles. "I'd like that a lot."

"Okay, then." She locked gazes with him. "It's complicated, but then so is everything else that's going on around us right now."

He leaned slightly and pressed his lips against hers. "If I wasn't so damned hungry, I'd stay out here and make out with you until daylight."

"If I wasn't about to succumb to hunger, I might do more than make out." She got out of the truck and went on ahead. "You bring the pizza. I'll have the beers ready when you get there."

She was sitting on the futon when he came through the doors with the flat pizza box in his hand. He set it down on the coffee table where the beers were already waiting, and opened it up. "Meat lovers," he groaned. "My favorite."

"Daddy's too. He probably ordered an assortment with a couple of extra-large meat lovers included." She picked up a slice and bit into it. "God, this tastes good."

Pax did the same and moaned his appreciation. "Maybe we should've had a pizza bar at the wedding reception."

"It's not too late," she said between bites. "Maybe we'll have some delivered to our room at the honeymoon hotel that first night."

Pax nodded as he chewed and then washed the bite down with a sip of beer. "I'm so glad that we met up at Mam's last winter and started talking."

"Me too," she told him. "But moving past what did happen and looking forward. We're going to have some arguments, you know."

"Yep, and that might involve make-up sex, right?" he asked.

"You've got a wicked twinkle in your eye, Mr. Callahan," she said.

"I'm talkin' about what I've heard from the guys." He shrugged. "I've never been with anyone long enough to have arguments and then make-up sex."

"Bullshit!" She almost choked on a mouthful of pizza.

"Truth." He held up his right hand. "I've always been a one-night-stand kind of guy. Commitment has always scared the hell out of me."

"Got to admit, I have dated, but it kind of scared me too," she said.

"By the way, do you kiss on the first date?" he joked.

"Not usually, but I've had the hots for you for a very long time, so I guess a few kisses wouldn't hurt," she shot back at him.

Her tongue darted out to moisten her lips when he moved closer to her. That tiny little motion created a stir behind his zipper. When his lips met hers, she groaned and wrapped her arms around his neck. Her fingers tangled up in his hair, and the kisses got deeper and deeper until neither of them could breathe.

"We didn't fight, so this can't be make-up sex," she panted as she took off her shirt and tossed it on the other side of the coffee table.

He started to unbutton his shirt. "If make-up sex is hotter than this, I'm not sure I can stand it."

She brushed his hands away and unfastened every single button for him. She unzipped his jeans and tugged them and his boots off in one fell swoop.

The first round was over way too quick to suit Pax. "That was only the warm-up," he said as he rolled to the side and drew her close to his body. "Are you ready for the real thing?"

"Bring it on, big boy," she teased.

To begin the second round, they took the time to explore each other's bodies, their hands finding all kinds of sweet spots that made the other one groan. Then when they actually did make love, it lasted long enough to leave them totally exhausted.

"Amazing," she said.

"Awesome," he managed.

She snuggled down onto his shoulder and promptly fell asleep. He stared his fill of her—long lashes fanned out on high cheekbones, a full mouth made for kissing, blond hair all messy, and a naked body made to fit right next to his. This game they were playing might turn into something wonderful, given time.

Chapter Sixteen

Alana woke up feeling grumpy on Friday morning, but then she and Pax hadn't left the tack room until 3:00 a.m. Sure, she'd slept after they'd had sex, or was it after they'd made love? Then her stomach lurched, and she barely grabbed the trash can beside her bed in time.

"Must've been some bad sausage on the pizza," she muttered as she rinsed her mouth and brushed her teeth.

When she got to the kitchen, she found a note on the table from her father saying that he and Lucas had gone to the cattle sale in Amarillo and not to expect them home until suppertime. She opened the refrigerator, took out the milk, and grabbed a box of Lucky Charms. She'd eaten only a few spoonfuls when she felt her stomach begin to disagree with her choice of breakfast, and this time she barely made it to the bathroom.

She was busy washing her face when it dawned on her that she should be starting her period that very morning, and it had been thirteen days since she and Paxton had had unprotected sex. She couldn't be pregnant, or could she? She grabbed her purse and headed out the door.

No way would she buy a pregnancy test at the tiny, local drugstore. The news would be all over town before she could even pee on the stick and find out for herself. Her hands sweated so badly that she had to keep wiping one and then the other on the legs of her jeans so she could grip the steering wheel. She told herself over and over that she had food poisoning from bad pizza. In between times of denial and worry, she scolded herself for drinking beer when there was even a remote possibility that she might be pregnant.

You said you could be a single mother, the voice in her head reminded her.

"But I didn't mean it," Alana argued out loud. "I'm terrified at the thought of having to run the ranch all by myself. How am I going to do that and raise a child on my own?"

Driving to Amarillo usually took about thirty minutes, but that day it seemed like a six-hour trip. When she finally arrived at the store, she couldn't make herself go inside. What if, by chance, someone like Trudy or Billy Ray saw her checking out with a pregnancy test? Folks from Daisy often went to Amarillo and to that particular Walmart. She had to be smart about this thing. She started her truck and drove to a CVS pharmacy on the other side of town, and went into the store without hesitating.

She found the aisle with the pregnancy test—only there were at least a dozen brands and all with different prices. Did the higher cost of the more expensive ones mean they would give her a more accurate result than a cheaper one? She wanted the damned thing to be able to tell her the absolute truth, so she picked up the one that cost the most.

She stared at the rest of them for a long time and finally

decided to buy one of each brand and take one an hour over the rest of the day. That way she could compare results; one of them would surely be correct. She put them all in her cart, covered them with a fluffy throw that was on sale, and headed for the checkout counter. She made double sure no one that she knew was in the store before she unloaded her purchases onto the conveyor belt.

A young kid who couldn't be more than sixteen didn't even give the tests a second look. He ran them through the scanner, bagged them like he would have if they'd been toothpaste. Then he found the tag on the throw, ran it over the scanner, and hit the total button. Alana handed him cash, got her change, and escaped out the door without being seen by anyone from Daisy—or so she hoped.

Of course, there was always the off-the-wall chance that the kid would go home that night and tell his mama that some tall blonde had come in the store and bought a dozen pregnancy tests. Thank God she'd paid with cash, so he couldn't go back and find out her name from the credit card receipt.

She drove straight home, and even though her stomach was growling, she didn't even stop for a doughnut at the little shop in Daisy. She poured a glass of sweet tea and made herself a piece of toast on her way through the kitchen. Then she took her bag of tests up to her bathroom and lined all of them up on the vanity—cheapest to most expensive.

I've got food poisoning, she told herself as she unwrapped the cheapest one and read the instructions. In three minutes, after performing the test, there would be two pink lines on the stick if she was pregnant. One pink line meant she wasn't and she would be able to breathe easy again.

She did what she was supposed to do and laid the test on the box it had come in. Three minutes wasn't that long, but every time she checked the clock beside her curling iron, only five to ten seconds had gone by. She was ready to throw the clock out the upstairs window when the time finally passed, and then she couldn't look at the stick.

"I should have thought this through," she said. "I need a friend, like Bridget, to look for me, but I can't call her out of the blue and tell her to come over here and see if there's two pink lines on the stick I just peed on." She rolled her eyes toward the ceiling. "I'm not pregnant. I'm proving that I'm certifiable goofy by the way I'm talking to myself."

She shut her eyes tightly and then opened them on the count of three. Two bright pink lines seemed to leap up at her, and she gasped. "It's cheap," she muttered. "A more expensive one will tell the truth." She picked up the one on the other end of the line, did what she had to do, and began the eternal wait again. The directions on this brand said to wait two minutes, and if she was pregnant, the plus sign would turn to blue. If not, the minus sign would turn colors.

"No one gets pregnant with one time of unprotected sex," she said out loud. "If they did, there'd be so many teenagers with babies that"—she checked the stick at one minute and nothing was showing—"see there, that first one was a false positive."

Two minutes later, the little plus sign was a nice bright blue. She took all of the remaining tests, one right after another. Pee and wait. Pee and wait. She finished her tea and went to the kitchen for a bottle of water. With each new positive sign, the process became more frustrating. When she'd finished all of the tests and not a one showed a negative reading, she was ready to throw them all in the trash.

Not even that many could be right. There had to be something else wrong with her. She groaned all the way from her bathroom to the desk in her bedroom. She opened up her laptop and researched the causes for false positives for pregnancy tests. According to the experts on the Internet, the most common cause for such a problem was a cancerous tumor.

She threw herself back on her bed, the back of her hand against her forehead. There was nothing to do but call Doctor Wilson that afternoon. She told Mary Beth, his receptionist, that it was an emergency that couldn't wait until next week.

"Honey, he's leaving for a round of golf at noon and won't be back until Monday," Mary Beth said. "What's wrong, Alana?"

"I think I've got cancer," she blurted out.

"Oh, honey, I doubt that, but I can work you in at eleven if you can get here in that time," she said.

"I'll be there." Alana tossed all of the sticks with their hateful pink lines and blue pluses back into the plastic bag and stuffed them into her purse. She hurried down the stairs, jogged to her truck, and drove into town. When she pushed her way into the doctor's office, she was a nervous wreck. Her hands shook so badly that she could barely hang on to her purse. Her pulse raced and her heart felt like a brick was perched on top of it.

Mary Beth pointed to a chair in the reception area. "Doc had an emergency come in a couple of minutes ago. He's stitching up Danielle Barlow's son. Keeton was showing off with a pocketknife and cut his finger to the bone. Bless his little heart, he's only four, and Danielle doesn't have any idea how he got his hands on one of Richie's pocketknives."

Danielle's husband, Richie Barlow, pushed through the front doors, and Mary Beth pointed down the hallway. "Third door on the left. Danielle will sure be glad you're here. I'd forgotten that the sight of blood makes her faint."

"It's a wonder y'all didn't have to sedate her," Richie said without slowing down.

Alana had never seen Richie move so fast. He was a big man and had been a big linebacker on the Daisy High School football team back in the day. His job had been to block, and he had done it well, but he usually moved like he had no place to go and all day to get there when he wasn't on the football field.

Danielle showed up in the waiting room pretty soon after he arrived. "God, I'm glad Richie is here." She collapsed into a chair beside Alana. "I can't stand the sight of blood. I thought for sure I'd pass out cold getting Keeton here to the doctor's office." She threw a hand over her forehead and closed her eyes. "What are you in here for?"

Alana quickly zipped her purse so Danielle couldn't see the bag of pregnancy tests. "My arm is still hurting from that fall at the reunion," she lied, but was glad she had a good excuse.

Danielle sat straight up and stared at the huge bruise on Alana's arm. "That Rachel can be a real bitch sometimes. I wish she'd never made the cheer team, because now we have to treat her practically like a sorority sister. She even insisted I let her be a bridesmaid when I married Richie. What could I do? I'd already asked the other cheerleaders, and she would have caused a helluva problem if I hadn't asked her."

"I can see that happening." Alana nodded.

"Then be damned if she didn't try to sleep with Richie after the rehearsal dinner," Danielle whispered. "I wish she'd find a rich husband, get married, and move off somewhere far away—maybe like Africa."

Alana couldn't keep the smile off her face. "Why would you wish that on those poor people?"

Danielle giggled. "You got a point there."

"Okay, Alana," Mary Beth said, "let's get you into a room and ready for Doc to see you. He should be done stitching up Keeton before too long."

"I hope Keeton gets along all right," Alana told Danielle as she picked up her purse and followed Mary Beth through a door and back to an examination room.

Danielle waved. "Thank you, and if you need any help with your wedding, call me."

Could you please kidnap Rachel and keep her in a remote place until the wedding is over? Alana thought, but she did a finger wave over her shoulder.

Mary Beth ushered her into a room and nodded toward a chair. "Of course, everything that comes through the office is confidential, but I want you to know that I'm real sorry about Matt. You've got my prayers, and, honey, I've got broad shoulders if you need to cry, and I've got listening ears if you need to talk. And you can rest assured, I don't gossip. Couldn't if I wanted to. Doc would fire me."

"Thank you." Alana managed a smile. "I might just give you a call sometime."

"Anytime at all." Mary Beth closed the door behind her.

Alana sat down and picked up a magazine. She flipped through its pages for all of thirty seconds, laid it down, and checked the time on her phone. She'd been sitting there for a whole minute now, and she could hear the doctor's deep voice talking about golfing with Richie in the next room.

"Small-town doctors," she grumbled. "They know everyone's history for generations back."

"Well, I believe that's got Keeton fixed up," she heard Doctor Wilson say. "Tell Mary Beth to give him a lollipop on the way out and make an appointment for a week from now to get the stitches removed."

"We'll be here." Richie's voice was as clear as if he'd been in the room with her.

"I'll buy Keeton a whole bag of lollipops if you'll hurry up and get the hell out of here," she muttered as she checked her phone again. Five minutes had passed. She could hardly breathe for the brick that was still on her heart. Her hands were sweating again, and her stomach was making noises. She scanned the room for a trash can and located one over beside the sink.

"Good to know that there's one here." She glared at her phone again. Six minutes had gone by.

"Well, Alana." The doctor breezed into the room with her chart in his hand. "Mary Beth tells me you have cancer. Why on earth would you think that?"

She brought the bag out of her purse. "Twelve tests, doctor, and every damn one of them is positive. The Internet says that cancer can cause a false positive."

"Have you been celibate the past month, Alana?" Dr. Wilson smiled. "Have you had unprotected sex with Pax? I'm not judging. You two are engaged after all."

"Once," she admitted.

"Once is all it takes." He peeked into the bag she had handed him. "I'll do some bloodwork, but, honey, from a positive result on that many tests I'd say you're pregnant."

"But Daddy has cancer and Mama had it, and..." She felt the tears before they even started running down her cheeks. "And I've got too much on my plate right now for a baby."

"Alana." Dr. Wilson laid a hand on her shoulder. "I've treated you since you were born. What your mama had started as skin cancer on her back and got into her blood before we knew it was there. The type of cancer your dad has might or might not be hereditary, but I'm pretty damn sure you don't have it. What you *do* have is a baby on the way, so go home and tell Pax he's going to be a father. If you want to wait until after the wedding to announce the good news, that's up to you, but Matt is going to be ecstatic, and you know it. He told me the last time I saw him that he wanted to see you settled down and know he was having grandchildren before he dies. I'll need to do a blood test to be absolutely sure, and after that we can do an ultrasound."

"Do the test." Alana held out her arm. "I'm not telling anyone, not Pax or Daddy, until it comes back positive."

Doc reached into a cabinet and pulled out a sample bottle of prenatal vitamins. "Start these tomorrow morning. I don't have to tell you about no alcohol, and if you have morning sickness, sweet tea and crackers before you get out of bed might give you some relief. Congratulations, Alana. You and Pax will make wonderful parents."

"I had a beer a week ago," she blurted.

"Then no alcohol from now on. I'll send my nurse in to get a blood sample. Now go home and stop worrying. Things have a way of working themselves out for the best." He gave her another pat on the shoulder and left the room.

She made up her mind right then not to accept the results of the tests she'd taken that morning, no matter if they had pink lines or blue plus signs. Until the results of the blood test came back on Monday and made it official, she was going to pretend that all of them were wrong. She would throw the bagful of the tests in the Dumpster behind the doctor's office and keep the news to herself.

* * *

Matt was sitting in the dining room when she got home at noon. His nose was in the morning paper and his coffee cup was empty. He looked up over the top of the paper and smiled at her. "The sale was a bust. The bull we were interested in sold before the sale even started, and nothing else looked good, so we came home. But..." His eyes twinkled. "You up for a little overnight road trip? Delbert, the foreman down at the Broken Arrow Ranch near Odessa, has a bull that I'd love to buy. The two of us got to talkin' and he said that he wouldn't sell it to just anyone, and he damn sure wouldn't bring it to any sale. Says it's as much a pet as it is a breeder, and he wants it to have a good home. I thought we might have a father-daughter trip. I can drive myself if you and Pax have plans. Since I got off that medicine, I'm pretty clear-headed."

A vision of her father sitting on the tailgate of his truck earlier in the week flashed through her mind. What if he got turned around on the four-hour trip and wound up halfway across New Mexico? Besides, it would take up one whole day of the weekend. That was one day that Pax wouldn't be able to see the worry in her face and ask questions.

"I'd love to have you all to myself for a little while," she told him. "When are we leaving?"

"My bag is packed," Matt said. "I figured we'd stop in Lubbock at that café we both like so well. I think I could eat one of those big old chicken-fried steaks. Then we'd drive on down to Odessa. I booked two rooms down there for the night. Delbert said we could see the bull about ten in the morning, so I figured, if we buy him, we can be home by suppertime or a little after."

"Give me ten minutes." Alana headed out of the room. She stopped halfway up the stairs and yelled. "Is Lucas hooking up the cattle trailer?"

"He'll have it around to the front of the house by the time you get packed. You want to invite Pax to go with us?" Matt raised his voice.

"No, let's have some time with just the two of us," she hollered as she went the rest of the way to the second floor. She threw a nightshirt, some underwear, a pair of jeans, and a shirt in a bag. She always kept a travel makeup and toiletry kit ready to go, so all she had to do was toss it in the bag and she was ready.

She toted the bag to the bottom of the stairs, picked up her purse, and followed her dad out the door. Lucas was standing by the fender of the truck, the ever-present cigarette in his hands. When they started across the lawn, he put it out on the heel of his boot and shoved the unsmoked remnant back in the pack.

"I can tell by the look in your eyes that you're going to fuss at me for smoking," he said. "And I know the damn things will kill me someday, but I'm seventy years old, and I done got the three score and seven that the good Lord promised, so I'm livin' on borrowed time anyway."

"Only thing I was about to say," Alana told him, "is that if the inside of that truck smells like smoke, I'm going to make you unhitch the trailer and put it on the back of my vehicle."

Lucas's wide smile showed off a mouthful of crooked teeth. "Darlin', I didn't light up until I was out of the truck, and I'm down to only two cigarettes a day. I been workin' on quittin' so I'll still be around and I can hold the grandbabies when they get here. All that other bullshit I said was to rile you up. I'm going to live to be a hundred years old and not kick the bucket until after Matt's first grandchild is born."

"I hope you do." Matt rounded the front of the truck and got in the passenger's side. "Giving up smoking was the toughest thing I ever did, but Joy told me if I didn't, she was going to make me wear a mask and a gown every time I held my new baby daughter."

"I remember that very well." Lucas followed him and leaned on the edge of the truck window. "Y'all have a good trip and don't worry about a thing. I kind of like bein' the boss man when you're both gone."

"I never worry when you're in charge," Matt told him. "We'll be home tomorrow evening."

Lucas stepped away from the truck, and Alana fired up the engine. "I never knew you smoked, Daddy."

"I told you that Paxton Callahan, even with his bad habits and cattin' around, couldn't outdo me in my younger days," he chuckled. "I'm glad that this trip came up on the fly. It's like the good old days when your mama would let me take you with me on a buying trip."

"I learned a lot on those trips." She expertly backed the truck and trailer around and then drove down the lane to the road.

"Did you call Pax and tell him you wouldn't be home tonight?" Matt asked. "It *is* Friday night and that's date night, isn't it? It's still not too late to ask him to go with us. I sure don't mind sitting in the backseat."

"No, Daddy, this is time for us to spend with each other." She couldn't very well tell him that she'd rather not see Pax until after Monday.

* * *

Dark clouds drifted back and forth over the sun that Friday morning. Stretching barbed wire and replacing fence posts was hot work, so Pax appreciated every minute of shade that the clouds offered him. He wouldn't have minded working through a little half-hour shower to cool things down, but so far there hadn't been a single drop of rain.

He had to keep cheering his two little work crews on if he wanted to get the job finished by noon. The first bunch got to the finish line, which was the corner of the pasture, a full five minutes before the second team made it. That meant each of them would get an extra ten dollars on their paycheck that evening.

"Okay, boys, time to drag out your lunches, find a shady spot, and take a nap for an hour. I'm goin' up to the house and refill our tea and water coolers." He removed his hat and wiped the sweat from his forehead with a blue bandanna. "This afternoon the bunch of you are going to work on the last section of the fence we want to replace this summer."

"You goin' to the Wild Cowboy tonight?" Jake, one of the older boys, asked.

"Might if Alana wants to get out and do some dancin'." Pax settled his hat back on his head and picked up the two empty orange coolers.

"Reckon you could let me tag along behind you?" Jake asked.

"How old are you?" Pax set the two containers in the backseat of the old farm truck.

"Seventeen, but I'll be eighteen in December," he said.

"Then I'll let you tag along in December," Pax answered.

"I told you he was a square shooter," one of the other boys said.

"Never hurts to ask," Jake sighed loudly. "Guess we'll all go to the pond after work and see who wants to go skinny-dippin' with us."

Pax didn't have a bit of trouble remembering back when he was seventeen and wanting to go to the Wild Cowboy on Friday nights. He'd gotten Maverick to help him with a fake ID so he could go with his older brother and the Baker boys. He shuddered at the idea of his own son doing the same thing.

"It's a wonder Mam didn't lock us up on weekends," he mumbled as he got into the truck. He started the engine, and his phone rang at the same time. He turned the air-conditioning up as high as it would go and picked up the phone from the passenger seat.

"Hello, darlin'," he said, "is this my girlfriend or my fiancée? I was thinkin' we might go to the Wild Cowboy tonight if it's my girlfriend."

"Sorry, honey," she said. "Daddy and I are on the way to Odessa to look at a bull. We won't be back until late tomorrow evening."

"You go spend as much time with him as you can," Pax said. "The Wild Cowboy ain't goin' nowhere, so we'll have lots of Friday nights to go there. Can I pick you up for church on Sunday morning?"

"Of course," she said. "I'll be ready at ten thirty. Daddy wanted me to invite y'all to Mama Jo's for dinner afterward. He's got a hankerin' for some of her chicken and dressin'."

"I'm accepting for all of us," Pax said. "Have a safe trip and call or text me when you can."

"Sure thing. Love you," she said.

"Me too," he answered, knowing that the words were for Matt's benefit.

Maverick's truck was parked in the backyard when Pax got to the house, but he was still sitting in it. He slung open the door, and the two of them got out at the same.

"It's going to rain. I can smell it," Maverick said as the first big drops hit the ground.

They jogged the rest of the way to the house with Pax taking the lead. "What's the weatherman saying?"

"One hundred percent chance all night," Maverick told him. "I sent my boys on home. You might as well give Jake a call and tell him to haul your crew back to town. Didn't they ride out with him?"

Pax darted into the house, made the call, and groaned. "I really wanted to get the last of the fencing done today. Once that's set, we'll have all the old wooden posts replaced with metal T-posts, and we won't have to mess with it for a couple of years."

"I guess this gives you all afternoon to get presentable and go out with Alana tonight." Maverick hung his hat on the hook by the back door. "Hey, where's my pretty girls. Y'all ready for Daddy to be in the house the rest of the day?"

Iris looked up from the stove, where she was stirring a pot of fresh green beans cooked with new potatoes. "Y'all are right on time," she said. "The chicken is all fried and ready to go on the table."

Bridget crossed the room and tiptoed to give Maverick a kiss. "We'll have dinner on the table by the time y'all get washed up."

Laela toddled over to Maverick and held up her arms for him to pick her up. The idea of starting a family a few weeks ago would have had Pax running like a jackrabbit toward the nearest mesquite thicket but seeing the happiness in his brother's eyes made him wish that he was already settled down and maybe even a father.

"Do I see a little jealousy?" Iris poked him on the arm with a wooden spoon.

"Yes, you do," Pax admitted.

"Well, maybe this time next year, I'll have another great-grandchild, and Laela will have a little cousin," Iris said.

"A very wise lady told me once not to count my chickens before they're hatched." Pax adjusted the water at the kitchen sink and lathered up his hands.

Bridget finished setting the table, took the baby from Maverick, and kissed him on the cheek. "Since it's raining, do you think we might go shopping this afternoon, darlin'? It's only two weeks until the wedding, and I still haven't bought a pair of boots."

"I'll keep Laela for you," Iris said. "Y'all make a day of it. Go shopping, have dinner somewhere nice, and then either go dancin' at the Wild Cowboy or maybe take in a movie."

"I'll help Mam babysit," Pax volunteered. "Alana has gone off on a road trip to Odessa with Matt, so I'm free until Sunday morning."

"It'll be good for Alana and Matt to have some time together before the wedding." Iris sat down at the table. "Things are about to change drastically over there at the Bar C. It's only been the two of them since Alana was ten years old, and now there'll be a third in the mix."

But you're so right, Pax thought. *A drastic change is definitely coming, and none of y'all have any idea how huge the change could very well be.*

Chapter Seventeen

Soft rain was falling outside when Alana awoke on Sunday morning. The drops sliding down the window reminded her of all the tears she'd shed in the past few weeks. Determined that she wouldn't cry anymore and that she'd be thankful for what time she had left with her father, she pushed back the covers and grabbed her robe from the back of a rocking chair. She was already in the bathroom when she realized that she wasn't the least bit sick that morning.

She brushed her teeth and laid a hand on her flat stomach and then glanced through the open door at her wedding dress, hanging on the back of the closet door. The preacher hadn't known how right he'd been when he had talked about tangled webs. If she hadn't asked Pax to pretend that they were getting married, none of this would be happening. What she'd created by telling her dad that she and Pax were involved would take years and years to unknot but seeing him so happy made it all worthwhile.

The smell of bacon and coffee hit her when she reached the bottom of the stairs, and she could hear her father humming before she reached the kitchen. She headed straight for the coffeepot and poured herself a mugful.

"You're in a good mood this morning," she said.

"Why wouldn't I be? We had a fantastic road trip, bought two good bulls that are going to bring new blood to our line, and today I get to have Sunday dinner with good friends. Life is good," he replied.

"What can I do to help with breakfast?" she asked.

"Not a thing," Matt answered. "Sit down and enjoy your coffee. Bacon is done and the waffle iron is hot. Breakfast will be on the table in five minutes. Do you realize that two weeks from right now, you'll be waking up with your brand-new husband in the honeymoon suite of a hotel in Amarillo? I arranged a little surprise for you."

"Another one?" she asked.

"Yep, but you know how hard it is for me to keep a secret so..." He shrugged as he poured batter into the waffle iron. "I've chartered a private plane to take y'all to Colorado so you won't have to spend the first day of your marriage driving."

Alana opened her mouth to argue, to remind him that she might need to get home in a hurry if he started feeling bad, but then she clamped it shut. If he could charter a plane to take them to Colorado, then if it became necessary, she could do the same to get back home. "That's so sweet of you, Daddy. You've thought of everything, haven't you?"

"If I haven't," he said with a grin, "I promise I'll do my best to do so before the weddin'. Let's keep this our little secret so we can at least surprise Pax with it."

"I hope he's not afraid of flying," she laughed.

* * *

Alana remembered her comment about Paxton's possible fear of flying when the choir director at church that morning asked everyone to turn their hymnals to "I'll Fly Away." She'd only flown a few times in her life, and she loved being as high as the clouds and higher. But usually she and her dad drove to rodeos or cattle sales, and more than likely, they would have a trailer hitched up to their truck with either a horse in it or plans to bring some sort of animal back with them.

"Have you ever flown anywhere?" she whispered in Pax's ear.

He shook his head. "Nope, always had too much gear."

"Shhh..." Iris poked him on the shoulder from the pew right behind them.

He gave Alana a slow, sexy wink and gently squeezed her hand. She nudged him with her shoulder and started singing again. When the song ended, the preacher stepped up behind the old oak lectern, cleared his throat, and started his sermon by reading the passage from Acts, the one about Ananias and Sapphira, a couple who were struck dead for lying.

"Did he not already speak on this a week or two ago?" she muttered under her breath.

Pax nodded and then shook his head.

That gesture meant that he agreed, but that he didn't feel like they were lying, or maybe he thought the preacher was talking to someone else in the congregation and not them. Alana wasn't so sure about that. She felt like the man was staring right at her. She made up her mind right then and there that she would tell her dad the truth after tomorrow. If she was pregnant, that might ease the blow of her having lied to him. If she had cancer, then they'd have more to worry about than canceling a wedding.

That decision made and knowing that she only had to live with the uncertainty and the guilt for another twenty-four hours brought peace to her heart. She was able to ignore the rest of the sermon and focus on Pax. The scent of his woodsy shaving lotion wafted over to her every time he moved and sent her thoughts back toward the tack room when she had awakened to find her naked body snuggled up to him on the futon.

The preacher jerked her back from the past when he asked her father to deliver the benediction. She'd been so lost in reliving those sexy moments with Pax that she had not heard the end of the sermon or any announcements.

"Amen," her father said, and everyone in the church said it right after him.

Then folks began to stand up, and the quietness was replaced with the hum of dozens of conversations all going on at the same time. Alana followed Pax to the end of the pew, and when she stepped out into the center aisle, she came face-to-face with Danielle Barlow. Richie was crowded in right behind her, and their son, Keeton, was holding on to his mother's arm, his hurt finger pointing straight up.

"How's he doin'?" Alana asked.

"Whinin', but then it was a deep cut," Danielle said. "I still don't know how he got into his father's gun safe and got his hands on that pocketknife."

"He probably watched me punch in the combination," Richie said. "I already changed it, and I'll be more careful where he is when I open that safe from now on."

Alana imagined a child of hers and Pax's being as precocious. Neither of them had ever been afraid of anything—

well, almost anything. They had both run from each other for a long time.

"So how's your arm?" Danielle asked.

Alana was sweating bullets, hoping the woman wouldn't mention seeing her at the doctor's office. "It's healin' up good. Nothing but a big ugly bruise. It'll probably be gone by the day of the wedding."

"Well, honey, if it's not, you call me. I've got some fantastic makeup that will cover it right up," Danielle said with a wink. "Richie's mama is expectin' us for dinner"— she lowered her voice—"so we're going to sneak out the side door. I'm sure she's going to blame me for her grandson gettin' hurt."

"Of course she will," Richie teased. "I'm the precious baby of the family that never does anything wrong."

Alana glanced over at Pax with a knowing look. He was the baby son, and Iris probably thought he didn't do anything wrong either, but Alana could educate her pretty quick on that issue.

The Barlow family headed toward the side door, but what Richie had said stayed with Alana. Even if she and Pax were to really get married, she wouldn't have a mother-in-law to have to deal with, and he'd have no in-laws at all. Tears welled up in her eyes again—Lord have mercy! She'd cried more over that weekend than she had her whole life, and a lot of those tears had been brought on by the thought that her baby would not have grandparents, aunts and uncles, or even cousins. She thought about Pax's family and all his extended friends out in Sunset who were like kinfolk. On that side, her child would have lots of relatives, so maybe she shouldn't throw away the idea of staying married to him. It would sure simplify things all around for her, but he might resent her for trapping him that way.

Besides, she was going to put a stop to the whole engagement charade tomorrow, anyway. She had already made that decision, and Alana Joy Carey never sat on a fence. Once she made a decision, she stuck with it.

Why, Lord, she looked up toward the high ceiling in the church, *does everything have to be so complicated and confusing?*

Your life has been simple and honest for twenty-nine years, girl. It wasn't until you told that first little lie that things got complicated and confusing. Don't blame God, or even ask Him a question like that. You know the answer all too well, the voice in her head scolded.

"Are you okay?" Pax asked. "You seem to be fighting with yourself today."

"I am," she admitted. "I can't do all this pretending and lying anymore. I'm going to come clean with Daddy tomorrow."

"No, you are not!" Pax said. "We've come this far, and it would break his heart to know that we've deceived him. It's only two more weeks, and we'll get through it together."

"Don't tell me what I can and can not do," she snapped.

"We'll talk after dinner," he said out of the side of his mouth. "We can't argue in church with so many people around us."

"Who's arguing?" Iris asked.

"We're trying to decide if we want the Sunday special or hamburgers," Alana lied and then worried that she was getting entirely too smooth at not telling the truth.

"You can get a burger any day of the week, but you can only get chicken and dressin' on Sunday," Matt said. "But it's up to you kids. Whatever you want, you can have it."

"Thanks, Daddy." Alana smiled.

* * *

Pax had put a lot of time and energy into their ruse, plus he'd discovered that he really liked Alana—a lot— so he intended to do his dead level best to talk her out of coming clean. If the time ever came when they wanted to break up, they could get a divorce then. Folks would stand in line to say "I told you he'd never settle down," or they might even say that Alana had only married him because her father was sick, and she didn't want to be alone. Pax didn't give a damn what rumors got spread about him on down the road. He wanted Matt to die a happy man, and if it took arguing with Alana until the cows came home to make that happen, he was up for the task.

"So what were you two kids really arguing about back there?" Matt asked when they were in Pax's truck and headed toward the café. "Don't try to lie to me about it, either. You know, you've never been able to pull the wool over my eyes, Alana Joy."

She glanced over at Pax, and the fire in her eyes said that she wasn't giving in to him or anyone else.

"Whether to have children when we first get married or wait a couple of years," Pax answered.

Her brown eyes looked like they might shoot flames at him at any time.

"If you want my advice, don't wait too long." Matt buckled his seat belt. "You want to have the energy to raise your kids, and the older you get, the less energy you have. Plus, if you wait two or three years, you'll be set in your ways and a baby kind of upsets things."

"That's exactly what I told Alana. If we want three or four kids, then we should have the first one pretty quick, and maybe one every eighteen months to two years after that. If we did that, we'd still be past fifty when the youngest one graduates high school." Pax thought of that old saying about getting hung for a sheep as well as a lamb came to mind. Since he was spinning a yarn anyway, he thought, he might as well make it a big one.

"You two aren't going to gang up on me." Alana crossed her arms over her chest and gave Pax another dirty look.

"We aren't, baby girl," Matt chuckled. "What're you naming the firstborn?"

"Something Joy if it's a girl," she answered.

"And maybe Thomas Matthew if it's a boy," Pax chimed in. He reached over and patted Alana on the shoulder. "If you want to wait a year to start our family, I'm good with that, darlin'. We could still be parents by the time we're thirty."

"Well, I can't think of any better names." Matt beamed. "Y'all need to make a decision and not fight about when to start. Just love each other and compromise. I know I've said it before, but I'm so happy about this wedding and knowing that y'all are going to be together."

Pax shot a knowing look at Alana, but she turned her head and looked out the side window. Big black clouds rolled in from the southwest. A long streak of lightning flashed through the sky, and a roll of thunder followed right on its tail. Pax's grandpa had always told him to count the seconds between the lightning and the thunder, and that would tell how many minutes he had to get inside before the storm hit. If that was the truth, then they barely had time to get parked and into the café without getting soaked.

"Looks like we're in for a frog strangler," Matt said when Pax parked the truck right in front of the café.

"Kind of does, don't it?" Pax agreed. "Y'all go on in and I'll get the truck parked and join you in the café."

"You best hurry," Matt said as he slammed the door shut.

Alana didn't even look at him, but slid out of the passenger seat and hurried toward the café.

Something told him that whatever squall was boiling in Alana's heart was going to be much bigger than what the weather could deliver that day.

* * *

Matt was already heading back to the table where Iris, Bridget, Maverick and Laela waited when Alana got into the café. She took two steps to follow him, but Danielle touched her arm and whispered, "I'm warning you that Rachel is really angry at you for not asking her to do something at the wedding. She called me on my way from the church to here."

"Well, maybe I should ask her to be on bathroom duty. She could hand out pretty monogrammed paper towels for the ladies to dry their hands on," Alana said with a saccharine smile.

Danielle giggled. "Are you really going to have someone do that?"

"Nope, but it would be a good job for her. Here comes Pax. Thanks for the heads-up," Alana said.

Pax came through the door and made his way right to her. He slipped his arm around her shoulders and said, "Glad y'all got inside before it started. The way the wind is picking up, it could be quite a storm out there in a few minutes. I'd hate for you to get your pretty dress all wet, darlin'."

The heat of his arm resting south of her shoulder made

her angry. She didn't want him to have that kind of effect on her emotions. What she wanted was for him to agree with her about putting an end to all the lies and start telling the truth. She didn't want to talk about baby names, not when she wasn't sure whether she was pregnant or had cancer. The latter would mean that she'd probably die young and never have children, so why pick out names for children she might never have.

"I took the privilege of ordering us all sweet tea," Iris said. "Our waitress will be back for our orders in a few minutes. I swear to God, the servers in this place get younger every year. The one who's waiting on us can't even be out of high school."

"No, she's not," Matt said. "That's Doc Wilson's granddaughter, and she's been working here all summer."

"Well, how about that," Iris crowed. "I like to see kids work. It teaches them responsibility. Now tell us what y'all were really arguing about at the church." Her grin faded as she stared across the round table at Alana and Pax.

"They're trying to decide whether they should start a family right after they get married or wait a year or two," Matt answered. "I already got it out of them, and guess what, Iris? When they have a son, they're going to name him Thomas Matthew, and when they have a daughter, her middle name is going to be Joy."

Iris's smile was so bright that it lit up the room. No one around the table even thought about the rain pouring down outside. "That's the most precious thing I've heard in months." She sighed. "Your grandpa would be so proud."

"Whoa!" Maverick threw up both hands. "Bridget and I were going to wait to tell all y'all, but if you're stealing my boy name, then we might as well let the cat out of the bag right now. We're expecting a second child in November.

And we've decided if it's a boy, we'd like to use the name Thomas."

"Oh. My. Goodness." Iris's hands went to her cheeks. "This is great news. Laela needs a sibling, and now I'll have two great-grandchildren."

Alana leaned over and gave Bridget a hug. "I'm so happy for you."

Pax pushed back his chair and hugged Bridget on his way to clamp a hand on his brother's shoulder. "Congratulations." Pax smiled. "We called the name first, but nothing says we can't turn our name around to Matthew Thomas, and both of us use Grandpa's name."

"He'd be bustin' the buttons off his shirt with pride," Iris said.

"Great news." Matt was on his feet next and shook hands with both Bridget and Maverick. "You kids are a lucky couple and some fine parents already."

"I might have a girl," Bridget reminded them.

"Or we might have one on our first try too," Pax said.

The conversation turned to whether Bridget would have her baby on Thanksgiving Day, since her due date was close to then. Iris wanted to know all the details, like when she'd been to the doctor and was she using Doctor Wilson.

Alana listened to the conversation going on around her, but she didn't care about all the particulars. She was glad that the spotlight was off what she and Pax had been arguing about. It was still her intention to come clean after her visit to Doctor Wilson, whatever the test results revealed. She simply couldn't carry the guilt of their deception another two weeks.

"Twenty-four hours," Pax whispered in her ear and then kissed her on the cheek.

"What are you talking about?" she asked.

"Give us until this time tomorrow to think about what you're about to do. If you're still set on telling Matt, then I'll go with you. He deserves to hear it from both of us," Pax said for her ears only.

Alana agreed with a nod. She hadn't planned to talk to her father until afternoon anyway, and Pax should be there when she did. True enough, it had been her idea, but Pax hadn't hesitated a single second when he agreed to play along. She would know for sure exactly what to tell both of them tomorrow.

"And one more thing while the attention is on Bridget. Have you taken a pregnancy test yet?" Pax asked, his head close to Alana's.

"Okay, you two lovebirds, what are you whispering about, now?" Bridget asked.

"I was telling Pax that we'll talk about when to start a family later. Right now, I'm starving and I want a big plate of chicken and dressing with all the sides," she answered. "I've never learned to make good dressing. I always put too much sage in it."

"I'll teach you at Thanksgiving," Iris offered. "It took me years to get it right. Here come our drinks. Better be making your decisions about dinner."

"Thank you." Alana wondered if Iris would even want her in the Callahan house when she found out what she and Pax had done.

The waitress passed their drinks around and then took out her order pad and pen. "Y'all ready?"

Pax went first. "I want the Sunday special, only instead of green beans, I want corn."

When she'd written down all their orders, the waitress rushed off to the kitchen.

Matt picked up his glass of tea. "A toast. To the new baby."

They all clinked glasses together and then took a sip of their tea.

Iris raised her glass. "Another toast. To Pax and Alana. We're glad you two finally woke up and realized you were meant to be together."

"Amen!" Matt touched his glass with Pax's. "Love her. Cherish her. And may y'all celebrate your fiftieth anniversary with your children beside you and your grandchildren playing in the front yard of the Bar C Ranch."

"Hear, hear!" Iris stood up and touched her glass to Alana's.

A visual popped into Alana's mind. Pax as sitting on the porch with her. Three or four of their grown children gathered around them, and a whole horde of little grandchildren playing chase on the front lawn. The picture warmed her heart. But it wasn't enough to keep her from feeling like the biggest hypocrite in the whole state of Texas.

Chapter Eighteen

Alana had read somewhere that guilt was the strongest of all the emotions, and the toughest to get past. The peace that she'd felt from making the decision to come clean with her father had been short-lived. Now it had been replaced by a heavy feeling in her chest that she was afraid would never leave, no matter what she did or didn't do.

Damned if you do; damned if you don't, went through her mind as she waited for the doctor to come into the examination room. The open-back gown barely came to her knees, and the sheet Mary Beth gave her to cover with wasn't doing a very good job. She inhaled deeply when she heard someone approaching out in the hallway. Her breath rushed out with a loud whoosh when Mary Beth pushed a cart with a computer on the top of it into the room.

"What's that?" Alana asked.

"Internal ultrasound machine," Mary Beth told her. "Doc

should be here in a few minutes. Just relax." She hurried out of the room and closed the door behind her.

Alana let out a long sigh. Cold chills that had nothing to do with the air-conditioning vent being right above her chased down her spine. Goose bumps popped up on her arms, and her breath came out in short gasps.

She couldn't give her father the truth. To keep from crying—again—she focused on a height and weight chart hanging on the wall. She was six feet tall, so according to the chart she should weigh 148 pounds. She'd tipped the doctor's scales at 145 that morning, so she was pretty close to normal.

That wouldn't last long, though, not if she was pregnant. Her stomach would swell faster than her skin could grow, and she would waddle like a duck, and Pax would think she was ugly. Poor man had sure gotten himself into a mess when he agreed to a fake marriage.

Voices outside her door took her attention away from the chart and the pictures she visualized in her mind showed how horrible she would look in a few months. Two people were arguing right outside the door. She leaned forward and listened so hard that her ears ached. One had to be Mary Beth, and she was not happy.

"I'm goin' in." Pax's voice came through loud and clear.

Her eyes widened and her breath caught in her throat when Pax pushed his way into the exam room with Mary Beth right behind him.

"What are you doin' here?" Alana asked.

He folded his arms over his chest. "I'm your fiancé, and I've got every right to be here."

She tugged the sheet up over her chest, only to leave her thighs and legs exposed. "How did you even know I was here?"

"I followed you," he said. "Are you pregnant? Is that why you've been acting so weird all weekend?"

The two of them were totally focused on each other, so Mary Beth took advantage of the situation and eased out of the room.

"I don't know." Alana pushed the sheet back down and twisted the corner into a knot. "The pregnancy tests I took were positive, but there's no way I can be pregnant. I wasn't ovulating. From what I read on the Internet, cancer will present a false positive, so I'm waiting for Doc to tell me what the blood work said."

"And you didn't tell me...why?" Pax crossed the small room in a couple of long strides and took Alana's hand in his. "If we were really engaged, my place would be right here with you. Hell, if we weren't doing more than dating and you thought you were pregnant, you still should have told me."

"I wanted to be sure." Wearing nothing but a backless gown and a sheet, Alana was sitting on the end of an exam table, and his touch still caused sparks to bounce off the light green walls.

"It doesn't matter what the doctor says, Alana." Pax brought her hand to his lips and kissed her knuckles. "I'm here for you. I'll be right here with you. I'm not going anywhere, darlin'."

Doctor Wilson pushed into the room with a chart in his hands. He laid it on the countertop and flipped it open to the first page. "Your blood work shows absolutely no abnormalities that would indicate cancer, and every sign that you are pregnant. Congratulations to both of you."

"Are you sure?" Alana whispered. "Do you need to do more tests?"

"No, you are definitely pregnant," he said again. "Now

lie back, put your heels in the stirrups, and we'll do an ultrasound. I'll push this screen closer to you so that you and Pax both can see your baby."

She stared up at Pax, and be damned if his eyes weren't twinkling.

"This will be a little cold. Sorry about that," Doc Wilson said. "And I don't usually do an internal ultrasound this early, but..." He pointed toward the screen. "That little bean right there is your baby. That's Matt Carey's first grandchild."

Alana couldn't take her eyes off the tiny blob on the screen. "That can't be a baby. It looks like one of those goldfish crackers. Are you sure it's not the beginning of a tumor?"

"Shhh..." Doc Wilson said and turned up the volume on the machine. "Must be because you are both good-size people. The baby is already pretty big for only two weeks."

"That's a good sign, right, Doc?" Pax's expression changed from happy to worried.

"Shhh..." he said again. "Listen carefully."

"All I hear is a whooshing noise," Pax said.

"Is that..." Alana covered her mouth with her hand.

"It's a heartbeat." Doc nodded. "It's early to detect one, but bigger babies do sound out earlier than the smaller ones. Since you know the day you got pregnant, I'd say you're two weeks right now, and right there"—he pointed to numbers on the bottom of the screen—"is your due date. Looks like you might have a Valentine's baby."

The doctor removed the apparatus, and the screen went dark.

"Put it back," Alana said. "I'm not finished looking at it. I'm really going to have a baby?"

"*We're* really going to have a baby," Pax corrected.

"Congratulations, again," Doc said. "And in a few seconds we'll have you some paper copies of your ultrasound. That should put your mind at ease about the idea of cancer."

Doc took a slip of paper on which were three copies of black-and-white pictures from a printer on the bottom shelf of the rolling cart and handed them to Alana. "Proof that you do not have cancer. I never knew a tumor to have a heart-beat," he chuckled. "I'll be going now. You can get dressed and go celebrate the good news. Make an appointment with Mary Beth to come back in a month. After the sixth month, I'll see you every two weeks, and after the eighth, it will be every week."

"We'll take care of that, Doc," Pax replied. "And I'll be here with her for every appointment."

Alana was staring so hard at what was in her hands that she didn't even know when the doctor left the room. "I thought things couldn't get any more complicated, but I was wrong," she whispered.

Pax leaned down and kissed her on the cheek. "Grandpa used to say when obstacles came along how you got over them or around them all depended on how you looked at them. Ten years from now, we might look back on this and see it as a blessing. I'm going to be right here with you to help raise this child, Alana. Boy or girl, I want to be a part of its life."

"A baby is a long-term commitment." She still couldn't believe something so small could have a heartbeat.

"I'm ready for that," he said.

"Are you sure?" She sat up and turned her head so that she could look right into his eyes.

He nodded without hesitation. "I'm very sure. I told you before I will always be a part of the life of any child

I father, and I meant it. I'll be there for this baby. I'll pay for the little one's food, clothing, shelter—whatever he or she needs. No matter what, I'll be right across the fence from you, and I'll be there in five minutes anytime you call."

"Do you realize that less than three weeks ago . . ." Her voice cracked.

"Yes, I do." He hugged her tightly. "And I also know that in only eleven days we're getting married. You got your vows written?"

"No, I have not," she declared. "Pax, what am I going to do? It would kill Daddy's soul to know that he was leaving me behind—pregnant . . ." She paused to wipe her eyes. "Dammit! All this is making me emotional."

Pax reached across her lap, pulled a tissue from a box on a nearby table, and wiped the tears from her eyes, "Don't cry, darlin'. We started this baby together, and we'll raise it together."

"Here's a scenario for you. We've decided to be only friends. You live over at Callahan Ranch, and I'm living on the Bar C. It's Saturday night, and you're about to head out to go to the Wild Cowboy for some fun. I call and tell you that the baby has a fever, and we need to rush to the emergency room. Or I call and tell you that our toddler got away from me out in the pasture and a bull trampled him. What do you do?" She had no control over the damn tears that kept rolling down her cheeks.

"In both cases, I go to the emergency room with you and forget about the bar bunnies," he answered. "Here's another scenario. We decide to get into a real relationship, not a false one, have three more kids, and then you leave me. Will you still let me be a part of my children's lives?"

"After what you've done for me, I could never shut you

out of our kids' lives," she told him. "But why would I leave you after we have four babies together?"

"Because you wake up one morning, take a look at me, and figure that you could have done so much better," he answered. "We could play this game all day, darlin', but why don't you get dressed. Let's go get some ice cream, or maybe even a burger and fries, and let this all soak in for an hour or so."

Alana nodded, but she still had a lump the size of an orange in her throat. Knowing that she was pregnant changed everything. She couldn't tell her dad about the lies, and she damn sure couldn't call off the wedding. All she could think about when she stepped behind the curtain to get dressed was that she was going to have one helluva time writing vows.

"Hey, did you remember that Daisy Days is this weekend?" Pax asked from the other side of the curtain. "Memorial Day weekend is coming right up, and then our wedding party will all be here in the middle of the next week. Think we should invite them to come a little early so they can enjoy the festival?"

How could he talk about a dumb old Texas celebration when her whole world had spun completely out of control? "Let's think about it tomorrow. I imagine that they'll be doing good to get away from their ranches for the rehearsal dinner and wedding, though."

"Fair enough," Pax agreed. "We gave our hired hands the weekend off. What are y'all doing over at your place?"

"Same thing." She pulled on her bikini underpants and splayed out the fingers of both hands on her stomach. If she had inherited enough of her mother's genes, she'd go back into shape fairly soon after the baby came, but there would be stretch marks. Few women got through a whole pregnancy without those battle scars. Would Pax even be able to look at her with her belly button turned inside out and all those ugly purple marks on her belly?

"I guess we won't be ridin' the Ferris wheel at the carnival, will we?" he asked.

Was he trying to take her mind or his off the fact that they were expecting a baby? Alana wondered. Learning that the two of them were going to have a baby had to have been as much of a shock to Pax as it had been to her. That had to be why he was jumping from one topic to another.

"No, and we won't be having a beer either, but we can eat funnel cakes and fried pickles," she answered.

"And cotton candy, and I'll even buy you a daisy to wear in your hair," he offered.

"That's right sweet." She pushed the curtain back and stepped out into the room. His eyes started at the toes of her cowboy boots and traveled up to her eyes. "Man, you are one beautiful woman."

"You won't be saying that come Christmas when I'm only about six weeks from delivery. I'll be looking like a baby elephant or maybe a beached whale, and I won't even be able to bend down and tie my shoes," she said.

Pax stood up and pulled her into his arms. "Darlin', you'll always be gorgeous in my eyes, and I'll tie your shoes for you any day of the week."

"I'll be holdin' you to that," she said.

"It's a promise," he told her, "and I'll even seal it with a kiss."

* * *

When their lips met, Pax's knees went more than a little bit weak and he could feel her heart thumping against his chest.

He had kissed a lot of women and gone to bed with his fair share, but a kiss from any of them had never affected him like this—up until that moment not even Alana's. Did that mean he was falling in love with her, in a real sense?

She took a short step back, ending the kiss, and smiled at him. "Okay, cowboy, you promised me food, so while we eat let's go talk about how we're going to tell Daddy this news."

"Burgers, Mexican, or a plate dinner from Mama Jo's?" he asked.

"The café," she said. "The Monday special is meat loaf and mashed potatoes, and I love the hot rolls they make there."

"Let's take my truck, and then I'll bring you back for yours when we're done." He laced his fingers with hers and led her out of the room. They stopped at the front desk, and Mary Beth handed them a card. "You will be back from your honeymoon by then, right?"

"Yes, ma'am." Pax tucked the card into the pocket of his chambray work shirt.

"What time?" Alana asked when they were outside.

"Nine in the morning," he answered. "But you've got enough on your mind, so it will be my job to remember this. When we get to the café, I'll put it on the calendar on my phone."

"Thank you." She butted him with her hip. "What else have you got on that calendar?"

"Well, there's our wedding, of course, the honeymoon information, and the..." He paused and wondered if he would be saying too much, but then he plowed right on, "The day that six weeks is up. That's June seventeenth."

"So it could be over by the time I come back to the doctor for my next visit." She sighed.

"Possibly, but miracles do still happen," he said as he helped her into his truck.

"I'd consider it a miracle if he made it to July Fourth," she said.

Pax wasn't about to tell her that he just hoped Matt was able to walk her down the aisle for her wedding. That seemed to have come to mean so much to her as well as to her father, but Matt was moving slower and shuffling more with each passing day. Would he still have the strength left to pick up his feet and walk Alana down the aisle on their wedding day?

He got behind the wheel and headed toward the three-block section of downtown and the little local café where they'd all had Sunday dinner the day before. "We could call your dad and have him meet us at the café and tell him there. I'd feel a lot better in a public place."

"Why's that?" she asked.

"He won't have access to a shotgun," Pax told her. "He and Mam have both teased us about starting a family, but I'm the cowboy that got your daddy's baby girl pregnant. He might not be too happy about that."

"I need some more time to wrap my mind around it," Alana said. "You sure are taking this calmly."

He parked in front of the café and went around to open the door for her. He offered a hand to help her out, and she took it. Then he put his hand on her back and guided her across the sidewalk and to the old-fashioned screen door. "I hope they never replace these old wood doors," he said. "It gives the place more character than the ones that are made of aluminum and glass that open automatically."

"Yep," Alana agreed but her tone was curt.

"Did I say or do something wrong?" he asked.

She took his hand and pulled him toward an empty booth at the back of the café. She slid all the way to the far end of one side and patted the seat beside her. "Sit beside me, not across from me."

"Yes, ma'am," he said. "Now, would you please answer my question?"

"You didn't do anything wrong," she said. "My brain is whirling around like one of those whirligigs we used to get when we were kids. We'd hang them out the back window of the truck, and they'd go so fast that they were a blur. Well, that's the way my thought patterns are right now. I want to grab something and hang on to it, to prove I'm sane, but everything's going at warp speed."

"Grab on to this." He leaned over and kissed her on the lips.

When he pulled back, her eyes looked different. Ever since he'd barged into the doctor's office, she'd had the look of a lone crippled prairie chicken at a coyote convention.

"That grounded me right quick." She picked up the menu from the table. "Thank you, Pax."

"Let's forget about the wedding, what we're enduring with your dad, and concentrate on baby names for the next hour. You really want to name our daughter Something?"

"What?" She frowned.

"I'm not too fond of these newfangled names folks are using, like Stormy or Rain. But, honey, Something, is sure way out there as far as weird goes." He tucked a strand of hair behind her ear and kissed the lobe. "I was thinkin' maybe we'd name her Anything instead of Something or maybe even Everything."

"What in the hell are you talking about?" She frowned. "Have you finally realized that you're going to be a daddy, and it's affecting your thinking?"

"You said yesterday that you wanted to name our baby girl Something Joy," he reminded her.

She slapped him on the thigh. "You know what I meant, but thanks for making me think about something—" Her sentence ended abruptly, and she stared at him with a blank look. "I forgot what I was saying."

"Are you talking about our daughter, Something?" he butted in with a chuckle.

"No, but every time I say that word from now on, I'll think of a cute little blond-haired girl," Alana said.

"Or maybe a little dark-haired one with your brown eyes." He laid a hand on her knee and squeezed gently.

The waitress brought over two glasses of water and set them on the table. "Can I get y'all some appetizers or something to drink other than water?"

"Sweet tea," Pax said.

"Lemonade, and maybe an order of fried green tomatoes. I'm ready to order now too," Alana said. "I'll have the meat loaf special with green beans, mashed potatoes, and brown gravy, and a side salad with ranch dressing."

"The same," Pax said.

"Have those drinks and tomatoes right out," the waitress said and hurried back toward the kitchen.

"Okay, now that we've discussed a girl's name, let's talk about the divorce issue," Pax said. "Can we stay married until the baby is born at least? I can't stand the thought of not being there with you. What if you fell or you wanted watermelon at two in the morning?"

"The longer we put it off, the harder it will get," she cautioned.

"Maybe," Pax agreed, "or maybe we'll both be ready to call it quits by then. I'll even sleep in a different room if that's what you want, so that at least you won't be in that big house all alone."

"That does scare me a little," she admitted. "Not that I haven't ever stayed alone, but to actually be there by myself if something were to happen where either you or the baby's concerned, spooks me a little. I can't believe we're talking about this, Pax. When I asked you to help me make Daddy happy with a fake engagement and wedding, I never intended for us to have sex, much less to do it without protection."

"I know sweetheart," he said. "But like our folks have told us for years, everything happens for a reason."

Chapter Nineteen

Is there such a thing as a lie not being a lie?

That's what Alana typed into the search engine on her phone as she and Pax drove back to the parking lot at the doctor's office so she could get her truck. The answer she got was exactly what she needed to hear, and it came from an educated psychiatrist: Lying is not harmful or deceptive if someone lies in order to refrain from hurting another's feelings or to help them over a difficult situation.

"I didn't have a malicious bone in my body when I set this little ball in motion," she muttered.

Pax turned down the volume on the radio "What did you say?"

"I just read this"—she read the exact quote from her phone—"and I said that I didn't tell Daddy that first lie with anything mean in my heart."

"Of course, you didn't." Pax took her hand in his. "I'm

a little worried about how we're goin' to tell him about the baby. We'll be together, but which one of us will actually say the words?"

"I'll do it," Alana said. "At least, it's the solid truth, and I've got the pictures to prove it."

He parked right beside her truck, and she kissed him on the cheek before she got out. "Thanks, again, for being there for me."

"Whoa, let's talk a minute," he said before she could slam the door shut.

"What about?" she asked.

"Are we telling him as soon as we get to the ranch, or tonight after supper, or when?"

"The sooner the better," she answered. "If he's in the house, we'll tell him right then. If he doesn't come in until supper, I'll give you a call, and you can come over and we'll tell him then. We'll have to play it by ear."

"Okay, then," he said with a smile.

The ranch was five miles from town, and Pax didn't seem to be in a bit of a hurry to get there. Alana was following him, and he drove slowly, probably so that the dust wouldn't boil up from the back of his truck and settle all over hers. But the recent rain had left the roads still a little wet, so when Pax turned down the dirt road leading to the ranch there was nothing to fly back. "The rain was kind of like today, and cleared up my mind," she said out loud. "I keep our deception to myself, and Daddy goes to his grave with peace in his heart, not turmoil over the lies I told in his final weeks."

She was singing along with the radio when she turned down the tree-lined lane to the Bar C ranch and smiled when she parked her truck. Pax hadn't gotten out of his yet, and she knew the reason. He thought it was bad luck to ever not finish listening to a song. He'd sit there until it ended, and from the way his head was bobbing, she figured he was listening to the same station she was. Travis Tritt was singing, "Best of Intentions," and although most of the lyrics didn't apply to their situation, the idea kind of did.

When the last piano note played, Pax got out of his truck and hurried around to open her door. "Had to hear the song to the end," he explained.

"I remember that from high school." She slid out of the seat. "Why do you think you always have to listen to the whole song?"

He picked up her hand and looped it through his arm. "Grandpa was superstitious about that, so I adopted it from him. When I was a little boy we'd be out in the barn or in the field, and he'd be listenin' to music. Depending on where we were, it might be the old red radio from the 1950s he kept in the tack room, or it might be the one in his truck. It didn't matter if Mam rang the dinner bell to call us in, or whatever was going on, he finished listenin' to the song. I always hoped that he didn't die in the middle of a tune. We found him with the radio blaring out an old George Jones tune called 'Who's Gonna Fill Their Shoes' the day he died."

"Hey, where y'all been?" Matt asked from the porch swing. "Had your dinner? There's a pot of chili keepin' warm on the back of the stove if you're hungry."

"We ate in town," Alana answered.

"Thanks, anyway." Pax dragged a couple of rocking chairs across the porch so that he and Alana could sit beside each other facing Matt.

"I'm worried, baby girl. Someone called me to say that your truck was parked at the doctor's office for hours this morning. You know that you can't hide anything from the gossips in Daisy, Texas."

When had her father's face gotten so wrinkled? Alana wondered. He wasn't even sixty years old, for God's sake. In their Christmas picture, he sure hadn't looked so old. She plopped down in one of the rockers.

"I'm pregnant," Alana blurted out. "Pax and I went to the doctor to be sure this morning. I'm only two weeks along. The baby is due sometime around Valentine's Day."

"Thank God!" Matt wiped a hand down over his face. "I was scared to death that maybe something was really wrong and you didn't want to tell me." Suddenly, he smiled and looked ten years younger. "This is the best news ever. We never told you, but your mother and I had to go through a fertility process to get you, and your mama could never have more children. I've been so worried that you might have inherited something like she had and wouldn't be able to have children. This is the best news ever. I can't wait to get to heaven and tell Joy that she's going to be a grandmother."

"Don't be in too big of a rush," Pax said. "We want you to stick around as long as possible, Matt."

Alana pushed up out of her chair and went to hug her father. "Daddy, I'm so sorry I worried you. I've kind of suspected all weekend, but I wanted to be sure before I said anything." No way would she tell him that she'd been scared out of her mind that she also had cancer. "Want to see the pictures?"

Huge tears rolled down Matt's cheeks when she pulled back and reached for her purse. "Of course. Even if it's a little peanut right now, at least I get to see my grandchild before I go to be with your mama."

"It's barely the size of a pea," Pax said, "and, Matt, we

promise that we'll do our best to be the kind of parents that you and Mam have been to us."

"I don't have a single doubt." Matt dragged a hanky out of his pocket and wiped his eyes. "Can't have the baby see her grandpa cryin' the first time he sees her."

"It might be a boy, Daddy," Alana said.

He shook his head slowly. "I want y'all to have a daughter first time around. God owes me that much for not letting me stick around to help raise her."

"And we'll name her Something Joy," Pax teased.

"Hush, right now!" Alana pointed a finger at him. "He's been teasing me all day."

"Your mama would be honored to have you keep the name Joy. That goes back about six generations in her family." Matt inhaled and let it out slowly. "I'm so blessed to have this bit of news."

"We feel the same way," Pax said. "And thank you for not dragging out the shotgun and forcing us to the church right now. We're kind of lookin' forward to the big wedding here at the Bar C."

Matt chuckled. "I might have done that if y'all were still in high school, but time and circumstances have changed a lot. Let's go have a beer to celebrate."

"Y'all can have a beer." Alana stood up and put her hand in Pax's. "I'll have lemonade."

"I'll have lemonade too," Pax said. "If you have to give up alcohol until the baby is born, it's only fair that I do the same."

Matt got to his feet and patted Pax on the back. "Now, there's a man worth ridin' the river with, girl."

"Amen," Alana agreed.

* * *

On Tuesday morning, Pax awoke to the sound of Laela giggling. His first thought as he sat up in bed was that next year at this time, he could be waking up to his own child's laughter. Strangely enough, the idea didn't give him hives or put him into flight-or-fight mode. He threw his long legs over the side of the bed, got dressed, and opened the door to find Laela chasing the cat toward the living room. Poor old Dolly was barely staying out of reach, as if she were playing a game with the baby.

Maverick and Bridget were both in the kitchen, as usual. Bridget was stirring a pan full of sausage gravy, and Maverick was setting the table. Pax leaned on the doorjamb for a little while and drank in the scene. He wanted what they had so bad that it left a bittersweet ache in his heart. But even if he and Alana stayed together for years for the baby's sake, he'd always wonder if she would have been happier with someone else.

Finally, he pushed away from the doorjamb and said, "Hey, y'all, I've got some news to share with you. Alana's pregnant."

Bridget dropped her spoon on the floor. Maverick had been putting a spoon on Laela's tray and he froze like a statue.

"Are you serious?" Bridget whispered.

"Yep," Pax answered. "She's only two weeks along right now, but she's definitely got a bun in the oven. We were at the doctor's yesterday, and we even heard the heartbeat. I would have told y'all last night, but..." he stammered.

"What happened last night?" Iris came into the kitchen with Laela in her arms.

"Looks like Pax and Alana weren't teasing at dinner on Sunday," Maverick said as he laid the spoon down.

"About what?" Iris asked.

"Alana is pregnant," Pax said. "We weren't sure until yesterday, and I waited to tell y'all until we could all be together. You were off all afternoon with your church friends, Mam."

"Congratulations," Iris said. "Now you don't have to argue about when to start your family, do you?"

"How do you feel about being a father?" Maverick clamped a hand on his shoulder.

"How did you?" Pax laid his hand over his brother's.

"I fell in love with Laela the minute I laid eyes on her," Maverick replied. "She might not be mine or Bridget's by blood, but by golly, she belongs to the both of us by heart. But you didn't answer my question."

"Great," Pax said. "Absolutely wonderful."

By birth, Laela belonged to another couple. Her mother had been Bridget's best friend, Deidre, over in Ireland. When she and Laela's father both died in a car accident, Bridget had taken Laela to raise. Maverick was in the process of adopting her and making her a true Callahan.

"And Matt?" Iris asked. "Does he know?"

"Yes, and he's happy about it," Pax said.

"You do know that fifty years ago, he might have gotten down his shotgun?" Iris said.

"Oh, yeah, I do." Pax nodded.

Bridget picked up the spoon she'd dropped, tossed it in the sink, and crossed the floor to give Paxton a hug. "This is wonderful news. Our new baby and yours will grow up together. Little cousins on ranches right next to each other. I can't think of anything more precious." She wiped at a tear with the tail of her apron. "Damn pregnancy hormones. They've got me weeping at the least little thing these days."

"Thank you all for your support." Pax had trouble swallowing the lump in his own throat.

"I guess I'll have to believe there will definitely be a wedding now," Maverick said.

"I've told you from the beginning that there would be." Pax poured four cups of coffee and carried them, two at a time, to the table.

The wedding had always been a definite thing, Pax thought. Now all he had to do was to convince Alana not to divorce him as soon as Matt had passed away. He didn't want to be a weekend father or even one who lived across the barbed-wire fence. He wanted to be there for every hour, every minute, every second, of his child's life.

* * *

"Hump Day." Alana covered a yawn with the back of her hand when she reached the kitchen that morning. "What do you have going today, Daddy?"

"I'm meeting with the committee for the Daisy Days Festival," he said. "We've got to iron out the final details about getting Main Street blocked off, rerouting any traffic around the carnival that will be set up in that area and extending on down to the park. Just take care of the last-minute things."

"They're goin' to miss you," she muttered.

"I'm glad to hear you say that, Alana," he said. "It means that you're accepting the inevitable and moving forward."

"We knew that Mama wasn't going to make it," Alana told him. "But that didn't stop the pain when it happened."

"But it eased it," Matt told her. "We didn't want her to suffer any more, so we let her go. It would have been selfish of us to want to keep her and let her suffer the way she was. I wish the two of us could have had another child or two. That way you'd have some siblings to help you get through all this. Thank God for Paxton and his family. I'll go in peace, knowing that you are in good hands."

Alana poured a cup of coffee and sat down at the table with him. "Maybe I'll go with you this morning."

"I'd like that," Matt said. "How about we go get some breakfast at the café before we go to the meeting?"

"Sounds great to me." Alana took a sip of her coffee and then pushed her chair back. "I can be ready in half an hour."

"That should work out fine," Matt said. "And Pax is coming with us. I'm going to resign today, and recommend they give you and Pax my job as coordinator of the whole festival. It's time you two stepped up and started helping with the community."

"Yes, sir," she said as she carried her coffee up to her room.

She stripped out of her clothing, turned on the shower, and laid a hand on her stomach. "I have to be an adult now, whether I'm ready or not. Three weeks ago, I thought my daddy would live to be an old man. I sure wouldn't have guessed that in less than a month, I'd be looking at the end of his life and the beginning of yours."

She talked to herself and the baby all through her shower and while she got ready. When she made it back downstairs, Pax was already there. He and Matt were deep in conversation and didn't even hear her coming. She stood in the foyer and watched them looking over a paper that had been rolled out and covered the coffee table. Matt pointed to one end, and Pax frowned.

"I think it might work better here," her fiancé said. "It's

on a little bit higher ground, and the trees won't be the problem that they would be in the park."

Matt pursed his lips and nodded. "You're right. This is why we need new blood on the committee." He picked up a pencil, erased a few lines, and penciled them in over at the other end.

"You guys going to talk about whatever that is, or are you going to take this hungry, pregnant woman to breakfast?" Alana asked.

Pax shot to his feet, crossed the room, and kissed her. "Good mornin', darlin'. You look fabulous."

"I hope you're still saying that at Christmas." She wasn't so sure anymore if they had or had not crossed the line from pretend to real.

Matt stood up, rolled up the paper they had been looking at, and secured it with a rubber band. "Oh, honey, he will be. Your mama was at her most beautiful when she was carrying you. The rush at the café should be over by now, so let's go get us a plate of bacon and eggs."

"Where's the meeting going to be held?" Pax asked.

"In the community room of the bank, right next door to the café," Matt answered. "There's about fifteen of us that's been on the committee for years. Some new young'uns to help carry on the tradition will be good." He settled his cowboy hat on his head. "We'll take Pax's truck, and I get the backseat. I kind of like being chauffeured around like a celebrity."

"Please don't ask me to trade my cowboy hat in on one of those chauffeur-type things," Pax chuckled.

"Never." Matt pretended to shudder. "That would be like blasphemy for a cowboy."

"How about you, darlin'?" Pax whispered. "Would you like me to wear a fancy little hat and polished shoes?"

"Not even if we were role-playin'," she said. "But now if you wanted to wear a pair of chaps and your cowboy hat and nothing else to bed"—she hip-butted him—"I wouldn't mind playing that game."

"Be careful what you ask for, sweetheart." Pax's green eyes twinkled. "You might get more than you bargained for."

Chapter Twenty

No one would ever doubt that Pax and Alana were truly engaged if they saw them walking through the blocked-off section of Main Street and the park that Saturday afternoon arm in arm, laughing and smiling at each other. They stopped by a vendor and got a small order of fried shrimp to share and by another one for jalapeño poppers. Then they had snow cones and later in the afternoon, they shared a funnel cake, with Paxton breaking pieces of it off with his fingers and feeding it to his bride-to-be. To anyone looking on, they were another couple madly in love. And throughout the whole day, Pax had the feeling that someone was watching him. Several times he whipped around and scanned the crowd to see if he could catch anyone following close behind them.

"What's wrong with you?" Alana finally asked.

"Guess I've been watching too many reruns of cop shows," he admitted. "It feels to me like someone is watching me or maybe even following us."

"Good," she sighed. "I've had the same feeling, but I didn't want to say anything. Must be the devil licking at our heels for all the lies we've told."

"Could be, but your dad is a happy man, and I kind of doubt that the feller with the pitchfork is that interested in us. He's got bigger fish to fry than to chase after a couple who are trying to make a man happy." Pax pulled a bite of funnel cake off and fed it to Alana, then popped another piece into his mouth.

"Honestly, I imagine we're feeling what we are because there are so many strangers in town," Alana said. "Some of them are the carnies and vendors, but folks from as far away as Midland and Dalhart come down here for the festival. We're used to walking down the streets and knowing everyone we meet and their families from two or three generations. And folks in Daisy have known us since we were babies."

"You got a point there, but I've still got an eerie feeling," he said.

Alana nudged him with her shoulder. "Think it might be that blond beach boy back there at the sunglasses vendor, lookin' for a new pair of shades?"

Pax turned around slowly. "Oh, yeah, that's him all right. He's got to be with the carnival with that shaggy blond hair and that scraggly beard. And would you look at his boots? Those aren't real cowboy boots, and I don't believe he's a genuine cowboy."

"What's the difference in those he's wearin' or what you would call real ones?" she asked.

"You see any bullshit on his boots? Any wear on the heels? His boots are brand-new and barely broken in. Not even a scuff mark on them."

She sat down on a park bench. "I sure don't. I'm guessin'

he's a lawyer by day and thinks he can two-step in a bar like the Wild Cowboy on Saturday night. He's hoping to show off his dancin' skills and take a bar bunny home with him for the night."

"With that hair and scraggly beard?" Pax sat down beside her and shook his head. "He's not even from Texas, and he's never been to a western bar. He's sure not a lawyer with that long hair. Maybe some kind of con artist."

"Who does he remind you of, anyway?" Alana asked.

"I don't know." Pax drew his dark brows down and tried to place the kid. "Maybe one of the hands by the name of Jake that's been helping out on our ranch this summer."

"No, Jake is just a kid. That man's got to be at least twenty-two or twenty-three." She shot another quick look his way. "I know who it is. He looks a little bit like Marty Deeks."

"Who in the hell is that?"

"He's a character on *NCIS: Los Angeles*," she said. "He's a detective with the Los Angeles Police Department on the show, and he's also a lawyer, so that kid could be an attorney even with that hair. He's a little taller than Deeks, and his hair is a shade or two lighter, but the rest of him sure looks like Marty."

"A Hollywood actor in Daisy, Texas? That would cause a big hullabaloo, wouldn't it? But I can see a little re- semblance to that character. Guess we've finally attracted the rich and famous to our little Daisy Days Festival." Pax loved playing games like this with Alana. "So what about that woman who's checkin' him out while he's checkin' out sunglasses? Is she fixin' to flirt with him?"

"Oh, yeah, she is," Alana said without hesitation. "And then she's going to go home this evening to whatever Podunk town she lives in to tell all her friends and neighbors that she saw a real movie star. But then, the way she's been lookin' at you, she'll probably not even see him." Alana finished off the last bite of funnel cake and threw the paper plate in a trash bin near the end of the bench. "I could sure use a root beer."

"Me too." Pax stood up and headed over to the concession trailer that happened to be parked right next to the sunglasses where Hollywood was still looking at shades. Then he turned and looked over his shoulder. "What size, darlin'?"

Her wicked grin told him a smart-ass remark was on the way. "Size doesn't usually matter, but I'd like a big one this time."

"Your wish and all that hogwash," he joked right back at her.

"What's hogwash?" the guy they'd been discussing asked.

"Nonsense," Pax told him. "You part of the carnival crew?"

"Nope. I just got into town and thought I'd see what all the fuss was about." The young man smiled and be damned if Pax couldn't see even more of that television character.

"Our annual Daisy Days Festival is always held on the Saturday before Memorial Day," Pax said. "You enjoyin' it?"

"I guess so. I'm Landon Griffin." The kid stuck out his hand.

"Paxton Callahan." Pax shook with him. "Enjoy your visit to our town."

"Thanks," Landon said. "I sure hope I will."

Pax got two large cups of root beer and carried them back to where Alana was sitting. "His name is Landon Griffin. Is that your Marty Deeks?"

"Nope, I looked it up while you were talking to him. In real life Marty is Eric Christian Olsen, and I found out that he's got a brother who is his stunt double. Interesting, huh?"

"Yep, but the guy is just a kid in town for the festival," Pax said.

"Okay, then how about that short brunette over there by the jewelry vendor? What's she doin' here? She looks like pictures I've seen of gypsies," Alana said.

"She'd definitely with the carnival." Pax played along.

"How do you know?" Alana asked.

"Her picture is on the poster that's been up all over town," Pax said with a straight face. "That's the fortune-teller."

The woman turned around, and Alana slapped Pax on the arm. "You had me believing you. That's Rachel."

Pax blew on his arm. "Mosquitoes do seem to be bad around here today," he joked and then leaned over to whisper, "maybe she'll run away with the carnival and *become* a gypsy fortune-teller."

"From your lips to the carnie owner's ears," Alana said.

* * *

The festival was a two-day affair. The carnival had moved into town on Friday evening, had gotten set up and ready for business. Saturday was the big day. Sunday was a little slower, but still not too bad. On Monday, the carnies broke down their equipment, packed up, and moved on to the next town, usually up to Goodnight, where the next big to-do would be held next weekend.

Time had been when neither Pax nor Alana would have gotten home on Saturday night until after midnight the weekend of the festival, but that evening they'd seen all they wanted to see and visited with everyone they knew by nine o'clock. The stars were dimmed by all the carnival lights, and the smell of so many foods mingling together wasn't so appealing anymore. Maverick and Bridget had gone home an hour before to put a tired and cranky Laela to bed. Iris had declared that she'd had enough and gone with them.

"Look at us," Alana said as Pax parked in front of her house. "We must be engaged tonight, because if we were dating, we'd be out until dawn."

"We're pregnant," he reminded her. "The baby needs its rest. I read an article this week that said if the mother stays up half the night, then the baby will do the same when it's born. So if you want to get much sleep after she gets here, then you better keep an early schedule until then."

"She?" Alana asked.

"Your dad seems pretty sure we're having a girl," Pax said.

"Well, if Daddy is wrong, don't you think it might give a boy a complex to hear himself referred to as *she* for nine months?" Alana undid her seat belt, slid over, and kissed him.

"Maybe not this early. Want to make a trip by the tack room?" *He* kissed *her* this time and teased her lips open with the tip of his tongue.

"Love to, but I'm flat out too tired," she said when the kiss ended. "Walk me to the door, like that old song says. Kiss me one more time, and then let me get some sleep. We'll sneak off to the tack room tomorrow after church. You can bring your chaps and boots."

He opened the door to his truck, stepped out, and leaned back inside. "Darlin', that would be more than you could stand."

"Try me." She flashed a brilliant smile at him.

He rounded the front end of the truck and opened the

door for her. Then he whistled the old tune about walking her to the door all the way to the porch. He stopped at the top of the steps, put his hands on her shoulders, and drew her lips to his for one more scalding hot kiss. "Who needs role-play when we have enough heat between us to burn down the state of Texas?"

"How about *I* wear chaps and boots and nothing else?" she teased.

Pax groaned. "You're killin' me, woman."

"Try to keep that picture out of your dreams tonight," she whispered seductively into his ear.

Dreams, hell! he thought as he kissed her once more. Then he jogged to his truck. He'd have trouble getting that vision out of his head in his *waking* moments, never mind in his dreams. He was still smiling at Alana's sassiness when he passed a guy walking along the edge of the road. The man had a backpack slung over his shoulder, a stocking hat on his head, and was wearing baggy jeans. *Not anyone from around here,* Pax thought, but the guy looked vaguely familiar. He wasn't thumbing a ride, and Pax was a full fifty yards down the road when his conscience got the best of him. He pulled over and waited until the man caught up and then rolled down the window.

"Where you headed, buddy?" Pax asked. "Need a ride? Did you have car trouble back down the road?" Pax asked.

"Headed to the Callahan Ranch," the guy said. "I'd love a ride. Didn't realize that five miles was so far away. Hey, I met you at the festival this afternoon."

Paxton finally recognized the guy as the kid he'd talked to back at the sunglass vendor. What did he say his name was? Marty Deeks? No, that was the character that Alana talked about on the television show. Landon...something or other.

"That's right. I remember you," Pax said as he shifted into gear and started off again.

"Yep, I heard y'all might be hirin' some help on your ranch," Landon said.

"We usually only take on summer help, and we've pretty much got all we need right now, but we can talk to my brother, Maverick, when we get to the house." Pax turned into the lane. "Where do you come from? Got any ranchin' experience?"

"I've lived in California all my life. I've worked on a ranch before, but it was a smaller one," he answered.

Where would they put this guy if they did hire him? Their summer help showed up for work at seven in the morning and left sometime in the afternoon around four or five, depending on the work they had to do that day. If Maverick decided they didn't need him, Pax would at least offer to haul him back to town. The kid didn't look too prosperous. If he didn't already have a room out at the Cowboy Motel, the only place in town where folks could stay, then Pax would get him one for the night. Anyone who was willing to walk five miles to ask for a job deserved that much.

"This is it," Pax said when he parked the truck in front of the house. "I'll be able to take you back to town if we decide that we can't use another hand."

"Thank you." Landon nodded. "I'm used to running five miles every morning, but this late in the evening, I'd appreciate the ride."

Maverick and Iris were sitting on the porch when Landon and Pax walked up. Pax sat down on the top porch step and left the last rocking chair for Landon. There was something about the fellow's green eyes that looked familiar, Pax thought, but then, he had watched reruns of *NCIS:*

Los Angeles a few times, so maybe it was the fact that he looked a lot like that character, Marty Deeks, that Alana had mentioned.

"This is Landon Griffin," Pax said by way of introduction and motioned toward the empty chair with a wave of his hand. "Have a seat. I found him walking out here from town."

"What brings you out here to our ranch?" Maverick asked.

"I'm here for three reasons." Landon reached down and started to unzip his backpack.

"Whoa!" Iris put up a hand. "You're a stranger here, son. I'm not stupid. You could have a gun in that bag, and be here to rob us or do us harm. Kick that thing over to Pax and let him take a look inside it before you go diggin' in it."

Landon used the toe of his boot to slide the backpack across the porch. "I promise I'm not here to hurt anyone. Go ahead and take a look. I've got nothing to hide from you people."

"You ain't from the South, are you?" Iris asked.

"No, ma'am," Landon said. "Never been in Texas before today. I've flown over it a few times, but on land, I've not been outside of California. Mother preferred an airplane to a car."

Pax found a stack of letters tied with a faded red ribbon and a manila envelope that contained a bunch of documents in the bag, plus a couple of books, but nothing suspicious. "It's all good," he said. "No guns, or knives or anything harmful."

"Okay, go on," Iris said.

"Mother said you were a character." Landon smiled.

"How'd your mama know me?" Iris eyed him with a frown on her face.

"First, let me give you these letters. They rightfully belong to you, not me," Landon said.

"Who are you?" Pax frowned.

"Those are the letters that you two guys wrote to your mother when you were little boys," he said. "I found them in her things. She died two weeks ago of lung cancer."

Pax took the bundle from him and immediately recognized his own handwriting from when he was a child. Big block letters on the top envelope said TERESA and below that was an address in California. He undid the ribbon and took out the ones he'd written, then passed the others over to Maverick. Pax clamped his teeth together so tightly that his jaws ached. He remembered putting those letters in the mailbox and waiting for days for something in return. The only thing that he and Maverick ever got back was an occasional birthday card. Even those had stopped after a couple of years. She had come to see them that first Christmas, but she'd only stayed a few hours. Two years later, she popped in for a little while on New Year's Eve. That had been the year that Pax was nine—or had he been ten? What a time to dredge up all those memories, right when he had so many things on his plate.

"How'd you come to have those?" Iris nodded toward the letters in Maverick's hand.

"Our mother is dead?" Maverick asked.

Pax cocked his head to one side. "How did you get these again?"

"Like I said, I was going through her stuff. She never was one to save anything, not money or anything else. Not even my high school diploma or pictures of me through the years. As far as money, it was all gone after I took care of her medical bills. I found a bank deposit key in a shoe box that only had pictures of her taken through the years of her life. When I went to the bank, those letters were in it with a few other things. Here's the next thing I want you to see, but it belongs to me. I knew you'd need proof, so I brought it and some other documents with me." He handed a legal paper to Pax.

"It's a birth certificate." Pax held it up to the porch light so he could read it. "'Landon Carl Griffin, born to Carl Griffin and Teresa Griffin on July 30, 1997.' That makes you twenty-two years old in a couple of months."

"And that makes him your half-brother," Iris said. "Teresa left here with a man named Carl Griffin."

"That's right," Landon said. "Carl Griffin was my dad. He died when I was ten. Mother died without ever telling me that I had brothers. Now, they are both gone and y'all are the only family I have left. I'm not here for a handout or to ask for anything other than a job. I sold my car for enough money to get here. I recently graduated from college with a business degree. I had no idea that Mother had spent every dime of the money Daddy left for me until she was gone, but that was her. I loved her, but she liked to live above her means." He stopped and blinked several times.

"You got any ranchin' experience," Maverick asked.

"Little bit," Landon answered with a nod. "Mother hated anything to do with ranching, but she sent me off to summer camp every year from the time I was five. When I was ten she let me choose which one I wanted to go to, and my friends and I picked a working ranch. Maybe she hoped that I'd get my fill of cowboys and hate it. My friends certainly did, but I loved it. When I got to be sixteen, they hired me as a counselor, and I got to work with underprivileged kids. I'm talking too much, but yes, I do have a little bit of experience. I'll work for room and board only if you'll have me. I've got no place to live or to go until I find a job where I can use my degree. I guess y'all don't need a business manager, do you?"

Pax knew he was staring at the fellow, but he couldn't stop. The young man had the same green eyes that he and Maverick had inherited from their mother. That's why those eyes had looked familiar when he met him at the park. Now that Pax had heard his story and seen his birth certificate he had no doubt that he was Teresa's son. The wide, full lips and shape of his face both were like hers.

"I wanted to tell you who I was back in town when you caught me following you," Landon told Pax, "but it didn't seem like the right place, and besides, I wanted to tell both of you at the same time. If that ride into town still stands, I might take you up on it, now. I've got a room for one night at that little Cowboy Motel. The rest of my stuff is there."

"Nonsense!" Iris said. "He's your family, and we don't turn family out in the cold. Me and the girls all were plannin' on stayin' over at the Bar C when they get here, anyway. I'll call Alana to come get me, and I'll go on over there tonight. I know she won't mind, and Landon here can have my room."

"Thank you," Landon said. "I meant it when I said I'd work for room and board. You guys are my half-brothers, but you don't owe me anything."

"Tell us about our mother." Maverick's voice sounded more than a little hoarse.

"She and my dad liked to be on the go, so I was left with a nanny a lot. Looking back, I wonder if I wasn't an accident or maybe the way to get my dad to marry her because he had money at the time. She was three months pregnant with me when they…" He shrugged and went silent for a minute or two. "The last year, when she knew she was dying, she kind of depended on me, and we got closer than we'd ever been. I hate to tell you this, but I never really knew her all that well. She never, ever told me about you guys. I found your letters after she was gone."

"How did you find us anyway?" Pax asked.

"The return address on the letters was a starting place, and then I made a few phone calls and found out that you still lived here on the ranch, so I bought a bus ticket. I got into town this morning," he said.

"How'd you know that I was your brother?" Pax asked.

Landon pulled a picture from a shirt pocket and handed it to him. "That's one of the photographs I found in the bank box. *Teresa and Barton on their wedding day* is written on the back. You're a dead ringer for your father."

"I always said the same thing." Iris stood up and headed toward the house. "I'll have my things ready when Alana gets here. Y'all have lots to talk about, I'm sure."

"We'll pay you minimum wage, like we do the kids who work for us," Maverick said, "and believe me, you will earn every dime of it."

"Yes, sir." Landon nodded. "I'm not allergic to hard work, and I'm glad to have the job. You won't have to bird-dog me."

"What did you say?" Iris stopped in her tracks.

"Point me in the direction for every thing that needs to be done," he explained.

"I know what bird-doggin' is," Iris said. "I haven't heard that expression used since my husband died."

"I worked with a salty old cowboy on the ranch where I spent my summers." Landon smiled for the first time. "He used it a lot."

"I see." Iris went into the house and left them alone on the porch.

"I'm sure you have more questions, so ask away," Landon said.

"She never told you about us?" Pax asked.

"Not one time," Landon answered.

"Did you ever wonder about her past? Where she came from? If you had siblings or maybe cousins, you might have on her side of the family—or even grandparents?" Maverick asked.

"She told me that she had been married before and talked a little about Iris, but she didn't mention that I had brothers," Landon said. "When I asked her to tell me more, she said she'd grown up in foster care. Do you know something different?"

"Little bit," Maverick said. "She had a brother who died when Pax and I were little kids. I remember going to his funeral. Mam told us when we asked about him years later that he had two kids with his wife, and twins by his mistress who were born at the same time as his last son with his wife. The wife took her two boys to Canada, where she was from originally, and the mistress was from North Dakota, so she went back there with her son and daughter. The family had lost track of them long before her brother died. So, we have four cousins out there in the wilds somewhere. Our grandparents on that side died sometime before I was born. She wasn't an orphan and she didn't grow up in foster care. She grew up in Dallas, Texas. Her dad worked for the sanitation department, and her mother was a kindergarten teacher. They both retired and died within a year of each other."

"Did y'all get to see them often?" Landon asked.

Pax shook his head. "Maybe a dozen times in our entire

lives. They didn't like our father. From what we've pieced together, they thought she married down when she wed a rancher."

"Nothing much surprises me about Mother anymore," Landon said. "She was a complicated woman. I often wondered if maybe she had some mental-health issues. When she was in a good mood, she was fun, but when she was in one of her bad moods, I stayed over at a friend's house."

"I have a question," Pax said. "What would you have done if we'd told you to get lost?"

"You don't owe me anything at all, so I would have gotten lost," Landon said. "I love being on a ranch. I like working outside with my hands. But if I was in your boots, I might have told you to hit the road. Our mother abandoned you and what attention she had to give anyone fell on me. You could resent me for that, but I'm glad you're willing to give me a chance."

"You've got a home here," Pax said. "I'm getting married and moving over to the Bar C Ranch next door in a little more than a week, so even with a new baby coming, there'll be plenty of room," Pax said. "Your first job will be to make the tack room into your own living quarters. You should only have to sleep on the sofa a couple of nights." As he finished talking Alana's truck pulled into their driveway.

She parked, got out of the truck, and crossed the lawn to the porch. "Where's Iris? I understand she's coming over to my place. She didn't say why, but if y'all have hurt her feelings, I'm here to whoop up on whoever did it."

"Meet our half-brother, Landon Griffin," Pax said, and then gave her the short version of what Landon had told them.

"We've got two extra beds out in the bunkhouse over

on the Bar C, and Lucas is always looking for experienced hands," Alana offered. "We could probably use his expertise a little later with the bookkeeping part of ranchin' if things work out. Get your stuff together, Landon. I'm stealing you from the Callahans."

Landon looked over at Pax with questions written all over his face. "Is your fiancée serious?"

"Yep," Pax answered, and then turned to Alana. "Are you sure?"

"Yep, I'm sure," Alana answered and turned to Landon. "I'll call Lucas right now and tell him you're comin' in a few minutes. Pax and I will be married, so you'll still be working for one of your brothers."

"Don't you need to check references?" Landon asked. "I have a list of them."

"We'll know by Tuesday night if you're the real deal or a wannabe cowboy," Alana said. "Two days with my foreman, Lucas, will tell the tale."

"A word please." Pax stood up, took Alana by the arm, and led her over behind her truck. "Are you absolutely sure about this?"

"Honey, he's your half-brother, and that means our child has another uncle, which is good. You don't really know him, and he could be some kind of con artist, so it's best that he doesn't live here on the Callahan Ranch with little Laela and your family. Lucas will see there's a man behind his words, and if there is, we can use him on the Bar C." She put her arms around his neck and brought his lips to hers. When the kiss ended, she said, "Let's give him a couple of days to prove himself. I'll feel better knowing he's out in the bunkhouse with Lucas instead of in this house with Bridget and the baby. If he is on the up-and-up, then it's all a win-win situation."

"Hey, do you think I could get that ride back to town to get my things?" Landon hollered across the lawn.

"Go on and get in my truck," Pax said and then turned his attention back to Alana. "Talk about tangled webs. Guess they extend farther back than the first of this month. I'll call you and tell you all about it later. The crazy thing is I still got a lump in my throat at the idea of my mother being dead. I haven't seen her since I was a little boy, but somehow, I never thought of her dying before I'd see her again."

"She was your mother," Alana said. "You only get one. Good, bad, or ugly, it's natural that you'd mourn for her a little."

"Woman, you've got a big heart, and you always know what to say and what to do in any situation." He kissed her on the cheek. "I'll call you in a little while."

"Don't call me. Come and sit on the porch with me a little while when you get our television star delivered to Lucas."

Pax chuckled and drew her close to him for another kiss. "Get us a couple of lemonades poured up, and I'll try to be there in twenty minutes."

"What's goin' on out here? Maverick said that there's been a change in plans, and I'm not leaving tonight," Iris asked as she stepped out onto the porch.

"Yes, ma'am." Alana raised her voice. "I stole the new ranch hand. He's going to live in my bunkhouse and work for us. Pax is taking him back to town for his stuff and then bringing him over to the Bar C to turn him over to Lucas."

"Wonderful idea," Iris hollered. "Welcome to Texas, Landon Griffin."

He had already started toward the truck, but he turned

and waved at her. "Thank you. I think I'm going to like it here fine."

"Whew!" Pax shook his head in disbelief. "Just when I thought we'd jumped the last hurdle..."

"There's another one," Alana finished the sentence for him. "But we're proving that we do a pretty good job of getting over them if we hold hands and jump together."

Chapter Twenty-One

"So how do you feel about this new kid brother?" Pax asked Maverick at the breakfast table the next morning.

"When I went to sleep last night, I was mad as hell," he said. "She threw us away like we were trash because her new husband didn't want to raise another man's children, or so she said. But it doesn't take a genius to know that she never wanted us, the way she left us with Mam and Grandpa so much of the time. Then she goes and has another baby less than a year after Daddy's death?"

"That's not Landon's fault," Bridget said as she put a platter of muffins on the table. "He didn't even know he had brothers. I didn't bloody well know you had secret cousins who could come out of the woodwork at any time. What are you going to do if your uncle's kids come around wanting jobs or even handouts?"

Bridget's Irish accent got thicker when she was excited, but she was right. He and Maverick hadn't talked about their cousins in years, had in fact kind of pushed them out of their minds when Teresa had forsaken them. But somewhere out there were three guy cousins and one girl who would be somewhere in the neighborhood of the same age as he and Maverick. Pax remembered a couple of them coming to visit a few times, but he hadn't been more than five years old at the time, and he couldn't even bring up their faces or names in his memories.

Maverick raised a shoulder in half a shrug. "She's right. It's not Landon's fault, but I have to admit that I'm glad Alana offered to house him at her place. I wasn't real comfortable about bringing a stranger into the house."

"I would have protected y'all." Iris set a platter of ham and eggs on the table. "I didn't have a bad feeling about that kid. I kind of felt sorry for him. I knew your mama very well, and Teresa was always high maintenance as you kids call it today. She was more into her looks than her marriage to y'all's father, and poor old Barton loved her too much to see past her narcissism. Landon had to live with her without the benefit of a brother or grandparents to help him get through it."

"Well, he's close enough now that we can get to know him better," Maverick said.

"Which is a good thing, and we owe Alana for that." Iris pulled out a chair and sat down.

And I owe her for so much more than that, Pax thought as he bowed his head for Iris to say grace.

* * *

The wedding folks arrived on Monday morning to begin to get the basic decorations up. Alana and Matt were in and out all day, making decisions and overseeing the work with Crystal. By evening, they were dragging and decided to have fried chicken delivered to the house instead of making supper.

Alana noticed that Matt had been sitting more than standing throughout the day, and that he often asked for spicy food when she gave him a choice. Tonight, he was content to sit in his recliner with his legs propped up, and he didn't even turn the television on.

"Just think, Alana. On Saturday you're going to be a married woman," Matt said.

And in two weeks from that day, your official time is up, she thought. *I'm praying you will be spared a little longer than that, but I don't want you to suffer.*

"Yep, and right now I wish it was all over. I never thought that a wedding would be so much work and trouble," she said.

"Trouble?" Matt frowned. "Honey, this has been so exciting, and these have been the happiest days that I ever imagined. You've given me a reason to keep going this month. I can't wait until all the girls are here on Thursday with their kids. It's going to be wonderful."

"It's going to be loud and noisy and crazy." Alana almost cried when she thought about almost telling him about the whole ruse. Lately, the line between what was real and what was part of the deception had blurred more and more. "You do realize that Retta has a toddler. Claire and Emily both have sons that aren't even crawling yet. And they're bringing Claire's coworker, Dixie, with them, too. She's got a little girl who's probably up and crawling. Bridget has promised that she'll come over in the evenings so we can all be together. Nikki and Rose are pregnant. It's going to be kids and women with pregnancy hormones,"

"This house was built for a big family, and it never got

to have one, so I'm going to love having the kids and the ladies here for a few days," he said. "Hell, I'd be happy if they all moved in permanently. I can't imagine anything better than having every bedroom in the place filled. I don't want you to worry about cooking while they're here, so I hired Trudy to come in on Thursday and Friday. Plus she'll be here to help out with whatever needs done until all this is over. It's almost here, Alana. My biggest dream is going to come true. Everything is going as planned and nothing is going to go wrong."

Alana giggled, and told him about the idea of putting Trudy on Rachel patrol for the wedding.

Matt narrowed his eyes and said, "That woman had better not ruin your wedding, and I agree, Trudy would be a good choice for that job. I'll talk to her about it, too. I never did like Rachel. She was mean to you when y'all were little girls."

There was something different in her father's voice when he spoke about Trudy, and Alana asked, "Daddy, why didn't you ever remarry?"

"Truth is I thought about asking Trudy out five years after your mother passed away. It had been a couple of years since her husband had left her with Bobby Ray to raise all by herself, and she's a nice-lookin' Christian woman. But I felt like I was cheating on your mother to even think such a thing, so I didn't. Besides, by then, you were fifteen, and we were settled into our own routine. I couldn't make myself bring a woman and a ten-year-old boy into our home," he answered.

Alana battled the tears welling up behind her eyes, but she lost the fight, and she grabbed a tissue. "You gave up any hope of companionship and a second chance at love for me?"

"And it was worth every bit of it," he said. "That chicken

better be here in five more minutes or I'm by damn going to complain that they're doin' false advertising. They said they'd be here in half an hour."

He had changed the subject to keep from crying with her, and she knew it. She wiped her eyes and said, "We'll give them an extra five, since we live a ways out of town, but if"—she stopped in the middle of the sentence and leaned to the left so she could hear better—"I hear a car coming and there's a truck right behind it."

"The truck will be Lucas. I told him to come eat with us tonight. We need to know how this new brother of Paxton's is working out after his first day on the job," Matt said. "Be nice if he could stay on, but if he's as worthless as panties on a hooker, then we'll send him packing."

"Daddy!" Alana exclaimed.

"He said he's got experience. If that's the truth and he's a hard worker, let him prove it, or get on down the road," Matt said. "Don't matter whose relative he is. I never liked that mother of his. Pax's daddy was as blind as a bat in broad daylight when it came to that woman and couldn't see her faults. And then she left them boys when they needed a mama. If Landon turns out to be like her, then Pax is better off not havin' him around."

Lucas came in the kitchen door before Alana could reply to her father's rant. "I got the chicken and paid the kid. Y'all come on in here and we'll eat."

"Bring it in here," Matt called out. "Alana, darlin', grab us some drinks, would you please? Is Pax coming over tonight?"

"That'll be him on the porch now." She got up from her chair.

"Hey, food arrived." She opened the door and stepped into his open arms. "Lucas is joining us."

"Great." Pax kissed the top of her head. "I want to hear how Landon worked out today. Maverick and I owe you big-time for taking him in."

"Honey," she whispered, "I believe giving your brother a job is nothing compared to what you're doing for me." She took his hand and led him into the living room, where the containers of food had already been opened on the coffee table.

"Help yourself," Matt said. "You'll have to get your own beer. Me and Lucas is set and we ain't gettin' up."

"I'll bring our drinks," Alana said. "Lemonade?"

"Sweet tea if you have it made," Pax answered. "Remember, Matt, I've given up alcohol until…" He looked over at Lucas.

"Until what?" Lucas asked.

"Alana, you want to tell him?" Pax removed his hat and hung it on a lampshade.

"I'm pregnant," Alana said.

Matt slapped Lucas on the back. "How about that for great news? We'd as soon it didn't get out until after the wedding, though. We don't want folks sayin' that's the reason Pax is marryin' her."

Lucas let out a whoop, removed his hat, and slung it in the air. It came down from the high cathedral ceiling and landed on a pair of steer horns hanging above the sofa. "That's the best news we've heard since we started talkin' about the wedding. A baby on the ranch!! I told you that I was goin' to live long enough to see a grandbaby, didn't I?"

"You sure did, and since you helped me raise Alana, I think our baby ought to call you Papa," Matt said.

Lucas puffed out his chest. "I would be honored to be the new baby's papa."

Alana brought two glasses full of sweat tea back to the

living room and sat down on the sofa beside Pax. "From all the noise, I guess Lucas knows now?"

"Yes, I do, and congratulations to both of you. Promise I can buy the baby its first pony like I did yours," Lucas said.

"We'd be honored." Pax picked up a paper plate and handed it to Alana. "How'd Landon do today?"

"You done good, Alana, when you stole that boy from next door," Lucas chuckled. "He's a hard worker. I set him to stringing barbed wire. When he finished the job, he moved on down the line without bein' told and started replacing the old wooden posts with metal ones. I wish I had a dozen like him. He's strong as an ox and kind of quiet. He sings when he's busy, though. Hasn't got a voice for shit, but he seems to enjoy it."

"What kind of songs does he sing?" Pax asked.

"It was George Jones today," Lucas answered. "I asked him why a kid from California would be singing Jones, and he said there was an old foreman on the ranch where he used to stay in the summer who loved country music. He admired the old guy and hung around him as much as he could. He got to listenin' to that kind of music and learned to like it, he said. He never even stopped stringin' barbed wire when he answered my questions. Damn near worked me to death today, tryin' to keep up with him. Tomorrow I'm going to give him a job and then go on about supervisin' somewhere else. That kid don't need bird-doggin'. He's got the kind of ethic that you and Maverick have always had."

"Sounds like he's going to do fine, then," Pax said. "Matt, you do know that he has a business degree, don't you? You could steal him from Lucas and get him to work in the office some of the time."

"Well, now, that's even more good news," Matt said.

"This winter, when things slow down a little, you might think about that, Alana."

There was a lot that she'd have to think about when winter came, Alana thought, like what is the best way to take care of a new baby, how to get past the grief of losing her father. Thank God she and Pax had decided to wait on the divorce. She wanted him beside her through the next few months. No, that wasn't right. She didn't only want him, she needed him in her life forever.

Chapter Twenty-Two

Matt got his wish on Thursday afternoon when seven women and four children all arrived at practically the same time. The big house went from quiet to crazy in a matter of minutes. He stuck around until after Trudy served a buffet supper of lasagna, hot rolls, and salad, and then he packed a bag and headed off to the bunkhouse to join Lucas and the guys.

Alana walked him out the back door, gave him a hug, and said, "Don't you want to stick around for the bachelorette party? You've been right up in the middle of all the plans. You might want to see all the filmy, see-through nightwear the girls will give me for the honeymoon."

"Honey, I'm going to leave you in charge of that. My face is getting hot thinkin' about what's in those gift bags that are sitting on the credenza out in the foyer. Y'all have fun." He kissed her on the cheek and disappeared into the darkness.

She called Lucas on the way back into the house. "Hey, Daddy has left the house to us tonight. Give me a call when he gets there."

"We surely will," Lucas chuckled. "We've invited Pax and the guys over here for a little party of our own. We're going to play some poker and see how many bottles of Jack we can put away. Don't worry, darlin', I'll be sure Pax gets home all right, and that he's sober for the weddin' on Saturday."

"If he's not, I'm going to feed you to the coyotes," Alana threatened.

Lucas laughed out loud. "You'll have to catch me first, and, honey, I've got lots of old women who'd love to hide me out. Here's your dad comin' in the door right now. You go on and enjoy your party and don't worry about him no more."

"Thanks, Lucas," she said.

"Anytime," Lucas said and ended the call.

Nothing about the universe had changed. The phases of the moon were so predictable that there were charts telling when it would be full or when it would be nothing but a sliver. Stars still twinkled in the sky. The sun still came up in the east and went down in the west. But after the wedding on Saturday, nothing in Alana's world would ever be the same. With a long sigh, she pasted on a smile and went back into the house.

Trudy was busy putting dollops of cream cheese frosting in the middles of thumbprint cookies that were lined up on the countertop. "I thought you girls might want something a little fancy this evening, so I made these this afternoon."

Alana pressed her cheek against Trudy's and gave her a side hug. "Thank you, Trudy, for everything."

"Honey, I'd do anything for you. Your mama was my

best friend all through school. You've got good friends in there in the living room waiting for you. Enjoy your time with them, and I hope your marriage works out to be as good as what your folks had. Now, go enjoy your time with the girls." Trudy stepped away and went back to squirting perfect little globs of icing on each cookie.

"When you finish up here, come on in and join us," Alana said.

"Are you sure about that?" Trudy beamed.

"Positive," Alana told her. "Can I help you, so you'll be done faster?"

"Oh, no." Trudy shook her head. "All I have to do is put these on plates and set them on the table. I made your favorite punch, so we'll have that and the cookies as a little dessert for after you open your presents. I'll join y'all in five minutes. Now go!" Trudy gave her a gentle little shove toward the living room.

"Here comes our bride." Emily smiled when Alana came into the room. "We would have planned a bigger party, but with everything happening so fast and so much distance between us, we couldn't get it all together."

Alana patted her friend on the shoulder and sat down beside her. "I'm glad you're all here, and to tell the truth, I like this intimate little gathering much better than something huge. That you came all this way and are staying with me until after the wedding is a big deal to me. It's been a whirlwind around here this past month...and..." she stammered, "...and I only found out a few days ago that I'm pregnant."

"Congratulations!" Emily squealed.

Alana looked around the room, her eyes landing on each of the women by turn, and she felt more love and appreciation for these wonderful friends than she ever had before.

Emily had been her friend the longest of any of them. Tall and red haired, raised on a huge ranch not far away, the two of them had bonded as children when they traveled with their fathers to various cattle affairs. Rose, medium height, strawberry blond hair, had lived in Tulia and been Emily's friend while she was there. When her family moved to Daisy, she and Alana had become sort-of friends. Rose's parents had been very strict and she had never been allowed to go anywhere other than school, but Alana had liked her. The rest of the ladies, she'd gotten to know when Emily married Justin Dawson. Claire, a tiny little woman with a big attitude, had been one of Emily's bridesmaids, and was married to Levi, the foreman at the Longhorn Canyon Ranch. Retta, a tall blonde with even more sass than Claire, was Emily's sister-in-law, and married to Cade Dawson.

Dixie was the youngest woman in the group, and the newest to become a part of the friendship. A few months ago, she and her daughter, Sally, had been homeless. They had taken refuge in an abandoned house that had caught on fire, and Rose's husband, Hud, who was a volunteer fireman, had rescued them. Now, Dixie worked for Claire in the quilt shop that she owned halfway across the state in Sunset.

Friends, becoming family, Alana was thinking when Trudy joined them. She was going to need all of them to help her get through the next few days and weeks.

An hour later, the presents had been opened. Alana still had what appeared to be a permanent blush on her face because of all the sexy lingerie that the women had given her. Dozens of cookies had been devoured, and the babies were having a good time with all the tissue paper scattered on the floor.

"So what's on the agenda for tomorrow?" Trudy asked.

"I'm planning to make breakfast and a light lunch. Rehearsal dinner will be tomorrow evening at the church. Iris has a caterer lined up for that."

"We have a lady bringing in the stuff to do mani-pedis in the morning," Alana answered. "Then in the afternoon a massage therapist is coming to give us all a full-body massage. Then we do a rehearsal at six o'clock and the dinner afterward. I'm getting nervous thinking about how fast the days are going."

"That's completely normal," Trudy said. "I'd worry more about you if you didn't get a little bit of bride jitters."

"Yep," Iris said. "Do you think that massage lady can work miracles and rub a few of these wrinkles out of my face?"

"Who said it's a massage *lady*?" Alana giggled and remembered teasing Pax about chaps. "Maybe it's a cowboy wearing nothing but chaps and boots."

"Oh, my!" Iris laid a hand on her chest. "If he's going to do that, then I'll be last."

"Why's that?" Alana asked.

"By then, he'll be too tired to laugh at the way gravity has claimed most of my skin," Iris answered.

"It's a middle-aged lady who's been doing this for years," Alana confessed. "All of y'all's husbands would kill me if I brought a hunky man in here to massage us."

"They might at that." Retta yawned. "But what a way to go. I don't know about the rest of you, but I'm taking my daughter, Miss Cranky Pants Annie, up to bed. It's early, but it was a long drive out here, and we've got a big day tomorrow. Lord, I'm lookin' forward to having my nails done and getting a massage, even if it won't be by a sexy cowboy. I would have driven all the way to California for that."

"Me too." Claire looked down at her nails. "It's so sweet of you to plan something like this for all of us."

"Daddy and the wedding planner did it," Alana admitted. "And Saturday morning, the hairdresser will be here to take care of all of us."

"Holy smokes!" Dixie exclaimed. "I hope someday I can have a wedding like this."

"What you want most," Claire said, "is a good marriage like we've all got and what Alana and Pax will have."

"You got that right," Dixie said.

* * *

The barn had been transformed into a fairy-tale setting by Friday evening when the entire wedding party arrived. Dixie, bless her heart, had volunteered to help out by staying at the ranch house and watching the children for both the rehearsal and the dinner afterward. Trudy had insisted on staying late to help, and Billy Ray had popped in at the last minute to see if his mama needed him for anything.

Iris volunteered to stand in for Alana during the rehearsal, since Matt kept to the idea that it was bad luck for the bride to walk down the aisle before the actual ceremony. Everything had pretty much been set in stone before Landon showed up on their doorstep, but Iris had insisted that he have a little part, so Alana asked him if he would do the scripture reading for the preacher.

Pax and the preacher walked down the aisle and took their places on the stage. The music began and one by one the bridesmaids came from the back of the barn, each on the arm of her husband. They slowly came down the aisle formed by the placement of a couple of dozen folding chairs reserved for the closest of their friends. They separated at the top of the steps with the bridesmaids going to the left and the groomsmen to the right.

The first run-through was a little off with the music, so Crystal insisted that they give it another try. "I want the music to end at the exact moment the last bridesmaid takes her place."

They went through it again, and Crystal clapped her hands. "Perfect. Do it exactly like that tomorrow evening. The place will look even better for the wedding when the flowers and the food are here."

"Yeah, and the bride will look like she stepped into a time machine and will be a helluva lot younger when you see her in her pretty dress," Iris said. "Before we leave, would any of the rest of you like to walk down the aisle with Matt? It'll do wonders for your looks," she joked.

Yes, Alana thought, *I'd like to step into your time machine and go back to my teenage years when I didn't want to spend time with my daddy. I'd like a redo on all the Saturday nights when I went to the Wild Cowboy instead of staying home with him.*

"No takers?" Iris chuckled. "Well, then let's all drive to the church fellowship hall and have some dinner. The caterers have it ready for us, and, Alana, darlin', it's bad luck for the groom to see you after midnight. So that's y'all's curfew tonight."

"Yes, ma'am." Pax saluted and then stepped off the stage to hold out a hand to his fiancée, who had been sitting on the bottom row of the bleachers.

She put her hand in his, stood up, and asked, "Do you have your vows written?"

"Yep, and memorized," he answered. "How about you?"

"Haven't even started them," she answered. "I'm worried

about making vows in front of God, the preacher, and my daddy that I don't intend to keep."

He gave a kiss on the forehead. "Just speak from your heart."

"Good advice, but it's hard to follow," she said.

* * *

Pax kissed Alana good night at the ranch house door and headed over to the Callahan Ranch. There would be cowboys in every bedroom, sacked out on the sofa in the living room, and even a couple in sleeping bags on the living room floor. He went over his vows as he drove home, went straight to his room, took a quick shower, and got into bed.

He closed his eyes, and hundreds of pictures flashed through his mind, beginning with his first solid memory of Alana. They couldn't have been more than three years old, and she was as tall as he was even then. Mam had left him in the nursery at church that Sunday morning. Alana was sitting in a small rocking chair with a stuffed horse in her arms, singing "Jesus Loves Me" to it. The thought of someone holding a stuffed horse had seemed strange to him, but he liked the idea that she was being nice to the little brown animal.

His next memory was of when they were in first grade, and they flashed on through the years until he got to the ones they'd made that very night. "I've been in love with her my whole life, and I'm just now realizing it," he said out loud.

He sat straight up in bed and held his head in his hand as his thoughts swirled around so fast they made him dizzy. "I love Alana Carey. I want to marry her for real. I want to have a family with her and grow old with her," he muttered.

He looked at the clock beside his bed—five minutes past eleven. He couldn't write anything in the stars in fifty-five minutes. Hell, he couldn't make even a simple wire halo in that amount of time.

"But I can speak my mind," he whispered as he picked up his phone and sent her a text: *Meet me at the tack room?*

One came back immediately: *On my way.*

Most of the guys were snoring when he slipped out the kitchen door and jogged across the pasture. He put a hand on a fence post, sailed over the top strand of barbed wire, and was out of breath when he reached the barn. Stopping for a minute to catch his breath, he checked the time again. He had forty-five minutes now to convince her his love was real. After all, it would be bad luck if he saw her on their wedding day before she walked down the aisle.

She met him right inside the barn doors. "Please don't tell me you've changed your mind."

He put his arms around her and drew her close to his body. "Not one bit. I had to see you before midnight. I had to tell you something, and it can't be done over the phone or by a text." He held her out at arm's length and gazed at her worried eyes. "I love you, Alana Carey."

She gasped. "What are you talking about?"

"I loved you when I was three years old, maybe even earlier, but that's my first memory of you. You had on a blue-and-white-checked dress, and you were rocking a little stuffed pony in the church nursery. I've loved you our whole lives, and I can't tell you the exact moment that I *fell* in love with you, but it's been sometime over this past month. You are the kindest, sweetest woman I've ever known—and the sassiest, most determined, and the most bullheaded."

"At least you aren't wearing rose-colored glasses and seeing only my good side," she joked.

"I know you, and you know me. We both see things as they are." He stopped long enough to kiss her. Could he really do this? Was he ready for a lifetime commitment?

When the kiss ended, he took both her hands in his and dropped down on one knee. "I love you. I'm *in* love with you. Let's make tomorrow real. Let's grow old together. Will you marry me, Alana Joy?"

She knelt before him, and he was afraid she was going to refuse until he saw the tears streaming down her face. "Yes. Yes, I will. I love you so much, Pax, and I'm in love with you, too."

He took her in his arms and held her, both of them on their knees and his tears blending with hers. "Cowboys aren't supposed to cry," he said, "but, darlin', you've made me the happiest man in the world tonight."

"Strong cowboys have strong emotions," she whispered as she brought his lips to hers.

Chapter Twenty-Three

I'm getting married today," Alana squealed when she awoke on Saturday morning. She threw off the covers and sent Pax a text: *We're getting married today.*

She got a message back with a dozen heart emojis and one word: *Yes!*

"Did I hear my new granddaughter yelling in here?" Iris carried breakfast into her room on a tray. "She sounded happy about something that's happenin' today."

"I'm in love with Pax," she said.

"Well, I would certainly hope so, since you'll be married to him in about twelve hours." Iris set the tray on the bed. "I wanted to do something really special for you today to welcome you into my family, so I made my cinnamon rolls for breakfast. You're gettin' these fresh from the oven, and there's plenty more in the kitchen for the rest of the girls."

"Oh, Iris." Alana opened her arms for a hug. "I've always envied Pax because he had you, and now you'll be my grandmother too, and our baby will have a great-grandmother. That's so exciting."

Iris bent and gave Alana a hug. "I'm a blessed woman to have both you and Bridget in my family and to see my boys both happy. Now eat up, and let's get this show on the road. We've got a lot to do today. The hairdresser will be here in an hour, and I expect it will take her several hours to take care of all of us."

She started toward the door and turned to say, "Trudy said to tell you that she's asked Rachel to help her during the wedding and for you not to worry about her one bit."

"What's Trudy going to be doing that she needs help?" Alana asked.

"She's volunteered to keep the nursery for all the little children," Iris said with a smile.

"Does Rachel know what she's going to be doing?"

"I have no idea." The smile turned into a giggle. "That's one way for her to keep that woman away from Billy Ray, isn't it?"

"Yep." Alana took a first bite of the warm, gooey cinnamon roll and moaned. "If I get married every day, will you make these for me? Matter of fact, there's lots of room in this house. You can come and live with me and Pax."

"Only if you marry my grandson every day," Iris answered. "And, honey, I'd love to come visit y'all, but I need my own space, like you and Paxton need yours. Especially, during this first year of marriage. Always remember, though, I'm less than an hour away if you need to talk to me."

"Thank you, Iris," Alana said.

"From now on, that will be Mam to you, not Iris," she said.

"Thank you most of all for that." Alana nodded and was happy that she could truly call her Mam—and that it wouldn't be a big fat lie.

She took a picture of the cinnamon roll with her phone and sent it to Pax with a note: *Iris says that I can call her Mam.*

She got back a picture of a dirty plate and a text that read: *I had three for breakfast. I love you!*

* * *

Pax expected the day to drag by like a turtle on crutches, but he was wrong. After Matt and Lucas had served up a big breakfast for all the guys in the Bar C bunkhouse, Matt told them all what they were going to do that morning. Lucas would give the other guys a tour of the ranch, but he and Paxton had business in town.

"You need me to go with you?" Landon asked. "He might have a hangin' tree between here and there. You could need some help escapin'."

"Don't think so," Matt said with a grin. "I been tryin' to get this cowboy in my family for years. Neither he nor my stubborn daughter would listen to anything any one of us had to say. We'll be back by noon and we'll be bringing in fried chicken from a little café in town for dinner. If y'all have any ranchin'-type advice, tell Lucas. We're always on the look out for ways to improve."

"Thank God, you weren't arranging a golf game this morning," Cade said.

"Why in the hell would I do that?" Matt asked.

"We read somewhere that that's what some groomsmen do on the day of the wedding so they won't get in the way, but we'd rather get a tour of your ranch," Levi said.

"Speak for yourselves," Landon piped up. "Next to surfing, I like golf pretty damn well. Maybe we could turn at least one pasture into a practice green, you know, a nice level area to tee up and flags to tell us how many yards our drives made. I could give the cowboys some lessons."

Lucas shook a finger at him. "You want to play golf, you can hitch a ride up to Amarillo. You want to learn more about ranchin', you can stick around here. Now get out there on one of them four-wheelers and let's go take a tour of this whole place."

"Yes, sir," Landon said as he followed the other cowboys outside.

Eight engines roared into life, and the machines kicked up a fair amount of dust when the cowboys followed Lucas's lead. Pax would have far rather been with them as going to town to talk to a lawyer. He had a pretty good idea that Matt was going to have him sign a prenup that said if he and Alana ever divorced, he would only take away from the Bar C Ranch what he'd brought to it. That, of course, would be only his clothing and his pickup truck. He was more than willing to sign such an agreement, but he wondered if Alana had anything to do with the idea.

The ride into town took a few minutes, but Pax wasn't worried a bit. He wasn't going to divorce Alana, but if they ever did, he wasn't the kind of man to take what wasn't his to begin with. The only other vehicle in the parking lot at the lawyer's office was an older model pickup. Pax pulled in beside it and turned to Matt. "This is Saturday. Randall isn't open today."

"He is for me." Matt got out of the truck and started toward the small building.

Randall Marshall stepped out onto the porch and waved. "I'm all ready for you. Come right in. Want a cup of coffee?"

"Would love one." Matt took the steps one at a time

and held on tightly to the railing. "Me and Pax both take it black."

"Does this visit have anything to do with a prenup?" Pax got ahead of Matt and opened the door for him.

"Nope," Matt answered. "But then maybe it does in a way, since you'll be signing the papers before your wedding tonight."

Two cups of coffee were already sitting on the edge of the lawyer's desk. Matt sank down in a buttery soft leather chair, picked up a cup, and took a sip. "So you've got the papers all drawn up like I asked? Lucas is to have the inheritance that we talked about and a twenty-thousand-dollar bonus for every year he stays on at the ranch and helps these two newlyweds out."

"It's all right here, like you want it," Randall told him. "Lucas gets his payments in a lump sum. The ranch is to be jointly owned by Paxton and Alana Joy Callahan, and a trust fund will be set up for any future grandchildren to be used for their education. Alana Joy signed the papers this morning, and all I need is yours and Paxton's signatures."

"What if we were to split up or get a divorce?" Pax asked.

"It won't happen. I can see how much y'all love each other." Matt signed the papers and slid them over to Pax. "You told me that you'd love and take care of her, and a cowboy always keeps his word."

"But, Matt, I'm half owner of the Callahan Ranch and Maverick needs me." Pax held the pen over the papers but couldn't make himself put his name on them. He couldn't forsake his brother. He didn't need to be half owner of the ranch—that was Alana's inheritance, not his.

"A man can't ride two horses with one ass," Matt said. "You'll have responsibilities at the Bar C. Lucas should have retired ten years ago. You can't do justice to either place if you divide all your time between them. And Alana can't do everything by herself, especially not after the baby gets here."

"I know I'm late to the party, Matt, but I wasn't payin' a bit of attention to the time." Iris pushed her way inside the room. "I've been tryin' to get you all alone for a week to talk to you about this, Pax, but something was always coming up." She sat down in the third chair and laid a hand on her grandson's arm. "I want you to sign your half of the Callahan Ranch over to Maverick. We're going to turn the tack room into a little living space, so in the next month, that's exactly what we're going to do. We'll have it all finished by the first of July, and then Billy Ray is going to live in it and take over as foreman for Maverick."

"I need a minute to think," Pax whispered.

"What's there to think about?" Iris asked. "You'll have a ranch, your brother will have a ranch, and I'm putting half the fair market price of the ranch into a trust fund for your new baby to use for her college expenses," Iris said. "That only seems fair to me."

"Why don't you put that money back for Laela and whatever other children Maverick and Bridget might have?" Matt suggested. "I've taken care of the grandchildren that will be raised on the Bar C."

"Great idea," Iris agreed. "Are you in agreement with that, Paxton?"

Pax put the pen to paper and scrawled out his name. "Yes, ma'am, I am."

"Good, then when y'all get back from your honeymoon, I'll have all the papers ready to do the transfers. I'll wait until the excitement of today is over before I tell Maverick, so keep this a secret between us until then." She gave Paxton's arm a gentle squeeze. "Now that we've got the property settlement done, let's go get ready for the wedding of the century."

* * *

Alana's blond hair flowed in soft curls down to her shoulders. Bridget and Dixie had done her makeup, and all she had to do was apply a little lipstick to her full lips, slip into her dress, and put on her boots. In one hour the wedding would start, but first the photographer wanted to take some candid pictures in the living room of the ranch house.

She stood in front of the floor-length mirror attached to the back of her bedroom door and held out her hands. Not even a tremor. This whole affair had surely started out on the wrong foot, but it was ending perfectly.

"My wedding." She smiled at her reflection. "Not daddy's wedding or even a fake one with intentions of divorce or annulment in a few weeks."

"Hey, are you ready for some help getting into that gorgeous dress?" Emily called from the other side of the door.

Alana took a step back and opened it wide. "I sure am. Is the photographer here?"

"Oh, yeah, and chompin' at the bit for you to come downstairs," Emily said. "But, honey, this is your day. My grandmother made me understand that on my wedding day. She said, 'Emily, I don't care if the elastic in your panty hose pops and your stockings fall down around your ankles. Kick them off to the side and remember that it's your day. Don't let anyone rush you or make you nervous. You want good memories.' I listened to her and so should you." She lowered her voice. "I didn't tell her that I wasn't wearing panty hose, but that I was wearing a little white lace thong with BRIDE embroidered across the front."

Alana slipped off her robe to show that she was wearing the same style thong.

Emily giggled and removed the dress from the bag and slipped it over Alana's head. "Who would have thought when we were little girls that we'd be marrying good friends?"

"I think I always knew I'd marry Pax someday," Alana said. "I'm glad that we finally came to our senses and realized that we were supposed to be together."

"Amen," Emily said.

At fifteen minutes until time to walk down the aisle, Alana watched six sparkling clean trucks drive up in front of the house. Each of the five groomsmen got out of his vehicle and escorted a bridesmaid across the lawn. Dixie and Landon were already at the barn. She was sitting at the guest table, and Landon was serving as usher until the ceremony began and it was time to do the scripture reading.

"Oh, darlin'," Matt's said from her doorway.

Alana turned around slowly.

"You look like an angel," her father whispered. "Your mama is smiling up there in heaven for sure tonight."

"I hope so, Daddy." She crossed the room and hugged him. "I'm so happy that I could cry."

"Don't you dare." Matt held out an envelope. "I want you to put this in your suitcase and don't read it until tonight or maybe you should wait until after the honeymoon. Your mama told me to give it to you on your wedding day. I've done my part, and now you can choose when to open it."

Tears welled up in Alana's eyes, but she kept them at bay as she tucked the envelope into the outside pocket of her suitcase. "Thank you, Daddy—for everything."

"Right backatcha, kid." He bent his arm, and she slipped hers into it.

Crystal was waiting for them when Matt parked his truck in the spot reserved for the bride. She put the bridal bouquet into Alana's hand and said, "Five minutes, and then the music will begin. The groom and the preacher will go up the aisle, like we practiced last night, then each bridesmaid will be escorted in by her husband. When you hear the first strands of the song you picked to come down the aisle to, I will part the filmy curtain, and you'll step into the barn. I'm giving you a brief rundown, so you won't forget."

"Thanks." Alana remembered telling Crystal that her dad's short-term memory was suffering and appreciated how she'd handled the issue.

"I'm going to step up to the front of this line and set things in motion. Two minutes, now," she said and hurried off.

"Nervous?" Matt asked.

"Not anymore," Alana answered. "You're right here with me, and Pax is waiting for me inside."

"That's my girl." Matt patted her hand and asked, "Aren't you walking down the aisle to the traditional wedding song?"

"No, Daddy, I'm not." Alana kissed him on the cheek. "This part is my surprise for Pax—and maybe for you as well."

Piano music started, and Crystal opened the curtains. Matt and Alana took their first step into the barn to "Bless the Broken Road" by Rascal Flatts. All of the words to the old song fit her and Pax perfectly, especially the words that said that every sign pointed her straight to him.

Everyone in the bleachers stood, but Alana didn't even hear the rustling. All she could see was Pax waiting for her at the end of the aisle. He wore a black tux, white shirt, peach-colored tie, a black cowboy hat, and his best boots. His eyes locked with hers and his smile made her feel beautiful. Like the words said, all the dreams she ever had were leading her straight to him.

"Perfect song," Matt whispered when he put her hand into Pax's. "Take care of her son, and I expect you to keep the promises you made to me about loving her."

"Yes, sir," Pax said as he helped her climb the three steps up onto the stage.

Alana handed her bouquet to Emily, faced Pax, and took both of his hands in hers. Landon stood up from the front pew, combed his scraggly blond hair with his fingertips, and took his place behind a lectern that had been set up over to one side. His deep voice carried throughout the barn as he read, "From Corinthians thirteen, love is kind. Love is patient. Love does not want its own way..."

Alana's eyes were still locked with Pax's, and as Landon read, they vowed to always love each other without uttering a single word. Later, they would say other vows out loud for the benefit of friends and family who'd come to help them celebrate the day, but what they were expressing with their eyes right then came from their hearts and went down deep into their souls.

When it came time to say those other vows, Pax didn't have to take notes from his vest pocket like Alana thought he might. Instead, he looked right into her eyes again and said, "It takes about two seconds to say 'I love you,' maybe five to ask 'Will you marry me?' but it will take a lifetime to show you *how much* I love you. We're getting married right now, and today is wonderful, but I intend to try to make every day of our lives together as great as this moment. When we're old and gray and we look back on our lives, I don't ever want you to have a single regret that you decided to ride this river of life with me."

With tears in her eyes, Alana said, "I believe I have loved you my whole life, Paxton, from as far back as I can remember. I'm glad that you asked me to marry you and that we can journey through life together. I want to grow old with you by my side and not only to spend the years we will have in this life with you, but to be with you for all of eternity, because it will take me that long to prove to you how much I really, really love you."

"And with that said, I think I can add a hearty amen," the preacher said. "I now pronounce you husband and wife. You may now kiss your bride, Paxton."

Pax didn't have to be told twice. He drew Alana to him, and said, "I love you," before their lips met in a long kiss that had some of the spectators whistling and yelling.

"I will love you, forever and ever, amen," she said softly when the kiss ended.

"Funny, you should say that," he whispered as a Randy Travis song by that title began to play. Instead of taking her by the hand and leading her down the aisle, he two-stepped with her all the way into the reception area.

"Perfect!" She smiled up at him when they were standing behind the wedding cake table. "Just like this whole day."

"Amen, darlin'." He pulled her against his side and kissed her on the forehead.

Chapter Twenty-Four

Eighteen months later

Pax came through the back door, removed his coat, gloves, and hat and rushed across the floor to take Alana in his arms. "Merry Christmas, darlin'. It's spittin' snow out there. I don't think it's enough for a white Christmas, but it gives us the holiday spirit."

"That sounds like something Daddy would say." She slipped her arms around his neck and brought his lips to hers for a long kiss.

"Merry Christmas to all!" Lucas and Landon pushed their way through the door. "I smell cinnamon rolls. Reminds me of all the past Christmases in this house."

Landon shed his coat and went straight to the high-chair. "How's my favorite nephew this morning?" he asked the ten-month old baby. "Are you ready for your mama's famous Christmas breakfast? Is your daddy going to let me take you outside so you can catch some snowflakes on your tongue?"

"Not on your life," Pax answered him. "It's a daddy's job to get to take his son outside to experience his first snow."

"And of course, he's your favorite nephew, since he's your only one. Bridget and Maverick have two girls." Alana removed the pan of cinnamon rolls from the oven, dumped them upside down on a tray, and then spread butter cream frosting on the top. When she finished, she set the whole thing in the middle of the table.

"I'll pour coffee for everyone," Pax said.

Alana patted Lucas on the shoulder as they all took their seats. "Lucas, will you say grace for us?"

All four heads bowed, but Alana didn't pay much attention to the words. She kept one eye on her son sitting beside her in the same highchair she'd sat in as a baby. When she found out that she was pregnant, she remembered laying her hand on her stomach and promising her unborn child that she would bring her grandfather to life for her through stories—or for him, whichever the case might be.

"Amen," Lucas said.

"Your grandpa used to say grace for us," Alana told Tommy as she separated the cinnamon rolls and put them on plates. "He was a lot like your daddy, and you have his smile and his eyes. Your grandma would have loved you so much. She left me a letter to be read on my wedding day. It made me cry a little bit, but it also reminded me what strong parents I had. You've got the same, baby boy, and someday you will be like your grandpa and your daddy."

Landon held out his plate for a cinnamon roll. "I have no doubt about that. I only knew your grandpa for a little while, buddy, but he was a fantastic guy. If you grow up to be half the rancher and cowboy he was, then you'll do well."

After breakfast Paxton cleaned Tommy's face, took him out of the high chair, and carried him into the living room. Pax picked up a picture of Alana, Matt, and himself taken on the wedding day and showed it to the baby.

"Mama, Daddy, and Poppa," he said as he pointed to the individuals.

"And you were already in Mama's tummy," Alana said as she slipped up behind them. Having Pax beside her after losing her father a few weeks after the wedding had softened the sorrow. She and Pax had made an agreement to make sure that Thomas Matthew knew what a great man his grandpa was. Pax had begun showing the baby the pictures from the day he was born.

"Yes, you were," Pax said.

"So, there's your whole family right there in the picture," Landon said.

"Yep, it is." Lucas nodded.

Pax's smile lit up the whole room. Alana could read his mind and nodded. After all it was Christmas, and what better time to tell their close friends and family the news.

"It's not our whole family," Pax said. "Next Christmas we'll have a five-month-old baby to add to the family. Alana is pregnant and due in July."

Lucas had carried his hat into the room, but suddenly it was flying through the air, finally landing on the presents under the tree. "Merry Christmas to us all. That's the best news ever. I hope we get twin girls."

Alana air slapped him on the arm. "There's only going to be seventeen months between Tommy and the new baby. Don't wish twins on me."

"I wouldn't mind one bit." Pax kissed her on the cheek.

"This is a big house, and your dad told me he'd love to see it filled with children."

"And love," Alana said. "He said that he wanted lots of love and grandkids in this place."

"Looks like we're making his wishes—and mine—come true." Pax looked up at the ceiling. "So Merry Christmas, Matt and Joy, and"—he slipped his free arm around Alana's shoulders—"to you, my darlin'. Life with you is the best present ever."

"Right back at you," she said. "I love you, Pax."

"I love you," he said.

Lucas wiped a tear from his cheek. "Y'all are making me cry."

Alana blinked away tears of her own as she leaned against Paxton and took Tommy's hand in hers. What had started out as a farce had sure turned out to be a blessing and a miracle, and she looked forward to fulfilling that dream she'd had—the one where she and Pax were sitting on the porch watching their grandchildren play on the front lawn of the Bar C Ranch.

Don't miss Dixie and Landon, whose
hearts begin to feel more than the
holiday spirit, in

A Little Country Christmas

Coming in Fall 2020

Sunrise Ranch

A Daisies in the Canyon Novella

Carolyn Brown

One determined woman must wait out her sexy, cowboy competitor if she wants to inherit the ranch they're both vying for...

Chapter One

Three little monkeys jumping on a bed.

The song echoed through Bonnie's head, but it brought about a good memory. Her mother had read that book about the little monkeys to her so many times that Bonnie had memorized it before she was three years old and knew when Vivien left out a single word. Maybe the memory was so strong because her mama soon left off reading to her, and there weren't many other books in their trailer house.

Bonnie smiled as she picked up her bottle of beer and took a long drink from it. "Three sassy sisters livin' on a ranch," she singsonged. "One got married and went away. Two sassy sisters livin' on a ranch, one got married and went away. One sassy sister livin' on a ranch"—she paused—"it's mine now. All I have to do is sit still for another six months and it's mine, and then I can sell it and go wherever I want. Whatever I decide I'll never have to get up at five o'clock in the morning to feed cows in the cold or heat again. Do I go east or west? Both have a beach. All I need is a sign to point me in the right direction."

The sun dipped below the crest of the Palo Duro Canyon, leaving streaks of purple, red, pink, and orange in its wake. Black Angus cattle grazed in the pasture between the Malloy ranch house and the horizon. A gentle breeze wafted the scent of red roses and honeysuckle across the porch.

The sun set every evening. Cattle roamed around the pastures in search of green grass every day. Flowers bloomed in June in the panhandle of Texas. Not a single sign in any of that.

"Hey, we're here," Abby Joy and Shiloh yelled at the same time as they came around the end of the house.

Bonnie looked up toward the fluffy white clouds moving slowly as the breeze shifted them across the sky. "Is this my sign?"

Six months before, the three half-sisters had showed up at the Malloy Ranch to attend Ezra Malloy's funeral. He was the father they'd never met, the one who'd sent each of their mothers away when she'd given birth to a daughter instead of a son. Then he'd left a will saying that all three daughters had to come back to the Palo Duro Canyon and live together on his ranch for a year if they wanted a share of the Malloy Ranch. If one of them moved away for any reason—love, misery, contention with the other two sisters—then she got a small lump sum of money, but not a share of his prized two thousand acres of land at the bottom of the Palo Duro Canyon.

With both sisters now married and moved away in the last six months, Bonnie was the last one standing. All she had to do was live on the ranch until the end of the year, and every bit of the red dirt, cactus, wildflowers, and scrub oak trees belonged to her. If she moved away from the ranch early, for any reason, then the whole shebang went to Rusty Dawson, the ranch foreman and evidently the closest thing to a son that Ezra ever had. Unless that cowboy had enough money in his pocket or credit at the bank, he could forget owning the ranch, because Bonnie had full intentions of selling it to the highest bidder.

She'd liked Rusty from the first time she laid eyes on him. He'd taught her and her sisters how to run a ranch—at least what he could in six months. At first, he'd seemed resigned to the fact that one or all of Ezra's daughters would own the place and had voiced his wishes to stay on as foreman at the end of a year. That had been the fun Rusty. After Abby Joy had married and left the ranch, Bonnie had seen a slight change in him—nothing so visible or even verbal, except for a hungry look in his eyes. Now that Shiloh had married Waylon and moved across the road to his ranch, he had changed even more.

Tall and just a little on the lanky side, he had dark hair, mossy green eyes that seemed even bigger behind his black-framed glasses, and a real nice smile. It didn't matter how handsome he was, he was out of luck if he thought he could get rid of Bonnie and inherit the ranch. No, sir! She'd already given up six months of her life and was willing to give up six more to have the money to reclaim her wings. She'd never planned to stay in this god-forsaken place to begin with, and now that her sisters were gone, she and Rusty were about to lock horns when it came to the ranch.

Abby Joy sank down into a chair and tucked a strand of blond hair back up into her ponytail. Even pregnant, she still had that military posture—back straight as a board, shoulders squared off.

Shiloh, the only dark-haired sister in the trio, headed off to the kitchen. "Got lemonade made?"

"There's a pitcher in the refrigerator. There's also cold beers and a bottle of wine. Take your choice," Bonnie answered.

"Lemonade for me please," Abby Joy yelled.

Shiloh brought out two tall glasses filled with ice and lemonade. She handed one to Abby Joy and then sat down in a lawn chair on the other side of Bonnie. "Everything sure looks different now than it did last winter when we got here, doesn't it?"

"Are we talkin' about Abby Joy's big old pregnant belly?" Shiloh teased.

"I think she meant the ranch," Abby Joy shot back. "I thought I'd dropped off the face of the earth into hell when I drove past Silverton that day. This was the most desolate place I'd ever seen, and I'd done tours in Afghanistan. If I hadn't been so damned hungry, I wouldn't have even come up here to the house after the funeral, but I heard someone mention food."

Bonnie laughed out loud. "I was starving too, but I sure didn't want y'all to know that."

"Why not?" Shiloh asked.

"I thought you'd look down on me even worse if you thought I was so poor I couldn't even buy food," she answered, "but I was."

Abby Joy took a sip of her drink and nodded. "I looked down the row at y'all at Ezra's funeral and figured I'd out-last both of you, but I got to admit that I was just a little scared of you, Bonnie. You looked like you could kill us all with that stone-cold stare of yours."

"I felt the same about y'all, and now you've both moved away." Bonnie drank down part of her beer.

"Yep." Abby Joy smiled. "I was the smart one. I left when I figured out right quick that love meant more than any money I would get from staying on the ranch."

"That old bastard Ezra treated all of our mothers like breeding heifers, not wives," Shiloh chimed in. "I've come a long way toward forgiving him, but he'll never be a father to me."

Abby Joy shook her head. "He's more like a sperm donor, isn't he?"

"That's kind of the way I feel, so why would I want this ranch?" Bonnie asked. "If he'd done right by us, or any one of us, then the ranch would mean something, but he didn't, so why shouldn't I just sell the damned place and get on with my life. I'm not like you two. I didn't get to settle down and grow up in one place. Mama moved whenever the mood struck her, so I'm used to traveling."

"You've got six months to decide what you want," Abby Joy said. "Give it some time. Don't rush into anything, but if you ever do decide you don't want your name attached to anything that Ezra had, you can come live with me."

"Are either of you sorry that you left?" Bonnie asked.

"Not me!" Shiloh turned up her glass of lemonade and took several gulps. "I was having second thoughts about staying on the ranch those last few weeks, but Abby Joy can't have you all the time if you leave. I get you at least half of the year."

Bonnie smiled. "I'm not stayin', and I'm probably not moving in with either of you, but I appreciate the offer. I'm going to sell the place and travel. I will come see you real often though. I don't want us to ever be apart for very long at one time..." Bonnie downed the rest of her beer and stood up. "Getting you two for sisters was definitely the one good thing Ezra did for us."

Bonnie pulled both her sisters in for a group hug, then stepped back and slapped at a mosquito on her arm. "These damn bugs are horrible this time of year."

"Everything's bigger in Texas," Shiloh joked.

"It's all that moisture we got in the spring." Abby Joy pushed up out of her chair and led the way into the kitchen. "Come July, Cooper says that we'll be begging for rain and even a mosquito or two."

"Not me." Shiloh picked up the dirty glasses and the beer bottle and followed her sister. "This canyon grows mosquitoes as big as buzzards. I don't believe that they'll all be dead in a month. They'll be hiding up in the rock formations, and they'll swoop down on us and suck all our blood out when we're not looking."

Was the fact that her half-sisters had figured out love meant more to them than the ranch the sign she was looking for? Abby Joy had given up her right to the place when she married Cooper Wilson, a cowboy rancher whose land was right next to the Malloy Ranch. Shiloh had married Waylon Stephens, the cowboy who owned the ranch across the road from the Malloy place, just a few weeks ago. From what Bonnie could see, neither of her sisters had a single regret for the decision they'd made.

But finding love and settling down wasn't the right thing for Bonnie. She was born to fly, not grow roots in the canyon, and by the time New Year's Day rolled around, she would spread her wings and take off. Maybe she'd start with going to Florida or California to see the ocean. She loved bringing up the site for a little hotel in the panhandle of Florida and listening to the sound of the ocean waves.

"Wouldn't it be something, after everything is said and done, if Rusty bought this place when I sell it?" Bonnie picked up the pitcher of lemonade and a platter of cookies and carried them to the living room.

"Wouldn't it be poetic justice if all Rusty's children were all daughters?" Shiloh plopped down on the sofa and picked up two cookies.

"Serve Ezra right for throwing away his own daughters." Abby Joy eased down into a rocking chair and reached for a cookie. "Y'all ever wonder why he brought us back anyway. He didn't want us when we were born because we weren't boys, so why would he even give us a chance to inherit his ranch?"

At least once a week, the sisters had an evening at one place or another, and tonight was Bonnie's turn. She might be the one who'd showed up at the ranch six months before with her things crammed into plastic bags, but she knew how to be a good hostess.

Shiloh raised her glass. "To all of us for not killing each other, like Ezra probably wanted."

"Hear, hear!" Bonnie said as all three sisters clinked their glasses together.

* * *

Rusty Dawson stopped at the small cemetery on the way home from his weekly poker game with several of the area ranchers. That night Cooper, Waylon, and Jackson Bailey had been over at Cooper's place, and they'd all four played until almost midnight. Rusty had walked away five dollars richer, which was unusual for him. Usually, he was at least a dollar or two in the hole when the last hand was played.

He sat down on a bench that faced Ezra's grave and stared at the inscription on the tombstone for a long time. By the light of the moon, it was just obscure dark lines. So much had happened in the six months since the man died and his daughters had showed up at the ranch. Pictures from the day of the funeral flashed through his mind. Abby Joy had arrived just seconds before the graveside service began. She'd shown up in full camouflage and combat boots, and she'd snapped to attention and nodded smartly when it was her turn to walk past the casket. He'd always wondered if maybe she was showing Ezra that she was every bit as brave and tough as any son he might've produced. Shiloh was already there, of course. She looked like she'd just walked away from a line dance in a bar like the Sugar Shack up on the other end of the Canyon—pearl snap shirt that hugged her curves, starched jeans, Tony Lama boots, and a black Stetson hat.

Bonnie, the youngest of the sisters, had put a little extra beat in his heart from the first time he laid eyes on her. She drove up in an old rattletrap of a truck with duct tape holding the passenger-side window together, tires so bald that he was amazed she hadn't had a blowout on the trip and rusted-out fenders. She was wearing tight jeans, a leather jacket, and some kind of lace-up boots. A fake diamond sparkled on the side of her nose. He figured anyone with such a sassy attitude would surely be the one who inherited the place, and he was beginning to believe he'd been right.

You just going to lay down, roll over, and let her have it, or are you going to fight for what I meant for you to have? Ezra's voice was so clean in Rusty's head that he whipped around to see if the old guy's ghost haunted the cemetery. *If you want the ranch, run her off it and take it for your own. Anything worth having is worth fighting for.*

At first, Rusty had hoped the sisters would all hate each other and disappear so that he could mourn for his old friend and boss in private. But they had all three moved right in and dug in their heels for what looked like was going to be the duration.

"You shouldn't have sent them away, Ezra. They've all got your traits, and I mean more than just your blue eyes. They're determined and hardworking and don't mind speakin' their minds. Bonnie is the only one left now." Rusty removed his glasses, rubbed at his tired, burning eyes, and shook his head. "But you're right. It's time I gave Bonnie a run for her money. That ranch is the only real home I've known. And I love this canyon. I couldn't stand seeing her sell it to some strangers, after all my years of hard work. If she's still here at Christmas, by damn, it won't be because I didn't try."

An owl hooted off in the distance and a coyote answered it. Crickets and tree frogs had set up a chorus all around him. He found himself feeling angry with Ezra for the first time—after all, the old guy had promised him the ranch. He was trying to put his feelings into words when Martha, one of the three dogs that lived on the ranch, cold nosed him on the hand. He jumped a good foot up off the bench and came back down with a thud. His glasses flew off and landed at the base of the tombstone. He retrieved them, blew the dust away from the lenses, and then put them back on.

"Dammit!" he muttered as he scratched the dog's ears. "You scared the crap out of me. Come on, you can ride up to the house with me."

The dog jumped into the truck as soon as Rusty opened the truck door. She rode in the passenger seat until he reached the house, and then licked him across the face as she bounded across his lap, hopped out of the vehicle, and ran to the porch.

"I thought she might have come to meet you," Bonnie said from the shadows. "Did you win or lose tonight?"

"Came away five dollars richer." Rusty joined her on the swing. "Couple more nights winnin' like this, and I'll have the money saved up to buy a square foot of this place when you sell it."

"Who told you that I'm selling out when I inherit the ranch?" She frowned.

"Of all y'all, you are the one who'd never make a rancher. You're the hardest working of the three and you soaked up what I've taught you, but I can see it in your eyes..." He took a deep breath.

"You can't see anything in my eyes," she argued. "I'm the best damn poker player among all of us. Get out the cards, and I'll prove it to you."

"No, thanks. I'm going to hold on to the five bucks I won tonight," Rusty said. "But, honey, you'll light a shuck out of here so fast at the end of this year that your sisters will wonder if you were ever even here. You never intended on staying any longer than you have to."

"Bullshit!" Bonnie smarted off. "You don't know me at all, and it would take more than six months to figure out a damn thing about me. I'll tell you this much, though, when and if I do sell this ranch, you better have more than five dollars in your pocket."

He crossed his arms over his chest. "I've been saving for a few years, and I've got good credit."

Bonnie glared at him for several seconds and then smiled. "Maybe I won't sell it at all. It will be mine to do with whatever I damn well please, and since it adjoins Abby Joy's place, and is right across the road from Shiloh's, I may divide it between the two of them."

Let Mr. Smarty-Cowboy roll that idea around in his

brain. Bonnie had no intentions of doing such a thing, but if Rusty wanted to play hard ball, she'd get out the bat and catcher's mitt.

"I'll talk to Cooper and Waylon, and buy it from them," Rusty said.

"I may look like I don't know anything to you, but, honey, I do know how to hire a lawyer that will put it in writing that my sisters can't sell it to anyone, and especially not you." She flashed an even meaner look at him.

Rusty grinned and smiled at her in a condescending way that she'd never seen before. "I figure you'll be gone long before you have to make those decisions. I've seen the antsy in you lately. You won't last six more months. I'm going to bed. You better be up early in the morning. We're going to be in the hay field when the sun comes up. With the spring rain we had, it looks like it might be a good one."

"Not me." She yawned. "Ezra's rules said that I don't have to do one thing but be here. I get a paycheck every week whether I lift a finger or not. Remember what the will said? So tomorrow morning I plan to sleep in as long as I want, and then maybe do my toenails. Oh, and you can get your own breakfast, too. I'll have a bowl of cereal when I decide to get up."

Chapter Two

Ezra hadn't believed in spending money on what he called frivolous things, so the old ranch house did not have central heat and air. A fireplace provided warmth in the winter, and a couple of window units worked well enough to keep the temperature out of the triple digits in the summer. The small bunkhouse where Rusty stayed was about the same, but it only had one window unit, and it only cooled his bedroom.

He paced the floor from the living room with bunk beds lining three of the walls, to the kitchen, through his bedroom, going from hot to cool several times. He was so angry with himself for letting Bonnie get under his skin. If her mother was anything at all like her then he couldn't blame Ezra for sending her away. Damned women—all of the species anyway—and damn Ezra for not letting him have the ranch like he'd said he would.

You want it, work for it. Ezra's gruff old voice popped back into his head.

"I did," Rusty growled.

Rusty hadn't grown up in the lap of luxury. He'd worked hard for everything he ever had. He'd gone into foster care when he was so little that he didn't even remember his parents. He was told that they both went to prison on drug charges and had died before he was in school. He ran away from the last one when he was fourteen, lied about his age, and got a job on a ranch. He'd been doing that kind of work ever since. Ezra had lured him away from Jackson Bailey after Rusty had been working over at the Lonesome Canyon Ranch a couple of years.

"We even had central air and heat in the bunkhouse over there, but Ezra paid better, and he hinted that since he didn't have a son to leave his ranch to, that I would inherit this place someday." He opened the ancient and rusted refrigerator and took out a gallon of milk.

He poured a glassful and continued to talk to himself. "Ezra demanded more hours out of me, but I didn't mind the work, since I was getting a paycheck and got plenty of food, and I had the run of the bunkhouse. He even let me decide who to hire for summer help, and..." He sighed. "Malloy Ranch would be mine when Ezra passed on."

He stared out the kitchen window after he finished drinking his milk. A huge moon hung in the sky right over the bunkhouse. Stars danced around it, and a few clouds shifted from one side to the other, blocking out a little light some of the time. All three dogs had rushed inside the second they had the opportunity, and Martha nosed his bare foot.

"One of you should stay at the house and protect Bonnie," he scolded them and then laughed. "Though she's tough enough that she don't need anyone to take care of her. What do you think, Vivien? Can she chew up railroad spikes and spit out staples? That's what Ezra said about her mama." He stooped down and scratched the ears of the part Catahoula dog that had been named for Bonnie's mother. The dog yipped and went to stretch out on the cool hardwood floor with Martha right behind her. Polly, the dog named for Shiloh's mother, stuck around begging for doggy treats.

"Lot of help you are," Rusty muttered as he gave her a Milk-Bone.

* * *

When the alarm went off the next morning, he rolled over to see three sets of eyes peering up at him over the side of the bed. "How'd it get to be morning so quick?"

All the dogs turned around and raced toward the door. He pushed back the covers and hurried across the large living room to let them out. In another week, there would be ten hired hands living here, mostly teenage boys he'd have to shake out of the bunk beds lining the walls every morning. When the boys arrived, the dogs would be perfectly happy to sleep outside.

Rusty dressed in work jeans, a faded chambray shirt that he left open at the throat, a faded T-shirt showing underneath, and a pair of tan work boots. He made himself a couple of peanut butter sandwiches, poured a thermos full of coffee and filled a large cooler with sweet tea and ice. Then he put together three bologna sandwiches and shoved them into a plastic bag.

When he reached the field that morning, the sun was just rising over the eastern crest of the canyon.

"Sunrise Ranch," he muttered. "I'm going to own this ranch if I have to mortgage my soul and all three of those dogs to get it, and I'm going to rename the place Sunrise

Ranch. It has a good ring to it, and Ezra can just weep and moan about it. He should've done right by me."

Don't you dare change the name of this place. Ezra's gruff old voice scolded him. *It started off as Malloy Ranch back at Texas statehood days, and by damn, it will stay that way until the crack of doom.*

Rusty knotted his hands into fists. He'd worked hard for Ezra, had given him an honest day's work for what he got paid. Ezra was dead. He could name the ranch whatever he pleased. When Ezra got sick and barely had the energy to go from his recliner to the kitchen, Rusty had run both the ranch and the house for the old guy. Then a week or so before he died, he'd called in the lawyer and changed his will. Rusty had been disappointed, but Ezra assured him that his daughters were like their worthless mothers and wouldn't last a week on the ranch.

Guess who was wrong, he thought as he crawled up into the tractor, ate his peanut butter sandwiches for breakfast, and waited for good daylight to begin his day.

* * *

Bonnie planned on keeping her word and sleeping until noon, but she had a restless night and was more than ready to crawl out of bed at five o'clock that morning. She ate a bowl of cereal and two muffins, then packed a lunch to take to the field. If she was honest, she missed Rusty coming in to eat with her that morning, but that didn't mean she wasn't still mad at him for his arrogance the night before.

What about your stubborn pride? Shiloh's voice whispered in her head. *Y'all are just alike. Neither one of you will give an inch*

"I'm up, and I'm going to the field. That's giving a mile,

not an inch," Bonnie said as she grabbed her sack and jug of sweet tea. "Stay on your side of the barbed wire, sister. I don't need your advice. I can take care of myself."

From day one, Bonnie had never given a damn what Ezra wanted done. He hadn't even cared enough to take a look at her when she was born her mother had told her, and he hadn't been around to see one single solitary accomplishment in her life, so he didn't deserve the right to call her daughter after he was dead.

As she crawled up into the driver's seat of the tractor that she usually drove, she remembered that Loretta, Jackson Bailey's wife from the adjoining ranch to the north, had welcomed them to the canyon, and said, "It's kind of bare right now, but in a few weeks, when the wildflowers pop up, it will be lovely. Bluebonnets, wild daisies, coreopsis, and flowering cactus sure give it a different look. And trust me when I say it grows on you. The sunsets and sunrises are beautiful, and pretty soon, you'll wonder why you ever wanted to live anywhere else."

Bonnie had admired Loretta's flaming red hair and her sweet smile, but she'd thought that the woman had rocks for brains. There was no way this barren place would ever grow on her. She would stick around for a year just to prove those two bitchy half-sisters who were looking down on her that she could hold her own. But Loretta had been right. The place might not have grown on her, but it did have a kind of beauty in the spring and early summer, and she'd come to love her sisters.

"Damn it to hell!" She slapped the steering wheel and then started up the tractor's engine. "I promised myself that I wouldn't stay six months ago, and I never go back on a promise I make to myself, but now a part of me wants to stay here, and that would mean being tied down."

Her mind went back to that first day she'd been in the canyon. Ezra's funeral was over and the neighbor, Jackson, had brought a copy of Ezra's will for each of the sisters to keep, and one for Rusty. He had cut past the legal jargon and told them that Rusty would pay each of them on Friday evening for forty hours of work at minimum wage. Room and board would be provided free of charge. Rusty would bring in staples once a week, but if they wanted anything other than what he had bought, they would have to buy it themselves.

Bonnie hadn't been expecting a salary, so that had made her happy. No way would she ever let either of her sisters know that she'd spent her last dollar on enough gas to get her to the funeral. She kept her mouth shut and listened as Jackson went on to tell them that they would get their salary whether they sat on the porch and did nothing or whether they pitched in and learned the business of ranching. It made no difference and was their decision.

"I should be doing that today just to prove to Rusty that I can," she muttered, "but it sounded too boring, and besides if I'm going to get a good price for this place, it should be kept up. God only knows that Rusty can't do it by himself."

Jackson had said that Rusty would teach them the ranching business, if they had a mind to learn. Then he'd told them that whichever daughter was still on the ranch one year from that day would inherit the whole place. If anyone left before the year was up, they got a one-time, lump sum payment from Ezra's estate, but they would relinquish any and all rights to the ranch. Abby Joy and Shiloh hadn't been allowed to disclose what their inheritance was when they'd left. For all Bonnie knew, it was anywhere from $500 to $50,000.

At noon she parked the tractor and got out of the cab. After doing a few stretching exercises and rolling the kinks out of her neck, she picked up her sack lunch and sat down under a shade tree. She'd only taken the first bite when Rusty joined her.

"What are you thinkin' about?" he asked. "You look like you're ready to fight a wild bull with nothing but a willow switch."

"Just going over in my mind what Jackson told us that first day I was here," she said honestly, but she didn't tell Rusty that she'd fought against an attraction for him since day one. No way was she going to admit that, not when they had crossed horns over the ranch like a couple of rangy old bulls. She admired his work ethic—getting up at the crack of dawn seven days a week to take care of things—but she also liked his kindness. Add that to his eyes and the way he filled out his jeans, and it was dang hard to fight the feelings that had grown for him.

"That was a strange time for sure," Rusty said.

"You didn't like any of us so well, did you?" she asked.

"I didn't figure any of you would last a week. Abby Joy would get tired of it, and Shiloh was way too prissy for ranchin'. I was wrong about all of you. I figured you'd sit on the porch and draw your pay. Never figured you'd pitch in and learn a damned thing, but y'all got out there doing your best," he chuckled. "But I could also see that the other two were determined to learn, and you were just passing time. You don't give a damn about this place."

"Nope, I don't," she admitted. "Only reason I learned anything at all was out of sheer boredom and to show my sisters that they weren't better than me. Why'd you come over here anyway? I thought we were mad at each other."

"Only shade tree around here," he replied.

"I was here first," she protested.

"Too bad." He shrugged.

She tipped up her chin and looked down her nose at him. "I'm going to take a lot of pleasure in getting out of this place."

"Then I'll get the whole shade tree to myself," he smarted off.

There weren't many times she'd been alone with Rusty. She stole a glance over at him. Bulging biceps, a flat tummy under a chambray work shirt that was wet with sweat. That some woman hadn't snatched him up already was a miracle. She'd have to be very careful in the next months to not let anyone know about the little flutters in her heart whenever he was around.

"You've gone all quiet again," Rusty said.

"Was Ezra a controlling person?" she asked.

"Where'd that question come from?"

"You probably knew him better than anyone, so tell me more about him?" she said.

"Oh, hell, yeah, and mean as a rattlesnake," Rusty said. "I mean, he named the dogs after your mothers, so that ought to tell you something. He always told me he was leaving the ranch to me. Then a week before he died, he called the lawyer and changed his will."

"He called you the son he never had," Bonnie said. "Was that to make us feel less worthy of the Malloy name? I just can't wrap my mind around why he changed his will and brought us here. If I could figure out why, then maybe I'd find some peace before I leave Texas. Seems like every time I think of him, all I feel is anger, and a little bit of fear that I might be like him in some way. Most of the time I don't even like my mother, but I love her. I can't imagine even liking Ezra."

Rusty shrugged. "That old fart had his own ways. He was good to me, and for that I loved him, but what he did to you girls was wrong. I'm mad at him this morning, so I don't want to talk about him."

"Why?" Bonnie was stunned.

Rusty never had anything but praise for Ezra.

"He popped into my head and fussed at me when I said I might change the name of the ranch, and it made me even madder when he changed his will," Rusty said.

"What were you going to change the name to?" she asked, "And how would Ezra feel about that? I thought y'all were best buddies."

"Sunrise Ranch," Rusty answered. "I love the way the sun comes up over the crest of the canyon every morning." Rusty paused. "Sometimes I can hear his voice in my head, and it's good advice, but he was on one of his mean streaks this morning."

Bonnie pulled a banana from her sack and peeled it. "My mama does that all the time. Out of nowhere, she pops into my head and has something to say about what I'm doin'. Most of the time it's to tell me that I'm not smart enough to do something. It makes me so mad that I make it my mission to prove her wrong. I'm glad you stood up to him, even if he's dead and just a voice in your head. Sunrise Ranch has a nice sound to it. Maybe you'll come up with the highest bid after all, since you said you'd change the name to something nice."

"One more cup of tea, and then I'm going to work. You have a choice in what you do. I don't," he said.

"You could move off the ranch. I bet I could kick any mesquite bush between here and Silverton and a dozen foremen would come running out lookin' for a job," she said.

"And wouldn't a one of them be as good as I am." He

settled his dusty old straw hat on his head and left without even looking back.

"Little egotistical there," she called out.

He waved over his shoulder but still didn't turn around.

You've met your match. Her mother was in her head again, and this time she was laughing out loud. Bonnie heaved a long sigh and wondered if he'd felt the same attraction and little shocks of desire that she did when they were together. If so, why was he holding back? Should she talk to her sisters about the way she felt?

She shook her head as she finished off the last sip of her tea. No, she wouldn't talk to anyone about anything until she sorted it all out herself. She might find that the old saying about being out of sight, out of mind worked in this instance.

Chapter Three

Rusty had no intentions of going to the Sugar Shack on Saturday night, not after spending the whole day sitting in a tractor seat. He was dog-tired and ready to throw back in Ezra's old recliner and watch *Longmire* on television. Ezra had bought the DVDs of both that and *Justified*, and Rusty had watched them many times. But neither show held his attention, and he was bored. He'd gotten soft in the past six months. Any old time he wanted company he could go up to the ranch house and visit with the sisters.

He went into the bathroom where he stared at his reflection in the mirror. Light brown hair that needed cutting, a couple of days' worth of scruff on his face. "I am a loner," he whispered. "I don't need a gaggle of women around me to keep me company."

He picked up his razor and shaved, then took a shower and put on a pair of pajama pants. He opened a can of chili, poured it into a bowl, and warmed it in the microwave.

Once that was done, he poured himself a glass of sweet tea, and carried both to the living room. He set it on the end table beside his recliner and settled in to watch something on Netflix. At the end of the first episode of *The Ranch*, he realized he hadn't been paying enough attention to it to even know what had happened, so he got up and turned off the television.

Feeling cooped up, he went outside to sit on the porch and pet the dogs, but they weren't anywhere to be found. "Probably at the ranch house," he muttered. "Since women came onto the ranch, they're gettin' plumb spoiled."

So are you. Ezra's voice was back in his head. *Since them girls came around, you've gotten spoiled to having company all the time.*

"Maybe so," Rusty agreed. "So what?"

Ezra didn't have an answer for that.

Rusty walked from the bunkhouse to the ranch house and found the dogs lyin' on the porch—right where he figured they would be. Martha opened one eye and yipped one time. Vivien and Polly didn't even bother to do that much.

"I'm going to the Sugar Shack," he announced and headed back to the bunkhouse to get dressed. "Maybe I'll feel better after a few beers and when I dance some leather off of my boots."

* * *

Bonnie's thoughts all through the day had been constantly on the ranch and the insane attraction she'd felt for Rusty. It seemed even stronger since they were the only ones left on the ranch. She had no intentions of ever doing anything about it, so why wouldn't it just disappear? Too bad there wasn't a delete button for times like this, or for just time in general. Push the button and the chemistry she felt for her foreman would disappear. Push it again, and a whole year would disappear. She'd be on a beach somewhere in a cute little bar—hell, she might even own the bar—drinking a margarita and dancing with handsome beach boys.

She'd been restless after she finished cutting hay all day, so she'd gone to the grocery store in Claude to buy food for the week. She was pushing her cart toward the checkout counter when the message came over the PA system saying that the store would be closing in fifteen minutes. "Bring your purchases to the front of the store, please."

Evidently she was the last remaining person in the store, because no one else was pushing a cart toward one of the three cashiers. Bonnie unloaded her cart onto the conveyor belt and then stuck the ranch credit card into the machine to pay for everything.

"Been a long day," she said in way of conversation.

"Yep, and I can't wait to get home, get my boots on, and go to the Sugar Shack for some excitement," the woman said. "The place don't get hoppin' until about nine, so I'll get there at just about the right time."

Bonnie just nodded. No way did she have enough energy to go to the Sugar Shack this evening, and besides, the last time she had gone there, she had had Shiloh with her. Going alone just didn't sound like much fun.

On the trip back down into the canyon, her thoughts went back to the Malloy Ranch again. "I've got to get away from the forest so I can see the trees, as Mama used to tell me when I was fretting about something. Maybe I will go to the Sugar Shack, have a beer, do a little line dancing, and not think about anything but having a good time."

Now that's my girl. That pesky voice that sounded like her mother's was back.

"You've always put having a good time ahead of everything else," Bonnie muttered as she turned off the highway and down the lane to the ranch. She just shook her head when she passed the cemetery where Ezra was buried. "How on earth the two of you ever got together is a mystery that I'll probably never understand."

She parked her truck and unloaded the groceries. The dogs were all waiting on the front porch, so she promised them that she'd bring out a surprise in a few minutes as she headed into the house. She put away the perishables, kicked off her shoes, and put on her only pair of cowboy boots. When she'd tucked the legs of her jeans down into them, she picked up a package wrapped in white butcher paper and took three big soup bones out to the dogs.

"See, I didn't forget you ladies," she said. "Y'all are welcome to carry these back to the bunkhouse. Rusty might even let you bring them inside if you promise to keep them on the floor."

She balled up the butcher paper and threw it into the bed of her beat-up truck. Then she got behind the wheel and headed back down the lane, made a right-hand turn out onto the highway, and traveled a few miles before making another turn. The Sugar Shack was in an old wooden building with a wide front porch, and the whole place looked like it had been sprayed down with that pink medicine Bonnie's mama had given her for a stomachache when she was a little girl. She could hear the jukebox music blasting away before she even got out of her vehicle. Tips of cigarettes flared red as a row of cowboys leaned against the front of the building and sucked in a drag.

She walked through a haze of smoke on the way into the bar and got a few catcalls and offers from guys who were willing to put out their cigarettes if she'd dance with them.

She'd grown up around folks a lot rougher than these cowboys, so she just ignored them, paid her cover fee, and went inside. Most of the place was dimly lit, but the bar area was at least semibright. She located an empty barstool and slid onto it, not paying a bit of attention to who was sitting in the one right next to her.

"What are you doin' here?" Rusty asked.

"I decided that I've been thinkin' about serious things way too much. I just need to have some fun, so here I am." She motioned for the bartender to bring her a beer. "What about you? You lookin' to get lucky tonight?" Saying the words caused a shot of jealousy to shoot through her heart.

"Maybe," he answered. "Are you?"

"Never know what beer and dancing might cause," she answered with a shrug.

The bartender brought her beer, and she tipped up the bottle and took a long drink.

A good-looking dark-haired cowboy tapped her on the shoulder. When she looked up, she recognized him as one of the guys who worked over on her brother-in-law's ranch.

"Want to dance?" he asked as Jason Aldean's "She's Counry" came on the jukebox.

"Sure!" She handed her beer to Rusty. "Finish it before it gets warm."

"Don't know if you remember me, but I'm Lake, and I work for Cooper." He took her hand and led her out onto the dance floor. He swung her out a way, then brought her back to his chest and began a fast two-step and swing dance combination. "This song sounds like it's about you," he said. "You ain't afraid to stay country like you was born and raised."

"I'm glad you noticed," she teased with a hip wiggle when he spun her out the next time. She glanced over at the bar to see if Rusty was even watching, only to see nothing but empty barstools. With a quick glance over Lake's shoulder, she saw that Rusty was on the floor hugged up to a cute little brunette so tight that air couldn't get between them.

The next song was "Down to the Honkytonk" by Jake Owen. One of the lines said something about him having a girl that went bat shit crazy on tequila.

"Do you get silly on tequila?" Lake asked as he kept Bonnie on the dance floor.

"Honey, I could drink you under the table any day of the week," she answered.

Before Lake could disagree with her, Rusty tapped him on the shoulder and took his place with Bonnie.

"Why'd you do that?" she asked.

"He's a player," Rusty said. "You don't want to get mixed up with him. He's only interested in one-night stands."

Rusty was by far the smoothest cowboy she'd ever two-stepped with. When that song ended, he took her by the hand and led her back to the bar. Having her hand in his caused little shots of desire to run through her body, but that didn't surprise her so much. Dancing with him was one more thing she'd have to be careful about.

"You're not the boss of me," she protested.

"Nope, I'm not," he said. "But I will warn you of danger when it's right under your nose."

"Like a big brother?" she asked.

"Something like that," he chuckled.

* * *

Rusty wondered if Bonnie felt the heat between them like he did. He'd been attracted to her wild, free spirit from the first time he saw her, and that had grown through the months.

He'd never let her know that though—not when he had to run her off to even get a chance at the ranch.

She was staring right into his eyes and then a woman touched him on the arm. "I've got a bone to pick with you, Rusty Dawson. You snuck out of the house without even tellin' me goodbye last month, and you never called me. I'm not just a one-night stand. I'm a good woman, and you're a bastard. I've waited four whole weeks to hear from you."

"You're drunk, Sandy," he said.

"Yeah, but I'll be sober tomorrow, and you'll still be a bastard." She turned her attention toward Bonnie. "You're one of Ezra's daughters, ain't you? Well, honey," she draped an arm around Bonnie's shoulders, "Rusty is just like Ezra, bastard to the bone. Don't let yourself get mixed up with him."

"Let's get out of here," Rusty said.

"I agree," Bonnie said.

"You'll wish you'd listened to me"—Sandy slurred her words—"because I know what I'm talkin' about. He might marry you, but it'll only be to get the ranch. He'll never be faithful. Every time your turn your back, he'll be lookin' to get some on the side. You mark my words."

"I'm so sorry about that," Rusty said as he walked across the parking lot with her. "She was drunk off her ass. I took her home, put her to bed, and left. She got the impression that we'd slept together, but we didn't."

"Hey, you don't owe me any apologies," Bonnie told him. "We all make mistakes."

"Tell me about yours." He grinned.

"I would if we had some of Ezra's moonshine, but that's all gone, so..." She shrugged.

"It's not Ezra's, but I've got a pint of blackberry 'shine in the bunkhouse. Want to share a few shots with me, and talk about all our mistakes?" He caged her with an arm on each side of her against the door of her truck.

"Are you flirtin' with me?" she asked bluntly.

He removed his hands and shook his head. "Nope. With all the noise around us, I had to lean in real close so you could hear me."

"You really think gettin' me drunk would make me tell all my secrets?" she giggled. "Honey, I'm not one of them sad drunks who talks about how the world's not treating her right. I'm a happy drunk, one who don't give a damn what she says or does." She was remembering the night that she and her two sisters had gotten drunk on the last of Ezra's 'shine. Or at least Shiloh and Abby Joy did—she herself had enough 'shine sense to take a few sips and leave it alone, being as how she'd made the stuff herself back in Kentucky, and she knew what a kick it had.

"I like a happy drunk." Rusty smiled.

"Well, then, let's just get to it." She ducked under his arm and came up on the other side. "I'll follow you to the bunkhouse. In the morning, if you can make it to the house, I'll sure enough brew up my hangover cure for you."

"Who says I'll have a hangover?" he teased.

"You will have one like you've never had before when I get finished making you a couple of real blackberry bombs." She got into her truck and slammed the door shut.

When they arrived at the ranch, all three dogs followed their vehicles to the bunkhouse. Once inside, Martha flopped down on the cool floor in front of the sofa. Vivien followed Rusty into the kitchen, and Polly headed for the rug in front of the fireplace.

"I guess they're our chaperones." Bonnie followed Rusty into the kitchen.

He got the blackberry moonshine and two shot glasses

down from the cabinet, set them on the table, and started
to pour.

"Oh, no, you don't." She hip-bumped him out of the way.
"If we're going to have a real drink, then I'll do the mixin'."
She reached for a bottle of tequila. "Looks like you're about
out of this."

"That and this pint of 'shine and six beers in the
refrigerator is all that's left in the bunkhouse. I don't keep
any alcohol in here when the summer help arrives. They're
mostly underage, and I sure don't want to get tossed in jail
for giving liquor to a minor," Rusty said.

"Then let's do this up right." Bonnie poured a cup of
moonshine into a blender, added all of the tequila, and
a twist of lemon. She put a few cubes of ice into the
blender and punched chop, then hit stop when its contents
were smoothie texture. She carried the blender and the two
glasses into the living room.

"We were going to talk about mistakes. You go first." She
settled down right in the middle of the well-worn sofa, set
the blender on the coffee table, and poured two shots.

He took one of the glasses from her, threw back its
contents like a shot of whiskey, and held out his glass to be
refilled. "I ran away from the last foster home when I was
fourteen and went to work on a ranch. I wish I'd finished
high school and taken some business courses. Ezra took
care of the finances, and it's been a struggle for me to learn
how to operate the computer and do all that. Your turn."

She drank her bomb and said, "I got in with a bad group
in eastern Kentucky. We got caught growing pot."

"Did you do jail time?" he asked.

"No, it was worse than that," she told him.

"I'm listening." He refilled her glass.

"In the county I was living in at the time, one family

owned the pot business, and no one cultivated marijuana without their permission—and they didn't give it to kids. They caught us harvesting it, took it all from us, and went to our parents. We didn't get taken to jail, but our folks had to pay them the equivalent of a fine. Mama had to cough up five hundred dollars, and I had to work as a waitress all summer to pay her back."

She'd downed that bomb, so he made her another one. "Surely you made more than that in three months."

Bonnie threw back the drink and held out her glass for more. Memories were stirred up in her mind that she thought she'd buried too deep to ever surface, and they brought about the same hurt feelings as they had all those years ago. If her mother could get her hands on a dollar, she'd figure out a way to rationalize taking it. Bonnie's feelings or needs seldom if ever played into the grand scheme of anything. "Yep, and she called the rest of the money I made the interest and the lesson—depending on whether she was drunk or high herself. Your turn."

They switched back and forth with their tales of woe until finally Bonnie leaned her head back on the sofa and began to snore. Rusty gently carried her to his bedroom, laid her on the bed, and covered her with a quilt. She roused up, moaned and threw her hand over her eyes.

He stretched out beside her and whispered, "Shhh...just sleep."

* * *

Bonnie was jerked awake the next morning when Vivien licked her hand that was dangling over the side of the bed. She opened her eyes wide, looked around, and didn't recognize a single thing other than the dog that was named for her mother. The light stung her eyes. Her head pounded so hard that she could hear every heartbeat in it.

"Good mornin'." Rusty brought in a tray with pancakes and coffee. "We've overslept. It's too late to go to church, so evidently we won't be able to ask forgiveness for our sins."

"I don't know about you, but I don't believe I did anything I have to repent for." She sat up in bed, checked to be sure she was wearing clothes, and threw back the quilt. "I only had a few sips from a shot of blackberry bomb."

"I had about three of those wicked bombs you brewed up. You drank the rest of that blender full." He put the tray over her lap and sat down beside her.

"Well, at least you didn't sneak out in the middle of the night and leave me like you did that Sandy woman. Are you going to call me?" Her tone was saccharine.

He poured syrup on the pancakes, cut into them, and took a bite.

"I thought this was my breakfast," she said.

"It's ours to share, like we did all our mistakes last night." He handed her the fork and his hand brushed against hers. His gentle touch sent sensations coursing through her body that made her want to throw off the sheet and drag him right back into bed with her.

She took a bite and wondered what in the hell she'd shared with him? Did she tell him about the sorry sucker who'd talked her out of her virginity and then told everyone in high school about it the next day? Did she tell him that she'd never been so glad to go home that evening and find her mother packing the car to move again?

"So, what did I share?" she asked.

"I know about you trying to grow pot." Compared to all the other scrapes she'd been in, that wasn't so bad.

"So, we exchanged a few stories, got drunk, and now we're sharing pancakes. That doesn't change jack crap about this ranch," she said.

"Nope, it sure doesn't. I might make breakfast, but I'm still going to do my best to make you hate this place and leave before Christmas," he said.

"Give it your best shot, cowboy," she told him.

Chapter Four

Bonnie was on her way out the door when her phone rang. The noise startled her so badly she fumbled when she tried to fetch it from her hip pocket and dropped it on the floor. Breathless, she finally answered it on the fourth ring.

"Hello, Shiloh," she said.

"Why weren't you in church this morning?" Shiloh asked.

"Overslept," Bonnie answered.

"You're out of breath. What were you doing?"

I got drunk and had a hangover and woke up in Rusty's bed, she thought and smiled. But she said, "I was on my way outside when the phone rang. It startled me."

"Abby Joy and I are going to Amarillo this afternoon. Want to go with us? We're leaving in about half an hour."

Rusty walked up behind her. "I'm going out to check the hay we cut yesterday. Want to go with me?"

"Did I hear someone say something in the background?" Shiloh asked.

"Rusty came in the back door and wanted to know if I wanted to go to the pasture with him, but I'd rather go shopping. I'll see you in thirty," Bonnie said.

"Hello to him. See you in thirty. Oh, and tell Rusty, the guys are watching the bull riding on television at Abby Joy's if he wants to go over there." Shiloh ended the call.

Bonnie turned around to find him so close that his warm breath tickled the side of her cheek. "You're invited to Cooper's to watch bull riding."

All those damned moonshine bombs had to be the reason he affected her the way he did that morning. Sure, she'd had a little secret crush on him, but she'd never had to fight against the desire to take a step forward and kiss him. "I'm going shopping with my sisters."

He brushed a sweet kiss across her cheek. "Thanks for the evening and the night."

Her legs felt like they had no bones. Her pulse began to race, and her heart thumped against her ribs. "You can sweet talk me, feed me breakfast, or get me drunk and I'm still not going to let you have this ranch unless you're the highest bidder."

He chuckled. "But I will keep trying until the very last second. Bring home a couple of steaks, and I'll grill them for us tonight."

"There are two in the fridge"—she waved over her shoulder—"that I bought in Claude last evening."

"Y'all have fun," he called out just as she slammed the door of her truck.

She gave him a thumbs-up sign.

"What in the hell have I done?" she moaned as she drove the short distance from the bunkhouse to the ranch house. "I haven't been that drunk in years. It's a wonder I didn't do something totally stupid, like have sex with him."

She took a quick shower and washed her hair, dried off in a hurry, and threw on a pair of clean jeans and a shirt. She usually let her hair dry naturally, but that afternoon she used a blow dryer before she whipped it up in a ponytail. Her phone rang just as she picked up her lipstick.

"Where are you?" she asked when she saw Abby Joy's name pop up on the screen. "I thought y'all said thirty minutes. I've been ready for a while now."

"We just passed the cemetery," Abby Joy said.

"I'm headed out now. You don't even have to honk." She ended the call and hurriedly put on her lipstick.

She'd just picked up her purse when she remembered that she hadn't fed the dogs, so she hurried back inside and filled their bowl with dry food. She thought her head would explode when she bent over and hoped that she'd remembered to refill the aspirin bottle that she carried in her purse. She took her time crossing the yard, but her head was still pounding when she got into the backseat of her sister's van.

"You're flushed like you've been runnin' around in circles," Shiloh said.

"I don't think it's from runnin'." Abby Joy shook her head as she backed the van out of the driveway. "She wasn't in church this morning, and she's glowing. I heard someone say that she was at the Sugar Shack last night and got into a little catfight with Sandy Hamilton. I betcha they were arguing over some good-lookin' cowboy, and our sister won. That look on her face"—Abby Joy looked up at her in the rearview—"tells me she brought that cowboy home with her, and the two of them had sex."

Shiloh turned around in her seat as far as the seat belt would allow and stared at her youngest sister. "Is that true? Who was it? Is he still in the house? What is Rusty goin' to think of that?" She fired off questions too fast for anyone to keep up with.

Bonnie shook her head and then grabbed it with both hands. "I don't kiss and tell. No one is in the house or was last night. I don't think I need Rusty's permission to bring a man home if I want to. After all, in six months the ranch will belong to me, and he'll be working for me if I decide to keep it."

What was the matter with her anyway? She had no intentions of keeping the ranch. The moment it was in her hands, she planned to have a Realtor put a sign out beside the road announcing that it was for sale.

"What makes you think he'll stick around? If you decide to stick around, you'd better be putting out some feelers for a new foreman," Shiloh said.

While Bonnie was mulling that over in her head, Abby Joy spoke up. "You went home with someone, didn't you? No one glows like you are right now if they haven't had sex for the first time since Christmas." She glanced up at her youngest sister in the rearview mirror again.

"Or unless they're pregnant," Shiloh said. "The both of you are glowing. I'm beginning to feel left out. Y'all are going to have babies that will grow up together, and my poor little children will be so much younger that they'll get picked on by their older cousins."

Bonnie wanted children someday, but not right now. She had some heavy decisions to make about her life, and a pregnancy at this point would complicate the hell out of things. Her upbringing had taught her that when she got ready to have kids she would settle down in one place. She damn sure wouldn't jerk them out of school in the middle of a semester. Bonnie had lost count after twenty at how many schools she'd attended from kindergarten through graduation.

"You got something to tell us, little sister?" Abby Joy asked.

"I am not pregnant, and I'm glowing because I just got out of a hot shower, and y'all are making me blush," Bonnie said.

"Good God!" Shiloh gasped. "Bonnie blushing? I didn't think she had it in her to do that."

"Don't make me laugh." Abby Joy giggled. "With this baby lyin' heavy on my bladder, if I laugh too hard we'll be turning around and goin' back home to get me a pair of dry underwear."

Bonnie crossed her arms over her chest. "Y'all are bad sisters today."

"We wouldn't be if you'd tell us who you went home with last night," Shiloh told her.

"I left the Sugar Shack and came home. End of story," Bonnie said.

"Well, dammit!" Shiloh sighed. "I wanted to hear a more exciting story than that on the way to the mall."

"Three sassy sisters livin' on a ranch, one got married and went away. Two sassy sisters livin' on a ranch, one got married and went away. One sassy sister livin' on a ranch, she's all confused and don't know what to do..." Bonnie said. "Is that story good enough for you?"

"Double dammit!" Abby Joy swore. "Now I've got that worm in my head about the little monkeys."

"Good." Bonnie smiled. "Serves y'all right. I hope that song haunts you all day."

"Seriously," Shiloh said, "have you given some thought to what you intend to do about the ranch."

"Yes, but I've got a question for both of you." Bonnie nodded. "Y'all fell in love with someone and left, so evidently, it isn't hard to move off the ranch. But do you have any regrets now that time has passed? Both of you could have been in love and still put off leaving until the year was up. You could have even spent a night away at a time now and then, like Shiloh did when Waylon was hurt. As long as you didn't actually move away, both of you could have still been in for a share of the ranch."

"I don't have a single regret," Abby Joy answered without hesitation. "But then, I was in love with Cooper, and love trumps all the dirt in Texas in my books."

"I don't have regrets either," Shiloh said. "Both of you know, I was having doubts about staying on the ranch anyway. Following the terms of that will made me feel like Ezra had control over my life, and even if I had half ownership with you, Bonnie, it was"—she paused—"I can't explain the feeling, but I can tell you that when I made up my mind to leave, it felt like the chains dropped off my heart. Like Abby Joy, I was in love with Waylon, so that had a bearing on it, I'm sure, but I was relieved that Ezra wasn't running my life anymore."

"He really was an old sumbitch, wasn't he?" Bonnie whispered. "Do you wonder why he made his will the way he did? Why would he even care if we ever knew each other? I mean"—she took a deep breath and let it out in a whoosh—"I'm glad we have gotten acquainted, but why?"

"Can't answer that," Abby Joy replied. "I'm glad I came to the funeral, and that y'all did too, but understanding why Ezra did anything he did is impossible, and I've tried."

"Me too." Shiloh nodded.

"Thanks for being honest." Bonnie turned to look out the side window. She tried to imagine simply moving off the ranch and relinquishing all her rights to it to Rusty, but she didn't want to leave him. They made a great team, and he needed her right now, here in the busy season.

* * *

Rusty knocked on the door of Cooper's ranch house and then poked his head inside. "Where are y'all at?"

"In the living room," Cooper called out. "Come on in. The bareback bronc riding is about to begin. Bull riding comes after that."

Rusty carried a six-pack of cold beer through the kitchen and the foyer and into the living room where Cooper and Waylon were already stretched out in a couple of recliners. He twisted the top off two bottles and handed one to each of them. Then he sat down on the sofa, propped his boots on an oversize hassock, and uncapped a beer for himself.

"Heard you didn't close down the Sugar Shack last night," Cooper said. "You sick or something?"

"Nope, just got bored with it. Sandy was drunk." Rusty took a long drink of his beer.

"Sandy's always drunk. Woman can't hold her liquor any better than she can a boyfriend." Waylon muted the commercial.

"She's clingy and thinks if you buy her a drink, you're in love with her and about to propose." Cooper nodded. "I told you not to ever get involved with her, Rusty."

"I didn't, but I can't convince her of that," he groaned.

Waylon hit the red button on the remote to turn the sound back on. "Damn, I wish I was still doin' the rodeo rounds. I liked the sounds of the crowd, the thrill of the rides, all of it."

"Marriage changes a cowboy," Cooper said.

"Yep, it does," Waylon agreed. "And when it comes down to the line, I'd rather be married as out there bustin' up bones and spendin' time in emergency rooms. Since I got that concussion a few weeks ago in the wreck, I'd be afraid to ride anyway. I don't ever want to get to where I wouldn't know Shiloh."

"Wait until you've got a baby comin' along." Cooper combed back his dark hair with his fingertips. "That *really* changes everything. I sure enough feel my responsibility to keep healthy. I'm not even running for sheriff next election. I'm just going to ranch."

The commercial ended and the bronc riding event started. All three guys yelled for their favorite contestant, who was trying to make it all the way to the National Professional Rodeo in Las Vegas in December.

Rusty slumped down on the sofa and watched one event after another, but his thoughts wandered back to the Malloy Ranch. Cooper had inherited the Lucky Seven from his grandparents. Waylon had started off with a small spread and renamed it the Wildflower Ranch. Then the elderly lady next door to his place died and left him her small acreage. When he and Shiloh got married, she doubled the size of their acreage by buying the adjoining ranch to the south.

Rusty loved living in the canyon. He'd put down roots at the Malloy Ranch. He finally belonged somewhere. About all he could do at this point was hope that when Bonnie sold the place, he was the high bidder and that a bank would back him.

Chapter Five

The next morning the window served as a picture frame for the most beautiful sunrise Bonnie had ever seen. She threw off the covers and stared out at the gorgeous sight for a long time before she finally got dressed and headed toward the kitchen. She was halfway down the hall when she got a whiff of cinnamon blended with the aroma of coffee.

"Good mornin'," Rusty said. "I made cinnamon toast for breakfast. Looks like we're goin' to have a good day to get the hay raked and baled."

Was this his new trick to get rid of her—be nice so she'd feel sorry for him and give him the ranch for a fraction of its price? Well, he was dead wrong, if that's what he thought.

"So this is how we're going to play it, is it?" She poured a cup of coffee and carried it to the table.

"Play what?" he asked. "I was hungry for cinnamon toast and we usually have breakfast together if we're not fighting."

"I was afraid things would be awkward between us after the bombs on Saturday night," she answered.

"Why would things be weird?" Rusty set a whole cookie sheet full of cinnamon toast on the table and then poured himself a cup of coffee and took a seat.

His long legs brushed against hers under the table and heat spread through her body like she was standing next to a raging bonfire. He bowed his head to say grace. Lord have mercy! How was she supposed to keep a divine thought in her head while he said a short prayer with his leg touching hers?

"Amen," he said, "and now let's eat and talk about why you think we should act any different than we did before. We're consenting adults and we both had a bit to drink. Now we're ranchers and we've got work to do."

No wonder Mama never remarried, Bonnie thought. Vivien's words came back to her in a flash. *Men are impossible to live with for any length of time. You just have a good time with 'em and then shove 'em out the door and go find another one. The thrill and excitement don't last long. Ezra Malloy proved that to me, and I ain't never forgot that lesson.*

Bonnie had heard that speech so many times when she and her mother were together that it was branded on her brain. She might not agree with her mama, but it had been a long time since she'd talked to her, so she made a mental note to give Vivien a call later that day.

"I'm thinking about leaving. If you aren't going to sell me the place when you inherit, I need to get some feelers out there for another job. Cooper already has a foreman, but he said he'd hire me as a hand, and so did Jackson."

"No! You can't do that!" Bonnie gasped.

"Yes, I can and yes, I will. No use in waiting around, and

then bein' jobless. Ranchers don't need many hands in the dead of winter. It would be easier to get one now and get settled into a place by Christmas," Rusty said.

Bonnie laid her toast down and picked up her coffee. If Rusty left, she'd be lost. She'd learned a lot in the last six months, but sweet Jesus, she couldn't run the ranch without him, not even with the summer help arriving in the next few days.

"Please don't do that," she whispered.

"I like you," he said, "a lot. When y'all first arrived here, I could see that you had spunk and determination. You've worked hard to learn this business. But with your decision to leave and sell out, it's time for me to take my dogs and move on to another job."

Bonnie set her coffee down and shook her finger at him. "You're not taking the dogs. They belong on this ranch."

"Those dogs were left to me in the will, so they're mine," Rusty told her. "Get serious. Whoever buys the place will bring in their own dogs, and they probably will fight with Vivien, Polly, and Martha. And, honey," he dragged out the endearment to at least six syllables, "those dogs go with me. They're mine." He pushed back from the table. "I'm going out to the field to rake the hay. I'll see you this evening."

"Will you be here tomorrow?" she asked.

"Will you?" he shot over his shoulder as he settled his straw hat on his head and slammed the screen door.

Vivien's drunk voice popped into her head again. *Men! Can't live with 'em, and it's against the law to shoot 'em.*

"Why is it against the law to shoot them?" Bonnie muttered as she picked up a second piece of toast. "We could have a season on them, say once every five years. One day only, women could buy a tag like when I hunted deer in Kentucky. Red tag could be shoot to kill for cheaters and beaters. Blue tag could be a grazing shot for drunks and—"

Her mother's special ring tone interrupted her. "Hello, Mama, I was going to call you after breakfast."

"Great minds and all that crap," Vivien chuckled. "So how are things there? Looks like you're going to own a ranch before too many months, don't it?"

"Not if I leave," she said.

"Holy smokin' shit!" Vivien gasped. "You just made me spew coffee all over the table. You've beat both your half-sisters out for the ranch. You'd be a fool to give up now. You deserve that place after the way Ezra did me and you."

"I didn't earn it, Mama, but if I'm honest with myself, Rusty really should have it. He put up with Ezra for years and took care of him when he was sick," Bonnie said.

"You *did* earn it. You've done without things other girls had, and you've had to work for everything you needed—and so did I," Vivien told her.

"Why'd you marry him?" Bonnie asked. "Did you love him? Was he charming? Did he make you feel good about yourself? What drew you two together?"

There was a long silence before Vivien answered. "I was in one of my phases when I thought I wanted to live in the wilds. Ezra was not charming. He was crude and downright salty, but he had a ranch, and at that time I didn't want to go back to Texas or Kentucky. I wanted to settle down and have a family, and Ezra wanted a son. I didn't love him, but we tolerated each other fairly well until you were born. I never went back to the ranch after I gave birth to you. He packed up all my personal things and had them shipped back to where my mother was living at the time. I left the hospital with you in my arms, a bus ticket, and a checkbook with a deposit equal to the prenup agreement, which was ten thousand dollars."

"Did you know I had two half-sisters?" she asked.

"Of course, I did," Vivien sighed. "He never mentioned them, but that's a small community down there in the canyon, so I knew."

"Why didn't you tell me?" Bonnie could feel anger rising up from her toes. "I had a right to know that, don't you think?"

"What good would it have done? I didn't know where they were living or even what their names were," Vivien answered. "And I damn sure didn't want to know their mothers. From what I heard, they were both on the hoity-toity side."

"Why didn't you ask for half the ranch?" Bonnie tried to push the anger down, but it didn't work.

"I signed a prenup. If I didn't produce a son, then I got ten grand and a bus ticket out of the canyon," she answered. "Figured I had a fifty-fifty chance, and I lost the bet."

"So I'm just the by-product of a bet?" Bonnie's voice went all high and squeaky.

"I know that tone, and I don't like it, so goodbye." Vivien ended the call.

Bonnie wanted to throw the phone at the wall, but she shoved it into her hip pocket and stood up so quickly that she knocked her chair over. She stomped across the kitchen floor to the back door, didn't even look back at the chair or the remainder of the toast and her half-empty cup of coffee on the table.

She'd wanted to talk to her mother about these feelings she had for Rusty, but the conversation had sure enough taken a different path. "So, Mama, the ultimate love 'em and leave 'em married Ezra for money and security, not love," she fumed as she got into her old truck and drove out to the hay field. "She hasn't changed much, except she's given up on security, and now it's a good time she looks for. Even at her age now, she's always looking out for thrills, and when she gets bored with whoever is providing her with drama and fun, she goes on the prowl for another one."

Rusty was in the adjoining field, and although she couldn't see his face, she wondered if he was as angry as she was. Or maybe he was using his man powers and simply putting it out of his mind, like brushing a piece of lint from the shoulder of his jacket. Sweet Jesus! She had to persuade him to stay throughout the summer and fall at the very least.

Bonnie parked her truck, rolled down the windows, and was still mumbling to herself when she opened the door to the cab of the tractor. A blast of heat that had the faint aroma of sweat and the smell of dogs hit her in the face. She hopped up into the driver's seat, turned on the engine, and adjusted the air conditioner.

"He can go if he wants to. I can hire another foreman and the summer help will be here next week, but he's damn sure not takin' the dogs," she declared as she put the tractor in gear and started raking the hay into windrows. She wiped tears from her cheeks. She didn't want him to leave, and it had a helluva lot more to do with her feelings for him than it did with finding another foreman. There she'd admitted it— she wanted more out of the cowboy than just having him as a foreman or even as a friend.

* * *

When Bonnie stormed across the distance between her truck and the tractor, Rusty could tell by her body language that the woman was still angry. Women were such strange critters. He thought she'd be happy that he was leaving the ranch.

All of the sisters had been fast learners, but Bonnie had been the one who'd caught on to everything the fastest. Maybe it was because she'd had a hardscrabble life, and hadn't ever been handed everything. Abby Joy had showed up with her stuff in duffel bags, and Shiloh with monogrammed luggage. Bonnie had arrived with her things packed in plastic Walmart bags, and not once had she let her older half-sisters intimidate her.

She could run the ranch standing on her head in ashes, Rusty thought, *and do a fine job of it. She don't need me anymore. In the last six months she's learned plenty enough to do the job until she can get a foreman.*

His phone rang, and he grabbed it without even looking at the name on the screen. "Hello, you ready to talk this through?" he asked.

"No, but maybe we should," Waylon chuckled.

"Sorry, I thought you were Bonnie. We had an argument this morning," Rusty told him.

"Over what, if you don't mind me asking?" Waylon asked.

"Me leaving the ranch in the next few weeks," Rusty replied.

"I'll gladly give you a job and pay you more than you're making over there. I could use an extra foreman with all the new property," Waylon said.

"Thanks for the offer. The idea just came to me this morning that I should probably leave the place, and I want to think on it a couple of weeks," Rusty said.

"Don't jump into anything without sleeping on it would be my advice, but I'd hire you in a minute if you make that decision," Waylon said. "But the reason I called is that

Shiloh and I are having a little barbecue for our hired hands tomorrow evening. We wanted to invite you and Bonnie. Cooper and Abby Joy are coming for sure. She's been craving barbecued ribs."

"I never turn down ribs," Rusty said. "What time and what can I bring?"

"You can bring a six-pack of beer. Shiloh says she's asking Bonnie to bring baked beans." Waylon chuckled again.

"What's so funny?" Rusty snapped.

"Just thinking about the arguments Shiloh and I had before we admitted we were in love. It was a tough time, but seems like we all have to go through it until we admit to our feelings. That's what Shiloh told me later when we talked about those days. I'm thinkin' maybe you and Bonnie might be fighting over more than that ranch," Waylon answered.

"Me and Bonnie in love," Rusty sputtered. "That's not damn likely."

"Just tellin' you about me and Shiloh. I'm putting you down for a six-pack of beer, but if y'all are still fightin', then maybe you should bring a pint of something harder." This time Waylon laughed out loud.

"I'll bring a damned twelve-pack," Rusty growled. "And you better make extra ribs because I eat a lot when I'm aggravated."

"I'll get another rack, then. See you tomorrow night." Waylon ended the call.

Rusty tossed the phone over on the passenger's seat. He had the offer of a really good job, and he would still be in the area with all his friends. Maybe whoever bought Malloy Ranch would hate the place, and he'd have the opportunity to buy it again sometime on down the road. All he had to do was load up his truck, move across the road, and settle into

Waylon's new bunkhouse. He wouldn't have a room all to himself, but he'd have a place to lay his head at night.

At noon, he parked the tractor and noticed that Bonnie had done the same. They each got into their vehicles without even a simple wave, like they always did when they were heading back to the house for dinner.

If that was the way she wanted to be, then Rusty would give her enough space to cool off. He didn't even slow down when he passed the house but drove straight to the bunkhouse. All three dogs waited on the porch, and he bent down to pet each one of them. When he straightened up and went inside, they followed him.

He headed straight to the refrigerator, took out a gallon of sweet tea, and drank at least a pint straight from the container. He could almost hear Ezra laughing and telling him that a woman wasn't worth forgetting to take water or tea to the field with him. He put the voice out of his head while he made himself a ham and cheese sandwich. When he'd gotten out potato chips and pickles, he sat down at the table and bowed his head, but he was too agitated to pray.

Finally, he looked up at the ceiling and said, "God, why did you make women so damned stubborn? Pardon the cuss word. And by the way, thanks for the food."

No booming voice came down to answer his question, but one of the dogs cold-nosed his hand and made him almost jump out of his chair. "Are you trying to tell me something, Vivien?" he asked the mutt.

She whimpered and wagged her tail on the floor.

"Is the woman you're named after as bullheaded as her daughter?" He took another long drink of tea and then picked up his sandwich. "I'd rather be eating with her, you know. I've always looked forward to an hour in the middle of the day when we could talk about anything and everything. She's always been the easiest one for me to visit with."

Vivien laid a paw on his foot and yipped.

"Why is she bein' so damned hard to get along with'? Is it because she misses her sisters? Or maybe because she's been havin' to work so hard? Well, that's ranchin' in a nutshell, and if she don't like it, maybe she should sell out," he said between bites.

He finished his meal and headed back to the field, driving slowly because all three dogs were running along beside the truck. Dust floated across and through the barbed wire fence from where Bonnie was already back at work. When he got out of his vehicle, he sneezed twice on the way to the tractor, but the dogs stayed right with him. He opened the cab door, and they all three got inside. Two shared the passenger's seat, and Vivien curled up in the floorboard.

"Hmmmph!" Rusty said as he started the engine. "She's got rocks for brains if she thinks I'm leaving a single one of you behind. We'll go to court if we have to."

Chapter Six

Any other time, Bonnie would have suggested that she and Rusty ride over to the Wildflower Ranch together, but not that Tuesday evening. They hadn't even spoken to each other since the day before, and she wasn't going to take the first step toward reconciliation. Not when he threatened her with the dogs.

She had spent a restless night, and that morning when she awoke, she had trouble separating reality from the visions she'd had in her sleep. Tears ran down her cheeks as she sat up in bed and wondered if she'd gotten the sign she'd asked for in the form of dreams. In the first one she'd crammed all her clothing into one big black garbage bag and the other small things she'd accumulated since she'd been on the Malloy Ranch into a box. She'd put them in the back of her truck and was driving past the cemetery when she saw Ezra sitting on the top of his tombstone. With a big grin on his face, a wicked mean look in his eyes, he waved goodbye to her.

Ezra had won. All three girls had lost. Plain and simple. She couldn't let him win. She just couldn't.

In the second dream, there was snow on the ground, and both sisters, Abby Joy and Shiloh, stood on the porch as she drove away. She watched them in the mirror and realized that they would grow closer and closer to each other, while she'd just be a stranger who dropped in every few months or years to say hello.

Ezra had won a second time. He'd put the sisters together only to split them up again.

Bonnie punched her pillow several times. She couldn't let him win, and she damn sure couldn't leave her sisters behind. What if they needed her? What if she needed them like she had several times in the past months?

"Dammit!" she muttered as she wiped even more tears away with the edge of the bedsheet. "When did I put down such deep roots?"

About half angry with herself for letting herself become so vulnerable that she'd let other people deep into her heart, she threw back the covers and crawled out of bed.

She spent the entire day going back and forth from trying to convince herself that she was crazy for letting two dreams affect her whole life, to being honest with herself and admitting that they had been signs. She wasn't a lot closer to making a final decision when the day ended, and she went back to the ranch house that evening. She took a long shower, dressed in clean jeans and a sleeveless shirt, and carried her baked beans out to the truck. The vehicle looked like crap on the outside, but it had new tires, bought with her first couple of weeks' paychecks back in the winter. "You've been a faithful old friend. No way I'm goin' to turn my back on you now." She set her big bowl of baked beans on the seat beside her and put the pecan pie she'd whipped up the night before on the floorboard on the passenger side. "If you could talk, would you tell me to tell Rusty to get on down the road and not let the door hit him in the ass? Or would you tell me to settle down and call this place home."

She shot a dirty look through the gate of the small family cemetery where Ezra was buried and drove on across the road to her sister's place. She discovered that she had a choice—park right beside Rusty's truck or go all the way to the end of the line of cars and trucks. No way was she going to let him think that he'd intimidated her. She pulled in beside his vehicle, got out, and circled around behind the bed of her truck. She opened the passenger door, and suddenly both Waylon and Cooper were right there to help. One picked up the pie and the other the beans.

She caught a quick glimpse of Rusty sitting in the shadows when she mounted the porch steps, but she didn't acknowledge his presence. "Hello, everyone."

"Miz Bonnie." A few of the hired hands tipped their hats.

"Howdy." A couple more raised a beer bottle.

Out of the corner of her eye, she saw that Rusty didn't do either one, which told her that he was still every bit as angry as she was. She passed Waylon and Cooper coming through the kitchen door on their way back out to the porch. Abby Joy and Shiloh were busy at the stove, so Bonnie grabbed an apron from a hook, slipped it over her head, and asked what she could do to help.

"The corn bread should be done." Shiloh pointed at the stove. "If you'll get it out of the oven and cut it into squares, we should be ready to put it on the table and call everyone in for supper. The pie looks amazing. Thanks for bringing it. Abby Joy made a cobbler, and I whipped up a cream puff cake, so we should have plenty."

"I'll get a few glasses of tea poured up," Abby Joy said.

"I assume we're doing this buffet style?" Bonnie shoved her hands into two oven mitts and pulled the big pan of corn bread from the oven.

"Yep, and before all those guys get in our way, tell me what's going on with you and Rusty. He's pouting and you've got that look on your face that you had right after Ezra's funeral," Abby Joy said.

"Waylon said they're fighting," Shiloh informed her older sister.

"Over what?" Abby Joy asked.

"The dogs," Bonnie answered.

"Why would you fight over the dogs? Didn't Ezra leave them to Rusty in his will?" Abby Joy clamped a hand over her mouth. "Is he moving off the ranch? Good God, girl, what will you do?"

"She's tough." Shiloh picked up a knife and cut the pie into ten pieces. "She'll hire a new foreman and keep runnin' the place. Waylon said he offered him a job, so if he leaves, the dogs will just be across the road."

"That's not why we're really fighting." Bonnie sighed. "I've been thinkin' about it all day long while I sat in a tractor. It's just something to fight about because neither of us will face our feelings."

"And what's that supposed to mean?" Shiloh asked.

"That we're attracted to each other and have been for months," Bonnie blurted out.

Shiloh winked at Abby Joy.

"What's the winking all about?" Bonnie cut the corn bread and made a pyramid of it on a platter with the squares.

"We saw the attraction between the two of you the first week we were at the ranch," Abby Joy told her.

"We've just been waiting for y'all to figure it out for yourselves," Shiloh added. "So, give us the short version of what caused the fight." She carried a bowl of coleslaw to the dining room table.

"We've been arguing about me selling the ranch for a week now. And now he's saying that he might as well leave, since it'll be hard to find a job on a ranch in the wintertime. Then he said he was taking the dogs. I don't want him to leave, and I'm terrified about putting down roots. What if I got my mama's genes and after six months me and Rusty got ourselves in a relationship, and then I decided that I wanted to sell out and leave. He was good to teach us and help us learn, and Ezra was a sumbitch for going back on his word about leavin' the ranch to Rusty."

"Then why are you arguing with yourself about selling it to him?" Shiloh asked.

"Hell, if I know." Bonnie shrugged. "I'm so damned confused I don't know whether to wind my butt or scratch my watch as my mama used to say." She went on to tell them about the two dreams.

"The dogs just gave you something to argue about when you're really angry with yourselves because you can't figure out what it is you want to do and why. And, honey, I believe in dreams. Mama used to tell me that God has visited folks in dreams since the beginning of time, and when He speaks, we should listen," Abby Joy said.

Cooper came into the kitchen, walked up behind Abby Joy, and slipped his arms around her. "It sure smells good in here. Is it about time to call in the hungry guys?"

Abby Joy turned around and kissed him on the cheek. "Bonnie will have the corn bread on the table in about five seconds, so go on and tell them it's ready."

"Yes, ma'am." Cooper bent and brushed a kiss across

his wife's lips. "And thanks to all three of you ladies for all you've done."

Bonnie had barely set the platter of corn bread on the table when the men started filing inside the house. Rusty was the last one in the line, and he stood back against the wall. Waylon removed his cowboy hat and bowed his head. The rest of the cowboys did the same.

When he'd said "Amen" at the end of the very short grace, Shiloh kissed him on the cheek.

In that moment, Bonnie began to doubt whether she really wanted to sell the ranch and travel or if she wanted what her sisters both had, roots and someone to love them.

"We don't have room for everyone to sit down in the house, but we've set up a couple of long tables out in the backyard," Shiloh said. "The silverware and napkins are already out there."

"Man, this looks good," Cooper said.

"Smells good too. I haven't had anything but sandwiches for two days." Rusty stepped forward, picked up a plate, and began to load it.

Bonnie shot a mean look across the table at him, but his eyes were on the food and the evil glare was wasted. Fixing her own plate, she wondered if he'd missed coming to the ranch house to eat with her as much as she'd missed having him there.

How on earth Rusty got behind her was a mystery, but suddenly, he was there, and he whispered softly in her ear, "We need to talk, don't you think?"

His warm breath on the soft part of her neck sent shivers down her spine. "You're not taking those dogs away from their home," she said. "They were raised on the ranch, and they'd be miserable anywhere else. I'll stay right there and never leave before you take them away. I won't even sell it until they've all passed away, and then I'm going to bury them right on top of Ezra. That way he'll have all three of his wives in the same grave with him."

"Let's talk about all of this tomorrow." Rusty set his plate down on the first table they came to.

"Where and when?" she asked.

"Neutral place," he answered. "In the barn at six o'clock."

"I'll be there." With a curt nod, she walked on past him and sat down at the second table with Abby Joy, Cooper, and a handful of hired hands.

"What was that all about?" Abby Joy whispered.

"Just setting up a meeting so we can talk," Bonnie answered.

"You've got a job right here anytime you want to move," Abby Joy said. "Just promise me you won't get a wild hair and leave the canyon. Sisters should stick together, and besides, this baby"—she laid her hand on her bulging stomach—"needs his aunts. I don't know a blessed thing about babies, so I'll need all the help I can get too."

Bonnie made up her mind right then and there to stick around until the dogs had all died, and so that she could be an aunt to Abby Joy's baby. Bonnie missed having family in her life, so she couldn't very well deny her little niece the same. "I promise."

She glanced over at the other table, where Shiloh and Waylon were sitting with the rest of the hired hands. Her mind went back to that first day when Cooper had told them that they'd need more than one napkin because the chicken was greasy. She had been glad that her two older half-sisters weren't bashful when it came to food. On first impression, Shiloh had seemed pretty prissy, and the older sister was without a doubt a force to be reckoned with, but when they all three gathered around in the kitchen that cold day, all three of them hadn't had any qualms about food.

Abby Joy bumped her on the arm. "What are you thinkin' about? You've hardly touched your barbecue, and I know you like it a lot."

"I've been thinkin' about our first day together a lot lately," she answered.

"You mean at Ezra's funeral?" Cooper asked. "I couldn't believe that all three of you showed up looking like you did at his graveside service."

"Oh?" Abby Joy raised an eyebrow.

"Think about it," Cooper chuckled. "You looked like you'd just come out of a war zone in all that camouflage and your combat boots. Shiloh, over there"—he nodded her way—"looked like she'd just left a rodeo, and I wasn't sure if you were a biker or a punk rocker, Bonnie."

"I couldn't believe those two were my sisters, either." Bonnie giggled. "I figured that Abby Joy was like Ezra, and Shiloh had to take after her mother, and that neither of them would last two days on a ranch. Shiloh would be afraid she'd break a fingernail, and Abby Joy would be..."

"I'd be what?" Abby Joy asked.

"Bored to tears on a ranch after the life you'd led in the military," Bonnie finished. "I didn't even know Ezra, but from what Mama told me when she was drinking too much and bitchin' about him, I figured you were the most like him."

"Hey, now, I'm the least like Ezra of all of us," Abby Joy declared.

Suddenly Bonnie had that antsy feeling that she only got when someone was staring at her. She glanced over at the other table and locked eyes with Rusty. She wished that she could fall into those sexy green eyes all the way to the bottom of his soul and find out what his real feelings were. Waylon nudged him with a shoulder, and he looked away just about the same time Abby Joy poked her on the arm with her forefinger.

"You don't have a smart-ass remark about me being the least like Ezra?" Abby Joy asked.

"Nope, but I've got a question for Cooper. You liked Ezra, right?"

Cooper nodded. "He was an eccentric old codger, but he was smart as a whip when it came to ranchin'. All of us around these parts could depend on him for advice—other than when it came to women."

"Guess that answers my question fairly well," Bonnie said. "Thanks."

Cooper's head bobbed in a quick nod, and then he changed the subject. "These beans are great. What's your secret?"

"A tablespoon of mustard," Bonnie answered. "It cuts the sweet of the brown sugar and ketchup."

And a little argument is good for a relationship, like mustard is good for beans. Her mother's voice popped into her head. *It cuts all that sweetness of flirting and sex. Every couple has to endure a few tests to see if the relationship will withstand the long journey.*

That just might be the smartest advice you have ever given me, Mama, Bonnie thought. *Why don't you apply it to your own relationships?*

Chapter Seven

Bonnie was sitting on a bale of hay in the corner of the barn, ready for their talk, when Rusty arrived. Several strands of blond hair had escaped from her ponytail and were stuck to her sweaty face. Pieces of hay were still stuck to her clothing from hauling bales from the field to the barn all day. With no one else to help, and refusing to work together, they'd each loaded their own truck bed full, driven it to the barn, and then unloaded and stacked it there. They'd gotten in what they'd baled the day before, and tomorrow, they'd move to another field and start cutting what was ready there.

"Why didn't Ezra ever get the machinery to make those big round bales?" She removed her work gloves and laid them beside her.

"He was old school." Rusty sat down on the running board of her truck. "He said that ranchers wasted enough hay to make half a dozen small bales with what they lost on every one they left out in the weather. I think that once we were set up the waste would be worth it in the long run because we'd save a ton of money in the summer." When Ezra was alive, Rusty wouldn't have doubted anything the old man said.

"How would that be saving money?" she asked.

"We wouldn't be payin' the summer help wages," he answered. "But we're really not here to talk about hay, are we?"

"No, but after loading and hauling this all day, I'm all for buying the new stuff for the big bales," she said. "I'll go first. The argument over the dogs was just so we didn't have to face the real problem, which is the fact that I really do like you. One minute we're arguing, and the next we get along pretty good. I don't know if you're just pretending to be nice so I'll sell you the ranch, or if you feel the same sparks I do when you're in the same room with me." She pushed a strand of hair from her sweaty face.

He was speechless at her honesty. "I like you too. Always have felt a connection between us, but I'm having second thoughts about this place. I've had a love-hate connection to the ranch, though. Seems like it's tainted when it comes to relationships. I don't care if I had ten daughters and no sons, I'd never send them away, and they'd all inherit an equal share of whatever I had when my days on this earth came to an end. And Ezra shouldn't have treated his wives the way he did. Far as I could tell, none of them did a thing wrong, and it wasn't their fault their first child wasn't a son. The second one might have been."

"You won't get an argument out of me on any of what you just said," Bonnie agreed, "but a ranch is basically just dirt and grass. Is it really worth losing a friend, or the love of your life, over? Neither of my older sisters thought it was."

"Sometimes the place is just dirt if we don't get rain when we need it," Rusty chuckled. "When y'all first got here, you were sure enough ready to put on the gloves and go to war for the ranch, and now all you can talk about is selling it and gettin' the hell out of Dodge, or the Palo Duro Canyon, as this case is."

"Yep, but then we bonded, and now I feel pretty alone. It's not the first time. Every time Mama moved us, I had this same feeling of not knowing anyone. I hated walking into a new school three or four times a year," she said. "But not putting down roots is part of me now, and I don't know if I can stay in one place and be happy, Rusty. I'm afraid to even give it a try, but my heart has grown roots here and I have sisters who are living close by. Plus, you and I need to make the decisions about what happens on this place. Ezra is gone, and he doesn't get a say-so anymore."

Rusty moved over to sit beside her. "No, he doesn't, but he's buried right here on the property."

"He left you his knowledge of ranchin'." Bonnie nudged him with her shoulder. "I inherited his blue eyes and stubborn will. That's all he should get credit for."

"If you stay, and I hope you do," Rusty said, "what will you tell your kids about him someday? You do realize, he'll be their grandfather."

"I'll tell them the absolute truth, and then I'll tell them that they have a father who is amazing and loves them, even if their grandfather wasn't a nice person," she answered.

"How can you make that kind of statement when you have no idea who the father of your kids will be?" Rusty turned and studied her face.

"Because I won't ever marry until I can find a man that I can truly say is amazing and that will love our children. I grew up without a father, for no other reason than I wasn't a boy. My kids, boys or girls, are going to have a daddy to love them, protect them, and provide for them, or I won't have a husband," Bonnie declared with so much conviction that Rusty could have sworn the temperature in the hot barn raised a few more degrees.

"Now, let's talk about you," Rusty said. "Are you staying or leaving?"

"Staying. I can't let Ezra win, and besides, I kind of like having roots, now that I realize how it feels," she answered. "Let's make a deal. We both stay until Christmas and see where this attraction between us goes. No rush. No hurry. But I want to talk to that lawyer who set up Ezra's will. Think you could arrange a meeting with him?"

"What do you want to talk to him about?" Rusty frowned.

"I want to understand a little more about the way the will is written," she answered. "Then we'll be ready for another talk. When can we visit with him?"

"I'll call him tomorrow morning and set up an appointment," Rusty answered. "Now we should be ready to talk honestly about *us*. I've missed you the last two days." He scooted over closer to her.

"I wouldn't want to run this place without you." She turned so they were facing each other. "And I like having you around. I missed you too."

He cupped her face in his hands and their lips met in a fiery kiss that warmed the barn right up to a full ninety-plus degrees. His hands trembled and his pulse raced when the kiss ended.

"So, we're good then?" He wanted to kiss her again, just to see if the second one stirred his feelings as much as the first one.

"Yes, we're good." She laid her head on his shoulder. "Can we go over this one more time, though? We've agreed that neither of us will leave the ranch, but we haven't talked about the dogs."

"According to the will, they are mine," he said, "but I'm willing to share them with you as long as you stay on the place." He leaned back and frowned. "Are you keeping me around just so you don't have to give up the dogs?"

She reached up and ruffled his dark hair. "You're smarter than you look."

He grabbed her hand and brought it to his lips to kiss each knuckle. "I've got lots of surprises to show you, since you've said you'll stick around for a while."

Chapter Eight

On the day of Ezra's funeral, Jackson Bailey had served as executor to Ezra's estate and handed each of the sisters a copy of his will. Bonnie shoved hers into the bottom dresser drawer in her new bedroom and never gave it another minute's thought. When she awoke on Thursday morning, the first thing she did was go straight to the dresser and get the blue binder.

She padded barefoot to the kitchen, where she made a pot of coffee and then sat down at the table to try to make heads and tails out of the legalese its pages contained. Most of it was so deep that she couldn't understand a word of it, but the language that said the sisters had to stay on the ranch for a year to share it was plain enough. If two of them left, it went to the third one—kind of like the last girl standing. Bonnie would have to have the lawyer verify what she thought that meant, but if it did, everything could change in a hurry. Because the way she read it said that if she was the last one on the ranch, then it went to her, even before the year was up.

"Good mornin'." Rusty came into the kitchen by the back door. "What have you got there? Coffee smells good. Let's have ham and cinnamon toast for breakfast."

"Ezra's will," she answered. "That sounds fine."

"I'll call that lawyer about nine. That's usually when businesses open up in Claude. Don't get your hopes up. He's an old guy, maybe Ezra's age or older, and he pretty much keeps hours when he wants to." Rusty poured two mugs of coffee and brought them to the table. "What's got you worried about it? I thought it was pretty straightforward."

"I can't understand anything I'm reading, but I wanted to at least have looked at it before we go into town to see the lawyer." She pushed it to the middle of the table. "What's on the agenda for today?" But then she cocked her head to one side and listened intently. "That sounds like a car or maybe a truck."

"I thought it was a tractor with a bad engine problem coming up the lane," Rusty said.

"Are we expecting company?" Bonnie asked.

She pushed back her chair and frowned as she started toward the door. When she stepped outside, she could see the dust boiling up as the old blue pickup truck drove down the lane. She heard the door open and close behind her and felt Rusty's presence even before he laid a hand on her shoulder.

"Friend of yours?" he asked.

"Holy crap on a cracker!" Bonnie sighed. "That would be my mother, arriving without notice. I guess she sold her car and got a truck." *Could the morning get any worse?* she thought as she took a step back. "Mama?"

"I've come to rescue you," Vivien yelled as she got out of

the truck and jogged across the yard. A tall blond woman, she was so thin that Bonnie used to tell her to put rocks in her pockets to keep a strong wind from blowing her away. She looked every one of her fifty-three years, but then she lived on cigarettes, coffee, booze, and an occasional joint or two.

Vivien opened up her arms, and Bonnie walked into them. "I don't need or want to be rescued," she said. "Mama meet Rusty. Rusty, this is my mother, Vivien Malloy."

"I'll stick around until tomorrow and maybe you'll change your mind." Vivien took in the house and surrounding area in one sweeping glance. "This place ain't changed since you was a baby."

Vivien released her daughter from the hug. "You don't have to live like this another day, darlin'. I've changed my mind about you staying here to get his worthless piece of dirt. I want you to take whatever the money is offered in the will and go with me to California. If this old truck won't make it, we'll stop and get another one or finish the trip on the bus."

Bonnie folded her arms over her chest and stepped in front of the door. "I'm not going anywhere."

Vivien looked rougher than usual. Her eyes were bloodshot, and her hair hung in limp strings. She reeked of whiskey and marijuana and smelled like she hadn't had a bath in a week.

"Have you been drinking and driving again?"

"Yep, but I didn't get caught, so it's all right," Vivien giggled. "And yes, I had a joint or two to relax me on the long drive, and now I'm coming down off it. You know what that means—munchies. What's in the kitchen?"

"We haven't had breakfast yet, and we'll be glad to have you join us. We were about to make cinnamon toast and fry up some ham to go with it. The coffee is ready. You ladies can have a cup and visit while I get the food ready. Come on in and make yourself at home." Rusty held the door open.

"So, you're Rusty," Vivien said as she pushed her way inside. "I need to clean up a bit. Don't worry about me. I still remember where everything is located in this god-forsaken place."

"In my wildest imagination I can't see Ezra married to her," Rusty whispered as he got down a loaf of bread and began to slather butter on each piece.

Bonnie got a slice of ham out of the refrigerator. "Her favorite men have been bikers who stick around for a few weeks or maybe even a couple of months and then they get into a big fight and we usually wind up moving somewhere else."

"And even after you got out of school, you moved with her?" Rusty asked.

Bonnie nodded. "I hold down a job better than she does, so she needed me."

"That's called an enabler." Rusty shook a mixture of cinnamon and sugar over the buttered bread and slid it into the oven.

"Well, well, ain't this cozy?" Vivien arrived back in the kitchen. "I don't remember Ezra ever helping me cook a damn thing. You sure ain't related to him in anyway, Rusty."

She wore a pair of Bonnie's newest jeans, one of her shirts, and she'd changed out her ratty sneakers for Bonnie's cowboy boots.

"You are welcome to take my things without asking," Bonnie said in a saccharine tone.

"Thank you." Vivien poured herself a mug of coffee and added three heaping spoonfuls of sugar. "I knew you wouldn't mind. We'll be traveling together anyway and sharing hotel rooms, so it's not like you won't get them back."

"I'm not going anywhere," Bonnie reaffirmed. "Why are you going to California? You've always stuck around Kentucky and east Texas."

"About two months ago, Big Ben came into the bar where I've been working since you left Kentucky. We hit it off." Vivien shrugged. "And then he cheated on me. I've always wanted to see the ocean, and you talked about it when you was a kid, so I sold everything I had and headed this way. With what you'll get, surely, we can get out there and rent us a trailer. We can always find a job as bartenders. Come on, Bonnie, have some sense. This damned ranch ruined my life. Don't let it tear yours up too."

Bonnie sat down at the table beside her mother and laid a hand on Vivien's arm. "Mama, you need to slow down. Why don't you stay a few days here with me and forget about California?"

Vivien jerked her arm free. "Honey, this is *my* life. I'll live it the way I want to. If you're smart, you'll come with me and do the same. It's exciting. Settling down ain't in my blood. I was glad that Ezra kicked us out. I would've probably left him before long anyway. I damn sure wasn't happy being here or being pregnant, and I vowed after you was born I'd never go through that again, not even to give him a son and get part of this ranch."

"You are going to get yourself killed," Bonnie scolded.

Vivien shook her head. "Maybe, but I'll die happy, not withered up on a worthless ranch doing something I hate. Rusty, darlin', if she stays with you when I leave, you just remember whose daughter she is before you go gettin' involved with her. What the hell good could come out of me and Ezra Malloy? You just think about that."

"I don't believe that our heritage determines our future," Rusty said. "Bonnie, if you'll take a step to the side, I'll get the toast out of the oven, and we can eat breakfast."

"And that's real sweet of you, Mama, to say that about me. Maybe I've done something you've never been willing to do like change for the better," Bonnie said through clenched teeth.

"You always were a smart-ass. Got that from your daddy," Vivien told her. "You wouldn't have a denim jacket around here somewhere, would you?"

Bonnie realized she would be relieved when her mother had breakfast and left. One minute she wanted to cry for her mother's bad choices in life; the next she wanted to send her to her bedroom without supper to punish her.

"Why do you want a denim jacket?" Bonnie asked.

"They say it gets cool in the evenings in California, and I left in such a hurry that I didn't pack a coat." Vivien helped her plate with three pieces of toast and a big chunk of the ham slice.

"Why'd you leave so fast?" Bonnie asked and then shook her head slowly. "You took all of that biker's money when you headed west, didn't you? Like you used to do when I was a little girl and you got tired of living with some guy."

"And his bag of pot and two bottles of whiskey. I drove all night to get here," she said. "And I came to get my baby girl so I can take her to see the ocean like she always wanted."

"No thanks," Bonnie said. "I like the ranchin' business too well to leave it."

"I swear to God, she's just like Ezra," Vivien said.

"I can call Cooper," Rusty whispered just for Bonnie's ears. "After all, he is still the county sheriff until the election is over."

Bonnie shook her head and turned her attention back to Vivien, who was eating so fast that she couldn't have enjoyed the food. "You think Big Bill will follow you here?"

"No, he'll just cut his losses and move in with that hussy from the bar that he's been flirtin' with. And it's Big Ben, not Big Bill. Come on, Bonnie. Let's go see whoever we need to talk to and get your money. Between us we can have a good time," Vivien said.

"For the last time," Bonnie said, "the answer is no." She couldn't help but wonder what the answer might have been a few days before if Vivien had arrived with the same offer.

Bonnie remembered the dreams again and the empty feeling she had when she left her sisters behind. She didn't ever want to experience that in real life.

And this is your third sign, that niggling little voice in her head said. *Your mother is offering you freedom. You need to make up your mind for sure about what you want, and never look back.*

"Your loss," Vivien said as matter-of-factly as if she were discussing whether or not Bonnie should have a beer or a shot of whiskey with her.

"More coffee anyone?" Rusty asked as he brought the second pan of toast to the table and sat down.

"Hey, where is everyone?" Shiloh yelled from the front door.

"In the kitchen," Bonnie called out.

"Who's here?" Abby Joy's voice preceded her into the kitchen.

Vivien looked up from the table and smiled when they entered the room. "I'm Vivien, Bonnie's mother."

"These are my sisters, Shiloh and Abby Joy," Bonnie said.

"Half-sisters," Vivien corrected her. "Glad to meet y'all."

"Same here." Shiloh and Abby Joy said in unison.

"We were taking the morning off to run into Amarillo to grocery shop. We stopped by to see if you want to go, but since you've got company..." Shiloh let the sentence trail off.

"Give me time to finish eating and then I'll be leaving. You should never miss a chance to get off this ranch, Bonnie. Even if it's just to go for groceries," Vivien said.

Shiloh poured herself a cup of coffee and sat down at the kitchen table. "So what brings you back to the canyon, Miz Vivien?"

"My daughter," Vivien answered and picked up another piece of toast. "I thought she'd be tired of this place, and she'd jump at the chance to go with me to California. Maybe y'all can talk sense to her."

Bonnie could have sworn that the look Shiloh shot her way was one of pure understanding. But how could her sister know anything about the way Bonnie and Vivien had lived? Both of them had had a fairly stable life.

"We don't know what we'd do without her." Abby Joy pulled up a chair and sat down. "I'm having a baby soon, and my child is going to need her aunts to be close by, and I need her to help me. I don't know anything about babies."

"Neither does she," Vivien said.

"But she knows me, and she can calm me down when I get scared." Abby Joy smiled.

Bonnie could have hugged her sister for saying that.

"And she promised she'd stay close to us even if she didn't stay on this ranch. We've kind of grown to like having siblings," Shiloh said.

Vivien glanced up at Bonnie. "You're going to be sorry.

Every evening, I'll watch the sun set over the ocean, and you could be with me."

"You're playin' a dangerous game," Bonnie warned her. "We have lovely sunsets right here, and you can get sober and clean, maybe even learn to put down some roots like I have."

"That ain't for me." Vivien shook her head. "But, honey, I'll call and check in when I get my new job. Maybe you and your boyfriend"—she nodded toward Rusty—"can come out and visit me. You know how I hate goodbyes, so don't follow me to the door and wave and all that crap. We'll keep in touch. See you later." She stood up, finished off the last swallow of coffee, and grinned. "You wouldn't have a spare bottle of Jim Beam for me to take along on the trip, would you?"

"No, I do not," Bonnie said quickly.

"Never know the answer if you don't ask." Vivien waved as she left the house. In a couple of minutes, Bonnie heard the front door slam and then she let out a loud whoosh of breath that she didn't even realize she'd been holding.

"I'm sorry." Bonnie looked straight at Rusty. "I owe you a big thank-you and an apology."

"You are welcome, but you don't have to be sorry." He stood up and carried empty plates to the sink. "I'm going to the barn to change the tire on the tractor you use. You ladies probably have a lot to talk about." His eyes twinkled. "Hey, I'm special. Now I've met both your parents."

"That's not saying a lot, now is it?" she told him.

Rusty shot her a grin and strode out the door with a wave.

"Had your mom been drinkin'?" Abby Joy asked. "Her eyes were bloodshot."

"She drove all night from Kentucky and is damn lucky she didn't get stopped for drunk driving and drugs, but that's my mama. I have to love her, but nothing says I have to like her all the time," she said. "I'd forgotten how crazy she can be. Do y'all ever wonder what it was in Ezra that made our mothers marry him? From what we saw of that old man in the casket, I can't see why any woman would want to vow to love him forever."

"I've wondered the same thing about my mother," Abby Joy said. "Since we never knew him, we'll never know the answer to that question."

"Do you think she'll get all the way to the West Coast in that truck?" Shiloh asked.

"If she doesn't there's lots of biker bars and truck stops between here and there. She'll find a way." Bonnie crossed her arms on the table and laid her head down. "Someday I'm going to get a message that says she's been killed unless she cleans up her act. God, I'm scared to death of..." She didn't finish.

"That wouldn't be your fault," Abby Joy said.

Shiloh patted her on the shoulder. "She's living a dare-devil life and it has consequences."

"Not her, I'm scared to ever have children," Bonnie said. "She told Rusty that I didn't have anything to draw on, and she's right. Look at my parents—Ezra and Vivien. At least y'all had good mothers to balance out what Ezra donated to the gene pool."

"Maybe, you take a lesson from them on how not to be," Shiloh offered. "Are you trying to tell me something?"

"If I'm pregnant, it'll be the new baby Jesus. I haven't had sex since I got here," Bonnie said bluntly. "I'm just saying that any man in his right mind would never want a relationship with me if they truly understood my back-ground."

"Don't be thinkin' that," Shiloh said. "I've seen the love

you shower on a baby calf, or even the dogs. You'll be a great mother."

"Amen." Abby Joy added her two cents. "And besides, we've all got each other to help us learn the ropes on parenthood. I, for one, am glad that you didn't let your mother talk you into leaving us. We've proved that we belong together right here in this canyon."

"Yep," Shiloh said.

"Thank you both." Bonnie raised her head and wiped away the tears flowing down her cheeks. "Right now, I can't imagine living anywhere else."

"Well, that's settled," Abby Joy declared. "So now let's get on with some grocery shopping and talking about these sparks I keep feeling between you and Rusty."

"Good Lord!" Bonnie said. "One thing at a time. I need to process all this before I move on to my feelings for Rusty."

"At least you admit and recognize that the feelings are there, so that's a start." Abby Joy reached for the last piece of toast.

"And that's a big step for me," Bonnie admitted.

Chapter Nine

Bonnie had a lot of time to think as she drove a tractor around the field that afternoon. Rusty was just over the barbed wire fence on the next twenty acres cutting hay, just like she was doing—like they'd both done the day before. The difference was that they weren't fighting now, and every so often, they were even close enough to wave at each other.

In between those times, she replayed the morning over and over again in her mind. It was so surreal that she could almost believe it had never happened—that it was just a bad nightmare. Of all the crazy stunts Vivien had ever pulled, this one was the most insane. Bonnie slapped the steering wheel with both hands when she realized that her mother was the very reason Rusty might want to be with *her*?

"It better not be because you felt sorry for me. I don't want your pity," she muttered.

Her phone rang and she picked it up from the passenger

seat. When her mother's name came up, she answered immediately. "Did you change your mind? Where are you? I'll come get you."

"Hell, no, I ain't changed my mind," Vivien said. "I'm on my way to California. I'm not about to change my mind. I'm stopped at a roadside rest outside of Clovis to catch a catnap in the bed of the truck. I brought along a sleeping bag, and I'm dog-tired. I'm calling to ask you one more time to come with me."

"Answer is still no. I'm happy right here where I am, Mama, but I'll drive to Clovis and get *you* if you'll change your mind. You can work with us here on the place or get a job in Claude or somewhere close and just live here if you don't want to do ranch work," Bonnie told her.

"No, thanks. I washed my hands of that place when you was born," Vivien said. "Rusty seems like a good guy, but Ezra trained him, so keep that in mind. Make him sign a prenup before you marry him so he don't steal half the place from you. Even good men ain't to be trusted. You be real careful. There ain't no such thing as an honest man."

Bonnie sucked in a long breath to say something else, but then she realized that her mother had hung up on her. She slapped the steering wheel again, stopped the engine, and got out of the tractor. Tears ran down her cheeks—Lord have mercy! She'd cried more in the past few days than she had in her whole life put together. She shook her fist at the sky. Just when she thought she had left the past behind her, its ugly old head had popped right up again, coming at her this time as doubts and fears. Cooper and Waylon were good, honest men for sure, and so was Rusty. Her mother was wrong—she just flat out had to be.

She caught a movement in her peripheral vision but didn't

realize it was Rusty until he and all three dogs surrounded her. He took her in his arms and eased the two of them down on the ground. "What's the matter? Is it Shiloh or Abby Joy?"

"It's Mama." She sobbed into his chest.

"Is she hurt? Did she change her mind?" He rattled off questions too fast for her to comprehend, much less answer.

Even after meeting her and after knowing now exactly what kind of mother Bonnie had, he was still concerned for the woman. For some strange reason, that was the final little bit of what it took to convince Bonnie that she was right where she belonged and gave her the courage to admit her feelings.

"Mama is fine. She just wanted to give me one more chance to go with her." Bonnie dried her eyes with the back of her hand.

Rusty laid his hands on her shoulders and looked deeply into her eyes. "Please don't go."

"I couldn't if I wanted to, which I don't," she whispered without blinking. "It would be too painful to leave this ranch, my sisters, and most of all, you. I love you, Rusty," she admitted. "It's too soon to say it, but there it is. I figured it out a few days ago, and I'm tired of fighting the feeling. I don't want to go another day, or even another hour, without saying the words. I think I fell in love with you right there on that first day, but ..."

He put his fingers over her lips. "There are no buts in real love, only ands. I love you, Bonnie, and I don't give a damn who your parents were. We don't have to be the by-products of our parents, darlin'. I'm a foster child, and I don't even remember my folks. We can build our own life right here in this place. We can take steps forward and never look over our shoulder at the past. And, honey, I believe I felt the same about you from the beginning, but I didn't want you to think it was just to get this place."

"Okay." She managed a weak smile through the tears. "I love you, and I'm never letting my mother or anyone else make me doubt myself again."

Rusty pulled her close to his chest. "What are we going to do about this?"

"Live together on this place for six months and figure it out a day at a time?" she suggested.

"That sounds good to me." He tipped up her chin for a long kiss that left her breathless.

"Maybe you could even move your things back into the ranch house?" She might be moving too fast, but she didn't want to waste time she could be spending with Rusty.

Vivien wedged her way between them and licked Bonnie's hand. "Somehow I feel like this dog loves me more than my mother does. Do you realize you're the first person who's ever said those three words to me, Rusty?" Tears began to stream down her cheeks, again.

He brushed a sweet kiss across her forehead. "I believe you're the first who ever said them to me too. And, I promise to tell you every day that I love you. Now, tell me what caused these tears." He pulled a red bandanna from his pocket and dried her cheeks.

"I've had to be tough my whole life, and I don't like to cry because it's a sign of weakness, but I'm so happy that I figured out where I belong. These are happy tears, Rusty."

He tucked the bandanna back into his hip pocket and slipped an arm under her shoulders. "I'd never be so stupid as to think that you were weak."

"Thank you," she whispered. "I meant it when I said I

love you, but"—she stopped and shook her head—"it goes deeper than that. I can't explain it."

"It's more like a soul mate kind of thing then, right?" he asked.

"That's right, and I like the feeling." She finally smiled.

"So do I, darlin'." He kissed her one more time.

Chapter Ten

Six months later

Bonnie awoke to find Rusty propped up on an elbow staring at her. She smiled and reached up to run a hand over his unshaven face. "Happy wedding day. Are we ready for this?"

"I hope so." He grinned. "There's a lot of people that's goin' to be mad as hell if we ain't at the church this afternoon at about two o'clock. They're going to have to wade through more than a foot of snow just to get to their trucks, but Cooper and Waylon said they'd take care of clearing the porch of the church and sidewalk."

"It's supposed to be bad luck for the bride and groom to see each other on their wedding day." He toyed with a strand of her hair. "Do you think maybe we should have just gone to the courthouse?"

"Nope. I've always wanted a wedding," Bonnie assured him. "I want to see the look in your eyes when I walk down the aisle, and I want to hold that memory in my heart forever."

"There's no way you could be more beautiful than you are right now." He pulled her lips to his for the first morning kiss. "Think your mother will show up and surprise you?"

"It would be a big surprise all right." Bonnie threw back the covers and got out of bed. "She's still runnin' with that motorcycle gang, and they've joined up with more bikers somewhere up near the Canadian border in Washington. She called yesterday and tried to talk me into gettin' on a plane and coming out there to live with them."

Rusty got out of bed and picked up a pair of jeans. Bonnie stopped what she was doing and stared at his fine naked body—all hardened muscles, a broad chest, and a heart inside that was so full of love for her that sometimes she still found it hard to believe. In only a few hours, she'd have a piece of paper that said he belonged to her. She full well intended to frame it and set it up on the mantel above the fireplace in the living room for the whole world to see.

"I'm a lucky woman," she whispered.

"What was that?" Rusty asked.

"I said I'm one lucky woman," she repeated.

"Not as lucky as I am." He grinned and rounded the end of the bed to take her in his arms. "I'd like to go back to bed with you, but we're kind of on a tight schedule here. We've got brunch at Shiloh's, and then we're supposed to go straight to the church."

"And Abby Joy says once I step foot in the church, I can't see you anymore until the wedding." She tugged on her jeans and stomped her feet down into her boots. "Let's go get the feeding chores done and then head over to Shiloh's."

"Lovers forever." She held up a pinky.

"Married couple from today until death parts us." He wrapped his pinky around hers.

"Ranchers together." They both said it at the same time and held up three fingers.

* * *

Rusty looked out over the congregation that Wednesday afternoon and thought again that New Year's Day was a strange day for a wedding, but there was no way he was going to argue with Bonnie. She wanted the ceremony to be on the very day when she took ownership of the ranch. After her mother had come for that crazy visit, they'd signed papers back in the summer, and those papers said that on the day they married, the Malloy Ranch would belong to the two of them—and that on that very day, the name of the place would be changed to Sunrise Ranch.

The pianist began to play "The Rose," and Shiloh came down the center aisle with her arm looped in Waylon's. Abby Joy and Cooper followed behind them. In less than an hour, Rusty would have two sisters-in-law and two brothers-in-law—he'd have family for the first time in his life. The preacher raised his arms for everyone to stand, and the pianist began to play the traditional wedding march. The double doors at the back of the church opened, and Bonnie came down the aisle alone. Jackson Bailey had offered to escort her, but she had refused. She told Rusty that she was giving herself to him in marriage, and she didn't need anyone else to do that for her.

She was wearing a lovely white lace dress that stopped at her ankles. Peeking out from under its hem were the same biker boots that she'd worn a year ago on that very first day that Rusty had laid eyes on her. *The day that I fell in love with her if I'm being honest about the whole thing,* he thought. His eyes met hers, and he couldn't wait for her to reach the front of the church. He met her halfway back down the aisle and hugged her tightly to his chest.

"I'm the luckiest man alive this day," he whispered.

"I'd say we've made our own luck," she said. "Now let's go get married so we can tell the whole world about this baby we're going to have in four months."

He tucked her free hand into his, and together, they stepped up in front of the preacher. She handed her bouquet to Shiloh and turned to face Rusty, just like they'd rehearsed, but the night before, she hadn't looked so much like an angel straight from the courts of heaven. Suddenly, he was tongue-tied and was glad that he'd written his vows on a piece of paper.

* * *

The party for just the wedding party after the reception was held at the newly named Sunrise Ranch. While the ladies were in the bedroom helping Bonnie get out of her fancy lace dress and into a pair of jeans, Rusty slipped away and walked down to the cemetery. The wind whistled through the bare tree branches and blew powdery snow up from the ground, which chilled the bare skin on his face. He pulled the collar of his fleece-lined jacket up to keep his ears warm and bent his head against the cold.

The gate into the cemetery squeaked loudly as if it were competing with the noise of tree limbs rattling against each other. He wasn't aware that the dogs had followed him until he had brushed away the snow and sat down on the bench in front of Ezra's tombstone, and the three of them gathered around him.

"My faithful old friends." He took time to pat each of them on the head with a gloved hand. "We've come together to tell him goodbye, haven't we?"

He sat there for a full minute before he began to talk to the tombstone, which was half covered by a drift of snow. "I'm here again, Ezra. It was a year ago today that we put you in the ground, and I doubt that you would believe how much things have changed. Why you did what you did is still a mystery to me, but I have to admit, there's three cowboys in this part of the canyon now who are mighty glad that you did it for whatever reason. When Abby Joy got married and left the ranch, the other two sisters came right here and talked to you. When Shiloh did the same, Bonnie came to talk to you. I figure now that everything is settled, it's my turn."

He patted the bench, and all three dogs jumped up on it with him.

"They never knew I saw them make their journey here, and I'll never know what they said to you, but I don't imagine any one of them was telling you that she loved you. I may never come back here again except when it's time to mow and keep the cemetery cleaned up. I owe you that much. But this will be our last conversation. Abby Joy has a beautiful little son, and Shiloh will be having a boy in a few months, so you see if you'd kept either of them around, you would have had a grandson to leave your ranch to, and it would most likely remain the Malloy Ranch. Bonnie and I got married today, and we're having a daughter. We just found out yesterday that it's a girl, and we're so excited about her. I don't care if we have all girls or if they want to be ranchers when they grow up or not.

I can't imagine some of them not wanting to take over for me and Bonnie when we get old, but that will be their choice. One thing for damned sure, they won't be sent out into the world to fend for themselves like your daughters were. They'll be raised right here on Sunrise Ranch. And another thing just as sure, they will be loved." Rusty ran out of words and sat silent for a time. "I just wanted to tell you that, Ezra, and to thank you for giving me a job, because now I have a family. Goodbye, now, and I don't know why I should, after the way you treated folks while you were here, but I hope you find peace somewhere along your eternal journey, because you sure brought happiness to a lot of us, whether you intended to or not."

He stood up and started back toward the house, the dogs following at his heels. When he closed the gate, it didn't squeak. The wind had stopped blowing and everything was eerily quiet. He looked up at the moon hanging in the sky just in time to see a shooting star streak across the darkness.

* * *

When everyone had left that evening, Bonnie slumped down on the sofa beside Rusty. "It was a wonderful day in spite of the snow." She sighed.

"You were a beautiful bride, and now you're *my* gorgeous wife," he said. "Maybe in the spring we can sneak away for a honeymoon." He took her hand in his and kissed her knuckles, one by one.

"Honey, in the spring I'll either be nine months pregnant or we'll already have a pretty little daughter. Our honeymoon will be right here in this house, starting tonight and lasting through all eternity," she told him. "Where did you disappear to while I was changing clothes?"

"I went to talk to Ezra and tell him that we'd changed the name of the ranch," he said. "Our new sign will be hung over the cattle guard as soon as the weather clears up. I forgot to tell him that."

She snuggled in closer to his side. "Shiloh and I've had a few talks with him during this past year."

"I know." He nodded. "Guess what? I saw a shooting star on the way back to the house."

"What did you wish for?" she asked.

"That you would always love me as much as you do right now," he said.

"Darlin', that was a wasted wish." She smiled.

"Oh? So, you're not going to love me always?"

She shifted her position until she was sitting in his lap. "No, I'm just not going to love you as much as I do right now. I plan to love you more every single moment of every single day. You had that already, so you should have wished for something else."

"A new tractor, maybe?" He brushed a kiss across her lips.

"Why not?" She grinned. "Sunrise Ranch could always use a new tractor."

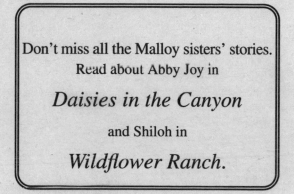

Don't miss all the Malloy sisters' stories.
Read about Abby Joy in

Daisies in the Canyon

and Shiloh in

Wildflower Ranch.

About the Author

Carolyn Brown is a *New York Times* and *USA Today* bestselling romance author and RITA finalist who has published more than one hundred books. She presently writes both women's fiction and cowboy romance. She has also written historical and contemporary romance, both stand-alone titles and series. She lives in southern Oklahoma with her husband, a former English teacher who is also an author of several mystery books. They have three children and enough grandchildren to keep them young.

For a complete listing of her books (in series order) and to sign up for her newsletter, check out her website at CarolynBrownBooks.com or catch her on Facebook/CarolynBrownBooks.

Looking for more hot cowboys?
Forever has you covered!

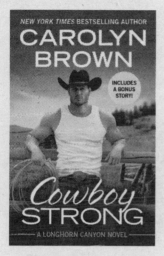

COWBOY STRONG
by Carolyn Brown

Alana Carey can out-rope and out-ride the toughest Texas cowboys. But she does have one soft spot—Paxton Callahan. So when her father falls ill, Alana presents Pax with a crazy proposal: to pretend to be her fiancé so her father can die in peace. But as the faux-wedding day draws near, Alana and Paxton must decide whether to come clean about their charade or finally admit their love is the real deal. Includes the bonus story *Sunrise Ranch*!

COWBOY COURAGE
by Carolyn Brown

Heading back to Texas to hold down the fort at her aunt's bed-and-breakfast will give Rose O'Malley just the break she needs from the military. But while she may speak seven languages, she can't repair a leaky sink to save her life. When Hudson Baker strides in like a hero and effortlessly figures out the fix, Rose can't help wondering if the boy she once crushed on as a kid could now be her saving grace. Includes the bonus story *Wildflower Ranch*!

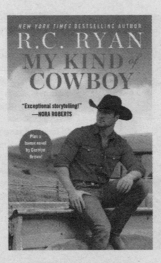

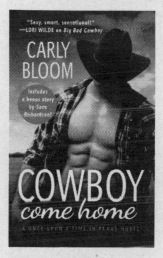

COWBOY COME HOME
by Carly Bloom

As far as Claire Kowalski is concerned, Big Verde, Texas, is perfect, except for one thing: the lack of eligible men. Some days it feels like she's dated every single one. It's too bad that the only man who ever tickled her fancy is the wandering, restless cowboy who took her heart with him when he left her father's ranch years ago. Just when she's resigned herself to never seeing him again, Ford Jarvis knocks on the door. Includes a bonus story by Sara Richardson!

FIRST KISS WITH A COWBOY
by Sara Richardson

With her carefully ordered life crumbling apart, shy and sensible Jane Harding welcomes the distraction of helping plan her best friend's wedding. When she discovers that the boy who once tempted her is now the best man, however, her distraction risks becoming a disaster. Toby Garrett may be the rodeo circuit's sexiest bull rider, but his kiss with Jane has never stopped fueling his fantasies. Can this sweet-talking cowboy prove that the passion still burning between them is worth braving the odds? Includes the bonus story *Cowboy to the Rescue* by A.J. Pine!

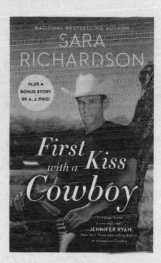

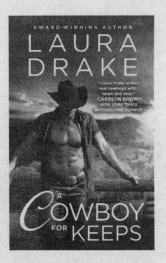

A COWBOY FOR KEEPS
by Laura Drake

Not much rattles a cowboy like Reese St. James—until his twin brother dies in a car accident, leaving behind a six-month-old daughter. Reese immediately heads to Unforgiven, New Mexico, to bring his niece home—but the girl's guardian, Lorelei West, refuses to let a hotshot cowboy like Reese take away her sister's baby. Only the more time they spend together, the harder it is to deny the attraction between them. Opening their hearts to a child is one thing—can they also open their hearts to a chance at happily-ever-after?

MY ONE AND ONLY COWBOY
by A.J. Pine

Sam Callahan is too busy trying to keep his new guest ranch afloat to spend any time on serious relationships—at least that's what he tells himself. But when a gorgeous blonde shows up insisting she owns half his property, Sam quickly realizes he's got bigger problems than Delaney's claim on the land: She could also claim his heart. Includes a bonus novel by Carolyn Brown!

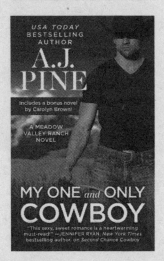